Y0-CWN-164

1 MONTH OF
FREE
READING

at

www.ForgottenBooks.com

By purchasing this book you are eligible for one month membership to ForgottenBooks.com, giving you unlimited access to our entire collection of over 1,000,000 titles via our web site and mobile apps.

To claim your free month visit:

www.forgottenbooks.com/free71335

* Offer is valid for 45 days from date of purchase. Terms and conditions apply.

ISBN 978-1-5283-6761-5
PIBN 10071335

This book is a reproduction of an important historical work. Forgotten Books uses state-of-the-art technology to digitally reconstruct the work, preserving the original format whilst repairing imperfections present in the aged copy. In rare cases, an imperfection in the original, such as a blemish or missing page, may be replicated in our edition. We do, however, repair the vast majority of imperfections successfully; any imperfections that remain are intentionally left to preserve the state of such historical works.

Forgotten Books is a registered trademark of FB &c Ltd.
Copyright © 2018 FB &c Ltd.
FB &c Ltd, Dalton House, 60 Windsor Avenue, London, SW19 2RR.
Company number 08720141. Registered in England and Wales.

For support please visit www.forgottenbooks.com

THE POISONED PEN

BY

ARTHUR B. REEVE

FRONTISPIECE BY
WILL FOSTER

HARPER & BROTHERS · PUBLISHERS
NEW YORK AND LONDON

THE POISONED PEN

Copyright, 1911, by HARPER & BROTHERS
Printed in the United States of America
A-T

CONTENTS

THE POISONED PEN

THE POISONED PEN

KENNEDY'S suit-case was lying open on the bed, and he was literally throwing things into it from his chiffonier, as I entered after a hurried trip up-town from the *Star* office in response to an urgent message from him.

"Come, Walter," he cried, hastily stuffing in a package of clean laundry without taking off the wrapping-paper, "I've got your suit-case out. Pack up whatever you can in five minutes. We must take the six o'clock train for Danbridge."

I did not wait to hear any more. The mere mention of the name of the quaint and quiet little Connecticut town was sufficient. For Danbridge was on everybody's lips at that time. It was the scene of the now famous Danbridge poisoning case—a brutal case in which the pretty little actress, Vera Lytton, had been the victim.

"I've been retained by Senator Adrian Willard," he called from his room, as I was busy packing in mine. "The Willard family believe that that young Dr. Dixon is the victim of a conspiracy—or at least Alma Willard does, which comes to the same thing, and—well, the senator called me up on long-distance and offered me anything I would name in reason to take the case. Are you ready? Come on, then. We've simply got to make that train."

As we settled ourselves in the smoking-compartment of the Pullman, which for some reason or other we had to ourselves, Kennedy spoke again for the first time since our frantic dash across the city to catch the train.

"Now let us see, Walter," he began. "We've both read a good deal about this case in the papers. Let's try to get our knowledge in an orderly shape before we tackle the actual case itself."

"Ever been in Danbridge?" I asked.

"Never," he replied. "What sort of place is it?"

"Mighty interesting," I answered; "a combination of old New England and new, of ancestors and factories, of wealth and poverty, and above all it is interesting for its colony of New-Yorkers—what shall I call it?—a literary-artistic-musical combination, I guess."

"Yes," he resumed, "I thought as much. Vera Lytton belonged to the colony. A very talented girl, too—you remember her in 'The Taming of the New Woman' last season? Well, to get back to the facts as we know them at present.

"Here is a girl with a brilliant future on the stage discovered by her friend, Mrs. Boncour, in convulsions—practically insensible—with a bottle of headache-powder and a jar of ammonia on her dressing-table. Mrs. Boncour sends the maid for the nearest doctor, who happens to be a Dr. Waterworth. Meanwhile she tries to restore Miss Lytton, but with no result. She smells the ammonia and then just tastes the headache-powder, a very foolish thing to do, for by the time Dr. Waterworth arrives he has two patients."

"No," I corrected, "only one, for Miss Lytton was dead when he arrived, according to his latest statement."

"Very well, then—one. He arrives, Mrs. Boncour is ill, the maid knows nothing at all about it, and Vera Lytton is dead. He, too, smells the ammonia, tastes the headache-powder—just the merest trace—and then he has two patients, one of them himself. We must see him, for his experience must have been appalling. How he ever did it I can't imagine, but he saved both himself and Mrs. Boncour from poisoning—cyanide, the papers say, but of course we can't accept that until we see. It seems to me, Walter, that lately the papers have made the rule in murder cases: When in doubt, call it cyanide."

Not relishing Kennedy in the humour of expressing his real opinion of the newspapers, I hastily turned the conversation back again by asking, "How about the note from Dr. Dixon?"

"Ah, there is the crux of the whole case—that note from Dixon. Let us see. Dr. Dixon is, if I am informed correctly, of a fine and aristocratic family, though not wealthy. I believe it has been established that while he was an interne in a city hospital he became acquainted with Vera Lytton, after her divorce from that artist Thurston. Then comes his removal to Danbridge and his meeting and later his engagement with Miss Willard. On the whole, Walter, judging from the newspaper pictures, Alma Willard is quite the equal of Vera Lytton for looks, only of a different style of beauty. Oh, well, we shall see. Vera decided to spend the spring and summer at Danbridge in the bungalow of her friend, Mrs. Boncour, the novelist. That's when things began to happen."

"Yes," I put in, "when you come to know Danbridge as I did after that summer when you were abroad, you'll understand, too. Everybody knows everybody else's business. It is the main occupation of a certain set, and the per-capita output of gossip is a record that would stagger the census bureau. Still, you can't get away from the note, Craig. There it is, in Dixon's own handwriting, even if he does deny it: 'This will cure your headache. Dr. Dixon.' That's a damning piece of evidence."

"Quite right," he agreed hastily; "the note was queer, though, wasn't it? They found it crumpled up in the jar of ammonia. Oh, there are lots of problems the newspapers have failed to see the significance of, let alone trying to follow up."

Our first visit in Danbridge was to the prosecuting attorney, whose office was not far from the station on the main street. Craig had wired him, and he had kindly waited to see us, for it was evident that Danbridge respected Senator Willard and every one connected with him.

"Would it be too much to ask just to see that note that was found in the Boncour bungalow?" asked Craig.

The prosecutor, an energetic young man, pulled out of a document-case a crumpled note which had been pressed flat again. On it in clear, deep black letters were the words, just as reported:

This will cure your headache.

DR. DIXON.

"How about the handwriting?" asked Kennedy.

The lawyer pulled out a number of letters. "I'm afraid they will have to admit it," he said with reluctance, as if down in his heart he hated to prosecute Dixon. "We have lots of these, and no handwriting expert could successfully deny the identity of the writing."

He stowed away the letters without letting Kennedy get a hint as to their contents. Kennedy was examining the note carefully.

"May I count on having this note for further examination, of course always at such times and under such conditions as you agree to?"

The attorney nodded. "I am perfectly willing to do anything not illegal to accommodate the senator," he said. "But, on the other hand, I am here to do my duty for the state, cost whom it may."

The Willard house was in a virtual state of siege. Newspaper reporters from Boston and New York were actually encamped at every gate, terrible as an army, with cameras. It was with some difficulty that we got in, even though we were expected, for some of the more enterprising had already fooled the family by posing as officers of the law and messengers from Dr. Dixon.

The house was a real, old colonial mansion with

tall white pillars, a door with a glittering brass knocker, which gleamed out severely at you as you approached through a hedge of faultlessly trimmed boxwoods.

Senator, or rather former Senator, Willard met us in the library, and a moment later his daughter Alma joined him. She was tall, like her father, a girl of poise and self-control. Yet even the schooling of twenty-two years in rigorous New England self-restraint could not hide the very human pallor of her face after the sleepless nights and nervous days since this trouble had broken on her placid existence. Yet there was a mark of strength and determination on her face that was fascinating. The man who would trifle with this girl, I felt, was playing fast and loose with her very life. I thought then, and I said to Kennedy afterward: "If this Dr. Dixon is guilty, you have no right to hide it from that girl. Anything less than the truth will only blacken the hideousness of the crime that has already been committed."

The senator greeted us gravely, and I could not but take it as a good omen when, in his pride of wealth and family and tradition, he laid bare everything to us, for the sake of Alma Willard. It was clear that in this family there was one word that stood above all others, "Duty."

As we were about to leave after an interview barren of new facts, a young man was announced, Mr. Halsey Post. He bowed politely to us, but it was evident why he had called, as his eye followed Alma about the room.

"The son of the late Halsey Post, of Post & Vance, silversmiths, who have the large factory in town, which you perhaps noticed," explained the senator. "My daughter has known him all her life. A very fine young man."

Later, we learned that the senator had bent every effort toward securing Halsey Post as a son-in-law, but his daughter had had views of her own on the subject.

Post waited until Alma had withdrawn before he disclosed the real object of his visit. In almost a whisper, lest she should still be listening, he said, "There is a story about town that Vera Lytton's former husband—an artist named Thurston—was here just before her death."

Senator Willard leaned forward as if expecting to hear Dixon immediately acquitted. None of us was prepared for the next remark.

"And the story goes on to say that he threatened to make a scene over a wrong he says he has suffered from Dixon. I don't know anything more about it, and I tell you only because I think you ought to know what Danbridge is saying under its breath."

We shook off the last of the reporters who affixed themselves to us, and for a moment Kennedy dropped in at the little bungalow to see Mrs. Boncour. She was much better, though she had suffered much. She had taken only a pinhead of the poison, but it had proved very nearly fatal.

"Had Miss Lytton any enemies whom you think of, people who were jealous of her professionally or personally?" asked Craig.

"I should not even have said Dr. Dixon was an enemy," she replied evasively.

"But this Mr. Thurston," put in Kennedy quickly. "One is not usually visited in perfect friendship by a husband who has been divorced."

She regarded him keenly for a moment. "Halsey Post told you that," she said. "No one else knew he was here. But Halsey Post was an old friend of both Vera and Mr. Thurston before they separated. By chance he happened to drop in the day Mr. Thurston was here, and later in the day I gave him a letter to forward to Mr. Thurston, which had come after the artist left. I'm sure no one else knew the artist. He was here the morning of the day she died, and—and—that's every bit I'm going to tell you about him, so there. I don't know why he came or where he went."

"That's a thing we must follow up later," remarked Kennedy as we made our adieus. "Just now I want to get the facts in hand. The next thing on my programme is to see this Dr. Waterworth."

We found the doctor still in bed; in fact, a wreck as the result of his adventure. He had little to correct in the facts of the story which had been published so far. But there were many other details of the poisoning he was quite willing to discuss frankly.

"It was true about the jar of ammonia?" asked Kennedy.

"Yes," he answered. "It was standing on her dressing-table with the note crumpled up in it, just as the papers said."

"And you have no idea why it was there?"

"I didn't say that. I can guess. Fumes of ammonia are one of the antidotes for poisoning of this kind."

"But Vera Lytton could hardly have known that," objected Kennedy.

"No, of course not. But she probably did know that ammonia is good for just that sort of faintness which she must have experienced after taking the powder. Perhaps she thought of sal volatile, I don't know. But most people know that ammonia in some form is good for faintness of this sort, even if they don't know anything about cyanides and——"

"Then it was cyanide?" interrupted Craig.

"Yes," he replied slowly. It was evident that he was suffering great physical and nervous anguish as the result of his too intimate acquaintance with the poisons in question. "I will tell you precisely how it was, Professor Kennedy. When I was called in to see Miss Lytton I found her on the bed. I pried open her jaws and smelled the sweetish odour of the cyanogen gas. I knew then what she had taken, and at the moment she was dead. In the next room I heard some one moaning. The maid said that it was Mrs. Boncour, and that she was deathly sick. I ran into her room, and though she was beside herself with pain I managed to control her, though she struggled desperately against me. I was rushing her to the bathroom, passing through Miss Lytton's room. 'What's wrong?' I asked as I carried her along. 'I took some of that,' she replied, pointing to the bottle on the dressing-table.

"I put a small quantity of its crystal contents on my tongue. Then I realised the most tragic truth of my life. I had taken one of the deadliest poisons in the world. The odour of the released gas of cyanogen was strong. But more than that, the metallic taste and the horrible burning sensation told of the presence of some form of mercury, too. In that terrible moment my brain worked with the incredible swiftness of light. In a flash I knew that if I added malic acid to the mercury—perchloride of mercury or corrosive sublimate—I would have calomel or subchloride of mercury, the only thing that would switch the poison out of my system and Mrs. Boncour's.

"Seizing her about the waist, I hurried into the dining-room. On a sideboard was a dish of fruit. I took two apples. I made her eat one, core and all. I ate the other. The fruit contained the malic acid I needed to manufacture the calomel, and I made it right there in nature's own laboratory. But there was no time to stop. I had to act just as quickly to neutralise that cyanide, too. Remembering the ammonia, I rushed back with Mrs. Boncour, and we inhaled the fumes. Then I found a bottle of peroxide of hydrogen. I washed out her stomach with it, and then my own. Then I injected some of the peroxide into various parts of her body. The peroxide of hydrogen and hydrocyanic acid, you know, make oxamide, which is a harmless compound.

"The maid put Mrs. Boncour to bed, saved. I went to my house, a wreck. Since then I have not left this bed. With my legs paralysed I lie here, expecting each hour to be my last."

"Would you taste an unknown drug again to discover the nature of a probable poison?" asked Craig.

"I don't know," he answered slowly, "but I suppose I would. In such a case a conscientious doctor has no thought of self. He is there to do things, and he does them, according to the best that is in him. In spite of the fact that I haven't had one hour of unbroken sleep since that fatal day, I suppose I would do it again."

When we were leaving, I remarked: "That is a martyr to science. Could anything be more dramatic than his willing penalty for his devotion to medicine?"

We walked along in silence. "Walter, did you notice he said not a word of condemnation of Dixon, though the note was before his eyes? Surely Dixon has some strong supporters in Danbridge, as well as enemies."

The next morning we continued our investigation. We found Dixon's lawyer, Leland, in consultation with his client in the bare cell of the county jail. Dixon proved to be a clear-eyed, clean-cut young man. The thing that impressed me most about him, aside from the prepossession in his favour due to the faith of Alma Willard, was the nerve he displayed, whether guilty or innocent. Even an innocent man might well have been staggered by the circumstantial evidence against him and the high tide of public feeling, in spite of the support that he was receiving. Leland, we learned, had been very active. By prompt work at the time of the young doctor's arrest he had managed to secure the greater part of Dr. Dixon's personal letters, though the prosecutor secured some, the contents of which had not been disclosed.

Kennedy spent most of the day in tracing out the movements of Thurston. Nothing that proved important was turned up, and even visits to near-by towns failed to show any sales of cyanide or sublimate to any one not entitled to buy them. Meanwhile, in turning over the gossip of the town, one of the newspapermen ran across the fact that the Boncour bungalow was owned by the Posts, and that Halsey Post, as the executor of the estate, was a more frequent visitor than the mere collection of the rent would warrant. Mrs. Boncour maintained a stolid silence that covered a seething internal fury when the newspaperman in question hinted that the landlord and tenant were on exceptionally good terms.

It was after a fruitless day of such search that we were sitting in the reading-room of the Fairfield Hotel. Leland entered. His face was positively white. Without a word he took us by the arm and led us across Main Street and up a flight of stairs to his office. Then he locked the door.

"What's the matter?" asked Kennedy.

"When I took this case," he said, "I believed down in my heart that Dixon was innocent. I still believe it, but my faith has been rudely shaken. I feel that you should know about what I have just found. As I told you, we secured nearly all of Dr. Dixon's letters. I had not read them all then. But I have been going through them to-night. Here is a letter from Vera Lytton herself. You will notice it is dated the day of her death."

He laid the letter before us. It was written in a curious greyish-black ink in a woman's hand, and read:

DEAR HARRIS:

Since we agreed to disagree we have at least been good friends, if no longer lovers. I am not writing in anger to reproach you with your new love, so soon after the old. I suppose Alma Willard is far better suited to be your wife than is a poor little actress—rather looked down on in this Puritan society here. But there is something I wish to warn you about, for it concerns us all intimately.

We are in danger of an awful mix-up if we don't look out. Mr. Thurston—I had almost said my husband, though I don't know whether that is the truth or not—who has just come over from New York, tells me that there is some doubt about the validity of our divorce. You recall he was in the South at the time I sued him, and the papers were served on him in Georgia. He now says the proof of service was fraudulent and that he can set aside the divorce. In that case you might figure in a suit for alienating my affections.

I do not write this with ill will, but simply to let you know how things stand. If we had married, I suppose I would be guilty of bigamy. At any rate, if he were disposed he could make a terrible scandal.

Oh, Harris, can't you settle with him if he asks anything? Don't forget so soon that we once thought we were going to be the happiest of mortals—at least I did. Don't desert me, or the very earth will cry out against you. I am frantic and hardly know what I am writing. My head aches, but it is my heart that is breaking. Harris, I am yours still, down in my heart, but not to be cast off like an old suit for a new one. You know the old saying about a woman scorned. I beg you not to go back on

Your poor little deserted

VERA.

As we finished reading, Leland exclaimed, "That never must come before the jury."

Kennedy was examining the letter carefully. "Strange," he muttered. "See how it was folded. It was written on the wrong side of the sheet, or rather folded up with the writing outside. Where have these letters been?"

"Part of the time in my safe, part of the time this afternoon on my desk by the window."

"The office was locked, I suppose?" asked Kennedy. "There was no way to slip this letter in among the others since you obtained them?"

"None. The office has been locked, and there is no evidence of any one having entered or disturbed a thing."

He was hastily running over the pile of letters as if looking to see whether they were all there. Suddenly he stopped.

"Yes," he exclaimed excitedly, "one of them *is* gone." Nervously he fumbled through them again. "One is gone," he repeated, looking at us, startled.

"What was it about?" asked Craig.

"It was a note from an artist, Thurston, who gave the address of Mrs. Boncour's bungalow—ah, I see you have heard of him. He asked Dixon's recommendation of a certain patent headache medicine. I thought it possibly evidential, and I asked Dixon about it. He explained it by saying that he did not have a copy of his reply, but as near as he could recall, he wrote that the compound would not cure a headache except at the expense of reducing heart action dangerously. He says he sent no prescription. Indeed, he thought it a scheme to extract advice without incurring the charge for an office call and answered it only because he thought Vera had become reconciled to Thurston again. I can't find that letter of Thurston's. It is gone."

We looked at each other in amazement.

"Why, if Dixon contemplated anything against Miss Lytton, should he preserve this letter from her?" mused Kennedy. "Why didn't he destroy it?"

"That's what puzzles me," remarked Leland. "Do you suppose some one has broken in and substituted this Lytton letter for the Thurston letter?"

Kennedy was scrutinising the letter, saying nothing. "I may keep it?" he asked at length. Leland was quite willing and even undertook to obtain some specimens of the writing of Vera Lytton. With these and the letter Kennedy was working far into the night and long after I had passed into a land troubled with many wild dreams of deadly poisons and secret intrigues of artists.

The next morning a message from our old friend First Deputy O'Connor in New York told briefly of locating the rooms of an artist named Thurston in one of the co-operative studio apartments. Thurston himself had not been there for several days and was reported to have gone to Maine to sketch. He had had a number of debts, but before he left they had all been paid—strange to say, by a notorious firm of shyster lawyers, Kerr & Kimmel. Kennedy wired back to find out the facts from Kerr & Kimmel and to locate Thurston at any cost.

Even the discovery of the new letter did not shake the wonderful self-possession of Dr. Dixon. He denied ever having received it and repeated his story of a letter from Thurston to which he had replied by sending an answer, care of Mrs. Boncour, as requested. He insisted that the engagement between Miss Lytton and himself had been broken before the announcement of his engagement with Miss Willard. As for Thurston, he said the man was little more than a name to him. He had known perfectly all the circumstances of the divorce, but had had no dealings with Thurston and no fear of him. Again and again he denied ever receiving the letter from Vera Lytton.

Kennedy did not tell the Willards of the new letter. The strain had begun to tell on Alma, and her father had had her quietly taken to a farm of his up in the country. To escape the curious eyes of reporters, Halsey Post had driven up one night in his closed car. She had entered it quickly with her father, and the journey had been made in the car, while Halsey Post had quietly dropped off on the outskirts of the town, where another car was waiting to take him back. It was evident that the Willard family relied implicitly on Halsey, and his assistance to them was most considerate. While he never forced himself forward, he kept in close touch with the progress of the case, and now that Alma was away his watchfulness increased proportionately, and twice a day he wrote a long report which was sent to her.

Kennedy was now bending every effort to locate the missing artist. When he left Danbridge, he seemed to have dropped out of sight completely. However, with O'Connor's aid, the police of all New England were on the lookout.

The Thurstons had been friends of Halsey's before Vera Lytton had ever met Dr. Dixon, we discovered from the Danbridge gossips, and I, at least, jumped to the conclusion that Halsey was shielding the artist, perhaps through a sense of friendship when he found that Kennedy was interested in Thurston's movement. I must say I rather liked Halsey, for he seemed very thoughtful of the Willards, and was never too busy to give an hour or so to any commission they wished carried out without publicity.

Two days passed with not a word from Thurston. Kennedy was obviously getting impatient. One day a rumour was received that he was in Bar Harbour; the next it was a report from Nova Scotia. At last, however, came the welcome news that he had been located in New Hampshire, arrested, and might be expected the next day.

At once Kennedy became all energy. He arranged for a secret conference in Senator Willard's house, the moment the artist was to arrive.

The senator and his daughter made a flying trip back to town. Nothing was said to any one about Thurston, but Kennedy quietly arranged with the district attorney to be present with the note and the jar of ammonia properly safeguarded. Leland of course came, although his client could not. Halsey Post seemed only too glad to be with Miss Willard, though he seemed to have lost interest in the case as soon as the Willards returned to look after it themselves. Mrs. Boncour was well enough to attend, and even Dr. Waterworth insisted on coming in a private ambulance which drove over from a near-by city especially for him. The time was fixed just before the arrival of the train that was to bring Thurston.

It was an anxious gathering of friends and foes of Dr. Dixon who sat impatiently waiting for Kennedy to begin this momentous exposition that was to establish the guilt or innocence of the calm young physician who sat impassively in the jail not half a mile from the room where his life and death were being debated.

"In many respects this is the most remarkable case that it has ever been my lot to handle," began Kennedy. "Never before have I felt so keenly my sense of responsibility. Therefore, though this is a somewhat irregular proceeding, let me begin by setting forth the facts as I see them.

"First, let us consider the dead woman. The question that arises here is, Was she murdered or did she commit suicide? I think you will discover the answer as I proceed. Miss Lytton, as you know, was, two years ago, Mrs. Burgess Thurston. The Thurstons had temperament, and temperament is quite often the highway to the divorce court. It was so in this case. Mrs. Thurston discovered that her husband was paying much attention to other women. She sued for divorce in New York, and he accepted service in the South, where he happened to be. At least it was so testified by Mrs. Thurston's lawyer.

" Now here comes the remarkable feature of the case. The law firm of Kerr & Kimmel, I find, not long ago began to investigate the legality of this divorce. Before a notary Thurston made an affidavit that he had never been served by the lawyer for Miss Lytton, as she was now known. Her lawyer is dead, but his representative in the South who served the papers is alive. He was brought to New York and asserted squarely that he had served the papers properly.

" Here is where the shrewdness of Mose Kimmel, the shyster lawyer, came in. He arranged to have the Southern attorney identify the man he had served the papers on. For this purpose he was engaged in conversation with one of his own clerks when the lawyer was due to appear. Kimmel appeared to act confused, as if he had been caught napping. The Southern lawyer, who had seen Thurston only once, fell squarely into the trap and identified the clerk as Thurston. There were plenty of witnesses to it, and it was point number two for the great Mose Kimmel. Papers were drawn up to set aside the divorce decree.

"In the meantime, Miss Lytton, or Mrs. Thurston, had become acquainted with a young doctor in a New York hospital, and had become engaged to him. It matters not that the engagement was later broken. The fact remains that if the divorce were set aside an action would lie against Dr. Dixon for alienating Mrs. Thurston's affections, and a grave scandal would result. I need not add that in this quiet little town of Danbridge the most could be made of such a suit."

Kennedy was unfolding a piece of paper. As he laid it down, Leland, who was sitting next to me, exclaimed under his breath:

"My God, he's going to let the prosecutor know about that letter. Can't you stop him?"

It was too late. Kennedy had already begun to read Vera's letter. It was damning to Dixon, added to the other note found in the ammonia-jar.

When he had finished reading, you could almost hear the hearts throbbing in the room. A scowl overspread Senator Willard's features. Alma Willard was pale and staring wildly at Kennedy. Halsey Post, ever solicitous for her, handed her a glass of water from the table. Dr. Waterworth had forgotten his pain in his intense attention, and Mrs. Boncour seemed stunned with astonishment. The prosecuting attorney was eagerly taking notes.

"In some way," pursued Kennedy in an even voice, "this letter was either overlooked in the original correspondence of Dr. Dixon or it was added to it later. I shall come back to that presently. My next point is that Dr. Dixon says he received a letter from Thurston on the day the artist visited the Boncour bungalow. It asked about a certain headache compound, and his reply was brief and, as nearly as I can find out, read, 'This compound will not cure your headache except at the expense of reducing heart action dangerously.'

"Next comes the tragedy. On the evening of the day that Thurston left, after presumably telling Miss Lytton about what Kerr & Kimmel had discovered, Miss Lytton is found dying with a bottle containing cyanide and sublimate beside her. You are all familiar with the circumstances and with the note discovered in the jar of ammonia. Now, if the prosecutor will be so kind as to let me see that note—thank you, sir. This is the identical note. You have all heard the various theories of the jar and have read the note. Here it is in plain, cold black and white—in Dr. Dixon's own handwriting, as you know, and reads: 'This will cure your headache. Dr. Dixon.'"

Alma Willard seemed as one paralysed. Was Kennedy, who had been engaged by her father to defend her fiancé, about to convict him?

"Before we draw the final conclusion," continued Kennedy gravely, "there are one or two points I wish to elaborate. Walter, will you open that door into the main hall?"

I did so, and two policemen stepped in with a prisoner. It was Thurston, but changed almost beyond recognition. His clothes were worn, his beard shaved off, and he had a generally hunted appearance.

Thurston was visibly nervous. Apparently he had heard all that Kennedy had said and intended he should hear, for as he entered he almost broke away from the police officers in his eagerness to speak.

"Before God," he cried dramatically, "I am as innocent as you are of this crime, Professor Kennedy."

"Are you prepared to swear before *me*," almost shouted Kennedy, his eyes blazing, "that you were never served properly by your wife's lawyers in that suit?"

The man cringed back as if a stinging blow had been delivered between his eyes. As he met Craig's fixed glare he knew there was no hope. Slowly, as if the words were being wrung from him syllable by syllable, he said in a muffled voice:

"No, I perjured myself. I was served in that suit. But——"

"And you swore falsely before Kimmel that you were not?" persisted Kennedy.

"Yes," he murmured. "But——"

"And you are prepared now to make another affidavit to that effect?"

"Yes," he replied. "If——"

"No buts or ifs, Thurston," cried Kennedy sarcastically. "What did you make that affidavit for? What is *your* story?"

"Kimmel sent for me. I did not go to him. He offered to pay my debts if I would swear to such a statement. I did not ask why or for whom. I swore to it and gave him a list of my creditors.

I waited until they were paid. Then my conscience "—I could not help revolting at the thought of conscience in such a wretch, and the word itself seemed to stick in his throat as he went on and saw how feeble an impression he was making on us—" my conscience began to trouble me. I determined to see Vera, tell her all, and find out whether it was she who wanted this statement. I saw her. When at last I told her, she scorned me. I can confirm that, for as I left a man entered. I now knew how grossly I had sinned, in listening to Mose Kimmel. I fled. I disappeared in Maine. I travelled. Every day my money grew less. At last I was overtaken, captured, and brought back here."

He stopped and sank wretchedly down in a chair and covered his face with his hands.

" A likely story," muttered Leland in my ear.

Kennedy was working quickly. Motioning the officers to be seated by Thurston, he uncovered a jar which he had placed on the table. The colour had now appeared in Alma's cheeks, as if hope had again sprung in her heart, and I fancied that Halsey Post saw his claim on her favour declining correspondingly.

" I want you to examine the letters in this case with me," continued Kennedy. " Take the letter which I read from Miss Lytton, which was found following the strange disappearance of the note from Thurston."

He dipped a pen into a little bottle, and wrote on a piece of paper:

What is your opinion about Cross's Headache Cure? Would you recommend it for a nervous headache?

BURGESS THURSTON,
c|o MRS. S. BONCOUR.

Craig held up the writing so that we could all see that he had written what Dixon declared Thurston wrote in the note that had disappeared. Then he dipped another pen into a second bottle, and for some time he scrawled on another sheet of paper. He held it up, but it was still perfectly blank.

"Now," he added, "I am going to give a little demonstration which I expect to be successful only in a measure. Here in the open sunshine by this window I am going to place these two sheets of paper side by side. It will take longer than I care to wait to make my demonstration complete, but I can do enough to convince you."

For a quarter of an hour we sat in silence, wondering what he would do next. At last he beckoned us over to the window. As we approached he said, "On sheet number one I have written with quinoline; on sheet number two I wrote with a solution of nitrate of silver."

We bent over. The writing signed "Thurston" on sheet number one was faint, almost imperceptible, but on paper number two, in black letters, appeared what Kennedy had written: "Dear Harris: Since we agreed to disagree we have at least been good friends."

"It is like the start of the substituted letter, and

the other is like the missing note," gasped Leland in a daze.

"Yes," said Kennedy quickly. "Leland, no one entered your office. No one stole the Thurston note. No one substituted the Lytton letter. According to your own story, you took them out of the safe and left them in the sunlight all day. The process that had been started earlier in ordinary light, slowly, was now quickly completed. In other words, there was writing which would soon fade away on one side of the paper and writing which was invisible but would soon appear on the other.

"For instance, quinoline rapidly disappears in sunlight. Starch with a slight trace of iodine writes a light blue, which disappears in air. It was something like that used in the Thurston letter. Then, too, silver nitrate dissolved in ammonia gradually turns black as it is acted on by light and air. Or magenta treated with a bleaching-agent in just sufficient quantity to decolourise it is invisible when used for writing. But the original colour reappears as the oxygen of the air acts upon the pigment. I haven't a doubt but that my analyses of the inks are correct and on one side quinoline was used and on the other nitrate of silver. This explains the inexplicable disappearance of evidence incriminating one person, Thurston, and the sudden appearance of evidence incriminating another, Dr. Dixon. Sympathetic ink also accounts for the curious circumstance that the Lytton letter was folded up with the writing apparently outside. It was outside and unseen until the sunlight brought it out and destroyed the other, inside, writing—a change, I suspeet, that was intended for the police to see after it was completed, not for the defence to witness as it was taking place."

We looked at each other aghast. Thurston was nervously opening and shutting his lips and moistening them as if he wanted to say something but could not find the words.

"Lastly," went on Craig, utterly regardless of Thurston's frantic efforts to speak, "we come to the note that was discovered so queerly crumpled up in the jar of ammonia on Vera Lytton's dressing-table. I have here a cylindrical glass jar in which I place some sal-ammoniac and quicklime. I will wet it and heat it a little. That produces the pungent gas of ammonia.

"On one side of this third piece of paper I myself write with this mercurous nitrate solution. You see, I leave no mark on the paper as I write. I fold it up and drop it into the jar—and in a few seconds withdraw it. Here is a very quick way of producing something like the slow result of sunlight with silver nitrate. The fumes of ammonia have formed the precipitate of black mercurous nitrate, a very distinct black writing which is almost indelible. That is what is technically called invisible rather than sympathetic ink."

We leaned over to read what he had written. It was the same as the note incriminating Dixon:

This will cure your headache.

DR. DIXON.

A servant entered with a telegram from New York. Scarcely stopping in his exposure, Kennedy tore it open, read it hastily, stuffed it into his pocket, and went on.

"Here in this fourth bottle I have an acid solution of iron chloride, diluted until the writing is invisible when dry," he hurried on. "I will just make a few scratches on this fourth sheet of paper—so. It leaves no mark. But it has the remarkable property of becoming red in vapour of sulpho-cyanide. Here is a long-necked flask of the gas, made by sulphuric acid acting on potassium sulpho-cyanide. Keep back, Dr. Waterworth, for it would be very dangerous for you to get even a whiff of this in your condition. Ah! See—the scratches I made on the paper are red."

Then hardly giving us more than a moment to let the fact impress itself on our minds, he seized the piece of paper and dashed it into the jar of ammonia. When he withdrew it, it was just a plain sheet of white paper again. The red marks which the gas in the flask had brought out of nothingness had been effaced by the ammonia. They had gone and left no trace.

"In this way I can alternately make the marks appear and disappear by using the sulpho-cyanide and the ammonia. Whoever wrote this note with Dr. Dixon's name on it must have had the doctor's reply to the Thurston letter containing the words, 'This will not cure your headache.' He carefully traced the words, holding the genuine note up to the light with a piece of paper over it, leaving out the word 'not' and using only such words as he needed. This note was then destroyed.

"But he forgot that after he had brought out the red writing by the use of the sulpho-cyanide, and though he could count on Vera Lytton's placing the note in the jar of ammonia and hence obliterating the writing, while at the same time the invisible writing in the mercurous nitrate involving Dr. Dixon's name would be brought out by the ammonia indelibly on the other side of the note—he forgot" —Kennedy was now speaking eagerly and loudly— "that the sulpho-cyanide vapours could always be made to bring back to accuse him the words that the ammonia had blotted out."

Before the prosecutor could interfere, Kennedy had picked up the note found in the ammonia-jar beside the dying girl and had jammed the state's evidence into the long-necked flask of sulpho-cyanide vapour.

"Don't fear," he said, trying to pacify the now furious prosecutor, "it will do nothing to the Dixon writing. That is permanent now, even if it is only a tracing."

When he withdrew the note, there was writing on both sides, the black of the original note and something in red on the other side.

We crowded around, and Craig read it with as much interest as any of us:

"Before taking the headache-powder, be sure to place the contents of this paper in a jar with a little warm water."

"Hum," commented Craig, "this was apparently written on the outside wrapper of a paper folded about some sal-ammoniac and quicklime. It goes on:

"'Just drop the whole thing in, *paper and all.* Then if you feel a faintness from the medicine the ammonia will quickly restore you. One spoonful of the headache-powder swallowed quickly is enough.'"

No name was signed to the directions, but they were plainly written, and "*paper and all*" was underscored heavily.

Craig pulled out some letters. "I have here specimens of writing of many persons connected with this case, but I can see at a glance which one corresponds to the writing on this red death-warrant by an almost inhuman fiend. I shall, however, leave that part of it to the handwriting experts to determine at the trial. Thurston, who was the man whom you saw enter the Boncour bungalow as you left—the constant visitor?"

Thurston had not yet regained his self-control, but with trembling forefinger he turned and pointed to Halsey Post.

"Yes, ladies and gentlemen," cried Kennedy as he slapped the telegram that had just come from New York down on the table decisively, "yes, the real client of Kerr & Kimmel, who bent Thurston to his purposes, was Halsey Post, once secret lover of Vera Lytton till threatened by scandal in Danbridge—Halsey Post, graduate in technology, student of sympathetic inks, forger of the Vera Lytton letter and the other notes, and dealer in cyanides in the silver-smithing business, fortune-hunter for the Willard millions with which to recoup the Post & Vance losses, and hence rival of Dr. Dixon for the love of Alma Willard. That is the man who wielded the poisoned pen. Dr. Dixon is innocent."

II

THE YEGGMAN

"HELLO! Yes, this is Professor Kennedy. I didn't catch the name—oh, yes—President Blake of the Standard Burglary Insurance Company. What—really? The Branford pearls—stolen? Maid chloroformed? Yes, I'll take the case. You'll be up in half an hour? All right, I'll be here. Good-bye."

It was through this brief and businesslike conversation over the telephone that Kennedy became involved in what proved to be one of the most dangerous cases he had ever handled.

At the mention of the Branford pearls I involuntarily stopped reading, and listened, not because I wanted to pry into Craig's affairs, but because I simply couldn't help it. This was news that had not yet been given out to the papers, and my instinct told me that there must be something more to it than the bare statement of the robbery.

"Some one has made a rich haul," I commented. "It was reported, I remember, when the Branford pearls were bought in Paris last year that Mrs. Branford paid upward of a million francs for the collection."

"Blake is bringing up his shrewdest detective to co-operate with me in the case," added Kennedy. "Blake, I understand, is the head of the Burglary

Insurance Underwriters' Association, too. This will be a big thing, Walter, if we can carry it through."

It was the longest half-hour that I ever put in, waiting for Blake to arrive. When he did come, it was quite evident that my surmise had been correct.

Blake was one of those young old men who are increasingly common in business to-day. There was an air of dignity and keenness about his manner that showed clearly how important he regarded the case. So anxious was he to get down to business that he barely introduced himself and his companion, Special Officer Maloney, a typical private detective.

"Of course you haven't heard anything except what I have told you over the wire," he began, going right to the point. "We were notified of it only this noon ourselves, and we haven't given it out to the papers yet, though the local police in Jersey are now on the scene. The New York police must be notified to-night, so that whatever we do must be done before they muss things up. We've got a clue that we want to follow up secretly. These are the facts."

In the terse, straightforward language of the up-to-date man of efficiency, he sketched the situation for us.

"The Branford estate, you know, consists of several acres on the mountain back of Montclair, overlooking the valley, and surrounded by even larger estates. Branford, I understand, is in the West with a party of capitalists, inspecting a reported find of potash salts. Mrs. Branford closed up the house a few days ago and left for a short stay at Palm Beach. Of course they ought to have put their valuables in a safe deposit vault. But they didn't. They relied on a safe that was really one of the best in the market—a splendid safe, I may say. Well, it seems that while the master and mistress were both away the servants decided on having a good time in New York. They locked up the house securely—there's no doubt of that—and just went. That is, they all went except Mrs. Branford's maid, who refused to go for some reason or other. We've got all the servants, but there's not a clue to be had from any of them. They just went off on a bust, that's clear. They admit it.

"Now, when they got back early this morning they found the maid in bed—dead. There was still a strong odour of chloroform about the room. The bed was disarranged as if there had been a struggle. A towel had been wrapped up in a sort of cone, saturated with chloroform, and forcibly held over the girl's nose. The next thing they discovered was the safe—blown open in a most peculiar manner. I won't dwell on that. We're going to take you out there and show it to you after I've told you the whole story.

"Here's the real point. It looks all right, so far. The local police say that the thief or thieves, whoever they were, apparently gained access by breaking a back window. That's mistake number one. Tell Mr. Kennedy about the window, Maloney."

"It's just simply this," responded the detective. "When I came to look at the broken window I found that the glass had fallen outside in such a way as it could not have fallen if the window had been broken from the outside. The thing was a blind. Whoever did it got into the house in some other way and then broke the glass later to give a false clue."

"And," concluded Blake, taking his cigar between his thumb and forefinger and shaking it to give all possible emphasis to his words, "we have had our agent at Palm Beach on long-distance 'phone twice this afternoon. Mrs. Branford did *not* go to Palm Beach. She did *not* engage rooms in any hotel there. And furthermore she never had any intention of going there. By a fortunate circumstance Maloney picked up a hint from one of the servants, and he has located her at the Grattan Inn in this city. In other words, Mrs. Branford has stolen her own jewels from herself in order to collect the burglary insurance—a common-enough thing in itself, but never to my knowledge done on such a large scale before."

The insurance man sank back in his chair and surveyed us sharply.

"But," interrupted Kennedy slowly, "how about——"

"I know—the maid," continued Blake. "I do not mean that Mrs. Branford did the actual stealing. Oh, no. That was done by a yeggman of experience. He must have been above the average, but everything points to the work of a yeggman.

She hired him. But he overstepped the mark when he chloroformed the maid."

For a moment Kennedy said nothing. Then he remarked: " Let us go out and see the safe. There must be some clue. After that I want to have a talk with Mrs. Branford. By the way," he added, as we all rose to go down to Blake's car, " I once handled a life insurance case for the Great Eastern. I made the condition that I was to handle it in my own way, whether it went for or against the company. That's understood, is it, before I undertake the case? "

" Yes, yes," agreed Blake. " Get at the truth. We're not seeking to squirm out of meeting an honest liability. Only we want to make a signal example if it is as we have every reason to believe. There has been altogether too much of this sort of fake burglary to collect insurance, and as president of the underwriters it is my duty and intention to put a stop to it. Come on."

Maloney nodded his head vigorously in assent with his chief. " Never fear," he murmured. " The truth is what will benefit the company, all right. She did it."

The Branford estate lay some distance back from the railroad station, so that, although it took longer to go by automobile than by train, the car made us independent of the rather fitful night train service and the local cabmen.

We found the house not deserted by the servants, but subdued. The body of the maid had been removed to a local morgue, and a police officer was patrolling the grounds, though of what use that could be I was at a loss to understand.

Kennedy was chiefly interested in the safe. It was of the so-called "burglar-proof" variety, spherical in shape, and looking for all the world like a miniature piece of electrical machinery.

"I doubt if anything could have withstood such savage treatment as has been given to this safe," remarked Craig as he concluded a cursory examination of it. "It shows great resistance to high explosives, chiefly, I believe, as a result of its rounded shape. But nothing could stand up against such continued assaults."

He continued to examine the safe while we stood idly by. "I like to reconstruct my cases in my own mind," explained Kennedy, as he took his time in the examination. "Now, this fellow must have stripped the safe of all the outer trimmings. His next move was to make a dent in the manganese surface across the joint where the door fits the body. That must have taken a good many minutes of husky work. In fact, I don't see how he could have done it without a sledge-hammer and a hot chisel. Still, he did it and then——"

"But the maid," interposed Maloney. "She was in the house. She would have heard and given an alarm."

For answer, Craig simply went to a bay-window and raised the curtain. Pointing to the lights of the next house, far down the road, he said, "I'll buy the best cigars in the state if you can make them hear you on a blustery night like last night.

No, she probably did scream. Either at this point, or at the very start, the burglar must have chloroformed her. I don't see any other way to explain it. I doubt if he expected such a tough proposition as he found in this safe, but he was evidently prepared to carry it through, now that he was here and had such an unexpectedly clear field, except for the maid. He simply got her out of the way, or his confederates did—in the easiest possible way, poor girl."

Returning to the safe, he continued: "Well, anyhow, he made a furrow perhaps an inch and a half long and a quarter of an inch wide and, I should say, not over an eighth of an inch deep. Then he commenced to burgle in earnest. Under the dent he made a sort of little cup of red clay and poured in the 'soup'—the nitroglycerin—so that it would run into the depression. Then he exploded it in the regular way with a battery and a fulminate cap. I doubt if it did much more than discolour the metal at first. Still, with the true persistency of his kind, he probably repeated the dose, using more and more of the 'soup' until the joint was stretched a little, and more of an opening made so that the 'soup' could run in.

"Again and again he must have repeated and increased the charges. Perhaps he used two or three cups at a time. By this time the outer door must have been stretched so as to make it easy to introduce the explosive. No doubt he was able to use ten or twelve ounces of the stuff at a charge. It must have been more like target-practice than safe-blowing. But the chance doesn't often come—an empty house and plenty of time. Finally the door must have bulged a fraction of an inch or so, and then a good big charge and the outer portion was ripped off and the safe turned over. There was still two or three inches of manganese steel protecting the contents, wedged in so tight that it must have seemed that nothing could budge it. But he must have kept at it until we have the wreck that we see here," and Kennedy kicked the safe with his foot as he finished.

Blake was all attention by this time, while Maloney gasped, "If I was in the safe-cracking business, I'd make you the head of the firm."

"And now," said Craig, "let us go back to New York and see if we can find Mrs. Branford."

"Of course you understand," explained Blake as we were speeding back, "that most of these cases of fake robberies are among small people, many of them on the East Side among little jewellers or other tradesmen. Still, they are not limited to any one class. Indeed, it is easier to foil the insurance companies when you sit in the midst of finery and wealth, protected by a self-assuring halo of moral rectitude, than under less fortunate circumstances. Too often, I'm afraid, we have good-naturedly admitted the unsolved burglary and paid the insurance claim. That has got to stop. Here's a case where we considered the moral hazard a safe one, and we are mistaken. It's the last straw."

Our interview with Mrs. Branford was about as awkward an undertaking as I have ever been concerned with. Imagine yourself forced to question a perfectly stunning woman, who was suspected of plotting so daring a deed and knew that you suspected her. Resentment was no name for her feelings. She scorned us, loathed us. It was only by what must have been the utmost exercise of her remarkable will-power that she restrained herself from calling the hotel porters and having us thrown out bodily. That would have put a bad face on it, so she tolerated our presence. Then, of course, the insurance company had reserved the right to examine everybody in the household, under oath if necessary, before passing on the claim.

"This is an outrage," she exclaimed, her eyes flashing and her breast rising and falling with suppressed emotion, "an outrage. When my husband returns I intend to have him place the whole matter in the hands of the best attorney in the city. Not only will I have the full amount of the insurance, but I will have damages and costs and everything the law allows. Spying on my every movement in this way—it is an outrage! One would think we were in St. Petersburg instead of New York."

"One moment, Mrs. Branford," put in Kennedy, as politely as he could. "Suppose——"

"Suppose nothing," she cried angrily. "I shall explain nothing, say nothing. What if I do choose to close up that lonely big house in the suburbs and come to the city to live for a few days—is it anybody's business except mine?"

"And your husband's?" added Kennedy, nettled at her treatment of him.

She shot him a scornful glance. "I suppose Mr. Branford went out to Arizona for the express purpose of collecting insurance on my jewels," she added sarcastically with eyes that snapped fire.

"I was about to say," remarked Kennedy as imperturbably as if he were an automaton, "that supposing some one took advantage of your absence to rob your safe, don't you think the wisest course would be to be perfectly frank about it?"

"And give just one plausible reason why you wished so much to have it known that you were going to Palm Beach when in reality you were in New York?" pursued Maloney, while Kennedy frowned at his tactless attempt at a third degree.

If she had resented Kennedy, she positively flew up in the air and commenced to aviate at Maloney's questioning. Tossing her head, she said icily: "I do not know that you have been appointed my guardian, sir. Let us consider this interview at an end. Good-night," and with that she swept out of the room, ignoring Maloney and bestowing one biting glance on Blake, who actually winced, so little relish did he have for this ticklish part of the proceedings.

I think we all felt like schoolboys who had been detected robbing a melon-patch or in some other heinous offence, as we slowly filed down the hall to the elevator. A woman of Mrs. Branford's stamp so readily and successfully puts one in the wrong that I could easily comprehend why Blake wanted to call on Kennedy for help in what otherwise seemed a plain case.

Blake and Maloney were some distance ahead of us, as Craig leaned over to me and whispered: "That Maloney is impossible. I'll have to shake him loose in some way. Either we handle this case alone or we quit."

"Right-o," I agreed emphatically. "He's put his foot in it badly at the very start. Only, be decent about it, Craig. The case is too big for you to let it slip by."

"Trust me, Walter. I'll do it tactfully," he whispered, then to Blake he added as we overtook them: "Maloney is right. The case is simple enough, after all. But we must find out some way to fasten the thing more closely on Mrs. Branford. Let me think out a scheme to-night. I'll see you to-morrow."

As Blake and Maloney disappeared down the street in the car, Kennedy wheeled about and walked deliberately back into the Grattan Inn again. It was quite late. People were coming in from the theatres, laughing and chatting gaily. Kennedy selected a table that commanded a view of the parlour as well as of the dining-room itself.

"She was dressed to receive some one—did you notice?" he remarked as we sat down and cast our eyes over the dizzy array of inedibles on the card before us. "I think it is worth waiting a while to see who it is."

Having ordered what I did not want, I glanced about until my eye rested on a large pier-glass at the other end of the dining-room.

"Craig," I whispered excitedly, "Mrs. B. is in

the writing-room—I can see her in that glass at the end of the room, behind you."

"Get up and change places with me as quietly as you can, Walter," he said quickly. "I want to see her when she can't see me."

Kennedy was staring in rapt attention at the mirror. "There's a man with her, Walter," he said under his breath. "He came in while we were changing places—a fine-looking chap. By Jove, I've seen him before somewhere. His face and his manner are familiar to me. But I simply can't place him. Did you see her wraps in the chair? No? Well, he's helping her on with them. They're going out. *Garçon, l'addition—vite.*"

We were too late, however, for just as we reached the door we caught a fleeting glimpse of a huge new limousine.

"Who was that man who just went out with the lady?" asked Craig of the negro who turned the revolving-door at the carriage entrance.

"Jack Delarue, sah—in 'The Grass Widower,' sah," replied the doorman. "Yes, sah, he stays here once in a while. Thank you, sah," as Kennedy dropped a quarter into the man's hand.

"That complicates things considerably," he mused as we walked slowly down to the subway station. "Jack Delarue—I wonder if he is mixed up in this thing also."

"I've heard that 'The Grass Widower' isn't such a howling success as a money-maker," I volunteered. "Delarue has a host of creditors, no doubt. By the way, Craig," I exclaimed, "don't you think it would be a good plan to drop down and see O'Connor? The police will have to be informed in a few hours now, anyhow. Maybe Delarue has a criminal record."

"A good idea, Walter," agreed Craig, turning into a drug-store which had a telephone booth. "I'll just call O'Connor up, and we'll see if he does know anything about it."

O'Connor was not at headquarters, but we finally found him at his home, and it was well into the small hours when we arrived there. Trusting to the first deputy's honour, which had stood many a test, Craig began to unfold the story. He had scarcely got as far as describing the work of the suspected hired yeggman, when O'Connor raised both hands and brought them down hard on the arms of his chair.

"Say," he ejaculated, "that explains it!"

"What?" we asked in chorus.

"Why, one of my best stool-pigeons told me to-day that there was something doing at a house in the Chatham Square district that we have been watching for a long time. It's full of crooks, and to-day they've all been as drunk as lords, a sure sign some one has made a haul and been generous with the rest. And one or two of the professional 'fences' have been acting suspiciously, too. Oh, that explains it all right."

I looked at Craig as much as to say, "I told you so," but he was engrossed in what O'Connor was saying.

"You know," continued the police officer, "there

is one particular 'fence' who runs his business under the guise of a loan-shark's office. He probably has a wider acquaintance among the big criminals than any other man in the city. From him crooks can obtain anything from a jimmy to a safe-cracking outfit. I know that this man has been trying to dispose of some unmounted pearls to-day among jewellers in Maiden Lane. I'll bet he has been disposing of some of the Branford pearls, one by one. I'll follow that up. I'll arrest this 'fence' and hold him till he tells me what yeggman came to him with the pearls."

"And if you find out, will you go with me to that house near Chatham Square, providing it was some one in that gang?" asked Craig eagerly.

O'Connor shook his head. "I'd better keep out of it. They know me too well. Go alone. I'll get that stool-pigeon—the Gay Cat is his name—to go with you. I'll help you in any way. I'll have any number of plain-clothes men you want ready to raid the place the moment you get the evidence. But you'll never get any evidence if they know I'm in the neighbourhood."

The next morning Craig scarcely ate any breakfast himself and made me bolt my food most unceremoniously. We were out in Montclair again before the commuters had started to go to New York, and that in spite of the fact that we had stopped at his laboratory on the way and had got a package which he carried carefully.

Kennedy instituted a most thorough search of the house from cellar to attic in daylight. What he expected to find, I did not know, but I am quite sure nothing escaped him.

" Now, Walter," he said after he had ransacked the house, " there remains just one place. Here is this little wall safe in Mrs. Branford's room. We must open it."

For an hour if not longer he worked over the combination, listening to the fall of the tumblers in the lock. It was a simple little thing and one of the old-timers in the industry would no doubt have opened it in short order. The perspiration stood out on his forehead, so intent was he in working the thing. At last it yielded. Except for some of the family silver, the safe was empty.

Carefully noting how the light shone on the wall safe, Craig unwrapped the package he had brought and disclosed a camera. He placed it on a writing-desk opposite the safe, in such a way that it was not at all conspicuous, and focused it on the safe.

" This is a camera with a newly-invented between-lens shutter of great illumination and efficiency," he explained. " It has always been practically impossible to get such pictures, but this new shutter has so much greater speed than anything ever invented before that it is possible to use it in detective work. I'll just run these fine wires like a burglar alarm, only instead of having an alarm I'll attach them to the camera so that we can get a picture. I've proved its speed up to one two-thousandth of a second. It may or it may not work. If it does we'll catch somebody, right in the act."

About noon we went down to Liberty Street, home

of burglary insurance. I don't think Blake liked it very much because Kennedy insisted on playing the lone hand, but he said nothing, for it was part of the agreement. Maloney seemed rather glad than otherwise. He had been combing out some tangled clues of his own about Mrs. Branford. Still, Kennedy smoothed things over by complimenting the detective on his activity, and indeed he had shown remarkable ability in the first place in locating Mrs. Branford.

"I started out with the assumption that the Branfords must have needed money for some reason or other," said Maloney. "So I went to the commercial agencies to-day and looked up Branford. I can't say he has been prosperous; nobody has been in Wall Street these days, and that's just the thing that causes an increase in fake burglaries. Then there is another possibility," he continued triumphantly. "I had a man up at the Grattan Inn, and he reports to me that Mrs. Branford was seen with the actor Jack Delarue last night. I imagine they quarrelled, for she returned alone, much agitated, in a taxi-cab. Any way you look at it, the clues are promising—whether she needed money for Branford's speculations or for the financing of that rake Delarue."

Maloney regarded Craig with the air of an expert who could afford to patronise a good amateur—but after all an amateur. Kennedy said nothing, and of course I took the cue.

"Yes," agreed Blake, "you see, our original hypothesis was a pretty good one. Meanwhile, of course, the police are floundering around in a bog of false scents."

"It would make our case a good deal stronger," remarked Kennedy quietly, "if we could discover some of the stolen jewellery hidden somewhere by Mrs. Branford herself." He said nothing of his own unsuccessful search through the house, but continued: "What do you suppose she has done with the jewels? She must have put them somewhere before she got the yeggman to break the safe. She'd hardly trust them in his hands. But she might have been foolish enough for that. Of course it's another possibility that he really got away with them. I doubt if she has them at Grattan Inn, or even if she would personally put them in a safe deposit vault. Perhaps Delarue figures in that end of it. We must let no stone go unturned."

"That's right," meditated Maloney, apparently turning something over in his mind as if it were a new idea. "If we only had some evidence, even part of the jewels that she had hidden, it would clinch the case. That's a good idea, Kennedy."

Craig said nothing, but I could see, or fancied I saw, that he was gratified at the thought that he had started Maloney off on another trail, leaving us to follow ours unhampered. The interview with Blake was soon over, and as we left I looked inquiringly at Craig.

"I want to see Mrs. Branford again," he said. "I think we can do better alone to-day than we did last night."

I must say I half expected that she would refuse

to see us and was quite surprised when the page returned with the request that we go up to her suite. It was evident that her attitude toward us was very different from that of the first interview. Whether she was ruffled by the official presence of Blake or the officious presence of Maloney, she was at least politely tolerant of us. Or was it that she at last began to realise that the toils were closing about her and that things began to look unmistakably black?

Kennedy was quick to see his advantage. "Mrs. Branford," he began, "since last night I have come into the possession of some facts that are very important. I have heard that several loose pearls which may or may not be yours have been offered for sale by a man on the Bowery who is what the yeggmen call a 'fence.'"

"Yeggmen—'fence'?" she repeated. "Mr. Kennedy, really I do not care to discuss the pearls any longer. It is immaterial to me what becomes of them. My first desire is to collect the insurance. If anything is recovered I am quite willing to deduct that amount from the total. But I must insist on the full insurance or the return of the pearls. As soon as Mr. Branford arrives I shall take other steps to secure redress."

A boy rapped at the door and brought in a telegram which she tore open nervously. "He will be here in four days," she said, tearing the telegram petulantly, and not at all as if she were glad to receive it. "Is there anything else that you wish to say?"

She was tapping her foot on the rug as if anxious

to conclude the interview. Kennedy leaned forward earnestly and played his trump card boldly.

"Do you remember that scene in 'The Grass Widower,'" he said slowly, "where Jack Delarue meets his runaway wife at the masquerade ball?"

She coloured slightly, but instantly regained her composure. "Vaguely," she murmured, toying with the flowers in her dress.

"In real life," said Kennedy, his voice purposely betraying that he meant it to have a personal application, "husbands do not forgive even rumours of—ah—shall we say affinities?—much less the fact."

"In real life," she replied, "wives do not have affinities as often as some newspapers and plays would have us believe."

"I saw Delarue after the performance last night," went on Kennedy inexorably. "I was not seen, but I saw, and he was with——"

She was pacing the room now in unsuppressed excitement. "Will you never stop spying on me?" she cried. "Must my every act be watched and misrepresented? I suppose a distorted version of the facts will be given to my husband. Have you no chivalry, or justice, or—or mercy?" she pleaded, stopping in front of Kennedy.

"Mrs. Branford," he replied coldly, "I cannot promise what I shall do. My duty is simply to get at the truth about the pearls. If it involves some other person, it is still my duty to get at the truth. Why not tell me all that you really know about the pearls and trust me to bring it out all right?"

She faced him, pale and haggard. "I have told,"

she repeated steadily. "I cannot tell any more—I know nothing more."

Was she lying? I was not expert enough in feminine psychology to judge, but down in my heart I knew that the woman was hiding something behind that forced steadiness. What was it she was battling for? We had reached an *impasse*.

It was after dinner when I met Craig at the laboratory. He had made a trip to Montclair again, where his stay had been protracted because Maloney was there and he wished to avoid him. He had brought back the camera, and had had another talk with O'Connor, at which he had mapped out a plan of battle.

"We are to meet the Gay Cat at the City Hall at nine o'clock," explained Craig laconically. "We are going to visit a haunt of yeggmen, Walter, that few outsiders have ever seen. Are you game? O'Connor and his men will be close by—hiding, of course."

"I suppose so," I replied slowly. "But what excuse are you going to have for getting into this yegg-resort?"

"Simply that we are two newspaper men looking for an article, without names, dates, or places—just a good story of yeggmen and tramps. I've got a little—well, we'll call it a little camera outfit that I'm going to sling over my shoulder. You are the reporter, remember, and I'm the newspaper photographer. They won't pose for us, of course, but that will be all right. Speaking about photographs, I got one out at Montclair that is interesting. I'll show it to you later in the evening—and in case anything should happen to me, Walter, you'll find the original plate locked here in the top drawer of my desk. I guess we'd better be getting downtown."

The house to which we were guided by the Gay Cat was on a cross street within a block or two of Chatham Square. If we had passed it casually in the daytime there would have been nothing to distinguish it above the other ramshackle buildings on the street, except that the other houses were cluttered with children and baby-carriages, while this one was vacant, the front door closed, and the blinds tightly drawn. As we approached, a furtive figure shambled from the basement areaway and slunk off into the crowd for the night's business of pocket-picking or second-story work.

I had had misgivings as to whether we would be admitted at all—I might almost say hopes—but the Gay Cat succeeded in getting a ready response at the basement door. The house itself was the dilapidated ruin of what had once been a fashionable residence in the days when society lived in the then suburban Bowery. The iron handrail on the steps was still graceful, though rusted and insecure. The stones of the steps were decayed and eaten away by time, and the front door was never opened.

As we entered the low basement door, I felt that those who entered here did indeed abandon hope. Inside, the evidences of the past grandeur were still more striking. What had once been a drawing-room was now the general assembly room of the resort. Broken-down chairs lined the walls, and the floor was generously sprinkled with sawdust. A huge pot-bellied stove occupied the centre of the room, and by it stood a box of sawdust plentifully discoloured with tobacco-juice.

Three or four of the "guests"—there was no "register" in this yeggman's hotel—were seated about the stove discussing something in a language that was English, to be sure, but of a variation that only a yegg could understand. I noted the once handsome white marble mantel, now stained by age, standing above the unused grate. Double folding-doors led to what, I imagine, was once a library. Dirt and grime indescribable were everywhere. There was the smell of old clothes and old cooking, the race odours of every nationality known to the metropolis. I recalled a night I once spent in a Bowery lodging-house for "local colour." Only this was infinitely worse. No law regulated this house. There was an atmosphere of cheerlessness that a half-blackened Welsbach mantle turned into positive ghastliness.

Our guide introduced us. There was a dead silence as eight eyes were craftily fixed on us, sizing us up. What should I say? Craig came to the rescue. To him the adventure was a lark. It was novel, and that was merit enough.

"Ask about the slang," he suggested. "That makes a picturesque story."

It seemed to me innocuous enough, so I engaged in conversation with a man whom the Gay Cat had introduced as the proprietor. Much of the slang

I already knew by hearsay, such as "bulls" for policemen, a "mouthpiece" for a lawyer to defend one when he is "ditched" or arrested; in fact, as I busily scribbled away I must have collected a lexicon of a hundred words or so for future reference.

"And names?" I queried. "You have some queer nicknames."

"Oh, yes," replied the man. "Now here's the Gay Cat—that's what we call a fellow who is the finder, who enters a town ahead of the gang. Then there's Chi Fat—that means he's from Chicago and fat. And Pitts Slim—he's from Pittsburgh and——"

"Aw, cut it," broke in one of the others. "Pitts Slim'll be here to-night. He'll give you the devil if he hears you talking to reporters about him."

The proprietor began to talk of less dangerous subjects. Craig succeeded in drawing out from him the yegg recipe for making "soup." "It's here in this cipher," said the man, drawing out a dirty piece of paper. "It's well known, and you can have this. Here's the key. It was written by 'Deafy' Smith, and the police pinched it."

Craig busily translated the curious document:

Take ten or a dozen sticks of dynamite, crumble it up fine, and put it in a pan or washbowl, then pour over it enough alcohol, wood or pure, to cover it well. Stir it up well with your hands, being careful to break all the lumps. Leave it set for a few minutes. Then get a few yards of cheesecloth and tear it up in pieces and strain the mixture through the cloth into another vessel. Wring the sawdust dry and throw it away. The remains will be the soup and alcohol mixed.

Next take the same amount of water as you used of alcohol and pour it in. Leave the whole set for a few minutes.

"Very interesting," commented Craig. "Safe-blowing in one lesson by correspondence school. The rest of this tells how to attack various makes, doesn't it?"

Just then a thin man in a huge, worn ulster came stamping upstairs from the basement, his collar up and his hat down over his eyes. There was something indefinably familiar about him, but as his face and figure were so well concealed, I could not tell just why I thought so.

Catching a glimpse of us, he beat a retreat across the opposite end of the room, beckoning to the proprietor, who joined him outside the door. I thought I heard him ask: "Who are those men? Who let them in?" but I could not catch the reply.

One by one the other occupants of the room rose and sidled out, leaving us alone with the Gay Cat. Kennedy reached over to get a cigarette from my case and light it from one that I was smoking.

"That's our man, I think," he whispered—"Pitts Slim."

I said nothing, but I would have been willing to part with a large section of my bank-account to be up on the Chatham Square station of the Elevated just then.

There was a rush from the half-open door behind us. Suddenly everything turned black before me; my eyes swam; I felt a stinging sensation on my head and a weak feeling about the stomach; I sank half-conscious to the floor. All was blank, but, dimly, I seemed to be dragged and dropped down hard.

How long I lay there I don't know. Kennedy says it was not over five minutes. It may have been so, but to me it seemed an age. When I opened my eyes I was lying on my back on a very dirty sofa in another room. Kennedy was bending over me with blood streaming from a long deep gash on his head. Another figure was groaning in the semi-darkness opposite; it was the Gay Cat.

"They blackjacked us," whispered Kennedy to me as I staggered to my feet. "Then they dragged us through a secret passage into another house. How do you feel?"

"All right," I answered, bracing myself against a chair, for I was weak from the loss of blood, and dizzy. I was sore in every joint and muscle. I looked about, only half comprehending. Then my recollection flooded back with a rush. We had been locked in another room after the attack, and left to be dealt with later. I felt in my pocket. I had left my watch at the laboratory, but even the dollar watch I had taken and the small sum of money in my pocketbook were gone.

Kennedy still had his camera slung over his shoulder, where he had fastened it securely.

Here we were, imprisoned, while Pitts Slim, the man we had come after, whoever he was, was making his escape. Somewhere across the street was O'Connor, waiting in a room as we had agreed. There was only one window in our room, and it opened on a miserable little dumbwaiter air-shaft.

It would be hours yet before his suspicions would be aroused and he would discover which of the houses we were held in. Meanwhile what might not happen to us?

Kennedy calmly set up his tripod. One leg had been broken in the rough-house, but he tied it together with his handkerchief, now wet with blood. I wondered how he could think of taking a picture. His very deliberation set me fretting and fuming, and I swore at him under my breath. Still, he worked calmly ahead. I saw him take the black box and set it on the tripod. It was indistinct in the darkness. It looked like a camera, and yet it had some attachment at the side that was queer, including a little lamp. Craig bent and attached some wires about the box.

At last he seemed ready. " Walter," he whispered, " roll that sofa quietly over against the door. There, now the table and that bureau, and wedge the chairs in. Keep that door shut at any cost. It's now or never—here goes."

He stopped a moment and tinkered with the box on the tripod. " Hello! Hello! Hello! Is that you, O'Connor? " he shouted.

I watched him in amazement. Was the man crazy? Had the blow affected his brain? Here he was, trying to talk into a camera. A little signalling-bell in the box commenced to ring, as if by spirit hands.

" Shut up in that room," growled a voice from outside the door. " By God, they've barricaded the door. Come on, pals, we'll kill the spies."

A smile of triumph lighted up Kennedy's pale face. "It works, it works," he cried as the little bell continued to buzz. "This is a wireless telephone you perhaps have seen announced recently—good for several hundred feet—through walls and everything. The inventor placed it in a box easily carried by a man, including a battery, and mounted on an ordinary camera tripod so that the user might well be taken for a travelling photographer. It is good in one direction only, but I have a signalling-bell here that can be rung from the other end by Hertzian waves. Thank Heaven, it's compact and simple.

"O'Connor," he went on, "it is as I told you. It was Pitts Slim. He left here ten or fifteen minutes ago—I don't know by what exit, but I heard them say they would meet at the Central freight-yards at midnight. Start your plain-clothes men out and send some one here, quick, to release us. We are locked in a room in the fourth or fifth house from the corner. There's a secret passage to the yegg-house. The Gay Cat is still unconscious, Jameson is groggy, and I have a bad scalp wound. They are trying to beat in our barricade. Hurry."

I think I shall never get straight in my mind the fearful five minutes that followed, the battering at the door, the oaths, the scuffle outside, the crash as the sofa, bureau, table, and chairs all yielded at once—and my relief when I saw the square-set, honest face of O'Connor and half a dozen plain-clothes men holding the yeggs who would certainly have murdered us this time to protect their pal in his getaway. The fact is I didn't think straight until we were halfway uptown, speeding toward the railroad freight-yards in O'Connor's car. The fresh air at last revived me, and I began to forget my cuts and bruises in the renewed excitement.

We entered the yards carefully, accompanied by several of the railroad's detectives, who met us with a couple of police dogs. Skulking in the shadow under the high embankment that separated the yards with their interminable lines of full and empty cars on one side and the San Juan Hill district of New York up on the bluff on the other side, we came upon a party of three men who were waiting to catch the midnight " side-door Pullman "—the fast freight out of New York.

The fight was brief, for we outnumbered them more than three to one. O'Connor himself snapped a pair of steel bracelets on the thin man, who seemed to be leader of the party.

" It's all up, Pitts Slim," he ground out from his set teeth.

One of our men flashed his bull's-eye on the three prisoners. I caught myself as in a dream.

Pitts Slim was Maloney, the detective.

An hour later, at headquarters, after the pedigrees had been taken, the " mugging " done, and the jewels found on the three yeggs checked off from the list of the Branford pearls, leaving a few thousand dollars' worth unaccounted for, O'Connor led the way into his private office. There were Mrs. Branford and Blake, waiting.

Maloney sullenly refused to look at his former

employer, as Blake rushed over and grasped Kennedy's hand, asking eagerly: "How did you do it, Kennedy? This is the last thing I expected."

Craig said nothing, but slowly opened a now crumpled envelope, which contained an untoned print of a photograph. He laid it on the desk. "There is your yeggman—at work," he said.

We bent over to look. It was a photograph of Maloney in the act of putting something in the little wall safe in Mrs. Branford's room. In a flash it dawned on me—the quick-shutter camera, the wire connected with the wall safe, Craig's hint to Maloney that if some of the jewels were found hidden in a likely place in the house, it would furnish the last link in the chain against her, Maloney's eager acceptance of the suggestion, and his visit to Montclair during which Craig had had hard work to avoid him.

"Pitts Slim, alias Maloney," added Kennedy, turning to Blake, "your shrewdest private detective, was posing in two characters at once very successfully. He was your trusted agent in possession of the most valuable secrets of your clients, at the same time engineering all the robberies that you thought were fakes, and then working up the evidence incriminating the victims themselves. He got into the Branford house with a skeleton key, and killed the maid. The picture shows him putting this shield-shaped brooch in the safe this afternoon—here's the brooch. And all this time he was the leader of the most dangerous band of yeggmen in the country."

"Mrs. Branford," exclaimed Blake, advancing and bowing most profoundly, "I trust that you understand my awkward position? My apologies cannot be too humble. It will give me great pleasure to hand you a certified check for the missing gems the first thing in the morning."

Mrs. Branford bit her lip nervously. Thc return of the pearls did not seem to interest her in the least.

"And I, too, must apologise for the false suspicion I had of you and—and—depend on me, it is already forgotten," said Kennedy, emphasising the "false" and looking her straight in the eyes.

She read his meaning and a look of relief crossed her face. "Thank you," she murmured simply, then dropping her eyes she added in a lower tone which no one heard except Craig: "Mr. Kennedy, how can I ever thank you? Another night, and it would have been too late to save me from myself."

III

THE GERM OF DEATH

By this time I was becoming used to Kennedy's strange visitors and, in fact, had begun to enjoy keenly the uncertainty of not knowing just what to expect from them next. Still, I was hardly prepared one evening to see a tall, nervous foreigner stalk noiselessly and unannounced into our apartment and hand his card to Kennedy without saying a word.

"Dr. Nicholas Kharkoff—hum—er, Jameson, you must have forgotten to latch the door. Well, Dr. Kharkoff, what can I do for you? It is evident something has upset you."

The tall Russian put his forefinger to his lips and, taking one of our good chairs, placed it by the door. Then he stood on it and peered cautiously through the transom into the hallway. "I think I eluded him this time," he exclaimed, as he nervously took a seat. "Professor Kennedy, I am being followed. Every step that I take somebody shadows me, from the moment I leave my office until I return. It is enough to drive me mad. But that is only one reason why I have come here to-night. I believe that I can trust you as a friend of justice—a friend of Russian freedom?"

He had included me in his earnest but somewhat vague query, so that I did not withdraw. Somehow, apparently, he had heard of Kennedy's rather liberal political views.

"It is about Vassili Saratovsky, the father of the Russian revolution, as we call him, that I have come to consult you," he continued quickly. "Just two weeks ago he was taken ill. It came on suddenly, a violent fever which continued for a week. Then he seemed to grow better, after the crisis had passed, and even attended a meeting of our central committee the other night. But in the meantime Olga Samarova, the little Russian dancer, whom you have perhaps seen, fell ill in the same way. Samarova is an ardent revolutionist, you know. This morning the servant at my own home on East Broadway was also stricken, and—who knows?—perhaps it will be my turn next. For to-night Saratovsky had an even more violent return of the fever, with intense shivering, excruciating pains in the limbs, and delirious headache. It is not like anything I ever saw before. Can you look into the case before it grows any worse, Professor?"

Again the Russian got on the chair and looked over the transom to be sure that he was not being overheard.

"I shall be only too glad to help you in any way I can," returned Kennedy, his manner expressing the genuine interest that he never feigned over a particularly knotty problem in science and crime. "I had the pleasure of meeting Saratovsky once in London. I shall try to see him the first thing in the morning."

Dr. Kharkoff's face fell. "I had hoped you

would see him to-night. If anything should happen——"

"Is it as urgent as that?"

"I believe it is," whispered Kharkoff, leaning forward earnestly. "We can call a taxicab—it will not take long, sir. Consider, there are many lives possibly at stake," he pleaded.

"Very well, I will go," consented Kennedy.

At the street door Kharkoff stopped short and drew Kennedy back. "Look—across the street in the shadow. There is the man. If I start toward him he will disappear; he is very clever. He followed me from Saratovsky's here, and has been waiting for me to come out."

"There are two taxicabs waiting at the stand," suggested Kennedy. "Doctor, you jump in the first, and Jameson and I will take the second. Then he can't follow us."

It was done in a moment, and we were whisked away, to the chagrin of the figure, which glided impotently out of the shadow in vain pursuit, too late even to catch the number of the cab.

"A promising adventure," commented Kennedy, as we bumped along over New York's uneven asphalt. "Have you ever met Saratovsky?"

"No," I replied dubiously. "Will you guarantee that he will not blow us up with a bomb?"

"Grandmother!" replied Craig. "Why, Walter, he is the most gentle, engaging old philosopher——"

"That ever cut a throat or scuttled a ship?" I interrupted.

"On the contrary," insisted Kennedy, somewhat nettled, "he is a patriarch, respected by every faction of the revolutionists, from the fighting organisation to the believers in non-resistance and Tolstoy. I tell you, Walter, the nation that can produce a man such as Saratovsky deserves and some day will win political freedom. I have heard of this Dr. Kharkoff before, too. His life would be a short one if he were in Russia. A remarkable man, who fled after those unfortunate uprisings in 1905. Ah, we are on Fifth Avenue. I suspect that he is taking us to a club on the lower part of the avenue, where a number of the Russian reformers live, patiently waiting and planning for the great 'awakening' in their native land."

Kharkoff's cab had stopped. Our quest had indeed brought us almost to Washington Square. Here we entered an old house of the past generation. As we passed through the wide hall, I noted the high ceilings, the old-fashioned marble mantels stained by time, the long, narrow rooms and dirty-white woodwork, and the threadbare furniture of black walnut and horsehair.

Upstairs in a small back room we found the venerable Saratovsky, tossing, half-delirious with the fever, on a disordered bed. His was a striking figure in this sordid setting, with a high intellectual forehead and deep-set, glowing coals of eyes which gave a hint at the things which had made his life one of the strangest among all the revolutionists of Russia and the works he had done among the most daring. The brown dye was scarcely yet out of his flowing white beard—a relic of his last trip back to his fatherland, where he had eluded the secret police in the disguise of a German gymnasium professor.

Saratovsky extended a thin, hot, emaciated hand to us, and we remained standing. Kennedy said nothing for the moment. The sick man motioned feebly to us to come closer.

"Professor Kennedy," he whispered, "there is some deviltry afoot. The Russian autocracy would stop at nothing. Kharkoff has probably told you of it. I am so weak——"

He groaned and sank back, overcome by a chill that seemed to rack his poor gaunt form.

"Kazanovitch can tell Professor Kennedy something, Doctor. I am too weak to talk, even at this critical time. Take him to see Boris and Ekaterina."

Almost reverently we withdrew, and Kharkoff led us down the hall to another room. The door was ajar, and a light disclosed a man in a Russian peasant's blouse, bending laboriously over a writing-desk. So absorbed was he that not until Kharkoff spoke did he look up. His figure was somewhat slight and his face pointed and of an ascetic mould.

"Ah!" he exclaimed. "You have recalled me from a dream. I fancied I was on the old mir with Ivan, one of my characters. Welcome, comrades."

It flashed over me at once that this was the famous Russian novelist, Boris Kazanovitch. I had not at first connected the name with that of the author of those gloomy tales of peasant life. Kazanovitch stood with his hands tucked under his blouse.

"Night is my favourite time for writing," he explained. "It is then that the imagination works at its best."

I gazed curiously about the room. There seemed to be a marked touch of a woman's hand here and there; it was unmistakable. At last my eye rested on a careless heap of dainty wearing apparel on a chair in the corner.

"Where is Nevsky?" asked Dr. Kharkoff, apparently missing the person who owned the garments.

"Ekaterina has gone to a rehearsal of the little play of Gershuni's escape from Siberia and betrayal by Rosenberg. She will stay with friends on East Broadway to-night. She has deserted me, and here I am all alone, finishing a story for one of the American magazines."

"Ah, Professor Kennedy, that is unfortunate," commented Kharkoff. "A brilliant woman is Mademoiselle Nevsky—devoted to the cause. I know only one who equals her, and that is my patient downstairs, the little dancer, Samarova."

"Samarova is faithful—Nevsky is a genius," put in Kazanovitch. Kharkoff said nothing for a time, though it was easy to see he regarded the actress highly.

"Samarova," he said at length to us, "was arrested for her part in the assassination of Grand Duke Sergius and thrown into solitary confinement in the fortress of St. Peter and St. Paul. They tortured her, the beasts—burned her body with their cigarettes. It was unspeakable. But she would not confess, and finally they had to let her go. Nevsky, who was a student of biology at the University of St. Petersburg when Von Plehve was assassinated, was arrested, but her relatives had sufficient influence to secure her release. They met in Paris, and Nevsky persuaded Olga to go on the stage and come to New York."

"Next to Ekaterina's devotion to the cause is her devotion to science," said Kazanovitch, opening a door to a little room. Then he added: "If she were not a woman, or if your universities were less prejudiced, she would be welcome anywhere as a professor. See, here is her laboratory. It is the best we—she can afford. Organic chemistry, as you call it in English, interests me too, but of course I am not a trained scientist—I am a novelist."

The laboratory was simple, almost bare. Photographs of Koch, Ehrlich, Metchnikoff, and a number of other scientists adorned the walls. The deeply stained deal table was littered with beakers and test-tubes.

"How is Saratovsky?" asked the writer of the doctor, aside, as we gazed curiously about.

Kharkoff shook his head gravely. "We have just come from his room. He was too weak to talk, but he asked that you tell Mr. Kennedy anything that it is necessary he should know about our suspicions."

"It is that we are living with the sword of Damocles constantly dangling over our heads, gentlemen," cried Kazanovitch passionately, turning toward us.

"You will excuse me if I get some cigarettes downstairs? Over them I will tell you what we fear."

A call from Saratovsky took the doctor away also at the same moment, and we were left alone.

"A queer situation, Craig," I remarked, glancing involuntarily at the heap of feminine finery on the chair, as I sat down before Kazanovitch's desk.

"Queer for New York; not for St. Petersburg," was his laconic reply, as he looked around for another chair. Everything was littered with books and papers, and at last he leaned over and lifted the dress from the chair to place it on the bed, as the easiest way of securing a seat in the scantily furnished room.

A pocketbook and a letter fell to the floor from the folds of the dress. He stooped to pick them up, and I saw a strange look of surprise on his face. Without a moment's hesitation he shoved the letter into his pocket and replaced the other things as he had found them.

A moment later Kazanovitch returned with a large box of Russian cigarettes. "Be seated, sir," he said to Kennedy, sweeping a mass of books and papers off a large divan. "When Nevsky is not here the room gets sadly disarranged. I have no genius for order."

Amid the clouds of fragrant light smoke we waited for Kazanovitch to break the silence.

"Perhaps you think that the iron hand of the Russian prime minister has broken the backbone of revolution in Russia," he began at length. "But because the Duma is subservient, it does not mean that all is over. Not at all. We are not asleep. Revolution is smouldering, ready to break forth at any moment. The agents of the government know it. They are desperate. There is no means they would not use to crush us. Their long arm reaches even to New York, in this land of freedom."

He rose and excitedly paced the room. Somehow or other, this man did not prepossess me. Was it that I was prejudiced by a puritanical disapproval of the things that pass current in Old World morality? Or was it merely that I found the great writer of fiction seeking the dramatic effect always at the cost of sincerity?

"Just what is it that you suspect?" asked Craig, anxious to dispense with the rhetoric and to get down to facts. "Surely, when three persons are stricken, you must suspect something."

"Poison," replied Kazanovitch quickly. "Poison, and of a kind that even the poison doctors of St. Petersburg have never employed. Dr. Kharkoff is completely baffled. Your American doctors—two were called in to see Saratovsky—say it is the typhus fever. But Kharkoff knows better. There is no typhus rash. Besides"—and he leaned forward to emphasise his words—"one does not get over typhus in a week and have it again as Saratovsky has."

I could see that Kennedy was growing impatient. An idea had occurred to him, and only politeness kept him listening to Kazanovitch longer.

"Doctor," he said, as Kharkoff entered the room again, "do you suppose you could get some perfectly clean test-tubes and sterile bouillon from Miss

Nevsky's laboratory? I think I saw a rack of tubes on the table."

"Surely," answered Kharkoff.

"You will excuse us, Mr. Kazanovitch," apologised Kennedy briskly, "but I feel that I am going to have a hard day to-morrow and—by the way, would you be so kind as to come up to my laboratory some time during the day, and continue your story."

On the way out Craig took the doctor aside for a moment, and they talked earnestly. At last Craig motioned to me.

"Walter," he explained, "Dr. Kharkoff is going to prepare some cultures in the test-tubes to-night so that I can make a microscopic examination of the blood of Saratovsky, Samarova, and later of his servant. The tubes will be ready early in the morning, and I have arranged with the doctor for you to call and get them if you have no objection."

I assented, and we started downstairs. As we passed a door on the second floor, a woman's voice called out, "Is that you, Boris?"

"No, Olga, this is Nicholas," replied the doctor. "It is Samarova," he said to us as he entered.

In a few moments he rejoined us. "She is no better," he continued, as we again started away. "I may as well tell you, Professor Kennedy, just how matters stand here. Samarova is head over heels in love with Kazanovitch—you heard her call for him just now? Before they left Paris, Kazanovitch showed some partiality for Olga, but now Nevsky has captured him. She is indeed a fascinating woman, but as for me, if Olga would consent to become Madame Kharkoff, it should be done to-morrow, and she need worry no longer over her broken contract with the American theatre managers. But women are not that way. She prefers the hopeless love. Ah, well, I shall let you know if anything new happens. Good-night, and a thousand thanks for your help, gentlemen."

Nothing was said by either of us on our journey uptown, for it was late and I, at least, was tired.

But Kennedy had no intention of going to bed, I found. Instead, he sat down in his easy chair and shaded his eyes, apparently in deep thought. As I stood by the table to fill my pipe for a last smoke, I saw that he was carefully regarding the letter he had picked up, turning it over and over, and apparently debating with himself what to do with it.

"Some kinds of paper can be steamed open without leaving any trace," he remarked in answer to my unspoken question, laying the letter down before me.

I read the address: "M. Alexander Alexandrovitch Orloff, — Rue de ——, Paris, France."

"Letter-opening has been raised to a fine art by the secret service agents of foreign countries," he continued. "Why not take a chance? The simple operation of steaming a letter open is followed by reburnishing the flap with a bone instrument, and no trace is left. I can't do that, for this letter is sealed with wax. One way would be to take a matrix of the seal before breaking the wax and then replace a duplicate of it. No, I won't risk it. I'll try a scientific way."

Between two pieces of smooth wood, Craig laid the letter flat, so that the edges projected about a thirty-second of an inch. He flattened the projecting edge of the envelope, then roughened it, and finally slit it open.

"You see, Walter, later I will place the letter back, apply a hair line of strong white gum, and unite the edges of the envelope under pressure. Let us see what we have here."

He drew out what seemed to be a manuscript on very thin paper, and spread it out flat on the table before us. Apparently it was a scientific paper on a rather unusual subject, "Spontaneous Generation of Life." It was in longhand and read:

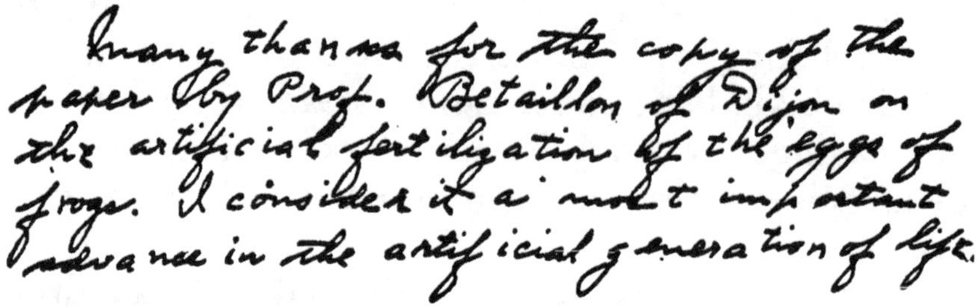
Many thanks for the copy of the paper by Prof. Betaillon of Dijon on the artificial fertilization of the eggs of frogs. I consider it a most important advance in the artificial generation of life.

I will not attempt to reproduce in facsimile the entire manuscript, for it is unnecessary, and, in fact, I merely set down part of its contents here because it seemed so utterly valueless to me at the time. It went on to say:

While Betaillon punctured the eggs with a platinum needle and developed them by means of electric discharges, Loeb in America placed eggs of the sea-urchin in a strong solution of sea water, then in a bath where they were subjected to the action of butyric acid. Finally they were placed in ordinary sea water again, where they developed in the natural manner. Delage at Roscorf used a liquid containing salts of magnesia and tannate of ammonia to produce the same result.

In his latest book on the Origin of Life Dr. Charlton Bastian tells of using two solutions. One consisted of two or three drops of dilute sodium silicate with eight drops of liquor ferri pernitratis to one ounce of distilled water. The other was composed of the same amount of the silicate with six drops of dilute phosphoric acid and six grains of ammonium phosphate. He filled sterilised tubes, sealed them hermetically, and heated them to 125 or 145 degrees, Centigrade, although 60 or 70 degrees would have killed any bacteria remaining in them.

Next he exposed them to sunlight in a south window for from two to four months. When the tubes were opened Dr. Bastian found organisms in them which differed in no way from real bacteria. They grew and multiplied. He contends that he has proved the possibility of spontaneous generation of life.

Then there were the experiments of John Butler Burke of Cambridge, who claimed that he had developed "radiobes" in tubes of sterilised bouillon by means of radium emanations. Daniel Berthelot in France last year announced that he had used the ultra-violet rays to duplicate nature's own process of chlorophyll assimilation. He has broken up carbon dioxide and water-vapour in the air in precisely the same way that the green cells of plants do it.

Leduc at Nantes has made crystals grow from an artificial "egg" composed of certain chemicals. These crystals show all the apparent vital phenomena without being actually alive. His work is interesting, for it shows the physical forces that probably control minute life cells, once they are created.

"What do you make of it?" asked Kennedy, noting the puzzled look on my face as I finished reading.

"Well, recent research in the problem of the origin of life may be very interesting," I replied.

"There are a good many chemicals mentioned here—I wonder if any of them is poisonous? But I am of the opinion that there is something more to this manuscript than a mere scientific paper."

"Exactly, Walter," said Kennedy in half raillery. "What I wanted to know was how you would suggest getting at that something."

Study as I might, I could make nothing out of it. Meanwhile Craig was busily figuring with a piece of paper and a pencil.

"I give it up, Craig," I said at last. "It is late. Perhaps we had better both turn in, and we may have some ideas on it in the morning."

For answer he merely shook his head and continued to scribble and figure on the paper. With a reluctant good-night I shut my door, determined to be up early in the morning and go for the tubes that Kharkoff was to prepare.

But in the morning Kennedy was gone. I dressed hastily, and was just about to go out when he hurried in, showing plainly the effects of having spent a sleepless night. He flung an early edition of a newspaper on the table.

"Too late," he exclaimed. "I tried to reach Kharkoff, but it was too late."

"Another East Side Bomb Outrage," I read. "While returning at a late hour last night from a patient, Dr. Nicholas Kharkoff, of —— East Broadway, was severely injured by a bomb which had been placed in his hallway earlier in the evening. Dr. Kharkoff, who is a well-known physician on the East Side, states that he has been constantly shadowed by some one unknown for the past week or two. He attributes his escape with his life to the fact that since he was shadowed he has observed extreme caution. Yesterday his cook was poisoned and is now dangerously ill. Dr. Kharkoff stands high in the Russian community, and it is thought by the police that the bomb was placed by a Russian political agent, as Kharkoff has been active in the ranks of the revolutionists."

"But what made you anticipate it?" I asked of Kennedy, considerably mystified.

"The manuscript," he replied.

"The manuscript? How? Where is it?"

"After I found that it was too late to save Kharkoff and that he was well cared for at the hospital, I hurried to Saratovsky's. Kharkoff had fortunately left the tubes there, and I got them. Here they are. As for the manuscript in the letter, I was going to ask you to slip upstairs by some strategy and return it where I found it, when you went for the tubes this morning. Kazanovitch was out, and I have returned it myself, so you need not go, now."

"He's coming to see you to-day, isn't he?"

"I hope so. I left a note asking him to bring Miss Nevsky, if possible, too. Come, let us breakfast and go over to the laboratory. They may arrive at any moment. Besides, I'm interested to see what the tubes disclose."

Instead of Kazanovitch awaiting us at the laboratory, however, we found Miss Nevsky, haggard and worn. She was a tall, striking girl with more of the Gaul than the Slav in her appearance. There was a slightly sensuous curve to her mouth, but on the whole her face was striking and intellectual. I felt that if she chose she could fascinate a man so that he would dare anything. I never before understood why the Russian police feared the women revolutionists so much. It was because they were themselves, plus every man they could influence.

Nevsky appeared very excited. She talked rapidly, and fire flashed from her grey eyes. "They tell me at the club," she began, "that you are investigating the terrible things that are happening to us. Oh, Professor Kennedy, it is awful! Last night I was staying with some friends on East Broadway. Suddenly we heard a terrific explosion up the street. It was in front of Dr. Kharkoff's house. Thank Heaven, he is still alive! But I was so unnerved I could not sleep. I fancied I might be the next to go.

"Early this morning I hastened to return to Fifth Avenue. As I entered the door of my room I could not help thinking of the horrible fate of Dr. Kharkoff. For some unknown reason, just as I was about to push the door farther open, I hesitated and looked —I almost fainted. There stood another bomb just inside. If I had moved the door a fraction of an inch it would have exploded. I screamed, and Olga, sick as she was, ran to my assistance—or perhaps she thought something had happened to Boris. It is standing there yet. None of us dares touch it. Oh, Professor Kennedy, it is dreadful, dreadful. And I cannot find Boris—Mr. Kazanovitch, I mean. Saratovsky, who is like a father to us all, is scarcely able to speak. Dr. Kharkoff is helpless in the hospital. Oh, what are we to do, what are we to do?"

She stood trembling before us, imploring.

"Calm yourself, Miss Nevsky," said Kennedy in a reassuring tone. "Sit down and let us plan. I take it that it was a chemical bomb and not one with a fuse, or you would have a different story to tell. First of all, we must remove it. That is easily done."

He called up a near-by garage and ordered an automobile. "I will drive it myself," he ordered, "only send a man around with it immediately."

"No, no, no," she cried, running toward him, "you must not risk it. It is bad enough that we should risk our lives. But strangers must not. Think, Professor Kennedy. Suppose the bomb should explode at a touch! Had we not better call the police and let them take the risk, even if it does get into the papers?"

"No," replied Kennedy firmly. "Miss Nevsky, I am quite willing to take the risk. Besides, here comes the automobile."

"You are too kind," she exclaimed. "Kazanovitch himself could do no more. How am I ever to thank you?"

On the back of the automobile Kennedy placed a peculiar oblong box, swung on two concentric rings balanced on pivots, like a most delicate compass.

We rode quickly downtown, and Kennedy hurried into the house, bidding us stand back. With a long pair of tongs he seized the bomb firmly. It was a tense moment. Suppose his hand should unnecessarily tremble, or he should tip it just a bit—it might explode and blow him to atoms. Keeping it perfectly horizontal he carried it carefully out to the waiting automobile and placed it gingerly in the box.

"Wouldn't it be a good thing to fill the box with water?" I suggested, having read somewhere that that was the usual way of opening a bomb, under water.

"No," he replied, as he closed the lid, "that wouldn't do any good with a bomb of this sort. It would explode under water just as well as in air. This is a safety bomb-carrier. It is known as the Cardan suspension. It was invented by Professor Cardono, an Italian. You see, it is always held in a perfectly horizontal position, no matter how you jar it. I am now going to take the bomb to some safe and convenient place where I can examine it at my leisure. Meanwhile, Miss Nevsky, I will leave you in charge of Mr. Jameson."

"Thank you so much," she said. "I feel better now. I didn't dare go into my own room with that bomb at the door. If Mr. Jameson can only find out what has become of Mr. Kazanovitch, that is all I want. What do you suppose has happened to him? Is he, too, hurt or ill?"

"Very well, then," Craig replied. "I will commission you, Walter, to find Kazanovitch. I shall be back again shortly before noon to examine the wreck of Kharkoff's office. Meet me there. Goodbye, Miss Nevsky."

It was not the first time that I had had a roving commission to find some one who had disappeared in New York. I started by inquiring for every possible place that he might be found. No one at the Fifth Avenue house could tell me anything definite, though they were able to give me a number of places where he was known. I consumed practically the whole morning going from one place to another on the East Side. Some of the picturesque haunts of the revolutionists would have furnished material for a story in themselves. But nowhere had they any word of Kazanovitch, until I visited a Polish artist who was illustrating his stories. He had been there, looking very worn and tired, and had talked vacantly about the sketches which the artist had showed him. After that I lost all trace of him again. It was nearly noon as I hurried to meet Craig at Kharkoff's.

Imagine my surprise to see Kazanovitch already there, seated in the wrecked office, furiously smoking cigarettes and showing evident signs of having something very disturbing on his mind. The moment he caught sight of me, he hurried forward.

"Is Professor Kennedy coming soon?" he inquired eagerly. "I was going up to his laboratory, but I called up Nevsky, and she said he would be here at noon." Then he put his hand up to my ear and whispered, "I have found out who it was who shadowed Kharkoff."

"Who?" I asked, saying nothing of my long search of the morning.

"His name is Revalenko—Feodor Revalenko. I

saw him standing across the street in front of the house last night after you had gone. When Kharkoff left, he followed him. I hurried out quietly and followed both of them. Then the explosion came. This man slipped down a narrow street as soon as he saw Kharkoff fall. As people were running to Kharkoff's assistance, I did the same. He saw me following him and ran, and I ran, too, and overtook him. Mr. Jameson, when I looked into his face I could not believe it. Revalenko—he is one of the most ardent members of our organisation. He would not tell me why he had followed Kharkoff. I could make him confess nothing. But I am sure he is an *agent provocateur* of the Russian government, that he is secretly giving away the plans that we are making, everything. We have a plot on now—perhaps he has informed them of that. Of course he denied setting the bomb or trying to poison any of us, but he was very frightened. I shall denounce him at the first opportunity."

I said nothing. Kazanovitch regarded me keenly to see what impression the story made on me, but I did not let my looks betray anything, except proper surprise, and he seemed satisfied.

It might be true, after all, I reasoned, the more I thought of it. I had heard that the Russian consul-general had a very extensive spy system in the city. In fact, even that morning I had had pointed out to me some spies at work in the public libraries, watching what young Russians were reading. I did not doubt that there were spies in the very inner circle of the revolutionists themselves.

At last Kennedy appeared. While Kazanovitch poured forth his story, with here and there, I fancied, an elaboration of a particularly dramatic point, Kennedy quickly examined the walls and floor of the wrecked office with his magnifying-glass. When he had concluded his search, he turned to Kazanovitch.

"Would it be possible," he asked, "to let this Revalenko believe that he could trust you, that it would be safe for him to visit you to-night at Saratovsky's? Surely you can find some way of reassuring him."

"Yes, I think that can be arranged," said Kazanovitch. "I will go to him, will make him think I have misunderstood him, that I have not lost faith in him, provided he can explain all. He will come. Trust me."

"Very well, then. To-night at eight I shall be there," promised Kennedy, as the novelist and he shook hands.

"What do you think of the Revalenko story?" I asked of Craig, as we started uptown again.

"Anything is possible in this case," he answered sententiously.

"Well," I exclaimed, "this all is truly Russian. For intrigue they are certainly the leaders of the world to-day. There is only one person that I have any real confidence in, and that is old Saratovsky himself. Somebody is playing traitor, Craig. Who is it?"

"That is what science will tell us to-night," was his brief reply. There was no getting anything out of Craig until he was absolutely sure that his proofs had piled up irresistibly.

Promptly at eight we met at the old house on Fifth Avenue. Kharkoff's wounds had proved less severe than had at first been suspected, and, having recovered from the shock, he insisted on being transferred from the hospital in a private ambulance so that he could be near his friends. Saratovsky, in spite of his high fever, ordered that the door to his room be left open and his bed moved so that he could hear and see what passed in the room down the hall. Nevsky was there and Kazanovitch, and even brave Olga Samarova, her pretty face burning with the fever, would not be content until she was carried upstairs, although Dr. Kharkoff protested vigorously that it might have fatal consequences. Revalenko, an enigma of a man, sat stolidly. The only thing I noticed about him was an occasional look of malignity at Nevsky and Kazanovitch when he thought he was unobserved.

It was indeed a strange gathering, the like of which the old house had never before harboured in all its varied history. Every one was on the *qui vive,* as Kennedy placed on the table a small wire basket containing some test-tubes, each tube corked with a small wadding of cotton. There was also a receptacle holding a dozen glass-handled platinum wires, a microscope, and a number of slides. The bomb, now rendered innocuous by having been crushed in a huge hydraulic press, lay in fragments in the box.

" First, I want you to consider the evidence of

the bomb," began Kennedy. "No crime, I firmly believe, is ever perpetrated without leaving some clue. The slightest trace, even a drop of blood no larger than a pin-head, may suffice to convict a murderer. The impression made on a cartridge by the hammer of a pistol, or a single hair found on the clothing of a suspected person, may serve as valid proof of crime.

"Until lately, however, science was powerless against the bomb-thrower. A bomb explodes into a thousand parts, and its contents suddenly become gaseous. You can't collect and investigate the gases. Still, the bomb-thrower is sadly deceived if he believes the bomb leaves no trace for the scientific detective. It is difficult for the chemist to find out the secrets of a shattered bomb. But it can be done.

"I examined the walls of Dr. Kharkoff's house, and fortunately was able to pick out a few small fragments of the contents of the bomb which had been thrown out before the flame ignited them. I have analysed them, and find them to be a peculiar species of blasting-gelatine. It is made at only one factory in this country, and I have a list of purchasers for some time back. One name, or rather the description of an assumed name, in the list agrees with other evidence I have been able to collect. Moreover, the explosive was placed in a lead tube. Lead tubes are common enough. However, there is no need of further evidence."

He paused, and the revolutionists stared fixedly at the fragments of the now harmless bomb before them.

"The exploded bomb," concluded Craig, "was composed of the same materials as this, which I found unexploded at the door of Miss Nevsky's room—the same sort of lead tube, the same blasting-gelatine. The fuse, a long cord saturated in sulphur, was merely a blind. The real method of explosion was by means of a chemical contained in a glass tube which was inserted after the bomb was put in place. The least jar, such as opening a door, which would tip the bomb ever so little out of the horizontal, was all that was necessary to explode it. The exploded bomb and the unexploded were in all respects identical—the same hand set both."

A gasp of astonishment ran through the circle. Could it be that one of their own number was playing false? In at least this instance in the warfare of the chemist and the dynamiter the chemist had come out ahead.

"But," Kennedy hurried along, "the thing that interests me most about this case is not the evidence of the bombs. Bombs are common enough weapons, after all. It is the evidence of almost diabolical cunning that has been shown in the effort to get rid of the father of the revolution, as you like to call him."

Craig cleared his throat and played with our feelings as a cat does with a mouse. "Strange to say, the most deadly, the most insidious, the most elusive agency for committing murder is one that can be obtained and distributed with practically no legal restrictions. Any doctor can purchase disease germs in quantities sufficient to cause thousands and thousands of deaths without giving any adequate explanation for what purpose he requires them. More than that, any person claiming to be a scientist or having some acquaintance with science and scientists can usually obtain germs without difficulty. Every pathological laboratory contains stores of disease germs, neatly sealed up in test-tubes, sufficient to depopulate whole cities and even nations. With almost no effort, I myself have actually cultivated enough germs to kill every person within a radius of a mile of the Washington Arch down the street. They are here in these test-tubes."

We scarcely breathed. Suppose Kennedy should let loose this deadly foe, these germs of death, whatever they were? Yet that was precisely what some fiend incarnate had done, and that fiend was sitting in the room with us.

"Here I have one of the most modern dark-field microscopes," he resumed. "On this slide I have placed a little pin-point of a culture made from the blood of Saratovsky. I will stain the culture. Now —er—Walter, look through the microscope under this powerful light and tell us what you see on the slide."

I bent over. "In the darkened field I see a number of germs like dancing points of coloured light," I said. "They are wriggling about with a peculiar twisting motion."

"Like a corkscrew," interrupted Kennedy, impatient to go on. "They are of the species known as Spirilla. Here is another slide, a culture from the blood of Samarova."

"I see them there, too," I exclaimed.

Every one was now crowding about for a glimpse, as I raised my head.

"What is this germ?" asked a hollow voice from the doorway.

We looked, startled. There stood Saratovsky, more like a ghost than a living being. Kennedy sprang forward and caught him as he swayed, and I moved up an armchair for him.

"It is the *spirillum Obermeieri,*" said Kennedy, "the germ of the relapsing fever, but of the most virulent Asiatic strain. Obermeyer, who discovered it, caught the disease and died of it, a martyr to science."

A shriek of consternation rang forth from Samarova. The rest of us paled, but repressed our feelings.

"One moment," added Kennedy hastily. "Don't be unnecessarily alarmed. I have something more to say. Be calm for a moment longer."

He unrolled a blue-print and placed it on the table.

"This," he continued, "is the photographic copy of a message which, I suppose, is now on its way to the Russian minister to France in Paris. Some one in this room besides Mr. Jameson and myself has seen this letter before. I will hold it up as I pass around and let each one see it."

In intense silence Kennedy passed before each of us, holding up the blue-print and searchingly scanning the faces. No one betrayed by any sign that he recognised it. At last it came to Revalenko himself.

"The checkerboard, the checkerboard!" he cried, his eyes half starting from their sockets as he gazed at it.

"Yes," said Kennedy in a low tone, "the checkerboard. It took me some time to figure it out. It is a cipher that would have baffled Poe. In fact, there is no means of deciphering it unless you chance to know its secret. I happened to have heard of it a long time ago abroad, yet my recollection was vague, and I had to reconstruct it with much difficulty. It took me all night to do it. It is a cipher, however, that is well known among the official classes of Russia.

"Fortunately I remember the crucial point, without which I should still be puzzling over it. It is that a perfectly innocent message, on its face, may be used to carry a secret, hidden message. The letters which compose the words, instead of being written continuously along, as we ordinarily write, have, as you will observe if you look twice, breaks, here and there. These breaks in the letters stand for numbers.

"Thus the first words are 'Many thanks.' The first break is at the end of the letter 'n,' between it and the 'y.' There are three letters before this break. That stands for the number 3.

"When you come to the end of a word, if the stroke is down at the end of the last letter, that means no break; if it is up, it means a break. The stroke at the end of the 'y' is plainly down. Therefore there is no break until after the 't.' That gives us the number 2. So we get 1 next, and again

1, and still again 1; then 5; then 5; then 1; and so on.

"Now, take these numbers in pairs, thus 3—2; 1—1; 1—5; 5—1. By consulting this table you can arrive at the hidden message."

He held up a cardboard bearing the following arrangement of the letters of the alphabet:

	1	2	3	4	5
1	A	B	C	D	E
2	F	G	H	IJ	K
3	L	M	N	O	P
4	Q	R	S	T	U
5	V	W	X	Y	Z

"Thus," he continued, "3—2 means the third column and second line. That is 'H.' Then 1—1 is 'A'; 1—5 is 'V'; 5—1 is 'E'—and we get the word 'Have.'"

Not a soul stirred as Kennedy unfolded the cipher. What was the terrible secret in that scientific essay I had puzzled so unsuccessfully over, the night before?

"Even this can be complicated by choosing a series of fixed numbers to be added to the real numbers over and over again. Or the order of the alphabet can be changed. However, we have the straight cipher only to deal with here."

"And what for Heaven's sake does it reveal?" asked Saratovsky, leaning forward, forgetful of the fever that was consuming him.

Kennedy pulled out a piece of paper on which he had written the hidden message and read:

"Have successfully inoculated S. with fever. Public opinion America would condemn violence. Think best death should appear natural. Samarova infected also. Cook unfortunately took dose in food intended Kharkoff. Now have three cases. Shall stop there at present. Dangerous excite further suspicion health authorities."

Rapidly I eliminated in my mind the persons mentioned, as Craig read. Saratovsky of course was not guilty, for the plot had centred about him. Nor was little Samarova, nor Dr. Kharkoff. I noted Revalenko and Kazanovitch glaring at each other and hastily tried to decide which I more strongly suspected.

"Will get K.," continued Kennedy. "Think bomb perhaps all right. K. case different from S. No public sentiment."

"So Kharkoff had been marked for slaughter," I thought. Or was "K." Kazanovitch? I regarded Revalenko more closely. He was suspiciously sullen.

"Must have more money. Cable ten thousand rubles at once Russian consul-general. Will advise you plot against Czar as details perfected here. Expect break up New York band with death of S."

If Kennedy himself had thrown a bomb or scattered broadcast the contents of the test-tubes, the effect could not have been more startling than his last quiet sentence—and sentence it was in two senses.

"Signed," he said, folding the paper up deliberately, "Ekaterina Nevsky."

It was as if a cable had snapped and a weight had fallen. Revalenko sprang up and grasped Kazanovitch by the hand. "Forgive me, comrade, for ever suspecting you," he cried.

"And forgive me for suspecting you," replied Kazanovitch, "but how did you come to shadow Kharkoff?"

"I ordered him to follow Kharkoff secretly and protect him," explained Saratovsky.

Olga and Ekaterina faced each other fiercely. Olga was trembling with emotion. Nevsky stood coldly, defiantly. If ever there was a consummate actress it was she, who had put the bomb at her own door and had rushed off to start Kennedy on a blind trail.

"You traitress," cried Olga passionately, forgetting all in her outraged love. "You won his affections from me by your false beauty—yet all the time you would have killed him like a dog for the Czar's gold. At last you are unmasked—you Azeff in skirts. False friend—you would have killed us all—Saratovsky, Kharkoff——"

"Be still, little fool," exclaimed Nevsky contemptuously. "The spirilla fever has affected your brains. Bah! I will not stay with those who are so ready to suspect an old comrade on the mere word of a charlatan. Boris Kazanovitch, do you stand there *silent* and let this insult be heaped upon me?"

For answer, Kazanovitch deliberately turned his

back on his lover of a moment ago and crossed the room. " Olga," he pleaded, " I have been a fool. Some day I may be worthy of your love. Fever or not, I must beg your forgiveness."

With a cry of delight the actress flung her arms about Boris, as he imprinted a penitent kiss on her warm lips.

" Simpleton," hissed Nevsky with curling lips. " Now you, too, will die."

" One moment, Ekaterina Nevsky," interposed Kennedy, as he picked up some vacuum tubes full of a golden-yellow powder, that lay on the table. " The spirilla, as scientists now know, belong to the same family as those which cause what we call, euphemistically, the ' black plague.' It is the same species as that of the African sleeping sickness and the Philippine yaws. Last year a famous doctor whose photograph I see in the next room, Dr. Ehrlich of Frankfort, discovered a cure for all these diseases. It will rid the blood of your victims of the Asiatic relapsing fever germs in forty-eight hours. In these tubes I have the now famous salvarsan."

With a piercing shriek of rage at seeing her deadly work so quickly and completely undone, Nevsky flung herself into the little laboratory behind her and bolted the door.

Her face still wore the same cold, contemptuous smile, as Kennedy gently withdrew a sharp scalpel from her breast.

" Perhaps it is best this way, after all," he said simply.

IV

THE FIREBUG

A BIG, powerful, red touring-car, with a shining brass bell on the front of it, was standing at the curb before our apartment late one afternoon as I entered. It was such a machine as one frequently sees threading its reckless course in and out among the trucks and street-cars, breaking all rules and regulations, stopping at nothing, the bell clanging with excitement, policemen holding back traffic instead of trying to arrest the driver—in other words, a Fire Department automobile.

I regarded it curiously for a moment, for everything connected with modern fire-fighting is interesting. Then I forgot about it as I was whisked up in the elevator, only to have it recalled sharply by the sight of a strongly built, grizzled man in a blue uniform with red lining. He was leaning forward, earnestly pouring forth a story into Kennedy's ear.

"And back of the whole thing, sir," I heard him say as he brought his large fist down on the table, "is a firebug—mark my words."

Before I could close the door, Craig caught my eye, and I read in his look that he had a new case—one that interested him greatly. "Walter," he cried, "this is Fire Marshal McCormick. It's all right, McCormick. Mr. Jameson is an accessory both before and after the fact in my detective cases."

A firebug!—one of the most dangerous of criminals. The word excited my imagination at once, for the newspapers had lately been making much of the strange and appalling succession of apparently incendiary fires that had terrorised the business section of the city.

"Just what makes you think that there is a firebug—one firebug, I mean—back of this curious epidemic of fires?" asked Kennedy, leaning back in his morris-chair with his finger-tips together and his eyes half closed as if expecting a revelation from some subconscious train of thought while the fire marshal presented his case.

"Well, usually there is no rhyme or reason about the firebug," replied McCormick, measuring his words, "but this time I think there is some method in his madness. You know the Stacey department-stores and their allied dry-goods and garment-trade interests?"

Craig nodded. Of course we knew of the gigantic dry-goods combination. It had been the talk of the press at the time of its formation, a few months ago, especially as it included among its organisers one very clever business woman, Miss Rebecca Wend. There had been considerable opposition to the combination in the trade, but Stacey had shattered it by the sheer force of his personality.

McCormick leaned forward and, shaking his forefinger to emphasise his point, replied slowly, "Practically every one of these fires has been directed against a Stacey subsidiary or a corporation controlled by them."

"But if it has gone as far as that," put in Kennedy, "surely the regular police ought to be of more assistance to you than I."

"I have called in the police," answered McCormick wearily, "but they haven't even made up their minds whether it is a single firebug or a gang. And in the meantime, my God, Kennedy, the firebug may start a fire that will get beyond control!"

"You say the police haven't a single clue to any one who might be responsible for the fires?" I asked, hoping that perhaps the marshal might talk more freely of his suspicions to us than he had already expressed himself in the newspaper interviews I had read.

"Absolutely not a clue—except such as are ridiculous," replied McCormick, twisting his cap viciously.

No one spoke. We were waiting for McCormick to go on.

"The first fire," he began, repeating his story for my benefit, although Craig listened quite as attentively as if he had not heard it already, "was at the big store of Jones, Green & Co., the clothiers. The place was heavily insured. Warren, the manager and real head of the firm, was out of town at the time."

The marshal paused as if to check off the strange facts in his mind as he went along.

"The next day another puzzling fire occurred. It was at the Quadrangle Cloak and Suit Co., on Fifth Avenue. There had been some trouble, I believe, with the employees, and the company had discharged a number of them. Several of the leaders have been arrested, but I can't say we have anything against any of them. Still, Max Bloom, the manager of this company, insists that the fire was set for revenge, and indeed it looks as much like a fire for revenge as the Jones-Green fire does " —here he lowered his voice confidentially—" for the purpose of collecting insurance.

" Then came the fire in the Slawson Building, a new loft-building that had been erected just off Fourth Avenue. Other than the fact that the Stacey interests put up the money for financing this building there seemed to be no reason for that fire at all. The building was reputed to be earning a good return on the investment, and I was at a loss to account for the fire. I have made no arrests for it—just set it down as the work of a pure pyromaniac, a man who burns buildings for fun, a man with an inordinate desire to hear the fire-engines screech through the streets and perhaps get a chance to show a little heroism in 'rescuing' tenants. However, the adjuster for the insurance company, Lazard, and the adjuster for the insured, Hartstein, have reached an agreement, and I believe the insurance is to be paid."

" But," interposed Kennedy, " I see no evidence of organised arson so far."

" Wait," replied the fire marshal. " That was only the beginning, you understand. A little later came a fire that looked quite like an attempt to mask a robbery by burning the building afterward. That was in a silk-house near Spring Street. But after a controversy the adjusters have reached an agreement on that case. I mention these fires because they show practically all the types of work of the various kinds of firebug—insurance, revenge, robbery, and plain insanity. But since the Spring Street fire, the character of the fires has been more uniform. They have all been in business places, or nearly all."

Here the fire marshal launched forth into a catalogue of fires of suspected incendiary origin, at least eight in all. I took them down hastily, intending to use the list some time in a box head with an article in the *Star*. When he had finished his list I hastily counted up the number of killed. There were six, two of them firemen, and four employees. The money loss ranged into the millions.

McCormick passed his hand over his forehead to brush off the perspiration. "I guess this thing has got on my nerves," he muttered hoarsely. "Everywhere I go they talk about nothing else. If I drop into the restaurant for lunch, my waiter talks of it. If I meet a newspaper man, he talks of it. My barber talks of it—everybody. Sometimes I dream of it; other times I lie awake thinking about it. I tell you, gentlemen, I've sweated blood over this problem."

"But," insisted Kennedy, "I still can't see why you link all these fires as due to one firebug. I admit there is an epidemic of fires. But what makes you so positive that it is all the work of one man?"

"I was coming to that. For one thing, he isn't like the usual firebug at all. Ordinarily they start their fires with excelsior and petroleum, or they smear the wood with paraffin or they use gasoline, benzine, or something of that sort. This fellow apparently scorns such crude methods. I can't say how he starts his fires, but in every case I have mentioned we have found the remains of a wire. It has something to do with electricity—but what, I don't know. That's one reason why I think these fires are all connected. Here's another."

McCormick pulled a dirty note out of his pocket and laid it on the table. We read it eagerly:

Hello, Chief! Haven't found the firebug yet, have you? You will know who he is only when I am dead and the fires stop. I don't suppose you even realise that the firebug talks with you almost every day about catching the firebug. That's me. I am the real firebug, that is writing this letter. I am going to tell you why I am starting these fires. There's money in it—an easy living. They never caught me in Chicago or anywhere, so you might as well quit looking for me and take your medicine.

A. SPARK.

"Humph!" ejaculated Kennedy, "he has a sense of humour, anyhow—A. Spark!"

"Queer sense of humour," growled McCormick, gritting his teeth. "Here's another I got to-day:

Say, Chief: We are going to get busy again and fire a big department-store next. How does that suit Your Majesty? Wait till the fun begins when the firebug gets to work again.

A. SPARK.

"Well, sir, when I got that letter," cried McCormick, "I was almost ready to ring in a double-nine alarm at once—they have me that bluffed out. But I said to myself, 'There's only one thing to do—see this man Kennedy.' So here I am. You see what I am driving at? I believe that firebug is an artist at the thing, does it for the mere fun of it and the ready money in it. But more than that, there must be some one back of him. Who is the man higher up—we must catch him. See?"

"A big department-store," mused Kennedy. "That's definite—there are only a score or so of them, and the Stacey interests control several. Mac, I'll tell you what I'll do. Let me sit up with you to-night at headquarters until we get an alarm. By George, I'll see this case through to a finish!"

The fire marshal leaped to his feet and bounded over to where Kennedy was seated. With one hand on Craig's shoulder and the other grasping Craig's hand, he started to speak, but his voice choked.

"Thanks," he blurted out huskily at last. "My reputation in the department is at stake, my promotion, my position itself, my—my family—er—er——"

"Not a word, sir," said Kennedy, his features working sympathetically. "To-night at eight I will go on watch with you. By the way, leave me those A. Spark notes."

McCormick had so far regained his composure as to say a hearty farewell. He left the room as if ten years had been lifted off his shoulders. A moment later he stuck his head in the door again. "I'll have one of the Department machines call for you, gentlemen," he said.

After the marshal had gone, we sat for several minutes in silence. Kennedy was reading and re-reading the notes, scowling to himself as if they presented a particularly perplexing problem. I said nothing, though my mind was teeming with speculations. At length he placed the notes very decisively on the table and snapped out the remark,

"Yes, it must be so."

"What?" I queried, still drumming away at my typewriter, copying the list of incendiary fires against the moment when the case should be complete and the story "released for publication," as it were.

"This note," he explained, picking up the first one and speaking slowly, "was written by a woman."

I swung around in my chair quickly. "Get out!" I exclaimed sceptically. "No woman ever used such phrases."

"I didn't say composed by a woman—I said written by a woman," he replied.

"Oh," I said, rather chagrined.

"It is possible to determine sex from handwriting in perhaps eighty cases out of a hundred," Kennedy went on, enjoying my discomfiture. "Once I examined several hundred specimens of writing to decide that point to my satisfaction. Just to test my conclusions I submitted the specimens to two professional graphologists. I found that our results were slightly different, but I averaged the thing up to four cases out of five correct. The so-called sex signs are found to be largely influenced by the amount of writing done, by age, and to a certain extent by practice and professional requirements, as in the conventional writing of teachers and the rapid hand of bookkeepers. Now in this case the person who wrote the first note was only an indifferent writer. Therefore the sex signs are pretty likely to be accurate. Yes, I'm ready to go on the stand and swear that this note was written by a woman and the second by a man."

"Then there's a woman in the case, and she wrote the first note for the firebug—is that what you mean?" I asked.

"Exactly. There nearly always is a woman in the case, somehow or other. This woman is closely connected with the firebug. As for the firebug, whoever it may be, he performs his crimes with cold premeditation and, as De Quincey said, in a spirit of pure artistry. The lust of fire propels him, and he uses his art to secure wealth. The man may be a tool in the hands of others, however. It's unsafe to generalise on the meagre facts we now have. Oh, well, there is nothing we can do just yet. Let's take a walk, get an early dinner, and be back here before the automobile arrives."

Not a word more did Kennedy say about the case during our stroll or even on the way downtown to fire headquarters.

We found McCormick anxiously waiting for us. High up in the sandstone tower at headquarters, we sat with him in the maze of delicate machinery with which the fire game is played in New York. In great glass cases were glistening brass and nickel machines with discs and levers and bells, tickers, sheets of paper, and annunciators without number.

This was the fire-alarm telegraph, the " roulette-wheel of the fire demon," as some one has aptly called it.

" All the alarms for fire from all the boroughs, both from the regular alarm-boxes and the auxiliary systems, come here first over the network of three thousand miles or more of wire nerves that stretch out through the city," McCormick was explaining to us.

A buzzer hissed.

" Here's an alarm now," he exclaimed, all attention.

" Three," " six," " seven," the numbers appeared on the annunciator. The clerks in the office moved as if they were part of the mechanism. Twice the alarm was repeated, being sent out all over the city. McCormick relapsed from his air of attention.

" That alarm was not in the shopping district," he explained, much relieved. " Now the fire-houses in the particular district where that fire is have received the alarm instantly. Four engines, two hook-and-ladders, a water-tower, the battalion chief, and a deputy are hurrying to that fire. Hello, here comes another."

Again the buzzer sounded. " One," " four," " five " showed in the annunciator.

Even before the clerks could respond, McCormick had dragged us to the door. In another instant we were wildly speeding uptown, the bell on the front of the automobile clanging like a fire-engine, the siren horn going continuously, the engine of the machine throbbing with energy until the water boiled in the radiator.

"Let her out, Frank," called McCormick to his chauffeur, as we rounded into a broad and now almost deserted thoroughfare.

Like a red streak in the night we flew up that avenue, turned into Fourteenth Street on two wheels, and at last were on Sixth Avenue. With a jerk and a skid we stopped. There were the engines, the hose-carts, the hook-and-ladders, the salvage corps, the police establishing fire lines—everything. But where was the fire?

The crowd indicated where it ought to be—it was Stacey's. Firemen and policemen were entering the huge building. McCormick shouldered in after them, and we followed.

"Who turned in the alarm?" he asked as we mounted the stairs with the others.

"I did," replied a night watchman on the third landing. "Saw a light in the office on the third floor back—something blazing. But it seems to be out now."

We had at last come to the office. It was dark and deserted, yet with the lanterns we could see the floor of the largest room littered with torn books and ledgers.

Kennedy caught his foot in something. It was a loose wire on the floor. He followed it. It led to an electric-light socket, where it was attached.

"Can't you turn on the lights?" shouted McCormick to the watchman.

"Not here. They're turned on from downstairs,

and they're off for the night. I'll go down if you want me to and——"

"No," roared Kennedy. "Stay where you are until I follow the wire to the other end."

At last we came to a little office partitioned off from the main room. Kennedy carefully opened the door. One whiff of the air from it was sufficient. He banged the door shut again.

"Stand back with those lanterns, boys," he ordered.

I sniffed, expecting to smell illuminating-gas. Instead, a peculiar, sweetish odour pervaded the air. For a moment it made me think of a hospital operating-room.

"Ether," exclaimed Kennedy. "Stand back farther with those lights and hold them up from the floor."

For a moment he seemed to hesitate as if at loss what to do next. Should he open the door and let this highly inflammable gas out or should he wait patiently until the natural ventilation of the little office had dispelled it?

While he was debating he happened to glance out of the window and catch sight of a drug-store across the street.

"Walter," he said to me, "hurry across there and get all the saltpeter and sulphur the man has in the shop."

I lost no time in doing so. Kennedy dumped the two chemicals into a pan in the middle of the main office, about three-fifths saltpeter and two-fifths sulphur, I should say. Then he lighted it. The mass burned with a bright flame but without explosion. We could smell the suffocating fumes from it, and we retreated. For a moment or two we watched it curiously at a distance.

"That's very good extinguishing-powder," explained Craig as we sniffed at the odour. "It yields a large amount of carbon dioxide and sulphur dioxide. Now—before it gets any worse—I guess it's safe to open the door and let the ether out. You see this is as good a way as any to render safe a room full of inflammable vapour. Come, we'll wait outside the main office for a few minutes until the gases mix."

It seemed hours before Kennedy deemed it safe to enter the office again with a light. When we did so, we made a rush for the little cubby-hole of an office at the other end. On the floor was a little can of ether, evaporated of course, and beside it a small apparatus apparently used for producing electric sparks.

"So, that's how he does it," mused Kennedy, fingering the can contemplatively. "He lets the ether evaporate in a room for a while and then causes an explosion from a safe distance with this little electric spark. There's where your wire comes in, McCormick. Say, my man, you can switch on the lights from downstairs, now."

As we waited for the watchman to turn on the lights I exclaimed, "He failed this time because the electricity was shut off."

"Precisely, Walter," assented Kennedy.

"But the flames which the night watchman saw,

what of them?" put in McCormick, considerably mystified. "He must have seen something."

Just then the lights winked up.

"Oh, that was before the fellow tried to touch off the ether vapour," explained Kennedy. "He had to make sure of his work of destruction first—and, judging by the charred papers about, he did it well. See, he tore leaves from the ledgers and lighted them on the floor. There was an object in all that. What was it? Hello! Look at this mass of charred paper in the corner."

He bent down and examined it carefully.

"Memoranda of some kind, I guess. I'll save this burnt paper and look it over later. Don't disturb it. I'll take it away myself."

Search as we might, we could find no other trace of the firebug, and at last we left. Kennedy carried the charred paper carefully in a large hat-box.

"There'll be no more fires to-night, McCormick," he said. "But I'll watch with you every night until we get this incendiary. Meanwhile I'll see what I can decipher, if anything, in this burnt paper."

Next day McCormick dropped in to see us again. This time he had another note, a disguised scrawl which read:

> Chief: I'm not through. Watch me get another store yet. I won't fall down this time.
>
> A. SPARK.

Craig scowled as he read the note and handed it to me. "The man's writing this time—like the second note," was all he said. "McCormick, since we know where the lightning is going to strike, don't you think it would be wiser to make our headquarters in one of the engine-houses in that district?"

The fire marshal agreed, and that night saw us watching at the fire-house nearest the department-store region.

Kennedy and I were assigned to places on the hose-cart and engine, respectively, Kennedy being in the hose-cart so that he could be with McCormick. We were taught to descend one of the four brass poles hand under elbow, from the dormitory on the second floor. They showed us how to jump into the "turn-outs"—a pair of trousers opened out over the high top boots. We were given helmets which we placed in regulation fashion on our rubber coats, turned inside out with the right armhole up. Thus it came about that Craig and I joined the Fire Department temporarily. It was a novel experience for us both.

"Now, Walter," said Kennedy, "as long as we have gone so far, we'll 'roll' to every fire, just like the regulars. We won't take any chances of missing the firebug at any time of night or day."

It proved to be a remarkably quiet evening with only one little blaze in a candy-shop on Seventh Avenue. Most of the time we sat around trying to draw the men out about their thrilling experiences at fires. But if there is one thing the fireman doesn't know it is the English language when talking about himself. It was quite late when we turned into the neat white cots upstairs.

We had scarcely fallen into a half doze in our

strange surroundings when the gong downstairs sounded. It was our signal.

We could hear the rapid clatter of the horses' hoofs as they were automatically released from their stalls and the collars and harness mechanically locked about them. All was stir, and motion, and shouts. Craig and I had bounded awkwardly into our paraphernalia at the first sound. We slid ungracefully down the pole and were pushed and shoved into our places, for scientific management in a New York fire-house has reached one hundred per cent. efficiency, and we were not to be allowed to delay the game.

The oil-torch had been applied to the engine, and it rolled forth, belching flames. I was hanging on for dear life, now and then catching sight of the driver urging his plunging horses onward like a charioteer in a modern Ben Hur race. The tender with Craig and McCormick was lost in the clouds of smoke and sparks that trailed behind us. On we dashed until we turned into Sixth Avenue. The glare of the sky told us that this time the firebug had made good.

"I'll be hanged if it isn't the Stacey store again," shouted the man next me on the engine as the horses lunged up the avenue and stopped at the allotted hydrant. It was like a war game. Every move had been planned out by the fire-strategists, even down to the hydrants that the engines should take at a given fire.

Already several floors were aflame, the windows glowing like open-hearth furnaces, the glass bulging and cracking and the flames licking upward and shooting out in long streamers. The hose was coupled up in an instant, the water turned on, and the limp rubber and canvas became as rigid as a post with the high pressure of the water being forced through it. Company after company dashed into the blazing "fireproof" building, urged by the hoarse profanity of the chief.

Twenty or thirty men must have disappeared into the stifle from which the police retreated. There was no haste, no hesitation. Everything moved as smoothly as if by clockwork. Yet we could not see one of the men who had disappeared into the burning building. They had been swallowed up, as it were. For that is the way with the New York firemen. They go straight to the heart of the fire. Now and then a stream of a hose spat out of a window, showing that the men were still alive and working. About the ground floors the red-helmeted salvage corps were busy covering up what they could of the goods with rubber sheets to protect them from water. Doctors with black bags and white trousers were working over the injured. Kennedy and I were busy about the engine, and there was plenty for us to do.

Above the shrill whistle for more coal I heard a voice shout, "Began with an explosion—it's the fire-bug, all right." I looked up. It was McCormick, dripping and grimy, in a high state of excitement, talking to Kennedy.

I had been so busy trying to make myself believe that I was really of some assistance about the engine that I had not taken time to watch the fire itself. It was now under control. The sharp and scientific attack had nipped what might have been one of New York's historic conflagrations.

"Are you game to go inside?" I heard McCormick ask.

For answer Kennedy simply nodded. As for me, where Craig went I went.

The three of us drove through the scorching door, past twisted masses of iron still glowing dull red in the smoke and steam, while the water hissed and spattered and slopped. The smoke was still suffocating, and every once in a while we were forced to find air close to the floor and near the wall. My hands and arms and legs felt like lead, yet on we drove.

Coughing and choking, we followed McCormick to what had been the heart of the fire, the office. Men with picks and axes and all manner of cunningly devised instruments were hacking and tearing at the walls and woodwork, putting out the last smouldering sparks while a thousand gallons of water were pouring in at various parts of the building where the fire still showed spirit.

There on the floor of the office lay a charred, shapeless, unrecognisable mass. What was that gruesome odour in the room? Burned human flesh? I recoiled from what had once been the form of a woman.

McCormick uttered a cry, and as I turned my eyes away, I saw him holding a wire with the insulation burned off. He had picked it up from the wreckage of the floor. It led to a bent and blackened can—that had once been a can of ether.

My mind worked rapidly, but McCormick blurted out the words before I could form them, "Caught in her own trap at last!"

Kennedy said nothing, but as one of the firemen roughly but reverently covered the remains with a rubber sheet, he stooped down and withdrew from the breast of the woman a long letter-file. "Come, let us go," he said.

Back in our apartment again we bathed our racking heads, gargled our parched throats, and washed out our bloodshot eyes, in silence. The whole adventure, though still fresh and vivid in my mind, seemed unreal, like a dream. The choking air, the hissing steam, the ghastly object under the tarpaulin —what did it all mean? Who was she? I strove to reason it out, but could find no answer.

It was nearly dawn when the door opened and McCormick came in and dropped wearily into a chair. "Do you know who that woman was?" he gasped. "It was Miss Wend herself."

"Who identified her?" asked Kennedy calmly.

"Oh, several people. Stacey recognised her at once. Then Hartstein, the adjuster for the insured, and Lazard, the adjuster for the company, both of whom had had more or less to do with her in connection with settling up for other fires, recognised her. She was a very clever woman, was Miss Wend, and a very important cog in the Stacey enterprises. And to think she was the firebug, after all. I can hardly believe it."

"Why believe it?" asked Kennedy quietly.

"Why believe it?" echoed McCormick. "Stacey has found shortages in his books due to the operation of her departments. The bookkeeper who had charge of the accounts in her department, a man named Douglas, is missing. She must have tried to cover up her operations by fires and juggling the accounts. Failing in that she tried to destroy Stacey's store itself, twice. She was one of the few that could get into the office unobserved. Oh, it's a clear case now. To my mind, the heavy vapours of ether—they are heavier than air, you know—must have escaped along the surface of the floor last night and become ignited at a considerable distance from where she expected. She was caught in a back-draught, or something of the sort. Well, thank God, we've seen the last of this firebug business. What's that?"

Kennedy had laid the letter-file on the table. "Nothing. Only I found this embedded in Miss Wend's breast right over her heart."

"Then she was murdered?" exclaimed McCormick.

"We haven't come to the end of this case yet," replied Craig evasively. "On the contrary, we have just got our first good clue. No, McCormick, your theory will not hold water. The real point is to find this missing bookkeeper at any cost. You must persuade him to confess what he knows. Offer him immunity—he was only a pawn in the hands of those higher up."

McCormick was not hard to convince. Tired

as he was, he grabbed up his hat and started off to put the final machinery in motion to wind up the long chase for the firebug.

"I must get a couple of hours' sleep," he yawned as he left us, "but first I want to start something toward finding Douglas. I shall try to see you about noon."

I was too exhausted to go to the office. In fact, I doubt if I could have written a line. But I telephoned in a story of personal experiences at the Stacey fire and told them they could fix it up as they chose and even sign my name to it.

About noon McCormick came in again, looking as fresh as if nothing had happened. He was used to it.

"I know where Douglas is," he announced breathlessly.

"Fine," said Kennedy, "and can you produce him at any time when it is necessary?"

"Let me tell you what I have done. I went down to the district attorney from here—routed him out of bed. He has promised to turn loose his accountants to audit the reports of the adjusters, Hartstein and Lazard, as well as to make a cursory examination of what Stacey books there are left. He says he will have a preliminary report ready to-night, but the detailed report will take days, of course.

"It's the Douglas problem that is difficult, though. I haven't seen him, but one of the central-office men, by shadowing his wife, has found that he is in hiding down on the East Side. He's safe there;

he can't make a move to get away without being arrested. The trouble is that if I arrest him, the people higher up will know it and will escape before I can get his confession and the warrants. I'd much rather have the whole thing done at once. Isn't there some way we can get the whole Stacey crowd together, make the arrest of Douglas and nab the guilty ones in the case, all together without giving them a chance to escape or to shield the real firebug?"

Kennedy thought a moment. "Yes," he answered slowly. "There is. If you can get them all together at my laboratory to-night at, say, eight o'clock, I'll give you two clear hours to make the arrest of Douglas, get the confession, and swear out the warrants. All that you'll need to do is to let me talk a few minutes this afternoon with the judge who will sit in the night court to-night. I shall install a little machine on his desk in the court, and we'll catch the real criminal—he'll never get a chance to cross the state line or disappear in any way. You see, my laboratory will be neutral ground. I think you can get them to come, inasmuch as they know the bookkeeper is safe and that dead women tell no tales."

When next I saw Kennedy it was late in the afternoon, in the laboratory. He was arranging something in the top drawer of a flat-top desk. It seemed to be two instruments composed of many levers and discs and magnets, each instrument with a roll of paper about five inches wide. On one was a sort of stylus with two silk cords attached at right angles to each other near the point. On the other was a capillary glass tube at the junction of two aluminum arms, also at right angles to each other.

It was quite like old times to see Kennedy at work in his laboratory preparing for a "séance." He said nothing as I watched him curiously, and I asked nothing. Two sets of wires were attached to each of the instruments, and these he carefully concealed and led out the window. Then he arranged the chairs on the opposite side of the desk from his own.

"Walter," he said, "when our guests begin to arrive I want you to be master of ceremonies. Simply keep them on the opposite side of the desk from me. Don't let them move their chairs around to the right or left. And, above all, leave the doors open. I don't want any one to be suspicious or to feel that he is shut in in any way. Create the impression that they are free to go and come when they please."

Stacey arrived first in a limousine which he left standing at the door of the Chemistry Building. Bloom and Warren came together in the latter's car. Lazard came in a taxicab which he dismissed, and Hartstein came up by the subway, being the last to arrive. Every one seemed to be in good humour.

I seated them as Kennedy had directed. Kennedy pulled out the extension on the left of his desk and leaned his elbow on it as he began to apologise for taking up their time at such a critical moment. As near as I could make out, he had quietly pulled out the top drawer of his desk on the right, the drawer in which I had seen him place the complicated apparatus. But as nothing further happened I almost forgot about it in listening to him. He began by referring to the burned papers he had found in the office.

"It is sometimes possible," he continued, "to decipher writing on burned papers if one is careful. The processes of colour photography have recently been applied to obtain a legible photograph of the writing on burned manuscripts which are unreadable by any other known means. As long as the sheet has not been entirely disintegrated positive results can be obtained every time. The charred manuscript is carefully arranged in as near its original shape as possible, on a sheet of glass and covered with a drying varnish, after which it is backed by another sheet of glass.

"By using carefully selected colour screens and orthochromatic plates a perfectly legible photograph of the writing may be taken, although there may be no marks on the charred remains that are visible to the eye. This is the only known method in many cases. I have here some burned fragments of paper which I gathered up after the first attempt to fire your store, Mr. Stacey."

Stacey coughed in acknowledgment. As for Craig, he did not mince matters in telling what he had found.

"Some were notes given in favour of Rebecca Wend and signed by Joseph Stacey," he said quietly. "They represent a large sum of money in the aggregate. Others were memoranda of Miss Wend's, and still others were autograph letters to Miss Wend of a very incriminating nature in connection with the fires by another person."

Here he laid the "A. Spark" letters on the desk before him. "Now," he added "some one, in a spirit of bravado, sent these notes to the fire marshal at various times. Curiously enough, I find that the handwriting of the first one bears a peculiar resemblance to that of Miss Wend, while the second and third, though disguised also, greatly suggest the handwriting of Miss Wend's correspondent."

No one moved. But I sat aghast. She had been a part of the conspiracy, after all, not a pawn. Had they played fair?

"Taking up next the remarkable succession of fires," resumed Kennedy, "this case presents some unique features. In short, it is a clear case of what is known as a 'firebug trust.' Now just what is a firebug trust? Well, it is, as near as I can make out, a combination of dishonest merchants and insurance adjusters engaged in the business of deliberately setting fires for profit. These arson trusts are not the ordinary kind of firebugs whom the firemen plentifully damn in the fixed belief that one-fourth of all fires are kindled by incendiaries. Such 'trusts' exist all over the country. They have operated in Chicago, where they are said to have made seven hundred and fifty thousand dollars in one year. Another group is said to have its headquarters in Kansas City. Others have worked in St. Louis, Pittsburgh, Cleveland, and Buffalo. The fire marshals of Illinois, Kentucky, Tennessee, and Ohio have investigated their work. But until recently New York has been singularly free from the organised work of this sort. Of course we have plenty of firebugs and pyromaniacs in a small way, but the big conspiracy has never come to my personal attention before.

"Now, the Jones-Green fire, the Quadrangle fire, the Slawson Building fire, and the rest, have all been set for one purpose—to collect insurance. I may as well say right here that some people are in bad in this case, but that others are in worse. Miss Wend was originally a party to the scheme. Only the trouble with Miss Wend was that she was too shrewd to be fooled. She insisted that she have her full share of the pickings. In that case it seems to have been the whole field against Miss Wend, not a very gallant thing, nor yet according to the adage about honour among thieves.

"A certain person whose name I am frank to say I do not know—yet—conceived the idea of destroying the obligations of the Stacey companies to Miss Wend as well as the incriminating evidence which she held of the 'firebug trust,' of which she was a member up to this time. The plan only partly succeeded. The chief coup, which was to destroy the Stacey store into the bargain, miscarried.

"What was the result? Miss Wend, who had been hand in glove with the 'trust,' was now a bitter enemy, perhaps would turn state's evidence. What more natural than to complete the conspiracy by carrying out the coup and at the same time get rid of the dangerous enemy of the conspirators? I believe that Miss Wend was lured under some pretext or other to the Stacey store on the night of the big fire. The person who wrote the second and third 'A. Spark' letters did it. She was murdered with this deadly instrument"—Craig laid the letter-file on the table—"and it was planned to throw the entire burden of suspicion on her by asserting that there was a shortage in the books of her department."

"Pooh!" exclaimed Stacey, smoking complacently at his cigar. "We have been victimised in those fires by people who have grudges against us, labour unions and others. This talk of an arson trust is bosh—yellow journalism. More than that, we have been systematically robbed by a trusted head of a department, and the fire at Stacey's was the way the thief took to cover—er—her stealings. At the proper time we shall produce the bookkeeper Douglas and prove it."

Kennedy fumbled in the drawer of the desk, then drew forth a long strip of paper covered with figures. "All the Stacey companies," he said, "have been suffering from the depression that exists in the trade at present. They are insolvent. Glance over that, Stacey. It is a summary of the preliminary report of the accountants of the district attorney who have been going over your books to-day."

Stacey gasped. "How did you get it? The report was not to be ready until nine o'clock, and it is scarcely a quarter past now."

"Never mind how I got it. Go over it with the adjusters, anybody. I think you will find that there was no shortage in Miss Wend's department, that you were losing money, that you were in debt to Miss Wend, and that she would have received the lion's share of the proceeds of the insurance if the firebug scheme had turned out as planned."

"We absolutely repudiate these figures as fiction," said Stacey, angrily turning toward Kennedy after a hurried consultation.

"Perhaps, then, you'll appreciate this," replied Craig, pulling another piece of paper from the desk. "I'll read it. 'Henry Douglas, being duly sworn, deposes and says that one'—we'll call him 'Blank' for the present—'with force and arms did feloniously, wilfully, and intentionally kill Rebecca Wend whilst said Blank was wilfully burning and setting on fire——'"

"One moment," interrupted Stacey. "Let me see that paper."

Kennedy laid it down so that only the signature showed. The name was signed in a full round hand, "Henry Douglas."

"It's a forgery," cried Stacey in rage. "Not an hour before I came into this place I saw Henry Douglas. He had signed no such paper then. He could not have signed it since, and you could not have received it. I brand that document as a forgery."

Kennedy stood up and reached down into the open drawer on the right of his desk. From it he lifted the two machines I had seen him place there early in the evening.

"Gentlemen," he said, "this is the last scene of the play you are enacting. You see here on the desk an instrument that was invented many years ago, but has only recently become really practical. It is the telautograph—the long-distance writer. In this new form it can be introduced into the drawer of a desk for the use of any one who may wish to make inquiries, say, of clerks without the knowledge of a caller. It makes it possible to write a message under these conditions and receive an answer concerning the personality or business of the individual seated at one's elbow without leaving the desk or seeming to make inquiries.

"With an ordinary pencil I have written on the paper of the transmitter. The silk cord attached to the pencil regulates the current which controls a pencil at the other end of the line. The receiving pencil moves simultaneously with my pencil. It is the principle of the pantagraph cut in half, one half here, the other half at the end of the line, two telephone wires in this case connecting the halves.

"While we have been sitting here I have had my right hand in the half-open drawer of my desk writing with this pencil notes of what has transpired in this room. These notes, with other evidence, have been simultaneously placed before Magistrate Brenner in the night court. At the same time, on this other, the receiving, instrument the figures of the accountants written in court have been reproduced here. You have seen them. Meanwhile,

Douglas was arrested, taken before the magistrate, and the information for a charge of murder in the first degree perpetrated in committing arson has been obtained. You have seen it. It came in while you were reading the figures."

The conspirators seemed dazed.

"And now," continued Kennedy, "I see that the pencil of the receiving instrument is writing again. Let us see what it is."

We bent over. The writing started: "County of New York. In the name of the People of the State of New York——"

Kennedy did not wait for us to finish reading. He tore the writing from the telautograph and waved it over his head.

"It is a warrant. You are all under arrest for arson. But you, Samuel Lazard, are also under arrest for the murder of Rebecca Wend and six other persons in fires which you have set. You are the real firebug, the tool of Joseph Stacey, perhaps, but that will all come out in the trial. McCormick, McCormick," called Craig, "it's all right. I have the warrant. Are the police there?"

There was no answer.

Lazard and Stacey made a sudden dash for the door, and in an instant they were in Stacey's waiting car. The chauffeur took off the brake and pulled the lever. Suddenly Craig's pistol flashed, and the chauffeur's arms hung limp and useless on the steering-wheel.

As McCormick with the police loomed up, a moment late, out of the darkness and after a short struggle clapped the irons on Stacey and Lazard in Stacey's own magnificently upholstered car, I remarked reproachfully to Kennedy: "But, Craig, you have shot the innocent chauffeur. Aren't you going to attend to him?"

"Oh," replied Kennedy nonchalantly, "don't worry about that. They were only rock-salt bullets. They didn't penetrate far. They'll sting for some time, but they're antiseptic, and they'll dissolve and absorb quickly."

V

THE CONFIDENCE KING

"SHAKE hands with Mr. Burke of the secret service, Professor Kennedy."

It was our old friend First Deputy O'Connor who thus in his bluff way introduced a well-groomed and prosperous-looking man whom he brought up to our apartment one evening.

The formalities were quickly over. "Mr. Burke and I are old friends," explained O'Connor. "We try to work together when we can, and very often the city department can give the government service a lift, and then again it's the other way—as it was in the trunk-murder mystery. Show Professor Kennedy the 'queer,' Tom."

Burke drew a wallet out of his pocket, and from it slowly and deliberately selected a crisp, yellow-backed hundred-dollar bill. He laid it flat on the table before us. Diagonally across its face from the upper left- to the lower right-hand corner extended two parallel scorings in indelible ink.

Not being initiated into the secrets of the gentle art of "shoving the queer," otherwise known as passing counterfeit money, I suppose my questioning look betrayed me.

"A counterfeit, Walter," explained Kennedy. "That's what they do with bills when they wish to preserve them as records in the secret service and yet render them valueless."

Without a word Burke handed Kennedy a pocket magnifying-glass, and Kennedy carefully studied the bill. He was about to say something when Burke opened his capacious wallet again and laid down a Bank of England five-pound note which had been similarly treated.

Again Kennedy looked through the glass with growing amazement written on his face, but before he could say anything, Burke laid down an express money-order on the International Express Company.

"I say," exclaimed Kennedy, putting down the glass, "stop! How many more of these are there?"

Burke smiled. "That's all," he replied, "but it's not the worst."

"Not the worst? Good heavens, man, next you'll tell me that the government is counterfeiting its own notes! How much of this stuff do you suppose has been put into circulation?"

Burke chewed a pencil thoughtfully, jotted down some figures on a piece of paper, and thought some more. "Of course I can't say exactly, but from hints I have received here and there I should think that a safe bet would be that some one has cashed in upward of half a million dollars already."

"Whew," whistled Kennedy, "that's going some. And I suppose it is all salted away in some portable form. What an inventory it must be—good bills, gold, diamonds, and jewellery. This is a stake worth playing for."

"Yes," broke in O'Connor, "but from my standpoint, professionally, I mean, the case is even worse than that. It's not the counterfeits that bother us. We understand that, all right. But," and he leaned forward earnestly and brought his fist down hard on the table with a resounding Irish oath, "the finger-print system, the infallible finger-print system, has gone to pieces. We've just imported this new 'portrait parlé' fresh from Paris and London, invented by Bertillon and all that sort of thing—it has gone to pieces, too. It's a fine case, this is, with nothing left of either scientific or unscientific criminal-catching to rely on. There—what do you know about that?"

"You'll have to tell me the facts first," said Kennedy. "I can't diagnose your disease until I know the symptoms."

"It's like this," explained Burke, the detective in him showing now with no effort at concealment. "A man, an Englishman, apparently, went into a downtown banker's office about three months ago and asked to have some English bank-notes exchanged for American money. After he had gone away, the cashier began to get suspicious. He thought there was something phoney in the feel of the notes. Under the glass he noticed that the little curl on the 'e' of the 'Five' was missing. It's the protective mark. The water-mark was quite equal to that of the genuine—maybe better. Hold that note up to the light and see for yourself.

"Well, the next day, down to the Custom House, where my office is, a man came who runs a swell gambling-house uptown. He laid ten brand-new bills on my desk. An Englishman had been betting on the wheel. He didn't seem to care about winning, and he cashed in each time with a new one-hundred-dollar bill. Of course he didn't care about winning. He cared about the change—that was his winning. The bill on the table is one of the original ten, though since then scores have been put into circulation. I made up my mind that it was the same Englishman in both cases.

"Then within a week, in walked the manager of the Mozambique Hotel—he had been stung with the fake International Express money-order—same Englishman, too, I believe."

"And you have no trace of him?" asked Kennedy eagerly.

"We had him under arrest once—we thought. A general alarm was sent out, of course, to all the banks and banking-houses. But the man was too clever to turn up in that way again. In one gambling-joint which women frequent a good deal, a classy dame who might have been a duchess or a—well, she was a pretty good loser and always paid with hundred-dollar bills. Now, you know women are *not* good losers. Besides, the hundred-dollar-bill story had got around among the gambling-houses. This joint thought it worth taking a chance, so they called me up on the 'phone, extracted a promise that I'd play fair and keep O'Connor from raiding them, but wouldn't I please come up and look over the dame of the yellow bills? Of course I made a jump at it. Sure enough, they were the same counterfeits. I could tell because the silk threads were drawn in with coloured ink. But instead of making an arrest I decided to trail the lady.

"Now, here comes the strange part of it. Let me see, this must have been over two months ago. I followed her out to a suburban town, Riverwood along the Hudson, and to a swell country house overlooking the river, private drive, stone gate, hedges, old trees, and all that sort of thing. A sporty-looking Englishman met her at the gate with one of those big imported touring-cars, and they took a spin.

"I waited a day or so, but nothing more happened, and I began to get anxious. Perhaps I was a bit hasty. Anyhow I watched my chance and made an arrest of both of them when they came to New York on a shopping expedition. You should have heard that Englishman swear. I didn't know such language was possible. But in his pocket we found twenty more of those hundred-dollar bills—that was all. Do you think he owned up? Not a bit of it. He swore he had picked the notes up in a pocketbook on the pier as he left the steamer. I laughed. But when he was arraigned in court he told the magistrate the same story and that he had advertised his find at the time. Sure enough, in the files of the papers we discovered in the lost-and-found column the ad., just as he claimed. We couldn't even prove that he had passed the bills. So the magistrate refused to hold them, and they were both released. But we had had them in our power long enough to take their finger-prints and get descriptions and measurements of them, particularly by this new 'portrait parlé' system. We felt we could send out a strange detective and have him pick them out of a crowd—you know the system, I presume?"

Kennedy nodded, and I made a mental note of finding out more about the "portrait parlé" later.

Burke paused, and O'Connor prompted, "Tell them about Scotland Yard, Tom."

"Oh, yes," resumed Burke. "Of course I sent copies of the finger-prints to Scotland Yard. Within two weeks they replied that one set belonged to William Forbes, a noted counterfeiter, who, they understood, had sailed for South Africa but had never arrived there. They were glad to learn that he was in America, and advised me to look after him sharply. The woman was also a noted character—Harriet Wollstone, an adventuress."

"I suppose you have shadowed them ever since?" Kennedy asked.

"Yes, a few days after they were arrested the man had an accident with his car. It was said he was cranking the engine and that it kicked back and splintered the bone in his forearm. Anyhow, he went about with his hand and arm in a sling."

"And then?"

"They gave my man the slip that night in their fast touring-car. You know automobiles have about made shadowing impossible in these days. The house was closed up, and it was said by the neighbours that Williams and Mrs. Williams—as they called themselves—had gone to visit a specialist in Philadelphia. Still, as they had a year's lease on the house, I detailed a man to watch it more or less all the time. They went to Philadelphia all right; some of the bills turned up there. But we saw nothing of them.

"A short time ago, word came to me that the house was open again. It wasn't two hours later that the telephone rang like mad. A Fifth Avenue jeweller had just sold a rope of pearls to an Englishwoman who paid for it herself in crisp new one-hundred-dollar bills. The bank had returned them to him that very afternoon—counterfeits. I didn't lose any time making a second arrest up at the house of mystery at Riverwood. I had the county authorities hold them—and, now, O'Connor, tell the rest of it. You took the finger-prints up there."

O'Connor cleared his throat as if something stuck in it, in the telling. "The Riverwood authorities refused to hold them," he said with evident chagrin. "As soon as I heard of the arrest I started up myself with the finger-print records to help Burke. It was the same man, all right—I'll swear to that on a stack of Bibles. So will Burke. I'll never forget that snub nose—the concave nose, the nose being the first point of identification in the 'portrait parlé.' And the ears, too—oh, it was the same man, all right. But when we produced the London finger-prints which tallied with the New York finger-prints which we had made—believe it or not, but it is a fact, the Riverwood finger-prints did not tally at all."

He laid the prints on the table. Kennedy examined them closely. His face clouded. It was quite evident that he was stumped, and he said so. "There are some points of agreement," he remarked, "but more points of difference. Any points of difference are usually considered fatal to the finger-print theory."

"We had to let the man go," concluded Burke. "We could have held the woman, but we let her go, too, because she was not the principal in the case. My men are shadowing the house now and have been ever since then. But the next day after the last arrest, a man from New York, who looked like a doctor, made a visit. The secret-service man on the job didn't dare leave the house to follow him, but as he never came again perhaps it doesn't matter. Since then the house has been closed."

The telephone rang. It was Burke's office calling him. As he talked we could gather that something tragic must have happened at Riverwood, and we could hardly wait until he had finished.

"There has been an accident up there," he remarked as he hung up the receiver rather petulantly. "They returned in the car this afternoon with a large package in the back of the tonneau. But they didn't stay long. After dark they started out again in the car. The accident was at the bad railroad crossing just above Riverwood. It seems Williams's car got stalled on the track just as the Buffalo express was due. No one saw it, but a man in a buggy around the bend in the road heard a woman scream. He hurried down. The train had smashed the car to bits. How the woman escaped was a miracle, but they found the man's body up the tracks, horribly mangled. It was Williams, they say. They identified him by the clothes and by letters in his pockets. But my man tells me he found a watch on him with 'W. F.' engraved on it. His hands and arms and head must have been right under the locomotive when it struck him, I judge."

"I guess that winds the case up, eh?" exclaimed O'Connor with evident chagrin. "Where's the woman?"

"They said she was in the little local hospital, but not much hurt. Just the shock and a few bruises."

O'Connor's question seemed to suggest an idea to Burke, and he reached for the telephone again. "Riverwood 297," he ordered; then to us as he waited he said: "We must hold the woman. Hello, 297? The hospital? This is Burke of the secret service. Will you tell my man, who must be somewhere about, that I would like to have him hold that woman who was in the auto smash until I can—what? Gone? The deuce!"

He hung up the receiver angrily. "She left with a man who called for her about half an hour ago," he said. "There must be a gang of them. Forbes is dead, but we must get the rest. Mr. Kennedy, I'm sorry to have bothered you, but I guess we can handle this alone, after all. It was the finger-prints that fooled us, but now that Forbes is out of the way it's just a straight case of detective work of the old style which won't interest you."

"On the contrary," answered Kennedy, "I'm just beginning to be interested. Does it occur to you that, after all, Forbes may not be dead?"

"Not dead?" echoed Burke and O'Connor together.

"Exactly; that's just what I said—not dead. Now stop and think a moment. Would the great Forbes be so foolish as to go about with a watch marked 'W. F.' if he knew, as he must have known, that you would communicate with London and by means of the prints find out all about him?"

"Yes," agreed Burke, "all we have to go by is his watch found on Williams. I suppose there is some possibility that Forbes may still be alive."

"Who is this third man who comes in and with whom Harriet Wollstone goes away so willingly?" put in O'Connor. "You said the house had been closed—absolutely closed?"

Burke nodded. "Been closed ever since the last arrest. There's a servant who goes in now and then, but the car hasn't been there before to-night, wherever it has been."

"I should like to watch that house myself for a while," mused Kennedy. "I suppose you have no objections to my doing so?"

"Of course not. Go ahead," said Burke. "I will go along with you if you wish, or my man can go with you."

"No," said Kennedy, "too many of us might spoil the broth. I'll watch alone to-night and will see you in the morning. You needn't even say anything to your man there about us."

"Walter, what's on for to-night?" he asked when they had gone. "How are you fixed for a little trip out to Riverwood?"

"To tell the truth, I had an engagement at the College Club with some of the fellows."

"Oh, cut it."

"That's what I intend to do," I replied.

It was a raw night, and we bundled ourselves up in old football sweaters under our overcoats. Half an hour later we were on our way up to Riverwood.

"By the way, Craig," I asked, "I didn't like to say anything before those fellows. They'd think I was a dub. But I don't mind asking you. What is this 'portrait parlé' they talk about, anyway?"

"Why, it's a word-picture—a 'spoken picture,' to be literal. I took some lessons in it at Bertillon's school when I was in Paris. It's a method of scientific apprehension of criminals, a sort of necessary addition and completion to the methods of scientific identification of them after they are arrested. For instance, in trying to pick out a given criminal from his mere description you begin with the nose. Now, noses are all concave, straight, or convex. This Forbes had a nose that was concave, Burke says. Suppose you were sent out to find him. Of all the people you met, we'll say, roughly, two-thirds wouldn't interest you. You'd pass up all with straight or convex noses. Now the next point to observe is the ear. There are four general kinds of ears—triangular, square, oval, and round, besides a number of other differences which are clear enough after you study ears. This fellow is a pale man with square ears and a peculiar lobe to his ear. So you wouldn't give a second glance to, say, three-fourths of the square-cared people. So by a process of elimination of various features, the eyes, the mouth, the hair, wrinkles, and so forth, you would be able to pick your man out of a thousand—that is, if you were trained."

"And it works?" I asked rather doubtfully.

"Oh, yes. That's why I'm taking up this case. I believe science can really be used to detect crime, any crime, and in the present instance I've just pride enough to stick to this thing until—until they begin to cut ice on the Styx. Whew, but it will be cold out in the country to-night, Walter—speaking about ice."

It was quite late when we reached Riverwood, and Kennedy hurried along the dimly lighted streets, avoiding the main street lest some one might be watching or following us. He pushed on, following the directions Burke had given him. The house in question was a large, newly built affair of concrete, surrounded by trees and a hedge, directly overlooking the river. A bitter wind swept in from the west, but in the shadow of an evergreen tree and of the hedge Kennedy established our watch.

Of all fruitless errands this seemed to me to be the acme. The house was deserted; that was apparent, I thought, and I said so. Hardly had I said it when I heard the baying of a dog. It did not come from the house, however, and I concluded that it must have come from the next estate.

"It's in the garage," whispered Kennedy. "I

can hardly think they would go away and leave a dog locked up in it. They would at least turn him loose."

Hour after hour we waited. Midnight passed, and still nothing happened. At last when the moon had disappeared under the clouds, Kennedy pulled me along. We had seen not a sign of life in the house, yet he observed all the caution he would have if it had been well guarded. Quickly we advanced over the open space to the house, approaching in the shadow as much as possible, on the side farthest from the river.

Tiptoeing over the porch, Kennedy tried a window. It was fastened. Without hesitation he pulled out some instruments. One of them was a rubber suction-cup, which he fastened to the window-pane. Then with a very fine diamond-cutter he proceeded to cut out a large section. It soon fell and was prevented from smashing on the floor by the string and the suction-cup. Kennedy put his hand in and unlatched the window, and we stepped in.

All was silent. Apparently the house was deserted.

Cautiously Kennedy pressed the button of his pocket storage-battery lamp and flashed it slowly about the room. It was a sort of library, handsomely furnished. At last the beam of light rested on a huge desk at the opposite end. It seemed to interest Kennedy, and we tiptoed over to it. One after another he opened the drawers. One was locked, and he saved that until the last.

Quietly as he could, he jimmied it open, muffling

the jimmy in a felt cloth that was on a table. Most people do not realise the disruptive force that there is in a simple jimmy. I didn't until I saw the solid drawer with its heavy lock yield with just the trace of a noise. Kennedy waited an instant and listened. Nothing happened.

Inside the drawer was a most nondescript collection of useless articles. There were a number of pieces of fine sponge, some of them very thin and cut in a flat oval shape, smelling of lysol strongly; several bottles, a set of sharp little knives, some paraffin, bandages, antiseptic gauze, cotton—in fact, it looked like a first-aid kit. As soon as he saw it Kennedy seemed astonished but not at a loss to account for it.

"I thought he left that sort of thing to the doctors, but I guess he took a hand in it himself," he muttered, continuing to fumble with the knives in the drawer. It was no time to ask questions, and I did not. Kennedy rapidly stowed away the things in his pockets. One bottle he opened and held to his nose. I could distinguish immediately the volatile smell of ether. He closed it quickly, and it, too, went into his pocket with the remark, "Somebody must have known how to administer an anæsthetic—probably the Wollstone woman."

A suppressed exclamation from Kennedy caused me to look. The drawer had a false back. Safely tucked away in it reposed a tin box, one of those so-called strong-boxes which are so handy in that they save a burglar much time and trouble in hunting all over for the valuables he has come after.

Kennedy drew it forth and laid it on the desk. It was locked.

Even that did not seem to satisfy Kennedy, who continued to scrutinise the walls and corners of the room as if looking for a safe or something of that sort.

"Let's look in the room across the hall," he whispered.

Suddenly a piercing scream of a woman rang out upstairs. "Help! Help! There's some one in the house! Billy, help!"

I felt an arm grasp me tightly, and for a moment a chill ran over me at being caught in the nefarious work of breaking and entering a dwelling-house at night. But it was only Kennedy, who had already tucked the precious little tin box under his arm.

With a leap he dragged me to the open window, cleared it, vaulted over the porch, and we were running for the clump of woods that adjoined the estate on one side. Lights flashed in all the windows of the house at once. There must have been some sort of electric-light system that could be lighted instantly as a "burglar-expeller." Anyhow, we had made good our escape.

As we lost ourselves in the woods I gave a last glance back and saw a lantern carried from the house to the garage. As the door was unlocked I could see, in the moonlight, a huge dog leap out and lick the hands and face of a man.

Quickly we now crashed through the frozen underbrush. Evidently Kennedy was making for the station by a direct route across country instead of the circuitous way by the road and town. Behind us we could hear a deep baying.

"By the Lord, Walter," cried Kennedy, for once in his life thoroughly alarmed, "it's a bloodhound, and our trail is fresh."

Closer it came. Press forward as we might, we could never expect to beat that dog.

"Oh, for a stream," groaned Kennedy, "but they are all frozen—even the river."

He stopped short, fumbled in his pocket, and drew out the bottle of ether.

"Raise your foot, Walter," he ordered.

I did so and he smeared first mine and then his with the ether. Then we doubled on our trail once or twice and ran again.

"The dog will never be able to pick up the ether as our trail," panted Kennedy; "that is, if he is any good and trained not to go off on wild-goose chases."

On we hurried from the woods to the now dark and silent town. It was indeed fortunate that the dog had been thrown off our scent, for the station was closed, and, indeed, if it had been open I am sure the station agent would have felt more like locking the door against two such tramps as we were, carrying a tin box and pursued by a dog, than opening it for us. The best we could do was to huddle into a corner until we succeeded in jumping a milk-train that luckily slowed down as it passed Riverwood station.

Neither of us could wait to open the tin box in our apartment, and instead of going uptown Kennedy decided it would be best to go to a hotel near the station. Somehow we succeeded in getting a room without exciting suspicion. Hardly had the bellboy's footsteps ceased echoing in the corridor than Kennedy was at work wrenching off the lid of the box with such leverage as the scanty furnishings of the room afforded.

At last it yielded, and we looked in curiously, expecting to find fabulous wealth in some form. A few hundred dollars and a rope of pearls lay in it. It was a good " haul," but where was the vast spoil the counterfeiters had accumulated? We had missed it. So far we were completely baffled.

" Perhaps we had better snatch a couple of hours' sleep," was all that Craig said, stifling his chagrin.

Over and over in my mind I was turning the problem of where they had hidden the spoil. I dozed off, still thinking about it and thinking that, even should they be captured, they might have stowed away perhaps a million dollars to which they could go back after their sentences were served.

It was still early for New York when Kennedy roused me by talking over the telephone in the room. In fact, I doubt if he had slept at all.

Burke was at the other end of the wire. His man had just reported that something had happened during the night at Riverwood, but he couldn't give a very clear account. Craig seemed to enjoy the joke immensely as he told his story to Burke.

The last words I heard were: " All right. Send a man up here to the station—one who knows all the descriptions of these people. I'm sure they will have to come into town to-day, and they will have to come by train, for their car is wrecked. Better watch at the uptown stations, also."

After a hasty breakfast we met Burke's man and took our places at the exit from the train platforms. Evidently Kennedy had figured out that the counterfeiters would have to come into town for some reason or other. The incoming passengers were passing us in a steady stream, for a new station was then being built, and there was only a temporary structure with one large exit.

"Here is where the 'portrait parlé' ought to come in, if ever," commented Kennedy as he watched eagerly.

And yet neither man nor woman passed us who fitted the description. Train after train emptied its human freight, yet the pale man with the concave nose and the peculiar ear, accompanied perhaps by a lady, did not pass us.

At last the incoming stream began to dwindle down. It was long past the time when the counterfeiters should have arrived if they had started on any reasonable train.

"Perhaps they have gone up to Montreal, instead," I ventured.

Kennedy shook his head. "No," he answered. "I have an idea that I was mistaken about the money being kept at Riverwood. It would have been too risky. I thought it out on the way back this morning. They probably kept it in a safe deposit vault here. I had figured that they would come down and get it and leave New York after last night's events. We have failed—they have got by us. Neither the 'portrait parlé' nor the ordinary photography nor any other system will suffice alone against the arch-criminal back of this, I'm afraid. Walter, I am sore and disgusted. What I should have done was to accept Burke's offer—surround the house with a posse if necessary, last night, and catch the counterfeiters by sheer force. I was too confident. I thought I could do it with finesse, and I have failed. I'd give anything to know what safe deposit vault they kept the fake money in."

I said nothing as we strolled away, leaving Burke's man still to watch, hoping against hope. Kennedy walked disconsolately through the station, and I followed. In a secluded part of the waiting-room he sat down, his face drawn up in a scowl such as I had never seen. Plainly he was disgusted with himself—with only himself. This was no bungling of Burke or any one else. Again the counterfeiters had escaped from the hand of the law.

As he moved his fingers restlessly in the pockets of his coat, he absently pulled out the little pieces of sponge and the ether bottle. He regarded them without much interest.

"I know what they were for," he said, diving back into his pocket for the other things and bringing out the sharp little knives in their case. I said nothing, for Kennedy was in a deep study. At last he put the things back into his pocket. As he did so his hand encountered something which he drew forth with a puzzled air. It was the piece of paraffin.

"Now, what do you suppose that was for?" he asked, half to himself. "I had forgotten that. What was the use of a piece of paraffin? Phew, smell the antiseptic worked into it."

"I don't know," I replied, rather testily. "If you would tell me what the other things were for I might enlighten you, but——"

"By George, Walter, what a chump I am!" cried Kennedy, leaping to his feet, all energy again. "Why did I forget that lump of paraffin? Why, of course—I think I can guess what they have been doing—of course. Why, man alive, he walked right past us, and we never knew it. Boy, boy," he shouted to a newsboy who passed, "what's the latest sporting edition you have?"

Eagerly he almost tore a paper open and scanned the sporting pages. "Racing at Lexington begins to-morrow," he read. "Yes, I'll bet that's it. We don't have to know the safe deposit vault, after all. It would be too late, anyhow. Quick, let us look up the train to Lexington."

As we hurried over to the information booth, I gasped, in a whirl: "Now, look here, Kennedy, what's all this lightning calculation? What possible connection is there between a lump of paraffin and one of the few places in the country where they still race horses?"

"None," he replied, not stopping an instant. "None. The paraffin suggested to me the possible way in which our man managed to elude us under our very eyes. That set my mind at work again. Like a flash it occurred to me: Where would they be most likely to go next to work off some of the bills? The banks are on, the jewellery-houses are on, the gambling-joints are on. Why, to the race-tracks, of course. That's it. Counterfeiters all use the bookmakers, only since racing has been killed in New York they have had to resort to other means here. If New York has suddenly become too hot, what more natural than to leave it? Here, let me see—there's a train that gets there early to-morrow, the best train, too. Say, is No. 144 made up yet?" he inquired at the desk.

"No. 144 will be ready in fifteen minutes. Track 8."

Kennedy thanked the man, turned abruptly, and started for the still closed gate at Track 8.

"Beg pardon—why, hulloa—it's Burke," he exclaimed as we ran plump into a man staring vacantly about.

It was not the gentleman farmer of the night before, nor yet the supposed college graduate. This man was a Western rancher; his broad-brimmed hat, long moustache, frock coat, and flowing tie proclaimed it. Yet there was something indefinably familiar about him, too. It was Burke in another disguise.

"Pretty good work, Kennedy," nodded Burke, shifting his tobacco from one side of his jaws to the other. "Now, tell me how your man escaped you this morning, when you can recognise me instantly in this rig."

"You haven't altered your features," explained Kennedy simply. "Our pale-faced, snub-nosed, peculiar-eared friend has. What do you think of the possibility of his going to the Lexington track, now that he finds it too dangerous to remain in New York?"

Burke looked at Kennedy rather sharply. "Say, do you add telepathy to your other accomplishments?"

"No," laughed Craig, "but I'm glad to see that two of us working independently have arrived at the same conclusion. Come, let us saunter over to Track 8—I guess the train is made up."

The gate was just opened, and the crowd filed through. No one who seemed to satisfy either Burke or Kennedy appeared. The train-announcer made his last call. Just then a taxicab pulled up at the street-end of the platform, not far from Track 8. A man jumped out and assisted a heavily veiled lady, paid the driver, picked up the grips, and turned toward us.

We waited expectantly. As he turned I saw a dark-skinned, hook-nosed man, and I exclaimed disgustedly to Burke: "Well, if they are going to Lexington they can't make this train. Those are the last people who have a chance."

Kennedy, however, continued to regard the couple steadily. The man saw that he was being watched and faced us defiantly, "Such impertinence!" Then to his wife, "Come, my dear, we'll just make it."

"I'm afraid I'll have to trouble you to show us what's in that grip," said Kennedy, calmly laying his hand on the man's arm.

"Well, now, did you ever hear of such blasted

impudence? Get out of my way, sir, this instant, or I'll have you arrested."

"Come, come, Kennedy," interrupted Burke. "Surely you are getting in wrong here. This can't be the man."

Craig shook his head decidedly. "You can make the arrest or not, Burke, as you choose. If not, I am through. If so—I'll take all the responsibility."

Reluctantly Burke yielded. The man protested; the woman cried; a crowd collected.

The train-gate shut with a bang. As it did so the man's demeanour changed instantly. "There," he shouted angrily, "you have made us miss our train. I'll have you in jail for this. Come on now to the nearest magistrate's court. I'll have my rights as an American citizen. You have carried your little joke too far. Knight is my name—John Knight, of Omaha, pork-packer. Come on now. I'll see that somebody suffers for this if I have to stay in New York a year. It's an outrage—an outrage."

Burke was now apparently alarmed—more at the possibility of the humorous publicity that would follow such a mistake by the secret service than at anything else. However, Kennedy did not weaken, and on general principles I stuck to Kennedy.

"Now," said the man surlily while he placed "Mrs. Knight" in as easy a chair as he could find in the judge's chambers, "what is the occasion of all this row? Tell the judge what a bad man from Bloody Gulch I am."

O'Connor had arrived, having broken all speed

laws and perhaps some records on the way up from headquarters. Kennedy laid the Scotland Yard finger-prints on the table. Beside them he placed those taken by O'Connor and Burke in New York.

"Here," he began, "we have the finger-prints of a man who was one of the most noted counterfeiters in Great Britain. Beside them are those of a man who succeeded in passing counterfeits of several kinds recently in New York. Some weeks later this third set of prints was taken from a man who was believed to be the same person."

The magistrate was examining the three sets of prints. As he came to the third, he raised his head as if about to make a remark, when Kennedy quickly interrupted.

"One moment, sir. You were about to say that finger-prints never change, never show such variations as these. That is true. There are finger-prints of people taken fifty years ago that are exactly the same as their finger-prints of to-day. They don't change—they are permanent. The finger-prints of mummies can be deciphered even after thousands of years. But," he added slowly, "you can change fingers."

The idea was so startling that I could scarcely realise what he meant at first. I had read of the wonderful work of the surgeons of the Rockefeller Institute in transplanting tissues and even whole organs, in grafting skin and in keeping muscles artificially alive for days under proper conditions. Could it be that a man had deliberately amputated his fingers and grafted on new ones? Was the stake sufficient for such a game? Surely there must be some scars left after such grafting. I picked up the various sets of prints. It was true that the third set was not very clear, but there certainly were no scars there.

"Though there is no natural changeability of finger-prints," pursued Kennedy, "such changes can be induced, as Dr. Paul Prager of Vienna has shown, by acids and other reagents, by grafting and by injuries. Now, is there any method by which lost finger-tips can be restored? I know of one case where the end of a finger was taken off and only one-sixteenth inch of the nail was left. The doctor incised the edges of the granulating surface and then led the granulations on by what is known in the medical profession as the 'sponge graft.' He grew a new finger-tip.

"The sponge graft consists in using portions of a fine Turkish surgical sponge, such I have here. I found these pieces in a desk at Riverwood. The patient is anæsthetised. An incision is made from side to side in the stump of the finger and flaps of skin are sliced off and turned up for the new end of the finger to develop in—a sort of shell of living skin. Inside this, the sponge is placed, not a large piece, but a very thin piece sliced off and cut to the shape of the finger-stump. It is perfectly sterilised in water and washed in green soap after all the stony particles are removed by hydrochloric acid. Then the finger is bound up and kept moist with normal salt solution.

"The result is that the end of the finger, instead

of healing over, grows into the fine meshes of the pieces of sponge, by capillary attraction. Of course even this would heal in a few days, but the doctor does not let it heal. In three days he pulls the sponge off gently. The end of the finger has grown up just a fraction of an inch. Then a new thin layer of sponge is added. Day after day this process is repeated, each time the finger growing a little more. A new nail develops if any of the matrix is left, and I suppose a clever surgeon by grafting up pieces of epidermis could produce on such a stump very passable finger-prints."

No one of us said anything, but Kennedy seemed to realise the thought in our minds and proceeded to elaborate the method.

"It is known as the 'education sponge method,' and was first described by Dr. D. J. Hamilton, of Edinburgh, in 1881. It has frequently been used in America since then. The sponge really acts in a mechanical manner to support the new finger-tissue that is developed. The meshes are filled in by growing tissue, and as it grows the tissue absorbs part of the sponge, which is itself an animal tissue and acts like catgut. Part of it is also thrown off. In fact, the sponge imitates what happens naturally in the porous network of a regular blood-clot. It educates the tissue to grow, stimulates it—new blood-vessels and nerves as well as flesh.

"In another case I know of, almost the whole of the first joint of a finger was crushed off, and the doctor was asked to amputate the stump of bone that protruded. Instead, he decided to educate the tissue to grow out to cover it and appear like a normal finger. In these cases the doctors succeeded admirably in giving the patients entire new finger-tips, without scars, and, except for the initial injury and operation, with comparatively little inconvenience except that absolute rest of the hands was required.

"That is what happened, gentlemen," concluded Kennedy. "That is why Mr. Forbes, alias Williams, made a trip to Philadelphia to be treated—for crushed finger-tips, not for the kick of an automobile engine. He may have paid the doctors in counterfeits. In reality this man was playing a game in which there was indeed a heavy stake at issue. He was a counterfeiter sought by two governments with the net closing about him. What are the tips of a few fingers compared with life, liberty, wealth, and a beautiful woman? The first two sets of prints are different from the third because they are made by different finger-tips—on the same man. The very core of the prints was changed. But the finger-print system is vindicated by the very ingenuity of the man who so cleverly has contrived to beat it."

"Very interesting—to one who is interested," remarked the stranger, "but what has that to do with detaining my wife and myself, making us miss our train, and insulting us?"

"Just this," replied Craig. "If you will kindly oblige us by laying your fingers on this inking-pad and then lightly on this sheet of paper, I think I can show you an answer."

Knight demurred, and his wife grew hysterical

at the idea, but there was nothing to do but comply. Kennedy glanced at the fourth set of prints, then at the third set taken a week ago, and smiled. No one said a word. Knight or Williams, which was it? He nonchalantly lit a cigarette.

"So you say I am this Williams, the counterfeiter?" he asked superciliously.

"I do," reiterated Kennedy. "You are also Forbes."

"I don't suppose Scotland Yard has neglected to furnish you with photographs and a description of this Forbes?"

Burke reluctantly pulled out a Bertillon card from his pocket and laid it on the table. It bore the front face and profile of the famous counterfeiter, as well as his measurements.

The man picked it up as if indeed it was a curious thing. His coolness nearly convinced me. Surely he should have hesitated in actually demanding this last piece of evidence. I had heard, however, that the Bertillon system of measurements often depended on the personal equation of the measurer as well as on the measured. Was he relying on that, or on his difference in features?

I looked over Kennedy's shoulder at the card on the table. There was the concave nose of the "portrait parlé" of Forbes, as it had first been described to us. Without looking further I involuntarily glanced at the man, although I had no need to do so. I knew that his nose was the exact opposite of that of Forbes.

"Ingenious at argument as you are," he remarked

quietly, "you will hardly deny that Knight, of Omaha, is the exact opposite of Forbes, of London. My nose is almost Jewish—my complexion is dark as an Arab's. Still, I suppose I am the sallow, snub-nosed Forbes described here, inasmuch as I have stolen Forbes's fingers and lost them again by a most preposterous method."

"The colour of the face is easily altered," said Kennedy. "A little picric acid will do that. The ingenious rogue Sarcey in Paris eluded the police very successfully until Dr. Charcot exposed him and showed how he changed the arch of his eyebrows and the wrinkles of his face. Much is possible to-day that would make Frankenstein and Dr. Moreau look clumsy and antiquated."

A sharp feminine voice interrupted. It was the woman, who had kept silent up to this time. "But I have read in one of the papers this morning that a Mr. Williams was found dead in an automobile accident up the Hudson yesterday. I remember reading it, because I am afraid of accidents myself."

All eyes were now fixed on Kennedy. "That body," he answered quickly, "was a body purchased by you at a medical school, brought in your car to Riverwood, dressed in Williams's clothes with a watch that would show he was Forbes, placed on the track in front of the auto, while you two watched the Buffalo express run it down, and screamed. It was a clever scheme that you concocted, but these facts do not agree."

He laid the measurements of the corpse obtained by Burke and those from the London police card side by side. Only in the roughest way did they approximate each other.

"Your honour, I appeal to your sense of justice," cried our prisoner impatiently. "Hasn't this farce been allowed to go far enough? Is there any reason why this fake detective should make fools out of us all and keep my wife longer in this court? I'm not disposed to let the matter drop. I wish to enter a charge against him of false arrest and malicious prosecution. I shall turn the whole thing over to my attorney this afternoon. The deuce with the races—I'll have justice."

The man had by this time raised himself to a high pitch of apparently righteous wrath. He advanced menacingly toward Kennedy, who stood with his shoulders thrown back, and his hands deep in his pockets, and a half amused look on his face.

"As for you, Mr. Detective," added the man, "for eleven cents I'd lick you to within an inch of your life. 'Portrait parlé,' indeed! It's a fine scientific system that has to deny its own main principles in order to vindicate itself. Bah! Take that, you scoundrel!"

Harriet Wollstone threw her arms about him, but he broke away. His fist shot out straight. Kennedy was too quick for him, however. I had seen Craig do it dozens of times with the best boxers in the "gym." He simply jerked his head to one side, and the blow passed just a fraction of an inch from his jaw, but passed it as cleanly as if it had been a yard away.

The man lost his balance, and as he fell forward

and caught himself, Kennedy calmly and deliberately slapped him on the nose.

It was an intensely serious instant, yet I actually laughed. The man's nose was quite out of joint, even from such a slight blow. It was twisted over on his face in the most ludicrous position imaginable.

"The next time you try that, Forbes," remarked Kennedy, as he pulled the piece of paraffin from his pocket and laid it on the table with the other exhibits, "don't forget that a concave nose built out to hook-nose convexity by injections of paraffin, such as the beauty-doctors everywhere advertise, is a poor thing for a White Hope."

Both Burke and O'Connor had seized Forbes, but Kennedy had turned his attention to the larger of Forbes's grips, which the Wollstone woman vociferously claimed as her own. Quickly he wrenched it open.

As he turned it up on the table my eyes fairly bulged at the sight. Forbes' suit-case might have been that of a travelling salesman for the Kimberley, the Klondike, and the Bureau of Engraving, all in one. Craig dumped the wealth out on the table—stacks of genuine bills, gold coins of two realms, diamonds, pearls, everything portable and tangible all heaped up and topped off with piles of counterfeits awaiting the magic touch of this Midas to turn them into real gold.

"Forbes, you have failed in your get-away," said Craig triumphantly. "Gentlemen, you have here a master counterfeiter, surely—a master counterfeiter of features and fingers as well as of currency."

VI

THE SAND-HOG

"INTERESTING story, this fight between the Five-Borough and the Inter-River Transit," I remarked to Kennedy as I sketched out the draft of an exposé of high finance for the Sunday *Star*.

"Then that will interest you, also," said he, throwing a letter down on my desk. He had just come in and was looking over his mail.

The letterhead bore the name of the Five-Borough Company. It was from Jack Orton, one of our intimates at college, who was in charge of the construction of a new tunnel under the river. It was brief, as Jack's letters always were. "I have a case here at the tunnel that I am sure will appeal to you, my own case, too," it read. "You can go as far as you like with it, but get to the bottom of the thing, no matter whom it hits. There is some deviltry afoot, and apparently no one is safe. Don't say a word to anybody about it, but drop over to see me as soon as you possibly can."

"Yes," I agreed, "that does interest me. When are you going over?"

"Now," replied Kennedy, who had not taken off his hat. "Can you come along?"

As we sped across the city in a taxicab, Craig remarked: "I wonder what is the trouble? Did you see in the society news this morning the announcement of Jack's engagement to Vivian Taylor, the daughter of the president of the Five-Borough?"

I had seen it, but could not connect it with the trouble, whatever it was, at the tunnel, though I did try to connect the tunnel mystery with my exposé.

We pulled up at the construction works, and a strapping Irishman met us. "Is this Professor Kennedy?" he asked of Craig.

"It is. Where is Mr. Orton's office?"

"I'm afraid, sir, it will be a long time before Mr. Orton is in his office again, sir. The doctor have just took him out of the medical lock, an' he said if you was to come before they took him to the 'orspital I was to bring you right up to the lock."

"Good heavens, man, what has happened?" exclaimed Kennedy. "Take us up to him quick."

Without waiting to answer, the Irishman led the way up and across a rough board platform until at last we came to what looked like a huge steel cylinder, lying horizontally, in which was a floor with a cot and some strange paraphernalia. On the cot lay Jack Orton, drawn and contorted, so changed that even his own mother would scarcely have recognised him. A doctor was bending over him, massaging the joints of his legs and his side.

"Thank you, Doctor, I feel a little better," he groaned. "No, I don't want to go back into the lock again, not unless the pain gets worse."

His eyes were closed, but hearing us he opened them and nodded.

"Yes, Craig," he murmured with difficulty, "this

is Jack Orton. What do you think of me? I'm a pretty sight. How are you? And how are you, Walter? Not too vigorous with the hand-shakes, fellows. Sorry you couldn't get over before this happened."

"What's the matter?" we asked, glancing blankly from Orton to the doctor.

Orton forced a half smile. "Just a touch of the 'bends' from working in compressed air," he explained.

We looked at him, but could say nothing. I, at least, was thinking of his engagement.

"Yes," he added bitterly, "I know what you are thinking about, fellows. Look at me! Do you think such a wreck as I am now has any right to be engaged to the dearest girl in the world?"

"Mr. Orton," interposed the doctor, "I think you'll feel better if you'll keep quiet. You can see your friends in the hospital to-night, but for a few hours I think you had better rest. Gentlemen, if you will be so good as to postpone your conversation with Mr. Orton until later it would be much better."

"Then I'll see you to-night," said Orton to us feebly. Turning to a tall, spare, wiry chap, of just the build for tunnel work, where fat is fatal, he added: "This is Mr. Capps, my first assistant. He will show you the way down to the street again."

"Confound it!" exclaimed Craig, after we had left Capps. "What do you think of this? Even before we can get to him something has happened. The plot thickens before we are well into it. I think I'll not take a cab, or a car either. How are you for a walk until we can see Orton again?"

I could see that Craig was very much affected by the sudden accident that had happened to our friend, so I fell into his mood, and we walked block after block scarcely exchanging a word. His only remark, I recall, was, "Walter, I can't think it was an accident, coming so close after that letter." As for me, I scarcely knew what to think.

At last our walk brought us around to the private hospital where Orton was. As we were about to enter, a very handsome girl was leaving. Evidently she had been visiting some one of whom she thought a great deal. Her long fur-coat was flying carelessly, unfastened in the cold night air; her features were pale, and her eyes had the fixed look of one who saw nothing but grief.

"It's terrible, Miss Taylor," I heard the man with her say soothingly, "and you must know that I sympathise with you a great deal."

Looking up quickly, I caught sight of Capps and bowed. He returned our bows and handed her gently into an automobile that was waiting.

"He might at least have introduced us," muttered Kennedy, as we went on into the hospital.

Orton was lying in bed, white and worn, propped up by pillows which the nurse kept arranging and rearranging to ease his pain. The Irishman whom we had seen at the tunnel was standing deferentially near the foot of the bed.

"Quite a number of visitors, nurse, for a new patient," said Orton, as he welcomed us. "First

Capps and Paddy from the tunnel, then Vivian"—he was fingering some beautiful roses in a vase on a table near him—"and now, you fellows. I sent her home with Capps. She oughtn't to be out alone at this hour, and Capps is a good fellow. She's known him a long time. No, Paddy, put down your hat. I want you to stay. Paddy, by the way, fellows, is my right-hand man in managing the 'sand-hogs' as we call the tunnel-workers. He has been a sand-hog on every tunnel job about the city since the first successful tunnel was completed. His real name is Flanagan, but we all know him best as Paddy."

Paddy nodded. "If I ever get over this and back to the tunnel," Orton went on, "Paddy will stick to me, and we will show Taylor, my prospective father-in-law and the president of the railroad company from which I took this contract, that I am not to blame for all the troubles we are having on the tunnel. Heaven knows that——"

"Oh, Mr. Orton, you ain't so bad," put in Paddy without the faintest touch of undue familiarity. "Look what I was when ye come to see me when I had the bends, sir."

"You old rascal," returned Orton, brightening up. "Craig, do you know how I found him? Crawling over the floor to the sink to pour the doctor's medicine down."

"Think I'd take that medicine," explained Paddy, hastily. "Not much. Don't I know that the only cure for the bends is bein' put back in the 'air' in the medical lock, same as they did with you, and bein' brought out slowly? That's the cure, that, an' grit, an' patience, an' time. Mark me wurds, gintlemen, he'll finish that tunnel an' beggin' yer pardon, Mr. Orton, marry that gurl, too. Didn't I see her with tears in her eyes right in this room when he wasn't lookin', and a smile when he was? Sure, ye'll be all right," continued Paddy, slapping his side and thigh. "We all get the bends more or less—all us sand-hogs. I was that doubled up meself that I felt like a big jack-knife. Had it in the arm, the side, and the leg all at once, that time be was just speakin' of. He'll be all right in a couple more weeks, sure, an' down in the air again, too, with the rest of his men. It's somethin' else he has on his moind."

"Then the case has nothing to do with your trouble, nothing to do with the bends?" asked Kennedy, keenly showing his anxiety to help our old friend.

"Well, it may and it may not," replied Orton thoughtfully. "I begin to think it has. We have had a great many cases of the bends among the men, and lots of the poor fellows have died, too. You know, of course, how the newspapers are roasting us. We are being called inhuman; they are going to investigate us; perhaps indict me. Oh, it's an awful mess; and now some one is trying to make Taylor believe it is my fault.

"Of course," he continued, "we are working under a high air-pressure just now, some days as high as forty pounds. You see, we have struck the very worst part of the job, a stretch of quicksand in the river-bed, and if we can get through this we'll strike pebbles and rock pretty soon, and then we'll be all right again."

He paused. Paddy quietly put in: "Beggin' yer pardon again, Mr. Orton, but we had intirely too many cases of the bends even when we were wurkin' at low pressure, in the rock, before we sthruck this sand. There's somethin' wrong, sir, or ye wouldn't be here yerself like this. The bends don't sthrike the ingineers, them as don't do the hard work, sir, and is careful, as ye know—not often."

"It's this way, Craig," resumed Orton. "When I took this contract for the Five-Borough Transit Company, they agreed to pay me liberally for it, with a big bonus if I finished ahead of time, and a big penalty if I exceeded the time. You may or may not know it, but there is some doubt about the validity of their franchise after a certain date, provided the tunnel is not ready for operation. Well, to make a long story short, you know there are rival companies that would like to see the work fail and the franchise revert to the city, or at least get tied up in the courts. I took it with the understanding that it was every man for himself and the devil take the hindmost."

"Have you yourself seen any evidences of rival influences hindering the work?" asked Kennedy.

Orton carefully weighed his reply. "To begin with," he answered at length, "while I was pushing the construction end, the Five-Borough was working with the state legislature to get a bill extending the time-limit of the franchise another year. Of course, if it had gone through it would have been fine for us. But some unseen influence blocked the company at every turn. It was subtle; it never came into the open. They played on public opinion as only demagogues of high finance can, very plausibly of course, but from the most selfish and ulterior motives. The bill was defeated."

I nodded. I knew all about that part of it, for it was in the article which I had been writing for the *Star*.

"But I had not counted on the extra year, anyhow," continued Orton, "so I wasn't disappointed. My plans were laid for the shorter time from the start. I built an island in the river so that we could work from each shore to it, as well as from the island to each shore, really from four points at once. And then, when everything was going ahead fine, and we were actually doubling the speed in this way, these confounded accidents"—he was leaning excitedly forward—"and lawsuits and delays and deaths began to happen."

Orton sank back as a paroxysm of the bends seized him, following his excitement.

"I should like very much to go down into the tunnel," said Kennedy simply.

"No sooner said than done," replied Orton, almost cheerfully, at seeing Kennedy so interested. "We can arrange that easily. Paddy will be glad to do the honours of the place in my absence."

"Indade I will do that same, sor," responded the faithful Paddy, "an' it's a shmall return for all ye've done for me."

"Very well, then," agreed Kennedy. "To-morrow morning we shall be on hand. Jack, depend on us. We will do our level best to get you out of this scrape."

"I knew you would, Craig," he replied. "I've read of some of your and Walter's exploits. You're a pair of bricks, you are. Good-bye, fellows," and his hands mechanically sought the vase of flowers which reminded him of their giver.

At home we sat for a long time in silence. "By George, Craig," I exclaimed at length, my mind reverting through the whirl of events to the glimpse of pain I had caught on the delicate face of the girl leaving the hospital, "Vivian Taylor is a beauty, though, isn't she?"

"And Capps thinks so, too," he returned, sinking again into his shell of silence. Then he suddenly rose and put on his hat and coat. I could see the old restless fever for work which came into his eyes whenever he had a case which interested him more than usual. I knew there would be no rest for Kennedy until he had finished it. Moreover, I knew it was useless for me to remonstrate with him, so I kept silent.

"Don't wait up for me," he said. "I don't know when I'll be back. I'm going to the laboratory and the university library. Be ready early in the morning to help me delve into this tunnel mystery."

I awoke to find Kennedy dozing in a chair, partly dressed, but just as fresh as I was after my sleep. I think he had been dreaming out his course of action. At any rate, breakfast was a mere incident in his scheme, and we were over at the tunnel works when the night shift were going off.

Kennedy carried with him a moderate-sized box of the contents of which he seemed very careful. Paddy was waiting for us, and after a hasty whispered conversation, Craig stowed the box away behind the switchboard of the telephone central, after attaching it to the various wires. Paddy stood guard while this was going on so that no one would know about it, not even the telephone girl, whom he sent off on an errand.

Our first inspection was of that part of the works which was above ground. Paddy, who conducted us, introduced us first to the engineer in charge of this part of the work, a man named Shelton, who had knocked about the world a great deal, but had acquired a taciturnity that was Sphinxlike. If it had not been for Paddy, I fear we should have seen very little, for Shelton was not only secretive, but his explanations were such that even the editor of a technical journal would have had to blue pencil them considerably. However, we gained a pretty good idea of the tunnel works above ground—at least Kennedy did. He seemed very much interested in how the air was conveyed below ground, the tank for storing compressed air for emergencies, and other features. It quite won Paddy, although Shelton seemed to resent his interest even more than he despised my ignorance.

Next Paddy conducted us to the dressing-rooms. There we put on old clothes and oilskins, and the tunnel doctor examined us and extracted a written statement that we went down at our own risk and released the company from all liability—much to the disgust of Paddy.

"We're ready now, Mr. Capps," called Paddy, opening an office door on the way out.

"Very well, Flanagan," answered Capps, barely nodding to us. We heard him telephone some one, but could not catch the message, and in a minute he joined us. By this time I had formed the opinion, which I have since found to be correct, that tunnel men are not as a rule loquacious.

It was a new kind of thrill to me to go under the "air," as the men called it. With an instinctive last look at the skyline of New York and the waves playing in the glad sunlight, we entered a rude construction elevator and dropped from the surface to the bottom of a deep shaft. It was like going down into a mine. There was the air-lock, studded with bolts, and looking just like a huge boiler, turned horizontally.

The heavy iron door swung shut with a bang as Paddy and Capps, followed by Kennedy and myself, crept into the air-lock. Paddy turned on a valve, and compressed air from the tunnel began to rush in with a hiss as of escaping steam. Pound after pound to the square inch the pressure slowly rose until I felt sure the drums of my ears would burst. Then the hissing noise began to dwindle down to a wheeze, and then it stopped all of a sudden. That meant that the air-pressure in the lock was the same as that in the tunnel. Paddy pushed open the door in the other end of the lock from that by which we had entered.

Along the bottom of the completed tube we followed Paddy and Capps. On we trudged, fanned by the moist breath of the tunnel. Every few feet an incandescent light gleamed in the misty darkness. After perhaps a hundred paces we had to duck down under a semicircular partition covering the upper half of the tube.

"What is that?" I shouted at Paddy, the nasal ring of my own voice startling me.

"Emergency curtain," he shouted back.

Words were economised. Later, I learned that should the tunnel start to flood, the other half of the emergency curtain could be dropped so as to cut off the inrushing water.

Men passed, pushing little cars full of "muck" or sand taken out from before the "shield"—which is the head by which this mechanical mole advances under the river-bed. These men and others who do the shovelling are the "muckers."

Pipes laid along the side of the tunnel conducted compressed air and fresh water, while electric light and telephone wires were strung all about. These and the tools and other things strewn along the tunnel obstructed the narrow passage to such an extent that we had to be careful in picking our way.

At last we reached the shield, and on hands and knees we crawled out into one of its compartments. Here we experienced for the first time the weird realisation that only the "air" stood between us and destruction from the tons and tons of sand and water overhead. At some points in the sand we could feel the air escaping, which appeared at the surface of the river overhead in bubbles, indicating to those passing in the river boats just how far each tunnel heading below had proceeded. When the loss of air became too great, I learned, scows would dump hundreds of tons of clay overhead to make an artificial river bed for the shield to stick its nose safely through, for if the river bed became too thin overhead the "air" would blow a hole in it.

Capps, it seemed to me, was unusually anxious to have the visit over. At any rate, while Kennedy and Paddy were still crawling about the shield, he stood aside, now and then giving the men an order and apparently forgetful of us.

My own curiosity was quickly satisfied, and I sat down on a pile of the segments out of which the successive rings of the tunnel were made. As I sat there waiting for Kennedy, I absently reached into my pocket and pulled out a cigarette and lighted it. It burned amazingly fast, as if it were made of tinder, the reason being the excess of oxygen in the compressed air. I was looking at it in astonishment, when suddenly I felt a blow on my hand. It was Capps.

"You chump!" he shouted as he ground the cigarette under his boot. "Don't you know it is dangerous to smoke in compressed air?"

"Why, no," I replied, smothering my anger at his manner. "No one said anything about it."

"Well, it is dangerous, and Orton's a fool to let greenhorns come in here."

"And to whom may it be dangerous?" I heard a voice inquire over my shoulder. It was Kennedy. "To Mr. Jameson or the rest of us?"

"Well," answered Capps, "I supposed everybody knew it was reckless, and that he would hurt himself more by one smoke in the air than by a hundred up above. That's all."

He turned on Kennedy sullenly, and started to walk back up the tunnel. But I could not help thinking that his manner was anything but solicitude for my own health. I could just barely catch his words over the tunnel telephone some feet away. I thought he said that everything was going along all right and that he was about to start back again. Then he disappeared in the mist of the tube without even nodding a farewell.

Kennedy and I remained standing, not far from the outlet of the pipe by which the compressed air was being supplied in the tunnel from the compressors above, in order to keep the pressure up to the constant level necessary. I saw Kennedy give a hurried glance about, as if to note whether any one were looking at us. No one was. With a quick motion he reached down. In his hand was a stout little glass flask with a tight-fitting metal top. For a second he held it near the outlet of the pipe; then he snapped the top shut and slipped it back into his pocket as quickly as he had produced it.

Slowly we commenced to retrace our steps to the air-lock, our curiosity satisfied by this glimpse of one of the most remarkable developments of modern engineering.

"Where's Paddy?" asked Kennedy, stopping suddenly. "We've forgotten him."

"Back there at the shield, I suppose," said I. "Let's whistle and attract his attention."

I pursed up my lips, but if I had been whistling for a million dollars I couldn't have done it.

Craig laughed. "Walter, you are indeed learning many strange things. You can't whistle in compressed air."

I was too chagrined to answer. First it was Capps; now it was my own friend Kennedy chaffing me for my ignorance. I was glad to see Paddy's huge form looming in the semi-darkness. He had seen that we were gone and hurried after us.

"Won't ye stay down an' see some more, gintlemen?" he asked. "Or have ye had enough of the air? It seems very smelly to me this mornin'—I don't blame ye. I guess them as doesn't have to stay here is satisfied with a few minutes of it."

"No, thanks, I guess we needn't stay down any longer," replied Craig. "I think I have seen all that is necessary—at least for the present. Capps has gone out ahead of us. I think you can take us out now, Paddy. I would much rather have you do it than to go with anybody else."

Coming out, I found, was really more dangerous than going in, for it is while coming out of the "air" that men are liable to get the bends. Roughly, half a minute should be consumed in coming out from each pound of pressure, though for such high pressures as we had been under, considerably more time was required in order to do it safely.

We spent about half an hour in the air-lock, I should judge.

Paddy let the air out of the lock by turning on a valve leading to the outside, normal atmosphere. Thus he let the air out rapidly at first until we had got down to half the pressure of the tunnel. The second half he did slowly, and it was indeed tedious, but it was safe. There was at first a hissing sound when he opened the valve, and it grew colder in the lock, since air absorbs heat from surrounding objects when it expands. We were glad to draw sweaters on over our heads. It also grew as misty as a London fog as the water-vapour in the air was condensed.

At last the hiss of escaping air ceased. The door to the modern dungeon of science grated open. We walked out of the lock to the elevator shaft and were hoisted up to God's air again. We gazed out across the river with its waves dancing in the sunlight. There, out in the middle, was a wreath of bubbles on the water. That marked the end of the tunnel, over the shield. Down beneath those bubbles the sand-hogs were rooting. But what was the mystery that the tunnel held in its dark, dank bosom? Had Kennedy a clue?

"I think we had better wait around a bit," remarked Kennedy, as we sipped our hot coffee in the dressing-room and warmed ourselves from the chill of coming out of the lock. "In case anything should happen to us and we should get the bends, this is the place for us, near the medical lock, as it is called—that big steel cylinder over there, where we found Orton. The best cure for the bends is to go back under the air—recompression they call it. The renewed pressure causes the gas in the blood to contract again, and thus it is eliminated—sometimes. At any rate, it is the best-known cure and considerably reduces the pain in the worst cases. When you have a bad case like Orton's it means that the damage is done; the gas has ruptured some veins. Paddy was right. Only time will cure that."

Nothing happened to us, however, and in a couple of hours we dropped in on Orton at the hospital where he was slowly convalescing.

"What do you think of the case?" he asked anxiously.

"Nothing as yet," replied Craig, "but I have set certain things in motion which will give us a pretty good line on what is taking place in a day or so."

Orton's face fell, but he said nothing. He bit his lip nervously and looked out of the sun-parlour at the roofs of New York around him.

"What has happened since last night to increase your anxiety, Jack?" asked Craig sympathetically.

Orton wheeled his chair about slowly, faced us, and drew a letter from his pocket. Laying it flat on the table he covered the lower part with the envelope.

"Read that," he said.

"Dear Jack," it began. I saw at once that it was from Miss Taylor. "Just a line," she wrote, "to let you know that I am thinking about you always and hoping that you are better than when I saw you this evening. Papa had the chairman of the board of directors of the Five-Borough here late to-night, and they were in the library for over an hour. For your sake, Jack, I played the eaves-dropper, but they talked so low that I could hear nothing, though I know they were talking about you and the tunnel. When they came out, I had no time to escape, so I slipped behind a portière. I heard father say: 'Yes, I guess you are right, Morris. The thing has gone on long enough. If there is one more big accident we shall have to compromise with the Inter-River and carry on the work jointly. We have given Orton his chance, and if they demand that this other fellow shall be put in, I suppose we shall have to concede it.' Mr. Morris seemed pleased that father agreed with him and said so. Oh, Jack, can't you *do* something to show them they are wrong, and do it quickly? I never miss an opportunity of telling papa it is not your fault that all these delays take place."

The rest of the letter was covered by the envelope, and Orton would not have shown it for worlds.

"Orton," said Kennedy, after a few moments' reflection, "I will take a chance for your sake—a long chance, but I think a good one. If you can pull yourself together by this afternoon, be over at your office at four. Be sure to have Shelton and Capps there, and you can tell Mr. Taylor that you have something very important to set before him. Now, I must hurry if I am to fulfil my part of the contract. Good-bye, Jack. Keep a stiff upper lip, old man. I'll have something that will surprise you this afternoon."

Outside, as he hurried uptown, Craig was silent, but I could see his features working nervously, and as we parted he merely said: "Of course, you'll be there, Walter. I'll put the finishing touches on your story of high finance."

Slowly enough the few hours passed before I found myself again in Orton's office. He was there already, despite the orders of his physician, who was disgusted at this excursion from the hospital. Kennedy was there, too, grim and silent. We sat watching the two indicators beside Orton's desk, which showed the air pressure in the two tubes. The needles were vibrating ever so little and tracing a red-ink line on the ruled paper that unwound from the drum. From the moment the tunnels were started, here was preserved a faithful record of every slightest variation of air pressure.

"Telephone down into the tube and have Capps come up," said Craig at length, glancing at Orton's desk clock. "Taylor will be here pretty soon, and I want Capps to be out of the tunnel by the time he comes. Then get Shelton, too."

In response to Orton's summons Capps and Shelton came into the office, just as a large town car pulled up outside the tunnel works. A tall, distinguished-looking man stepped out and turned again toward the door of the car.

"There's Taylor," I remarked, for I had seen him often at investigations before the Public Service Commission.

"And Vivian, too," exclaimed Orton excitedly. "Say, fellows, clear off these desks. Quick, before she gets up here. In the closet with these blue-prints, Walter. There, that's a little better. If I had known she was coming I would at least have had the place swept out. Puff! look at the dust on this desk of mine. Well, there's no help for it. There they are at the door now. Why, Vivian, what a surprise."

"Jack!" she exclaimed, almost ignoring the rest of us and quickly crossing to his chair to lay a restraining hand on his shoulder as he vainly tried to stand up to welcome her.

"Why didn't you tell me you were coming?" he asked eagerly. "I would have had the place fixed up a bit."

"I prefer it this way," she said, looking curiously around at the samples of tunnel paraphernalia and the charts and diagrams on the walls.

"Yes, Orton," said President Taylor, "she would come—dropped in at the office and when I tried to excuse myself for a business appointment, demanded which way I was going. When I said I was coming here, she insisted on coming, too."

Orton smiled. He knew that she had taken this simple and direct means of being there, but he said nothing, and merely introduced us to the president and Miss Taylor.

An awkward silence followed. Orton cleared his throat. "I think you all know why we are here," he began. "We have been and are having altogether too many accidents in the tunnel, too many cases of the bends, too many deaths, too many delays to the work. Well—er—I—er—Mr. Kennedy has something to say about them, I believe."

No sound was heard save the vibration of the air-compressors and an occasional shout of a workman at the shaft leading down to the air-locks.

"There is no need for me to say anything about caisson disease to you, gentlemen, or to you, Miss Taylor," began Kennedy. "I think you all know how it is caused and a good deal about it already. But, to be perfectly clear, I will say that there are five things that must, above all others, be looked after in tunnel work: the air pressure, the amount of carbon dioxide in the air, the length of the shifts which the men work, the state of health of the men as near as physical examination can determine it, and the rapidity with which the men come out of the 'air,' so as to prevent carelessness which may cause the bends.

"I find," he continued, "that the air pressure is not too high for safety. Proper examinations for carbon dioxide are made, and the amount in the air is not excessive. The shifts are not even as long as those prescribed by the law. The medical inspection is quite adequate and as for the time taken in coming out through the locks the rules are stringent."

A look of relief crossed the face of Orton at this commendation of his work, followed by a puzzled expression that plainly indicated that he would like to know what was the matter, if all the crucial things were all right.

"But," resumed Kennedy, "the bends are still hitting the men, and there is no telling when a fire or a blow-out may occur in any of the eight headings that are now being pushed under the river. Quite often the work has been delayed and the tunnel partly or wholly flooded. Now, you know the theory of the bends. It is that air—mostly the nitrogen in the air—is absorbed by the blood under the pressure. In coming out of the 'air' if the nitrogen is not all eliminated, it stays in the blood and, as the pressure is reduced, it expands. It is just as if you take a bottle of charged water and pull the cork suddenly. The gas rises in big bubbles. Cork it again and the gas bubbles cease to rise and finally disappear. If you make a pin-hole in the cork the gas will escape slowly, without a bubble. You must decompress the human body slowly, by stages, to let the super-saturated blood give up its nitrogen to the lungs, which can eliminate it. Otherwise these bubbles catch in the veins, and the result is severe pains, paralysis, and even death. Gentlemen, I see that I am just wasting time telling you this, for you know it all well. But consider."

Kennedy placed an empty corked flask on the table. The others regarded it curiously, but I recalled having seen it in the tunnel.

"In this bottle," explained Kennedy, "I collected some of the air from the tunnel when I was down there this morning. I have since analysed it. The quantity of carbon dioxide is approximately what it should be—not high enough of itself to cause trouble. But," he spoke slowly to emphasise his words, "I found something else in that air beside carbon dioxide."

"Nitrogen?" broke in Orton quickly, leaning forward.

"Of course; it is a constituent of air. But that is not what I mean."

"Then, for Heaven's sake, what did you find?" asked Orton.

"I found in this air," replied Kennedy, "a very peculiar mixture—an explosive mixture."

"An explosive mixture?" echoed Orton.

"Yes, Jack, the blow-outs that you have had at the end of the tunnel were not blow-outs at all, properly speaking. They were explosions."

We sat aghast at this revelation.

"And, furthermore," added Kennedy, "I should, if I were you, call back all the men from the tunnel until the cause for the presence of this explosive mixture is discovered and remedied."

Orton reached mechanically for the telephone to give the order, but Taylor laid his hand on his arm. "One moment, Orton," he said. "Let's hear Professor Kennedy out. He may be mistaken, and there is no use frightening the men, until we are certain."

"Shelton," asked Kennedy, "what sort of flash oil is used to lubricate the machinery?"

"It is three-hundred-and-sixty-degree Fahrenheit flash test," he answered tersely.

"And are the pipes leading air down into the tunnel perfectly straight?"

"Straight?"

"Yes, straight—no joints, no pockets where oil, moisture, and gases can collect."

"Straight as lines, Kennedy," he said with a sort of contemptuous defiance.

They were facing each other coldly, sizing each other up. Like a skilful lawyer, Kennedy dropped that point for a moment, to take up a new line of attack.

"Capps," he demanded, turning suddenly, "why do you always call up on the telephone and let some one know when you are going down in the tunnel and when you are coming out?"

"I don't," replied Capps, quickly recovering his composure.

"Walter," said Craig to me quietly, "go out in the outer office. Behind the telephone switchboard you will find a small box which you saw me carry in there this morning and connect with the switchboard. Detach the wires, as you saw me attach them, and bring it here."

No one moved, as I placed the box on a drafting-table before them. Craig opened it. Inside he disclosed a large disc of thin steel, like those used by some mechanical music-boxes, only without any perforations. He connected the wires from the box to a sort of megaphone. Then he started the disc revolving.

Out of the little megaphone horn, sticking up like a miniature talking-machine, came a voice: "Number please. Four four three o, Yorkville. Busy, I'll call you. Try them again, Central. Hello, hello, Central——"

Kennedy stopped the machine. "It must be further along on the disc," he remarked. "This, by the way, is an instrument known as the telegraphone, invented by a Dane named Poulsen. It records conversations over a telephone on this plain metal disc by means of localised, minute electric charges."

Having adjusted the needle to another place on the disc he tried again. "We have here a record of the entire day's conversations over the telephone, preserved on this disc. I could wipe out the whole thing by pulling a magnet across it, but, needless to say, I wouldn't do that—yet. Listen."

This time it was Capps speaking. "Give me Mr. Shelton. Oh, Shelton, I'm going down in the south tube with those men Orton has sent nosing around here. I'll let you know when I start up again. Meanwhile—you know—don't let anything happen while I am there. Good-bye."

Capps sat looking defiantly at Kennedy, as he stopped the telegraphone.

"Now," continued Kennedy suavely, "what *could* happen? I'll answer my own question by telling what actually did happen. Oil that was smoky at a lower point than its flash was being used in the machinery—not really three-hundred-and-sixty-degree oil. The water-jacket had been tampered with, too. More than that, there is a joint in the pipe leading down into the tunnel, where explosive gases can collect. It is a well-known fact in the use of compressed air that such a condition is the best possible way to secure an explosion.

"It would all seem so natural, even if discovered," explained Kennedy rapidly. "The smoking oil—smoking just as an automobile often does—is passed into the compressed-air pipe. Condensed oil, moisture, and gases collect in the joint, and perhaps they line the whole distance of the pipe. A spark from the low-grade oil—and they are ignited. What takes place is the same thing that occurs in the cylinder of an automobile where the air is compressed with gasoline vapour. Only here we have compressed air charged with vapour of oil. The flame proceeds down the pipe—exploding through the pipe, if it happens to be not strong enough. This pipe, however, is strong. Therefore, the flame in this case shoots out at the open end of the pipe, down near the shield, and if the air in the tunnel happens also to be surcharged with oil-vapour, an explosion takes place in the tunnel—the river bottom is blown out—then God help the sand-hogs!

"That's how your accidents took place, Orton," concluded Kennedy in triumph, "and that impure air—not impure from carbon dioxide, but from this oil-vapour mixture—increased the liability of the men for the bends. Capps knew about it. He was careful while he was there to see that the air was made as pure as possible under the circumstances. He was so careful that he wouldn't even let Mr. Jameson smoke in the tunnel. But as soon as he went to the surface, the same deadly mixture was pumped down again—I caught some of it in this flask, and——"

"My God, Paddy's down there now," cried

Orton, suddenly seizing his telephone. "Operator, give me the south tube—quick—what—they don't answer?"

Out in the river above the end of the heading, where a short time before there had been only a few bubbles on the surface of the water, I could see what looked like a huge geyser of water spouting up. I pulled Craig over to me and pointed.

"A blow-out," cried Kennedy, as he rushed to the door, only to be met by a group of blanched-faced workers who had come breathless to the office to deliver the news.

Craig acted quickly. "Hold these men," he ordered, pointing to Capps and Shelton, "until we come back. Orton, while we are gone, go over the entire day's record on the telegraphone. I suspect you and Miss Taylor will find something there that will interest you."

He sprang down the ladder to the tunnel air-lock, not waiting for the elevator. In front of the closed door of the lock, an excited group of men was gathered. One of them was peering through the dim, thick, glass porthole in the door.

"There he is, standin' by the door with a club, an' the men's crowdin' so fast that they're all wedged so's none can get in at all. He's beatin' 'em back with the stick. Now, he's got the door clear and has dragged one poor fellow in. It's Jimmy Rourke, him with the eight childer. Now he's dragged in a Polack. Now he's fightin' back a big Jamaica nigger who's tryin' to shove ahead of a little Italian."

"It's Paddy," cried Craig. "If he can bring them all out safely without the loss of a life he'll save the day yet for Orton. And he'll do it, too, Walter."

Instantly I reconstructed in my mind the scene in the tunnel—the explosion of the oil-vapour, the mad race up the tube, perhaps the failure of the emergency curtain to work, the frantic efforts of the men, in panic, all to crowd through the narrow little door at once; the rapidly rising water—and above all the heroic Paddy, cool to the last, standing at the door and single-handed beating the men back with a club, so that they could go through one at a time.

Only when the water had reached the level of the door of the lock, did Paddy bang it shut as he dragged the last man in. Then followed an interminable wait for the air in the lock to be exhausted. When, at last, the door at our end of the lock swung open, the men with a cheer seized Paddy and, in spite of his struggles, hoisted him on to their shoulders, and carried him off, still struggling, in triumph up the construction elevator to the open air above.

The scene in Orton's office was dramatic as the men entered with Paddy. Vivian Taylor was standing defiantly, with burning eyes, facing Capps, who stared sullenly at the floor before him. Shelton was plainly abashed.

"Kennedy," cried Orton, vainly trying to rise, "listen. Have you still that place on the telegraphone record, Vivian?"

Miss Taylor started the telegraphone, while we all crowded around leaning forward eagerly.

"Hello. Inter-River? Is this the president's office? Oh, hello. This is Capps talking. How are you? Oh, you've heard about Orton, have you? Not so bad, eh? Well, I'm arranging with my man Shelton here for the final act this afternoon. After that you can compromise with the Five-Borough on your own terms. I think I have argued Taylor and Morris into the right frame of mind for it, if we have one more big accident. What's that? How is my love affair? Well, Orton's in the way yet, but you know why I went into this deal. When you put me into his place after the compromise, I think I will pull strong with her. Saw her last night. She feels pretty bad about Orton, but she'll get over it. Besides, the pater will never let her marry a man who's down and out. By the way, you've got to do something handsome for Shelton. All right. I'll see you to-night and tell you some more. Watch the papers in the meantime for the grand finale. Good-bye."

An angry growl rose from one or two of the more quick-witted men. Kennedy reached over and pulled me with him quickly through the crowd.

"Hurry, Walter," he whispered hoarsely, "hustle Shelton and Capps out quick before the rest of the men wake up to what it's all about, or we shall have a lynching instead of an arrest."

As we shoved and pushed them out, I saw the rough and grimy sand-hogs in the rear move quickly aside, and off came their muddy, frayed hats. A dainty figure flitted among them toward Orton. It was Vivian Taylor.

"Papa," she cried, grasping Jack by both hands and turning to Taylor, who followed her closely, "Papa, I told you not to be too hasty with Jack."

VII

THE WHITE SLAVE

KENNEDY and I had just tossed a coin to decide whether it should be a comic opera or a good walk in the mellow spring night air and the opera had won, but we had scarcely begun to argue the vital point as to where to go, when the door buzzer sounded—a sure sign that some box-office had lost four dollars.

It was a much agitated middle-aged couple who entered as Craig threw open the door. Of our two visitors, the woman attracted my attention first, for on her pale face the lines of sorrow were almost visibly deepening. Her nervous manner interested me greatly, though I took pains to conceal the fact that I noticed it. It was quickly accounted for, however, by the card which the man presented, bearing the name "Mr. George Gilbert" and a short scribble from First Deputy O'Connor:

> Mr. and Mrs. Gilbert desire to consult you with regard to the mysterious disappearance of their daughter, Georgette. I am sure I need say nothing further to interest you than that the M. P. Squad is completely baffled.
>
> O'CONNOR.

"H—m," remarked Kennedy; "not strange for the Missing Persons Squad to be baffled—at least, at this case."

"Then you know of our daughter's strange—er—departure?" asked Mr. Gilbert, eagerly scanning Kennedy's face and using a euphemism that would fall less harshly on his wife's ears than the truth.

"Indeed, yes," nodded Craig with marked sympathy: "that is, I have read most of what the papers have said. Let me introduce my friend, Mr. Jameson. You recall we were discussing the Georgette Gilbert case this morning, Walter?"

I did, and perhaps before I proceed further with the story I should quote at least the important parts of the article in the morning *Star* which had occasioned the discussion. The article had been headed, "When Personalities Are Lost," and with the Gilbert case as a text many instances had been cited which had later been solved by the return of the memory of the sufferer. In part the article had said:

Mysterious disappearances, such as that of Georgette Gilbert, have alarmed the public and baffled the police before this, disappearances that in their suddenness, apparent lack of purpose, and inexplicability, have had much in common with the case of Miss Gilbert.

Leaving out of account the class of disappearances such as embezzlers, blackmailers, and other criminals, there is still a large number of recorded cases where the subjects have dropped out of sight without apparent cause or reason and have left behind them untarnished reputations. Of these a small percentage are found to have met with violence; others have been victims of a suicidal mania; and sooner or later a clue has come to light, for the dead are often easier to find than the living. Of the remaining small proportion there are on record a number of carefully authenticated cases where the subjects have been the victims of a sudden and complete loss of memory.

This dislocation of memory is a variety of aphasia known as amnesia, and when the memory is recurrently lost and restored it is an "alternating personality." The psychical researchers and psychologists have reported many cases of alternating personality. Studious efforts are being made to understand and to explain the strange type of mental phenomena exhibited in these cases, but no one has as yet given a final, clear, and comprehensive explanation of them. Such cases are by no means always connected with disappearances, but the variety known as the ambulatory type, where the patient suddenly loses all knowledge of his own identity and of his past and takes himself off, leaving no trace or clue, is the variety which the present case calls to popular attention.

Then followed a list of a dozen or so interesting cases of persons who had vanished completely and had, some several days and some even years later, suddenly "awakened" to their first personality, returned, and taken up the thread of that personality where it had been broken.

To Kennedy's inquiry I was about to reply that I recalled the conversation distinctly, when Mr. Gilbert shot an inquiring glance from beneath his bushy eyebrows, quickly shifting from my face to Kennedy's, and asked, "And what was your conclusion—what do you think of the case? Is it aphasia or amnesia, or whatever the doctors call it, and do you think she is wandering about somewhere unable to recover her real personality?"

"I should like to have all the facts at first hand before venturing an opinion," Craig replied with precisely that shade of hesitancy that might reassure the anxious father and mother, without raising a false hope.

Mr. and Mrs. Gilbert exchanged glances, the purport of which was that she desired him to tell the story.

"It was day before yesterday," began Mr. Gilbert, gently touching his wife's trembling hand that sought his arm as he began rehearsing the tragedy that had cast its shadow across their lives, "Thursday, that Georgette—er—since we have heard of Georgette." His voice faltered a bit, but he proceeded: "As you know, she was last seen walking on Fifth Avenue. The police have traced her since she left home that morning. It is known that she went first to the public library, then that she stopped at a department store on the avenue, where she made a small purchase which she had charged to our family account, and finally that she went to a large book-store. Then—that is the last."

Mrs. Gilbert sighed, and buried her face in a lace handkerchief as her shoulders shook convulsively.

"Yes, I have read that," repeated Kennedy gently, though with manifest eagerness to get down to facts that might prove more illuminating. "I think I need hardly impress upon you the advantage of complete frankness, the fact that anything you may tell me is of a much more confidential nature than if it were told to the police. Er—r, had Miss Gilbert any—love affair, any trouble of such a nature that it might have preyed on her mind?"

Kennedy's tactful manner seemed to reassure both the father and the mother, who exchanged another glance.

"Although we have said no to the reporters," Mrs. Gilbert replied bravely in answer to the nod of approval from her husband, and much as if she herself were making a confession for them both, "I fear that Georgette had had a love affair. No doubt you have heard hints of Dudley Lawton's name in connection with the case? I can't imagine how they could have leaked out, for I should have said that that old affair had long since been forgotten even by the society gossips. The fact is that shortly after Georgette 'came out,' Dudley Lawton, who is quite on the road to becoming one of the rather notorious members of the younger set, began to pay her marked attentions. He is a fascinating, romantic sort of fellow, one that, I imagine, possesses much attraction for a girl who has been brought up as simply as Georgette was, and who has absorbed a surreptitious diet of modern literature such as we now know Georgette did. I suppose you have seen portraits of Georgette in the newspapers and know what a dreamy and artistic nature her face indicates?"

Kennedy nodded. It is, of course, one of the cardinal tenets of journalism that all women are beautiful, but even the coarse screen of the ordinary newspaper half-tone had not been able to conceal the rather exceptional beauty of Miss Georgette Gilbert. If it had, all the shortcomings of the newspaper photographic art would have been quickly glossed over by the almost ardent descriptions by those ladies of the press who come along about the second day after an event of this kind with signed articles analysing the character and motives, the life and gowns of the latest actors in the front-page stories.

"Naturally both my husband and myself opposed his attentions from the first. It was a hard struggle, for Georgette, of course, assumed the much-injured air of some of the heroines of her favourite novels. But I, at least, believed that we had won and that Georgette finally was brought to respect and, I hoped, understand our wishes in the matter. I believe so yet. Mr. Gilbert in a roundabout way came to an understanding with old Mr. Dudley Lawton, who possesses a great influence over his son, and—well, Dudley Lawton seemed to have passed out of Georgette's life. I believed so then, at least, and I see no reason for not believing so yet. I feel that you ought to know this, but really I don't think it is right to say that Georgette had a love affair. I should rather say that she had *had* a love affair, but that it had been forgotten, perhaps a year ago."

Mrs. Gilbert paused again, and it was evident that though she was concealing nothing she was measuring her words carefully in order not to give a false impression.

"What does Dudley Lawton say about the newspapers bringing his name into the case?" asked Kennedy, addressing Mr. Gilbert.

"Nothing," replied he. "He denies that he has

even spoken to her for nearly a year. Apparently he has no interest in the case. And yet I cannot quite believe that Lawton is as uninterested as he seems. I know that he has often spoken about her to members of the Cosmos Club where he lives, and that he reads practically everything that the newspapers print about the case."

"But you have no reason to think that there has ever been any secret communication between them? Miss Georgette left no letters or anything that would indicate that her former infatuation survived?"

"None whatever," repeated Mr. Gilbert emphatically. "We have gone over her personal effects very carefully, and I can't say they furnish a clue. In fact, there were very few letters. She rarely kept a letter. Whether it was merely from habit or for some purpose, I can't say."

"Besides her liking for Dudley Lawton and her rather romantic nature, there are no other things in her life that would cause a desire for freedom?" asked Kennedy, much as a doctor might test the nerves of a patient. "She had no hobbies?"

"Beyond the reading of some books which her mother and I did not altogether approve of, I should say no—no hobbies."

"So far, I suppose, it is true that neither you nor the police have received even a hint as to where she went after leaving the book-store?"

"Not a hint. She dropped out as completely as if the earth had swallowed her."

"Mrs. Gilbert," said Kennedy, as our visitors

rose to go, "you may rest assured that if it is humanly possible to find your daughter I shall leave no stone unturned until I have probed to the bottom of this mystery. I have seldom had a case that hung on more slender threads, yet if I can weave other threads to support it I feel that we shall soon find that the mystery is not so baffling as the Missing Persons Squad has found it so far."

Scarcely had the Gilberts left when Kennedy put on his hat, remarking: "We'll at least get our walk, if not the show. Let's stroll around to the Cosmos Club. Perhaps we may catch Lawton in."

Luckily we chanced to find him there in the reading-room. Lawton was, as Mrs. Gilbert had said, a type that is common enough in New York and is very fascinating to many girls. In fact, he was one of those fellows whose sins are readily forgiven because they are always interesting. Not a few men secretly admire though publicly execrate the Lawton type.

I say we chanced to find him in. That was about all we found. Our interview was most unsatisfactory. For my part, I could not determine whether he was merely anxious to avoid any notoriety in connection with the case or whether he was concealing something that might compromise himself.

"Really, gentlemen," he drawled, puffing languidly on a cigarette and turning slowly toward the window to watch the passing throng under the lights of the avenue, "really I don't see how I can be of any assistance. You see, except for a mere passing acquaintance Miss Gilbert and I had drifted entirely apart—entirely apart—owing to circumstances over which I, at least, had no control."

"I thought perhaps you might have heard from her or about her, through some mutual friend," remarked Kennedy, carefully concealing under his nonchalance what I knew was working in his mind—a belief that, after all, the old attachment had not been so dead as the Gilberts had fancied.

"No, not a breath, either before this sad occurrence or, of course, after. Believe me, if I could add one fact that would simplify the search for Georgette—ah, Miss Gilbert—ah—I would do so in a moment," replied Lawton quickly, as if desirous of getting rid of us as soon as possible. Then perhaps as if regretting the brusqueness with which he had tried to end the interview, he added, "Don't misunderstand me. The moment you have discovered anything that points to her whereabouts, let me know immediately. You can count on me—provided you don't get me into the papers. Goodnight, gentlemen. I wish you the best of success."

"Do you think he could have kept up the acquaintance secretly?" I asked Craig as we walked up the avenue after this baffling interview. "Could he have cast her off when he found that in spite of her parents' protests she was still in his power?"

"It's impossible to say what a man of Dudley Lawton's type could do," mused Kennedy, "for the simple reason that he himself doesn't know until he has to do it. Until we have more facts, anything is both possible and probable."

There was nothing more that could be done that

night, though after our walk we sat up for an hour or two discussing probabilities. It did not take me long to reach the end of my imagination and give up the case, but Kennedy continued to revolve the matter in his mind, looking at it from every angle and calling upon all the vast store of information that he had treasured up in that marvellous brain of his, ready to be called on almost as if his mind were card-indexed.

" Murders, suicides, robberies, and burglaries are, after all, pretty easily explained," he remarked, after a long period of silence on my part, " but the sudden disappearance of people out of the crowded city into nowhere is something that is much harder to explain. And it isn't so difficult to disappear as some people imagine, either. You remember the case of the celebrated Arctic explorer whose picture had been published scores of times in every illustrated paper. He had no trouble in disappearing and then reappearing later, when he got ready.

"Yet experience has taught me that there is always a reason for disappearances. It is our next duty to discover that reason. Still, it won't do to say that disappearances are not mysterious. Disappearances except for money troubles are all mysterious. The first thing in such a case is to discover whether the person has any hobbies or habits or fads. That is what I tried to find out from the Gilberts. I can't tell yet whether I succeeded."

Kennedy took a pencil and hastily jotted down something on a piece of paper which he tossed over to me. It read:

1. Love, family trouble.
2. A romantic disposition.
3. Temporary insanity, self-destruction.
4. Criminal assault.
5. Aphasia.
6. Kidnapping.

"Those are the reasons why people disappear, eliminating criminals and those who have financial difficulties. Dream on that and see if you can work out the answer in your subliminal consciousness. Good-night."

Needless to say, I was no further advanced in the morning than at midnight, but Kennedy seemed to have evolved at least a tentative programme. It started with a visit to the public library, where he carefully went over the ground already gone over by the police. Finding nothing, he concluded that Miss Gilbert had not found what she wanted at the library and had continued the quest, even as he was continuing the quest of herself.

His next step was to visit the department-store. The purchase had been an inconsequential affair of half a dozen handkerchiefs, to be sent home. This certainly did not look like a premeditated disappearance; but Craig was proceeding on the assumption that this purchase indicated nothing except that there had been a sale of handkerchiefs which had caught her eye. Having stopped at the library first and a book-shop afterward, he assumed that she had also visited the book-department of the store. But here again nobody seemed to recall her or that she had asked for anything in particular.

Our last hope was the book-shop. We paused for a moment to look at the display in the window, but only for a moment, for Craig quickly pulled me along inside. In the window was a display of books bearing the sign:

BOOKS ON NEW THOUGHT, OCCULTISM, CLAIRVOYANCE, MESMERISM

Instead of attempting to go over the ground already traversed by the police, who had interrogated the numerous clerks without discovering which one, if any, had waited on Miss Gilbert, Kennedy asked at once to see the record of sales of the morning on which she had disappeared. Running his eye quickly down the record, he picked out a work on clairvoyance and asked to see the young woman who had made the sale. The clerk was, however, unable to recall to whom she had sold the book, though she finally admitted that she thought it might have been a young woman who had some difficulty in making up her mind just which one of the numerous volumes she wanted. She could not say whether the picture Kennedy showed her of Miss Gilbert was that of her customer, nor was she sure that the customer was not escorted by some one. Altogether it was nearly as hazy as our interview with Lawton.

"Still," remarked Kennedy cheerfully, "it may furnish a clue, after all. The clerk at least was not positive that it was *not* Miss Gilbert to whom she sold the book. Since we are down in this neighbourhood, let us drop in and see Mr. Gilbert again. Perhaps something may have happened since last night."

Mr. Gilbert was in the dry-goods business in a loft building in the new dry-goods section on Fourth Avenue. One could almost feel that a tragedy had invaded even his place of business. As we entered, we could see groups of clerks, evidently discussing the case. It was no wonder, I felt, for the head of the firm was almost frantic, and beside the loss of his only daughter the loss of his business would count as nothing, at least until the keen edge of his grief was worn off.

"Mr. Gilbert is out," replied his secretary, in answer to our inquiry. "Haven't you heard? They have just discovered the body of his daughter in a lonely spot in the Croton Aqueduct. The report came in from the police just a few minutes ago. It is thought that she was murdered in the city and carried there in an automobile."

The news came with a stinging shock. I felt that, after all, we were too late. In another hour the extras would be out, and the news would be spread broadcast. The affair would be in the hands of the amateur detectives, and there was no telling how many promising clues might be lost.

"Dead!" exclaimed Kennedy, as he jammed his hat on his head and bolted for the door. "Hurry, Walter. We must get there before the coroner makes his examination."

I don't know how we managed to do it, but by dint of subway, elevated, and taxicab we arrived on the scene of the tragedy not very long after the coroner. Mr. Gilbert was there, silent, and looking as if he had aged many years since the night before; his hand shook and he could merely nod recognition to us.

Already the body had been carried to a rough shanty in the neighbourhood, and the coroner was questioning those who had made the discovery, a party of Italian labourers on the water improvement near by. They were a vicious looking crew, but they could tell nothing beyond the fact that one of them had discovered the body in a thicket where it could not possibly have lain longer than overnight. There was no reason, as yet, to suspect any of them, and indeed, as a much travelled automobile road ran within a few feet of the thicket, there was every reason to believe that the murder, if murder it was, had been committed elsewhere and that the perpetrator had taken this means of getting rid of his unfortunate victim.

Drawn and contorted were the features of the poor girl, as if she had died in great physical agony or after a terrific struggle. Indeed, marks of violence on her delicate throat and neck showed only too plainly that she had been choked.

As Kennedy bent over the form of the once lovely Georgette, he noted the clenched hands. Then he looked at them more closely. I was standing a little behind him, for though Craig and I had been through many thrilling adventures, the death of a human being, especially of a girl like Miss Gilbert, filled me with horror and revulsion. I could see, however, that he had noted something unusual. He pulled out a little pocket magnifying glass and made an even more minute examination of the hands. At last he rose and faced us, almost as if in triumph. I could not see what he had discovered—at least it did not seem to be anything tangible, like a weapon.

Quickly he opened the pocketbook which she had carried. It seemed to be empty, and he was about to shut it when something white, sticking in one corner, caught his eye. Craig pulled out a clipping from a newspaper, and we crowded about him to look at it. It was a large clipping from the section of one of the metropolitan journals which carries a host of such advertisements as "spirit medium," "psychic palmist," "yogi mediator," "magnetic influences," "crystal gazer," "astrologer," "trance medium," and the like. At once I thought of the sallow, somewhat mystic countenance of Dudley, and the idea flashed, half-formed, in my mind that somehow this clue, together with the purchase of the book on clairvoyance, might prove the final link necessary.

But the first problem in Kennedy's mind was to keep in touch with what the authorities were doing. That kept us busy for several hours, during which Craig was in close consultation with the coroner's physician. The physician was of the opinion that Miss Gilbert had been drugged as well as strangled, and for many hours, down in his laboratory, his chemists were engaged in trying to discover from tests of her blood whether the theory was true.

One after another the ordinary poisons were climinated, until it began to look hopeless.

So far Kennedy had been only an interested spectator, but as the different tests failed, he had become more and more keenly alive. At last it seemed as if he could wait no longer.

"Might I try one or two reactions with that sample?" he asked of the physician who handed him the test tube in silence.

For a moment or two Craig thoughtfully regarded it, while with one hand he fingered the bottles of ether, alcohol, distilled water, and the many reagents standing before him. He picked up one and poured a little liquid into the test tube. Then, removing the precipitate that was formed, he tried to dissolve it in water. Not succeeding, he tried the ether and then the alcohol. Both were successful.

"What is it?" we asked as he held the tube up critically to the light.

"I can't be sure yet," he answered slowly. "I thought at first that it was some alkaloid. I'll have to make further tests before I can be positive just what it is. If I may retain this sample I think that with other clues that I have discovered I may be able to tell you something definite soon."

The coroner's physician willingly assented, and Craig quickly dispatched the tube, carefully sealed, to his laboratory.

"That part of our investigation will keep," he remarked as we left the coroner's office. "To-night I think we had better resume the search which was so unexpectedly interrupted this morning. I suppose you have concluded, Walter, that we can be reasonably sure that the trail leads back through the fortune-tellers and soothsayers of New York,—which one, it would be difficult to say. The obvious thing, therefore, is to consult them all. I think you will enjoy that part of it, with your newspaperman's liking for the bizarre."

The fact was that it did appeal to me, though at the moment I was endeavouring to formulate a theory in which Dudley Lawton and an accomplice would account for the facts.

It was early in the evening as we started out on our tour of the clairvoyants of New York. The first whom Kennedy selected from the advertisements in the clipping described himself as "Hata, the Veiled Prophet, born with a double veil, educated in occult mysteries and Hindu philosophy in Egypt and India." Like all of them his advertisement dwelt much on love and money:

> The great questions of life are quickly solved, failure turned to success, sorrow to joy, the separated are brought together, foes made friends. Truths are laid bare to his mysterious mind. He gives you power to attract and control those whom you may desire, tells you of living or dead, your secret troubles, the cause and remedy. Advice on all affairs of life, love, courtship, marriage, business, speculations, investments. Overcomes rivals, enemies, and all evil influences. Will tell you how to attract, control, and change the thought, intentions, actions, or character of any one you desire.

Hata was a modest adept who professed to be able to explain the whole ten stages of Yoga. He had established himself on a street near Times Square, just off Broadway, and there we found several automobiles and taxicabs standing at the curb, a mute testimony to the wealth of at least some of his clientele.

A solemn-faced coloured man ushered us into a front parlour and asked if we had come to see the professor. Kennedy answered that we had.

"Will you please write your names and addresses on the outside sheet of this pad, then tear it off and keep it?" asked the attendant. "We ask all visitors to do that simply as a guarantee of good faith. Then if you will write under it what you wish to find out from the professor I think it will help you concentrate. But don't write while I am in the room, and don't let me see the writing."

"A pretty cheap trick," exclaimed Craig when the attendant had gone. "That's how he tells the gullible their names before they tell him. I've a good notion to tear off two sheets. The second is chemically prepared, with paraffin, I think. By dusting it over with powdered charcoal you can bring out what was written on the first sheet over it. Oh, well, let's let him get something across, anyway. Here goes, our names and addresses, and underneath I'll write, 'What has become of Georgette Gilbert?'"

Perhaps five minutes later the negro took the pad, the top sheet having been torn off and placed in Kennedy's pocket. He also took a small fee of two dollars. A few minutes later we were ushered into the awful presence of the "Veiled Prophet," a tall, ferret-eyed man in a robe that looked suspiciously like a brocaded dressing-gown much too large for him.

Sure enough, he addressed us solemnly by name and proceeded directly to tell us why we had come.

"Let us look into the crystal of the past, present, and future and read what it has to reveal," he added solemnly, darkening the room, which was already only dimly lighted. Then Hata, the crystal-gazer, solemnly seated himself in a chair. Before him, in his hands, reposing on a bag of satin, lay a huge oval piece of glass. He threw forward his head and riveted his eyes on the milky depths of the crystal. In a moment he began to talk, first ramblingly, then coherently.

"I see a man, a dark man," he began. "He is talking earnestly to a young girl. She is trying to avoid him. Ah—he seizes her by both arms. They struggle. He has his hand at her throat. He is choking her."

I was thinking of the newspaper descriptions of Lawton, which the fakir had undoubtedly read, but Kennedy was leaning forward over the crystal-gazer, not watching the crystal at all, nor with his eyes on the clairvoyant's face.

"Her tongue is protruding from her mouth, her eyes are bulging——"

"Yes, yes," urged Kennedy. "Go on."

"She falls. He strikes her. He flees. He goes to——"

Kennedy laid his hand ever so lightly on the arm of the clairvoyant, then quickly withdrew it.

"I cannot see where he goes. It is dark, dark. You will have to come back to-morrow when the vision is stronger."

The thing stung me by its crudity. Kennedy, however, seemed elated by our experience as we gained the street.

"Craig," I remonstrated, "you don't mean to say you attach any importance to vapourings like that? Why, there wasn't a thing the fellow couldn't have imagined from the newspapers, even the clumsy description of Dudley Lawton."

"We'll see," he replied cheerfully, as we stopped under a light to read the address of the next seer, who happened to be in the same block.

It proved to be the psychic palmist who called himself "the Pandit." He also was "born with a strange and remarkable power—not meant to gratify the idle curious, but to direct, advise, and help men and women"—at the usual low fee. He said in print that he gave instant relief to those who had trouble in love, and also positively guaranteed to tell your name and the object of your visit. He added:

> Love, courtship, marriage. What is more beautiful than the true unblemished love of one person for another? What is sweeter, better, or more to be desired than perfect harmony and happiness? If you want to win the esteem, love, and everlasting affection of another, see the Pandit, the greatest living master of the occult science.

Inasmuch as this seer fell into a passion at the other incompetent soothsayers in the next column (and almost next door) it seemed as if we must surely get something for our money from the Pandit.

Like Hata, the Pandit lived in a large brownstone house. The man who admitted us led us into a parlour where several people were seated about as if waiting for some one. The pad and writing process was repeated with little variation. Since we were the latest comers we had to wait some time before we were ushered into the presence of the Pandit, who was clad in a green silk robe.

The room was large and had very small windows of stained glass. At one end of the room was an altar on which burned several candles which gave out an incense. The atmosphere of the room was heavy with a fragrance that seemed to combine cologne with chloroform.

The Pandit waved a wand, muttering strange sounds as he did so, for in addition to his palmistry, which he seemed not disposed to exhibit that night, he dealt in mysteries beyond human ken. A voice, quite evidently from a phonograph buried in the depths of the altar, answered in an unknown language which sounded much like "Al-ya wa-aa haal-ya waa-ha." Across the dim room flashed a pale blue light with a crackling noise, the visible rays from a Crookes tube, I verily believe. The Pandit, however, said it was the soul of a saint passing through. Then he produced two silken robes, one red, which he placed on Kennedy's shoulders, and one violet, which he threw over me.

From the air proceeded strange sounds of weird

music and words. The Pandit seemed to fall asleep, muttering. Apparently, however, Kennedy and I were bad subjects, for after some minutes of this he gave it up, saying that the spirits had no revelation to make to-night in the matter in which we had called. Inasmuch as we had not written on the pad just what that matter was, I was not surprised. Nor was I surprised when the Pandit laid off his robe and said unctuously, "But if you will call to-morrow and concentrate, I am sure that I can secure a message that will be helpful about your little matter."

Kennedy promised to call, but still he lingered. The Pandit, anxious to get rid of us, moved toward the door. Kennedy sidled over toward the green robe which the Pandit had laid on a chair.

"Might I have some of your writings to look over in the meantime?" asked Craig as if to gain time.

"Yes, but they will cost you three dollars a copy—the price I charge all my students," answered the Pandit with just a trace of a gleam of satisfaction at having at last made an impression.

He turned and entered a cabinet to secure the mystic literature. The moment he had disappeared Kennedy seized the opportunity he had been waiting for. He picked up the green robe and examined the collar and neck very carefully under the least dim of the lights in the room. He seemed to find what he wished, yet he continued to examine the robe until the sound of returning footsteps warned him to lay it down again. He had not been quite quick enough. The Pandit eyed us suspiciously, then he rang a bell. The attendant appeared instantly, noiselessly.

"Show these men into the library," he commanded with just the faintest shade of trepidation. "My servant will give you the book," he said to Craig. "Pay him."

It seemed that we had suddenly been looked upon with disfavour, and I half suspected he thought we were spies of the police, who had recently received numerous complaints of the financial activities of the fortune tellers, who worked in close harmony with certain bucket-shop operators in fleecing the credulous of their money by inspired investment advice. At any rate, the attendant quickly opened a door into the darkness. Treading cautiously I followed Craig. The door closed behind us. I clenched my fists, not knowing what to expect.

"The deuce!" exclaimed Kennedy. "He passed us out into an alley. There is the street not twenty feet away. The Pandit is a clever one, all right."

It was now too late to see any of the other clairvoyants on our list, so that with this unceremonious dismissal we decided to conclude our investigations for the night.

The next morning we wended our way up into the Bronx, where one of the mystics had esconced himself rather out of the beaten track of police protection, or persecution, one could not say which. I was wondering what sort of vagary would come next. It proved to be "Swami, the greatest clairvoyant, psychic palmist, and Yogi mediator of them all.'" He also stood alone in his power, for he asserted:

> Names friends, enemies, rivals, tells whom and when you will marry, advises you upon love, courtship, marriage, business, speculation, transactions of every nature. If you are worried, perplexed, or in trouble come to this wonderful man. He reads your life like an open book; he overcomes evil influences, reunites the separated, causes speedy and happy marriage with the one of your choice, tells how to influence any one you desire, tells whether wife or sweetheart is true or false. Love, friendship, and influence of others obtained and a greater share of happiness in life secured. The key to success is that marvellous, subtle, unseen power that opens to your vision the greatest secrets of life. It gives you power which enables you to control the minds of men and women.

The Swami engaged to explain the "wonderful Karmic law," and by his method one could develop a wonderful magnetic personality by which he could win anything the human heart desired. It was therefore with great anticipation that we sought out the wonderful Swami and, falling into the spirit of his advertisement, posed as "come-ons" and pleaded to obtain this wonderful magnetism and a knowledge of the Karmic law—at a ridiculously low figure, considering its inestimable advantages to one engaged in the pursuit of criminal science. Naturally the Swami was pleased at two such early callers, and his narrow, half-bald head, long slim nose, sharp grey eyes, and sallow, unwholesome complexion showed his pleasure in every line and feature.

Rubbing his hands together as he motioned us

into the next room, the Swami seated us on a circular divan with piles of cushions upon it. There were clusters of flowers in vases about the room, which gave it the odour of the renewed vitality of the year.

A lackey entered with a silver tray of cups of coffee and a silver jar in the centre. Talking slowly and earnestly about the "great Karmic law," the Swami bade us drink the coffee, which was of a vile, muddy, Turkish variety. Then from the jar he took a box of rock crystal containing a sort of greenish compound which he kneaded into a little gum—gum tragacanth, I afterward learned,—and bade us taste. It was not at all unpleasant to the taste, and as nothing happened, except the suave droning of the mystic before us, we ate several of the gum pellets.

I am at a loss to describe adequately just the sensations that I soon experienced. It was as if puffs of hot and cold air were alternately blown on my spine, and I felt a twitching of my neck, legs, and arms. Then came a subtle warmth. The whole thing seemed droll; the noise of the Swami's voice was most harmonious. His and Kennedy's faces seemed transformed. They were human faces, but each had a sort of animal likeness back of it, as Lavater has said. The Swami seemed to me to be the fox, Kennedy the owl. I looked in the glass, and I was the eagle. I laughed outright.

It was sensuous in the extreme. The beautiful paintings on the walls at once became clothed in flesh and blood. A picture of a lady hanging near me caught my eye. The countenance really smiled and laughed and varied from moment to moment. Her figure became rounded and living and seemed to stir in the frame. The face was beautiful but ghastly. I seemed to be borne along on a sea of pleasure by currents of voluptuous happiness.

The Swami was affected by a profound politeness. As he rose and walked about the room, still talking, he salaamed and bowed. When I spoke it sounded like a gun, with an echo long afterward rumbling in my brain. Thoughts came to me like fury, bewildering, sometimes as points of light in the most exquisite fireworks. Objects were clothed in most fantastic garbs. I looked at my two animal companions. I seemed to read their thoughts. I felt strange affinities with them, even with the Swami. Yet it was all by the psychological law of the association of ideas, though I was no longer master but the servant of those ideas.

As for Kennedy, the stuff seemed to affect him much differently than it did myself. Indeed, it seemed to rouse in him something vicious. The more I smiled and the more the Swami salaamed, the more violent I could see Craig getting, whereas I was lost in a maze of dreams that I would not have stopped if I could. Seconds seemed to be years; minutes ages. Things at only a short distance looked much as they do when looked at through the inverted end of a telescope. Yet it all carried with it an agreeable exhilaration which I can only describe as the heightened sense one feels on the first spring day of the year.

At last the continued plying of the drug seemed to be too much for Kennedy. The Swami had made a profound salaam. In an instant Kennedy had seized with both hands the long flowing hair at the back of the Swami's bald forehead, and he tugged until the mystic yelled with pain and the tears stood in his eyes.

With a leap I roused myself from the train of dreams and flung myself between them. At the sound of my voice and the pressure of my grasp, Craig sullenly and slowly relaxed his grip. A vacant look seemed to steal into his face, and seizing his hat, which lay on a near-by stool, he stalked out in silence, and I followed.

Neither of us spoke for a moment after we had reached the street, but out of the corner of my eye I could see that Kennedy's body was convulsed as if with suppressed emotion.

"Do you feel better in the air?" I asked anxiously, yet somewhat vexed and feeling a sort of lassitude and half regret at the reality of life and not of the dreams.

It seemed as if he could restrain himself no longer. He burst out into a hearty laugh. "I was just watching the look of disgust on your face," he said as he opened his hand and showed me three or four of the gum lozenges that he had palmed instead of swallowing. "Ha, ha! I wonder what the Swami thinks of his earnest effort to expound the Karmic law."

It was beyond me. With the Swami's concoction still shooting thoughts like sky rockets through my brain I gave it up and allowed Kennedy to engineer our next excursion into the occult.

One more seer remained to be visited. This one professed to " hold your life mirror " and by his " magnetic monochrome," whatever that might be, he would " impart to you an attractive personality, mastery of being, for creation and control of life conditions."

He described himself as the " Guru," and, among other things, he professed to be a sun-worshipper. At any rate, the room into which we were admitted was decorated with the four-spoked wheel, or wheel and cross, the winged circle, and the winged orb. The Guru himself was a swarthy individual with a purple turban wound around his head. In his inner room were many statuettes, photographs of other Gurus of the faith, and on each of the four walls were mysterious symbols in plaster representing a snake curved in a circle, swallowing his tail, a five-pointed star, and in the centre another winged sphere.

Craig asked the Guru to explain the symbols, to which he replied with a smile: " The snake represents eternity, the star involution and evolution of the soul, while the winged sphere—eh, well, that represents something else. Do you come to learn of the faith? "

At this gentle hint Craig replied that he did, and the utmost amicability was restored by the purchase of the Green Book of the Guru, which seemed to deal with everything under the sun, and particularly the revival of ancient Asiatic fire-worship with many forms and ceremonies, together with posturing and breathing that rivalled the "turkey trot," the "bunny hug," and the "grizzly bear." The book, as we turned over its pages, gave directions for preparing everything from food to love-philtres and the elixir of life. One very interesting chapter was devoted to "electric marriage," which seemed to come to those only who, after searching patiently, at last found perfect mates. Another of the Guru's tenets seemed to be purification by eliminating all false modesty, bathing in the sun, and while bathing engaging in any occupation which kept the mind agreeably occupied. On the first page was the satisfying legend, "There is nothing in the world that a disciple can give to pay the debt to the Guru who has taught him one truth."

As we talked, it seemed quite possible to me that the Guru might exert a very powerful hypnotic influence over his disciples or those who came to seek his advice. Besides this indefinable hypnotic influence, I also noted the more material lock on the door to the inner sanctuary.

"Yes," the Guru was saying to Kennedy, "I can secure you one of the love-pills from India, but it will cost you—er—ten dollars." I think he hesitated, to see how much the traffic would bear, from one to one hundred, and compromised with only one zero after the unit. Kennedy appeared satisfied, and the Guru departed with alacrity to secure the specially imported pellet.

In a corner was a sort of dressing-table on which lay a comb and brush. Kennedy seemed much interested in the table and was examining it when the Guru returned. Just as the door opened he managed to slip the brush into his pocket and appear interested in the mystic symbols on the wall opposite.

"If that doesn't work," remarked the Guru in remarkably good English, "let me know, and you must try one of my charm bottles. But the love-pills are fine. Good-day."

Outside Craig looked at me quizzically. "You wouldn't believe it, Walter, would you?" he said. "Here in this twentieth century in New York, and in fact in every large city of the world—love-philtres, love-pills, and all the rest of it. And it is not among the ignorant that these things are found, either. You remember we saw automobiles waiting before some of the places."

"I suspect that all who visit the fakirs are not so gullible, after all," I replied sententiously.

"Perhaps not. I think I shall have something interesting to say to-night as a result of our visits, at least."

During the remainder of the day Kennedy was closely confined in his laboratory with his microscopes, slides, chemicals, test-tubes, and other apparatus. As for myself, I put in the time speculating which of the fakirs had been in some mysterious way connected with the case and in what manner. Many were the theories which I had formed and the situations I conjured up, and in nearly all I had one central figure, the young man whose escapades had been the talk of even the fast set of a fast society.

That night Kennedy, with the assistance of First Deputy O'Connor, who was not averse to taking any action within the law toward the soothsayers, assembled a curiously cosmopolitan crowd in his laboratory. Besides the Gilberts were Dudley Lawton and his father, Hata, the Pandit, the Swami, and the Guru—the latter four persons in high dudgeon at being deprived of the lucrative profits of a Sunday night.

Kennedy began slowly, leading gradually up to his point: "A new means of bringing criminals to justice has been lately studied by one of the greatest scientific detectives of crime in the world, the man to whom we are indebted for our most complete systems of identification and apprehension." Craig paused and fingered the microscope before him thoughtfully. "Human hair," he resumed, "has recently been the study of that untiring criminal scientist, M. Bertillon. He has drawn up a full, classified, and graduated table of all the known colours of the human hair, a complete palette, so to speak, of samples gathered in every quarter of the globe. Henceforth burglars, who already wear gloves or paint their fingers with a rubber composition for fear of leaving finger-prints, will have to wear close-fitting caps or keep their heads shaved. Thus he has hit upon a new method of identification of those sought by the police. For instance, from time to time the question arises whether hair is human or animal. In such cases the microscope tells the answer truthfully.

"For a long time I have been studying hair,

taking advantage of those excellent researches by M. Bertillon. Human hair is fairly uniform, tapering gradually. Under the microscope it is practically always possible to distinguish human hair from animal. I shall not go into the distinctions, but I may add that it is also possible to determine very quickly the difference between all hair, human or animal, and cotton with its corkscrew-like twists, linen with its jointed structure, and silk, which is long, smooth, and cylindrical."

Again Kennedy paused as if to emphasise this preface. "I have here," he continued, "a sample of hair." He had picked up a microscope slide that was lying on the table. It certainly did not look very thrilling—a mere piece of glass, that was all. But on the glass was what appeared to be merely a faint line. "This slide," he said, holding it up, "has what must prove an unescapable clue to the identity of the man responsible for the disappearance of Miss Gilbert. I shall not tell you yet who he is, for the simple reason that, though I could make a shrewd guess, I do not yet know what the verdict of science is, and in science we do not guess where we can prove.

"You will undoubtedly remember that when Miss Gilbert's body was discovered, it bore no evidence of suicide, but on the contrary the marks of violence. Her fists were clenched, as if she had struggled with all her power against a force that had been too much for her. I examined her hands, expecting to find some evidence of a weapon she had used to defend herself. Instead, I found what was more valuable. Here on this slide are several hairs that I found tightly grasped in her rigid hands."

I could not help recalling Kennedy's remark earlier in the case—that it hung on slender threads. Yet how strong might not those threads prove!

"There was also in her pocketbook a newspaper clipping bearing the advertisements of several clairvoyants," he went on. "Mr. Jameson and myself had already discovered what the police had failed to find, that on the morning of the day on which she disappeared Miss Gilbert had made three distinct efforts, probably, to secure books on clairvoyance. Accordingly, Mr. Jameson and myself have visited several of the fortune-tellers and practitioners of the occult sciences in which we had reason to believe Miss Gilbert was interested. They all, by the way, make a specialty of giving advice in money matters and solving the problems of lovers. I suspect that at times Mr. Jameson has thought that I was demented, but I had to resort to many and various expedients to collect the specimens of hair which I wanted. From the police, who used Mr. Lawton's valet, I received some hair from his head. Here is another specimen from each of the advertisers, Hata, the Swami, the Pandit, and the Guru. There is just one of these specimens which corresponds in every particular of colour, thickness, and texture with the hair found so tightly grasped in Miss Gilbert's hand."

As Craig said this I could feel a sort of gasp of astonishment from our little audience. Still he was not quite ready to make his disclosure.

"Lest I should be prejudiced," he pursued evenly, "by my own rather strong convictions, and in order that I might examine the samples without fear or favour, I had one of my students at the laboratory take the marked hairs, mount them, number them, and put in numbered envelopes the names of the persons who furnished them. But before I open the envelope numbered the same as the slide which contains the hair which corresponds precisely with that hair found in Miss Gilbert's hand—and it is slide No. 2——" said Kennedy, picking out the slide with his finger and moving it on the table with as much coolness as if he were moving a chessman on a board instead of playing in the terrible game of human life, "before I read the name I have still one more damning fact to disclose."

Craig now had us on edge with excitement, a situation which I sometimes thought he enjoyed more keenly than any other in his relentless tracing down of a criminal.

"What was it that caused Miss Gilbert's death?" asked Kennedy. "The coroner's physician did not seem to be thoroughly satisfied with the theory of physical violence alone. Nor did I. Some one, I believe, exerted a peculiar force in order to get her into his power. What was that force? At first I thought it might have been the hackneyed knock-out drops, but tests by the coroner's physician eliminated that. Then I thought it might be one of the alkaloids, such as morphine, cocaine, and others. But it was not any of the usual things that was used to entice her away from her family and friends.

From tests that I have made I have discovered the one fact necessary to complete my case, the drug used to lure her and against which she fought in deadly struggle."

He placed a test tube in a rack before us. "This tube," he continued, "contains one of the most singular and, among us, least known of the five common narcotics of the world—tobacco, opium, coca, betel nut, and hemp. It can be smoked, chewed, used as a drink, or taken as a confection. In the form of a powder it is used by the narghile smoker. As a liquid it can be taken as an oily fluid or in alcohol. Taken in any of these forms, it literally makes the nerves walk, dance, and run. It heightens the feelings and sensibilities to distraction, producing what is really hysteria. If the weather is clear, this drug will make life gorgeous; if it rains, tragic. Slight vexation becomes deadly revenge; courage becomes rashness; fear, abject terror; and gentle affection or even a passing liking is transformed into passionate love. It is the drug derived from the Indian hemp, scientifically named *Cannabis Indica,* better known as hashish, or bhang, or a dozen other names in the East. Its chief characteristic is that it has a profound effect on the passions. Thus, under its influence, natives of the East become greatly exhilarated, then debased, and finally violent, rushing forth on the streets with the cry, 'Amok, amok,'—'Kill, kill'—as we say, 'running amuck.' An overdose of this drug often causes insanity, while in small quantities our doctors use it as a medicine. Any one who has read the brilliant Théophile Gautier's 'Club des Hachichens' or Bayard Taylor's experience at Damascus knows something of the effect of hashish, however.

"In reconstructing the story of Georgette Gilbert, as best I can, I believe that she was lured to the den of one of the numerous cults practised in New York, lured by advertisements offering advice in hidden love affairs. Led on by her love for a man whom she could not and would not put out of her life, and by her affection for her parents, she was frantic. This place offered hope, and to it she went in all innocence, not knowing that it was only the open door to a life such as the most lurid disorderly resorts of the metropolis could scarcely match. There her credulity was preyed upon, and she was tricked into taking this drug, which itself has such marked and perverting effect. But, though she must have been given a great deal of the drug, she did not yield, as many of the sophisticated do. She struggled frantically, futilely. Will and reason were not conquered, though they sat unsteadily on their thrones. The wisp of hair so tightly clasped in her dead hand shows that she fought bitterly to the end."

Kennedy was leaning forward earnestly, glaring at each of us in turn. Lawton was twisting uneasily in his chair, and I could see that his fists were doubled up and that he was holding himself in leash as if waiting for something, eyeing us all keenly. The Swami was seized with a violent fit of trembling, and the other fakirs were staring in amazement.

Quickly I stepped between Dudley Lawton and

Kennedy, but as I did so, he leaped behind me, and before I could turn he was grappling wildly with some one on the floor.

"It's all right, Walter," cried Kennedy, tearing open the envelope on the table. "Lawton has guessed right. The hair was the Swami's. Georgette Gilbert was one victim who fought and rescued herself from a slavery worse than death. And there is one mystic who could not foresee arrest and the death house at Sing Sing in his horoscope."

VIII

THE FORGER

WE were lunching with Stevenson Williams, a friend of Kennedy's, at the Insurance Club, one of the many new downtown luncheon clubs, where the noon hour is so conveniently combined with business.

"There isn't much that you can't insure against nowadays," remarked Williams when the luncheon had progressed far enough to warrant a tentative reference to the obvious fact that he had had a purpose in inviting us to the club. "Take my own company, for example, the Continental Surety. We have lately undertaken to write forgery insurance."

"Forgery insurance?" repeated Kennedy. "Well, I should think you'd be doing a ripping business—putting up the premium rate about every day in this epidemic of forgery that seems to be sweeping over the country."

Williams, who was one of the officers of the company, smiled somewhat wearily, I thought. "We are," he replied drily. "That was precisely what I wanted to see you about."

"What? The premiums or the epidemic?"

"Well—er—both, perhaps. I needn't say much about the epidemic, as you call it. To you I can admit it; to the newspapers, never. Still, I suppose you know that it is variously estimated that the forgers of the country are getting away with from ten to fifteen million dollars a year. It is just one case that I was thinking about—one on which the regular detective agencies we employ seem to have failed utterly so far. It involves pretty nearly one of those fifteen millions."

"What? One case? A million dollars?" gasped Kennedy, gazing fixedly at Williams as if he found it difficult to believe.

"Exactly," replied Williams imperturbably, "though it was not done all at one fell swoop, of course, but gradually, covering a period of some months. You have doubtless heard of the By-Products Company of Chicago?"

Craig nodded.

"Well, it is their case," pursued Williams, losing his quiet manner and now hurrying ahead almost breathlessly. "You know they own a bank out there also, called the By-Products Bank. That's how we come to figure in the case, by having insured their bank against forgery. Of course our liability runs up only to $50,000. But the loss to the company as well as to its bank through this affair will reach the figure I have named. They will have to stand the balance beyond our liability and, well, fifty thousand is not a small sum for us to lose, either. We can't afford to lose it without a fight."

"Of course not. But you must have some suspicions, some clues. You must have taken some action in tracing the thing out, whatever is back of it."

"Surely. For instance, only the other day we had the cashier of the bank, Bolton Brown, arrested, though he is out on bail now. We haven't anything directly against him, but he is suspected of complicity on the inside, and I may say that the thing is so gigantic that there must have been some one on the inside concerned with it. Among other things we have found that Bolton Brown has been leading a rather fast life, quite unknown to his fellow-officials. We know that he has been speculating secretly in the wheat corner that went to pieces, but the most significant thing is that he has been altogether too intimate with an adventuress, Adele DeMott, who has had some success as a woman of high finance in various cities here and in Europe and even in South America. It looks bad for him from the commonsense standpoint, though of course I'm not competent to speak of the legal side of the matter. But, at any rate, we know that the insider must have been some one pretty close to the head of the By-Products Company or the By-Products Bank."

"What was the character of the forgeries?" asked Kennedy.

"They seem to have been of two kinds. As far as we are concerned it is the check forgeries only that interest the Surety Company. For some time, apparently, checks have been coming into the bank for sums all the way from a hundred dollars to five thousand. They have been so well executed that some of them have been certified by the bank, all of them have been accepted when they came back from other banks, and even the officers of the company don't seem to be able to pick any flaws in them except as to the payee and the amounts for which they were drawn. They have the correct safety tint on the paper and are stamped with rubber stamps that are almost precisely like those used by the By-Products Company.

"You know that banking customs often make some kinds of fraud comparatively easy. For instance no bank will pay out a hundred dollars or often even a dollar without identification, but they will certify a check for almost any office boy who comes in with it. The common method of forgers lately has been to take such a certified forged check, deposit it in another bank, then gradually withdraw it in a few days before there is time to discover the forgery. In this case they must have had the additional advantage that the insider in the company or bank could give information and tip the forger off if the forgery happened to be discovered."

"Who is the treasurer of the company?" asked Craig quickly.

"John Carroll—merely a figurehead, I understand. He's in New York now, working with us, as I shall tell you presently. If there is any one else besides Brown in it, it might be Michael Dawson, the nominal assistant but really the active treasurer. There you have another man whom we suspect, and, strangely enough, can't find. Dawson was the assistant treasurer of the company, you understand, not of the bank."

"You can't find him? Why?" asked Kennedy, considerably puzzled.

"No, we can't find him. He was married a few days ago, married a pretty prominent society girl in the city, Miss Sibyl Sanderson. It seems they kept the itinerary of their honeymoon secret, more as a joke on their friends than anything else, they said, for Miss Sanderson was a well-known beauty and the newspapers bothered the couple a good deal with publicity that was distasteful. At least that was his story. No one knows where they are or whether they'll ever turn up again.

"You see, this getting married had something to do with the exposure in the first place. For the major part of the forgeries consists not so much in the checks, which interest my company, but in fraudulently issued stock certificates of the By-Products Company. About a million of the common stock was held as treasury stock—was never issued.

"Some one has issued a large amount of it, all properly signed and sealed. Whoever it was had a little office in Chicago from which the stock was sold quietly by a confederate, probably a woman, for women seem to rope in the suckers best in these get-rich-quick schemes. And, well, if it was Dawson the honeymoon has given him a splendid chance to make his get-away, though it also resulted in the exposure of the forgeries. Carroll had to take up more or less active duty, with the result that a new man unearthed the—but, say, are you really interested in this case?"

Williams was leaning forward, looking anxiously at Kennedy and it would not have taken a clairvoyant to guess what answer he wanted to his abrupt question.

"Indeed I am," replied Craig, "especially as there seems to be a doubt about the guilty person on the inside."

"There is doubt enough, all right," rejoined Williams, "at least I think so, though our detectives in Chicago who have gone over the thing pretty thoroughly have been sure of fixing something on Bolton Brown, the cashier. You see the blank stock certificates were kept in the company's vault in the bank to which, of course, Brown had access. But then, as Carroll argues, Dawson had access to them, too, which is very true—more so for Dawson than for Brown, who was in the bank and not in the company. I'm all at sea. Perhaps if you're interested you'd better see Carroll. He's here in the city and I'm sure I could get you a good fee out of the case if you cared to take it up. Shall I see if I can get him on the wire?"

We had finished luncheon and, as Craig nodded, Williams dived into a telephone booth outside the dining-room and in a few moments emerged, perspiring from the closeness. He announced that Carroll requested that we call on him at an office in Wall Street, a few blocks away, where he made his headquarters when he was in New York. The whole thing was done with such despatch that I could not help feeling that Carroll had been waiting to hear from his friend in the insurance company. The look of relief on Williams's face when Kennedy said he would go immediately showed plainly that the insurance man considered the cost of the luncheon, which had been no slight affair, in the light of a good investment in the interest of his company, which was " in bad " for the largest forgery insurance loss since they had begun to write that sort of business.

As we hurried down to Wall Street, Kennedy took occasion to remark, " Science seems to have safeguarded banks and other institutions pretty well against outside robbery. But protection against employees who can manipulate books and records does not seem to have advanced as rapidly. Sometimes I think it may have lessened. Greater temptations assail the cashier or clerk with greater opportunity for speculation, and the banks, as many authorities will agree, have not made enough use of the machinery available to put a stop to embezzlement. This case is evidently one of the results. The careless fellows at the top, like this man Carroll whom we are going to see, generally put forward as excuse the statement that the science of banking and of business is so complex that a rascal with ingenuity enough to falsify the books is almost impossible of detection. Yet when the cat is out of the bag as in several recent cases the methods used are often of the baldest and most transparent sort, fictitious names, dummies, and all sorts of juggling and kiting of checks. But I hardly think this is going to prove one of those simple cases."

John Carroll was a haggard and unkempt sort of man. He looked to me as if the defalcations had preyed on his mind until they had become a veritable obsession. It was literally true that they were all that he could talk about, all that he was thinking about. He was paying now a heavy penalty for having been a dummy and honorary officer.

"This thing has become a matter of life and death with me," he began eagerly, scarcely waiting for us to introduce ourselves, as he fixed his unnaturally bright eyes on us anxiously. "I've simply got to find the man who has so nearly wrecked the By-Products Bank and Company. Find him or not, I suppose I am a ruined man, myself, but I hope I may still prove myself honest."

He sighed and his eyes wandered vacantly out of the window as if he were seeking rest and could not find it.

"I understand that the cashier, Bolton Brown, has been arrested," prompted Kennedy.

"Yes, Bolton Brown, arrested," he repeated slowly, "and since he has been out on bail he, too, seems to have disappeared. Now let me tell you about what I think of that, Kennedy. I know it looks bad for Brown. Perhaps he's the man. The Surety Company says so, anyway. But we must look at this thing calmly."

He was himself quite excited, as he went on, "You understand, I suppose, just how much Brown must have been reasonably responsible for passing the checks through the bank? He saw personally about as many of them as—as I did, which was none until the exposure came. They were deposited in other banks by people whom we can't identify but who must have opened accounts for the purpose of finally putting through a few bad checks. Then they came back to our bank in the regular channels and were accepted. By various kinds of juggling they were covered up. Why, some of them looked so good that they were even certified by our bank before they were deposited in the other banks. Now, as Brown claims, he never saw checks unless there was something special about them and there seemed at the time to be nothing wrong about these.

"But in the public mind I know there is prejudice against any bank official who speculates or leads a fast life, and of course it is warranted. Still, if Brown should clear himself finally the thing will come back to Dawson and even if he is guilty, it will make me the—er—the ultimate goat. The upshot of it all will be that I shall have to stand the blame, if not the guilt, and the only way I can atone for my laxity in the past is by activity in catching the real offender and perhaps by restoring to the company and the bank whatever can yet be recovered."

"But," asked Kennedy sympathetically, "what makes you think that you will find your man, whoever he proves to be, in New York?"

"I admit that it is only a very slight clue that I have," he replied confidentially. "It is just a hint Dawson dropped once to one of the men with whom he was confidential in the company. This clerk told me that a long time ago Dawson said he had always wanted to go to South America and that perhaps on his honeymoon he might get a chance. This is the way I figured it out. You see, he is clever and some of these South American countries have no extradition treaties with us by which we could reach him, once he got there."

"Perhaps he has already arrived in one of them with his wife. What makes you think he hasn't sailed yet?"

"No, I don't think he has. You see, she wanted to spend a part of the honeymoon at Atlantic City. I learned that indirectly from her folks, who profess to know no better than we do where the couple are. That was an additional reason why I wanted to see if by coming to New York I might not pick up some trace of them, either here or in Atlantic City."

"And have you?"

"Yes, I think I have." He handed us a letter-gram which he had just received from Chicago. It read: "Two more checks have come in to-day from Atlantic City and New York. They seem to be in payment of bills, as they are for odd amounts. One is from the Lorraine at Atlantic City and the other from the Hotel Amsterdam of New York. They were dated the 19th and 20th."

"You see," he resumed as we finished reading, "it is now the 23rd, so that there is a difference of three days. He was here on the 20th. Now the next ship that he could take after the 20th sails from Brooklyn on the 25th. If he's clever he won't board that ship except in a disguise, for he will know that by that time some one must be watching. Now I want you to help me penetrate that disguise. Of course we can't arrest the whole shipload of passengers, but if you, with your scientific knowledge, could pick him out, then we could hold him and have breathing space to find out whether he is guilty alone or has been working with Bolton Brown."

Carroll was now pacing the office with excitement as he unfolded his scheme which meant so much for himself.

"H—m," mused Kennedy. "I suppose Dawson was a man of exemplary habits? They almost always are. No speculating or fast living with him as with Brown?"

Carroll paused in his nervous tread. "That's another thing I've discovered. On the contrary, I think Dawson was a secret drug fiend. I found that out after he left. In his desk at the By-Products office we discovered hypodermic needles and a whole outfit—morphine, I think it was. You know how cunningly a real morphine fiend can cover up his tracks."

Kennedy was now all attention. As the case unrolled it was assuming one new and surprising aspect after another.

"The lettergram would indicate that he had been stopping at the Lorraine in Atlantic City," remarked Kennedy.

"So I would infer, and at the Amsterdam in New York. But you can depend on it that he has not been going under his own name nor, I believe as far as I can find out, even under his own face. I think the fellow has already assumed a disguise, for nowhere can I find any description that even I could recognise."

"Strange," murmured Kennedy. "I'll have to

look into it. And only two days in which to do it, too. You will pardon me if I excuse myself now? There are certain aspects of the case that I hope I shall be able to shed some light on by going at them at once."

"You'll find Dawson clever, clever as he can be," said Carroll, not anxious to have Kennedy go as long as he would listen to the story which was bursting from his overwrought mind. "He was able to cover up the checks by juggling the accounts. But that didn't satisfy him. He was after something big. So he started in to issue the treasury stock, forging the signatures of the president and the treasurer, that is, my signature. Of course that sort of game couldn't last forever. Some one was going to demand dividends on his stock, or transfer it, or ask to have it recorded on the books, or something that would give the whole scheme away. From each person to whom he sold stock I believe he demanded some kind of promise not to sell it within a certain period, and in that way we figure that he gave himself plenty of time to realise several hundred thousand dollars quietly. It may be that some of the forged checks represented fake interest payments. Anyhow, he's at the end of his rope now. We've had an exciting chase. I had followed down several false clues before the real significance of the hint about South America dawned on me. Now I have gone as far as I dare with it without calling in outside assistance. I think now we are up with him at last—with your help."

Kennedy was anxious to go, but he paused long

enough to ask another question. "And the girl?" he broke in. "She must be in the game or her letters to some of her friends would have betrayed their whereabouts. What was she like?"

"Miss Sanderson was very popular in a certain rather flashy set in Chicago. But her folks were bounders. They lived right up to the limit, just as Dawson did, in my opinion. Oh, you can be sure that if a proposition like this were put up to her she'd take a chance to get away with it. She runs no risks. She didn't do it anyhow, and as for her part, after the fact, why, a woman is always pretty safe—more sinned against than sinning, and all that. It's a queer sort of honeymoon, hey?"

"Have you any copies of the forged certificates?" asked Craig.

"Yes, plenty of them. Since the story has been told in print they have been pouring in. Here are several."

He pulled several finely engraved certificates from his pocket and Kennedy scrutinised them minutely.

"I may keep these to study at my leisure?" he asked.

"Certainly," replied Carroll, "and if you want any more I can wire to Chicago for them."

"No, these will be sufficient for the present, thank you," said Craig. "I shall keep in touch with you and let you know the moment anything develops."

Our ride uptown to the laboratory was completed in silence which I did not interrupt, for I could see that Kennedy was thinking out a course of action. The quick pace at which he crossed the campus to the Chemistry Building told me that he had decided on something.

In the laboratory Craig hastily wrote a note, opened a drawer of his desk, and selected one from a bunch of special envelopes which he seemed to be saving for some purpose. He sealed it with some care, and gave it to me to post immediately. It was addressed to Dawson at the Hotel Amsterdam.

On my return I found him deeply engrossed in the examination of the forged shares of stock. Having talked with him more or less in the past about handwriting I did not have to be told that he was using a microscope to discover any erasures and that photography both direct and by transmitted light might show something.

"I can't see anything wrong with these documents," he remarked at length. "They show no erasures or alterations. On their face they look as good as the real article. Even if they are tracings they are remarkably fine work. It certainly is a fact, however, that they superimpose. They might all have been made from the same pair of signatures of the president and treasurer.

"I need hardly to say to you, Walter, that the microscope in its various forms and with its various attachments is of great assistance to the document examiner. Even a low magnification frequently reveals a drawing, hesitating method of production, or patched and reinforced strokes as well as erasures by chemicals or by abrasion. The stereoscopic microscope, which is of value in studying abrasions and alterations since it gives depth, in this case tells me that there has been nothing of that sort practised. My colour comparison microscope, which permits the comparison of the ink on two different documents or two places on one document at the same time, tells me something. This instrument with new and accurately coloured glasses enables me to measure the tints of the ink of these signatures with the greatest accuracy and I can do what was hitherto impossible—determine how long the writing has been on the paper. I should say it was all very recent, approximately within the last two months or six weeks, and I believe that whenever the stock may have been issued it at least was all forged at the same time.

"There isn't time now to go into the thing more deeply, but if it becomes necessary I can go back to it with the aid of the camera lucida and the microscopic enlarger, as well as this specially constructed document camera with lenses certified by the government. If it comes to a show-down I suppose I shall have to prove my point with the micrometer measurements down to the fifty-thousandth part of an inch.

"There is certainly something very curious about these signatures," he concluded. "I don't know what measurements would show, but they are really too good. You know a forged signature may be of two kinds—too bad or too good. These are, I believe, tracings. If they were your signature and mine, Walter, I shouldn't hesitate to pronounce them tracings. But there is always some slight room for doubt in these special cases where a man sits down and is in the habit of writing his signature over and over again on one stock or bond after another. He may get so used to it that he does it automatically and his signatures may come pretty close to superimposing. If I had time, though, I think I could demonstrate that there are altogether too many points of similarity for these to be genuine signatures. But we've got to act quickly in this case or not at all, and I see that if I am to get to Atlantic City to-night I can't waste much more time here. I wish you would keep an eye on the Hotel Amsterdam while I am gone, Walter, and meet me here, to-morrow. I'll wire when I'll be back. Good-bye."

It was well along in the afternoon when Kennedy took a train for the famous seaside resort, leaving me in New York with a roving commission to do nothing. All that I was able to learn at the Hotel Amsterdam was that a man with a Van Dyke beard had stung the office with a bogus check, although he had seemed to come well recommended. The description of the woman with him who seemed to be his wife might have fitted either Mrs. Dawson or Adele DeMott. The only person who had called had been a man who said he represented the By-Products Company and was the treasurer. He had questioned the hotel people rather closely about the whereabouts of the couple who had paid their expenses with the worthless slip of paper. It was not difficult to infer that this man was Carroll who had been hot on the trail, especially as he said that he personally would see the check paid if the hotel people would keep a sharp watch for the return of the man who had swindled them.

Kennedy wired as he promised and returned by an early train the next day.

He seemed bursting with news. "I think I'm on the trail," he cried, throwing his grip into a corner and not waiting for me to ask him what success he had had. "I went directly to the Lorraine and began frankly by telling them that I represented the By-Products Company in New York and was authorised to investigate the bad check which they had received. They couldn't describe Dawson very well—at least their description would have fitted almost any one. One thing I think I did learn and that was that his disguise must include a Van Dyke beard. He would scarcely have had time to grow one of his own and I believe when he was last seen in Chicago he was clean-shaven."

"But," I objected, "men with Van Dyke beards are common enough." Then I related my experience at the Amsterdam.

"The same fellow," ejaculated Kennedy. "The beard seems to have covered a multitude of sins, for while every one could recall that, no one had a word to say about his features. However, Walter, there's just one chance of making his identification sure, and a peculiar coincidence it is, too. It seems that one night this man and a lady who may have been the former Miss Sanderson, though the description of her like most amateur descriptions wasn't very accurate, were dining at the Lorraine. The Lorraine is getting up a new booklet about its accommodations and a photographer had been engaged to take a flashlight of the dining-room for the booklet.

"No sooner had the flash been lighted and the picture taken than a man with a Van Dyke beard—your friend of the Amsterdam, no doubt, Walter,—rushed up to the photographer and offered him fifty dollars for the plate. The photographer thought at first it was some sport who had reasons for not wishing to appear in print in Atlantic City, as many have. The man seemed to notice that the photographer was a little suspicious and he hastened to make some kind of excuse about 'wanting the home folks to see how swell he and his wife were dining in evening dress.' It was a rather lame excuse, but the fifty dollars looked good to the photographer and he agreed to develop the plate and turn it over with some prints all ready for mailing the next day. The man seemed satisfied and the photographer took another flashlight, this time with one of the tables vacant.

"Sure enough, the next day the man with a beard turned up for the plate. The photographer tells me that he had it all wrapped up ready to mail, just to call the fellow's bluff. The man was equal to the occasion, paid the money, wrote an address on the package which the photographer did not see, and as there was a box for mailing packages right at the door on the boardwalk there was no excuse for not mailing it directly. Now if I could get hold of that plate or a print from it I could identify Dawson in his disguise in a moment. I've started the post-office trying to trace that package both at Atlantic City and in Chicago, where I think it must have been mailed. I may hear from them at any moment—at least, I hope."

The rest of the afternoon we spent in canvassing the drug stores in the vicinity of the Amsterdam, Kennedy's idea being that if Dawson was a habitual morphine fiend he must have replenished his supply of the drug in New York, particularly if he was contemplating a long journey where it might be difficult to obtain.

After many disappointments we finally succeeded in finding a shop where a man posing as a doctor had made a rather large purchase. The name he gave was of course of no importance. What did interest us was that again we crossed the trail of a man with a Van Dyke beard. He had been accompanied by a woman whom the druggist described as rather flashily dressed, though her face was hidden under a huge hat and a veil. "Looked very attractive," as the druggist put it, "but she might have been a negress for all I could tell you of her face."

"Humph," grunted Kennedy, as we were leaving the store. "You wouldn't believe it, but it is the hardest thing in the world to get an accurate description of any one. The psychologists have said enough about it, but you don't realise it until you are up against it. Why, that might have been the DeMott woman just as well as the former Miss Sanderson, and the man might have been Bolton Brown as well as Dawson, for all we know. They've both disappeared now. I wish we could get some word about that photograph. That would settle it."

In the last mail that night Kennedy received back the letter which he had addressed to Michael Dawson. On it was stamped "Returned to sender. Owner not found."

Kennedy turned the letter over slowly and looked at the back of it carefully.

"On the contrary," he remarked, half to himself, "the owner was found. Only he returned the letter back to the postman after he had opened it and found that it was just a note of no importance which I scribbled just to see if he was keeping in touch with things from his hiding-place, wherever it is."

"How do you know he opened it?" I asked.

"Do you see those blots on the back? I had several of these envelopes prepared ready for use when I needed them. I had some tannin placed on the flap and then covered thickly with gum. On the envelope itself was some iron sulphate under more gum. I carefully sealed the letter, using very little moisture. The gum then separated the two prepared parts. Now if that letter were steamed open the tannin and the sulphate would come together, run, and leave a smudge. You see the blots? The inference is obvious."

Clearly, then, our chase was getting warmer. Dawson had been in Atlantic City at least within a few days. The fruit company steamer to South America on which Carroll believed he was booked to sail under an assumed name and with an assumed face was to sail the following noon. And still we had no word from Chicago as to the destination of the photograph, or the identity of the man in the Van Dyke beard who had been so particular to disarm suspicion in the purchase of the plate from the photographer a few days before.

The mail also contained a message from Williams of the Surety Company with the interesting information that Bolton Brown's attorney had refused to say where his client had gone since he had been released on bail, but that he would be produced when wanted. Adele DeMott had not been seen for several days in Chicago and the police there were of the opinion that she had gone to New York, where it would be pretty easy for her to pass unnoticed. These facts further complicated the case and made the finding of the photograph even more imperative.

If we were going to do anything it must be done quickly. There was no time to lose. The last of the fast trains for the day had left and the photograph, even though it were found, could not possibly reach us in time to be of use before the steamer sailed from Brooklyn. It was an emergency such as Kennedy had never yet faced, apparently physically insuperable.

But, as usual, Craig was not without some resource, though it looked impossible to me to do anything but make a hit or miss arrest at the boat. It was late in the evening when he returned from a conference with an officer of the Telegraph and Telephone Company to whom Williams had given him a card of introduction. The upshot had been that he had called up Chicago and talked for a long time with Professor Clark, a former classmate of ours who was now in the technology school of the university out there. Kennedy and Clark had been in correspondence for some time, I knew, about some technical matters, though I had no idea what it was they concerned.

"There's one thing we can always do," I remarked as we walked slowly over to the laboratory from our apartment.

"What's that?" he asked absent-mindedly, more from politeness than anything else.

"Arrest every one with a Van Dyke beard who goes on the boat to-morrow," I replied.

Kennedy smiled. "I don't feel prepared to stand a suit for false arrest," he said simply, "especially as the victim would feel pretty hot if we caused him to miss his boat. Men with beards are not so uncommon, after all."

We had reached the laboratory. Linemen were stringing wires under the electric lights of the campus from the street to the Chemistry Building and into Kennedy's sanctum.

That night and far into the morning Kennedy was working in the laboratory on a peculiarly complicated piece of mechanism consisting of electromagnets, rolls, and a stylus and numerous other contrivances which did not suggest to my mind anything he had ever used before in our adventures. I killed time as best I could watching him adjust the thing with the most minute care and precision.

Finally I came to the conclusion that as I was not likely to be of the least assistance, even if I had been initiated into what was afoot, I had as well retire.

"There is one thing you can do for me in the morning, Walter," said Kennedy, continuing to work over a delicate piece of clockwork which formed a part of the apparatus. "In case I do not see you then, get in touch with Williams and Carroll and have them come here about ten o'clock with an automobile. If I am not ready for them then I'm afraid I never shall be, and we shall have to finish the job with the lack of finesse you suggested by arresting all the bearded men."

Kennedy could not have slept much during the night, for though his bed had been slept in he was up and away before I could see him again. I made a hurried trip downtown to catch Carroll and Williams and then returned to the laboratory, where Craig had evidently just finished a satisfactory preliminary test of his machine.

"Still no message," he began in reply to my unspoken question. He was plainly growing restless with the inaction, though frequent talks over long-distance with Chicago seemed to reassure him. Thanks to the influence of Williams he had at least a direct wire from his laboratory to the city which was now the scene of action.

As nearly as I could gather from the one-sided conversations I heard and the remarks which Kennedy dropped, the Chicago post-office inspectors were still searching for a trace of the package from

Atlantic City which was to reveal the identity of the man who had passed the bogus checks and sold the forged certificates of stock. Somewhere in that great city was a photograph of the promoter and of the woman who was aiding him to escape, taken in Atlantic City and sent by mail to Chicago. Who had received it? Would it be found in time to be of use? What would it reveal? It was like hunting for a needle in a haystack, and yet the latest reports seemed to encourage Kennedy with the hope that the authorities were at last on the trail of the secret office from which the stock had been sold. He was fuming and wishing that he could be at both ends of the line at once.

"Any word from Chicago yet?" appealed an anxious voice from the doorway.

We turned. There were Carroll and Williams who had come for us with an automobile to go over to watch at the wharf in Brooklyn for our man. It was Carroll who spoke. The strain of the suspense was telling on him and I could readily imagine that he, like so many others who had never seen Kennedy in action, had not the faith in Craig's ability which I had seen tested so many times.

"Not yet," replied Kennedy, still busy about his apparatus on the table. "I suppose you have heard nothing?"

"Nothing since my note of last night," returned Williams impatiently. "Our detectives still insist that Bolton Brown is the man to watch, and the disappearance of Adele DeMott at this time certainly looks bad for him."

"It does, I admit," said Carroll reluctantly. "What's all this stuff on the table?" he asked, indicating the magnets, rolls, and clockwork.

Kennedy did not have time to reply, for the telephone bell was tinkling insistently.

"I've got Chicago on the wire," Craig informed us, placing his hand over the transmitter as he waited for long-distance to make the final connection. "I'll try to repeat as much of the conversation as I can so that you can follow it. Hello—yes—this is Kennedy. Is that you, Clark? It's all arranged at this end. How's your end of the line? Have you a good connection? Yes? My synchroniser is working fine here, too. All right. Suppose we try it. Go ahead."

As Kennedy gave a few final touches to the peculiar apparatus on the table, the cylindrical drum before us began slowly to revolve and the stylus or needle pressed down on the sensitised paper with which the drum was covered, apparently with varying intensity as it turned. Round and round the cylinder revolved like a graphophone.

"This," exclaimed Kennedy proudly, "is the 'electric eye,' the telelectrograph invented by Thorne Baker in England. Clark and I have been intending to try it out for a long time. It at last makes possible the electric transmission of photographs, using the telephone wires because they are much better for such a purpose than the telegraph wires."

Slowly the needle was tracing out a picture on the paper. It was only a thin band yet, but gradually it was widening, though we could not guess what it was about to reveal as the ceaseless revolutions widened the photographic print.

"I may say," explained Kennedy as we waited breathlessly, "that another system known as the Korn system of telegraphing pictures has also been in use in London, Paris, Berlin, and other cities at various times for some years. Korn's apparatus depends on the ability of the element selenium to vary the strength of an electric current passing through it in proportion to the brightness with which the selenium is illuminated. A new field has been opened by these inventions which are now becoming more and more numerous, since the Korn system did the pioneering.

"The various steps in sending a photograph by the Baker telelectrograph are not so difficult to understand, after all. First an ordinary photograph is taken and a negative made. Then a print is made and a wet plate negative is printed on a sheet of sensitised tinfoil which has been treated with a single-line screen. You know a halftone consists of a photograph through a screen composed of lines running perpendicular to each other—a coarse screen for newspaper work, and a fine screen for better work, such as in magazines. Well, in this case the screen is composed of lines running parallel in one direction only, not crossing at right angles. A halftone is composed of minute points, some light, some dark. This print is composed of long shaded lines, some parts light, others dark, giving the effect of a picture, you understand?"

"Yes, yes," I exclaimed, thoroughly excited. "Go on."

"Well," he resumed as the print widened visibly, "this tinfoil negative is wrapped around a cylinder at the other end of the line and a stylus with a very delicate, sensitive point begins passing over it, crossing the parallel lines at right angles, like the other lines of a regular halftone. Whenever the point of the stylus passes over one of the lighter spots on the photographic print it sends on a longer electrical vibration, over the darker spots a shorter vibration. The ever changing electrical current passes up through the stylus, vibrates with ever varying degrees of intensity over the thousand miles of telephone wire between Chicago and this instrument here at the other end of the line.

"In this receiving apparatus the current causes another stylus to pass over a sheet of sensitised chemical paper such as we have here. The receiving stylus passes over the paper here synchronously with the transmitting stylus in Chicago. The impression which each stroke of the receiving stylus makes on the paper is black or light, according to the length of the very quickly changing vibrations of the electric current. White spots on the photographic print come out as black spots here on the sensitised paper over which this stylus is passing, and vice versa. In that way you can see the positive print growing here before your very eyes as the picture is transmitted from the negative which Clark has prepared and is sending from Chicago."

As we bent over eagerly we could indeed now

see what the thing was doing. It was reproducing faithfully in New York what could be seen by the mortal eye only in Chicago.

"What is it?" asked Williams, still half incredulous in spite of the testimony of his eyes.

"It is a photograph which I think may aid us in deciding whether it is Dawson or Brown who is responsible for the forgeries," answered Kennedy, "and it may help us to penetrate the man's disguise yet, before he escapes to South America or wherever he plans to go."

"You'll have to hurry," interposed Carroll, nervously looking at his watch. "She sails in an hour and a half and it is a long ride over to the pier even with a fast car."

"The print is almost ready," repeated Kennedy calmly. "By the way, it is a photograph which was taken at Atlantic City a few days ago for a booklet which the Lorraine was getting out. The By-Products forger happened to get in it and he bribed the photographer to give him the plate and take another picture for the booklet which would leave him out. The plate was sent to a little office in Chicago, discovered by the post-office inspectors, where the forged stock certificates were sold. I understood from what Clark told me over the telephone before he started to transmit the picture that the woman in it looked very much like Adele DeMott. Let us see."

The machine had ceased to revolve. Craig stripped a still wet photograph off the telelectrograph instrument and stood regarding it with intense satisfaction. Outside, the car which had been engaged to hurry us over to Brooklyn waited.

"Morphine fiends," said Kennedy as he fanned the print to dry it, "are the most unreliable sort of people. They cover their tracks with almost diabolical cunning. In fact they seem to enjoy it. For instance, the crimes committed by morphinists are usually against property and character and based upon selfishness, not brutal crimes such as alcohol and other drugs induce. Kleptomania, forgery, swindling, are among the most common.

"Then, too, one of the most marked phases of morphinism is the pleasure its victims take in concealing their motives and conduct. They have a mania for leading a double life, and enjoy the deception and mask which they draw about themselves. Persons under the influence of the drug have less power to resist physical and mental impressions and they easily succumb to temptations and suggestions from others. Morphine stands unequalled as a perverter of the moral sense. It creates a person whom the father of lies must recognise as kindred to himself. I know of a case where a judge charged a jury that the prisoner, a morphine addict, was mentally irresponsible for that reason. The judge knew what he was talking about. It subsequently developed that he had been a secret morphine fiend himself for years."

"Come, come," broke in Carroll impatiently, "we're wasting time. The ship sails in an hour and unless you want to go down the bay on a tug you've got to catch Dawson now or never. The morphine business explains, but it does not excuse. Come on, the car is watiing. How long do you think it will take us to get over to——"

"Police headquarters?" interrupted Craig. "About fifteen minutes. This photograph shows, as I had hoped, the real forger. John Carroll, this is a peculiar case. You have forged the name of the president of your company, but you have also traced your own name very cleverly to look like a forgery. It is what is technically known as auto-forgery, forging one's own handwriting. At your convenience we'll ride down to Centre Street directly."

Carroll was sputtering and almost frothing at the mouth with rage which he made no effort to suppress. Williams was hesitating, nonplussed, until Kennedy reached over unexpectedly and grasped Carroll by the arm. As he shoved up Carroll's sleeve he disclosed the forearm literally covered with little punctures made by the hypodermic needle.

"It may interest you," remarked Kennedy, still holding Carroll in his vise-like grip, while the drug fiend's shattered nerves caused him to cower and tremble, "to know that a special detective working for me has located Mr. and Mrs. Dawson at Bar Harbor, where they are enjoying a quiet honeymoon. Brown is safely in the custody of his counsel, ready to appear and clear himself as soon as the public opinion which has been falsely inflamed against him subsides. Your plan to give us the slip at the last moment at the wharf and board the steamer for South America has miscarried. It is now too late to catch it, but I shall send a wireless that will cause the arrest of Miss DeMott the moment the ship touches an American port at Colon, even if she succeeds in eluding the British authorities at Kingston. The fact is, I don't much care about her, anyway. Thanks to the telelectrograph here we have the real criminal."

Kennedy slapped down the now dry print that had come in over his "seeing over a wire" machine. Barring the false Van Dyke beard, it was the face of John Carroll, forger and morphine fiend. Next him in the picture in the brilliant and fashionable dining-room of the Lorraine was sitting Adele DeMott who had used her victim, Bolton Brown, to shield her employer, Carroll.

IX

THE UNOFFICIAL SPY

"CRAIG, do you see that fellow over by the desk, talking to the night clerk?" I asked Kennedy as we lounged into the lobby of the new Hotel Vanderveer one evening after reclaiming our hats from the plutocrat who had acquired the checking privilege. We had dined on the roof garden of the Vanderveer apropos of nothing at all except our desire to become acquainted with a new hotel.

"Yes," replied Kennedy, "what of him?"

"He's the house detective, McBride. Would you like to meet him? He's full of good stories, an interesting chap. I met him at a dinner given to the President not long ago and he told me a great yarn about how the secret service, the police, and the hotel combined to guard the President during the dinner. You know, a big hotel is the stamping ground for all sorts of cranks and crooks."

The house detective had turned and had caught my eye. Much to my surprise, he advanced to meet me.

"Say,—er—er—Jameson," he began, at last recalling my name, though he had seen me only once and then for only a short time. "You're on the *Star*, I believe?"

"Yes," I replied, wondering what he could want.

"Well—er—do you suppose you could do the

house a little—er—favour?" he asked, hesitating and dropping his voice.

"What is it?" I queried, not feeling certain but that it was a veiled attempt to secure a little free advertising for the Vanderveer. "By the way, let me introduce you to my friend Kennedy, McBride."

"Craig Kennedy?" he whispered aside, turning quickly to me. I nodded.

"Mr. Kennedy," exclaimed the house man deferentially, "are you very busy just now?"

"Not especially so," replied Craig. "My friend Jameson was telling me that you knew some interesting yarns about hotel detective life. I should like to hear you tell some of them, if you are not yourself too——"

"Perhaps you'd rather see one instead?" interrupted the house detective, eagerly scanning Craig's face.

"Indeed, nothing could please me more. What is it—a 'con' man or a hotel 'beat'?"

McBride looked about to make sure that no one was listening. "Neither," he whispered. "It's either a suicide or a murder. Come upstairs with me. There isn't a man in the world I would rather have met at this very instant, Mr. Kennedy, than yourself."

We followed McBride into an elevator which he stopped at the fifteenth floor. With a nod to the young woman who was the floor clerk, the house detective led the way down the thickly carpeted hall, stopping at a room which, we could see through the transom, was lighted. He drew a bunch of keys from his pocket and inserted a pass key into the lock.

The door swung open into a sumptuously fitted sitting-room. I looked in, half fearfully, but, although all the lights were turned on, the room was empty. McBride crossed the room quickly, opened a door to a bedroom, and jerked his head back with a quick motion, signifying his desire for us to follow.

Stretched lifeless on the white linen of the immaculate bed lay the form of a woman, a beautiful woman she had been, too, though not with the freshness which makes American women so attractive. There was something artificial about her beauty, the artificiality which hinted at a hidden story of a woman with a past.

She was a foreigner, apparently of one of the Latin races, although at the moment in the horror of the tragedy before us I could not guess her nationality. It was enough for me that here lay this cold, stony, rigid beauty, robed in the latest creations of Paris, alone in an elegantly furnished room of an exclusive hotel where hundreds of gay guests were dining and chatting and laughing without a suspicion of the terrible secret only a few feet distant from them.

We stood awestruck for the moment.

"The coroner ought to be here any moment," remarked McBride and even the callousness of the regular detective was not sufficient to hide the real feelings of the man. His practical sense soon returned, however, and he continued, "Now, Jameson, don't you think you could use a little influence with the newspaper men to keep this thing off the front pages? Of course something has to be printed about it. But we don't want to hoodoo the hotel right at the start. We had a suicide the other day who left an apologetic note that was played up by some of the papers. Now comes this affair. The management are just as anxious to have the crime cleared up as any one—if it is a crime. But can't it be done with the soft pedal? We will stop at nothing in the way of expense—just so long as the name of the Vanderveer is kept in the background. Only, I'm afraid the coroner will try to rub it in and make the thing sensational."

"What was her name?" asked Kennedy. "At least, under what name was she registered?"

"She was registered as Madame de Nevers. It is not quite a week now since she came here, came directly from the steamer *Tripolitania*. See, there are her trunks and things, all pasted over with foreign labels, not an American label among them. I haven't the slightest doubt that her name was fictitious, for as far as I can see all the ordinary marks of identification have been obliterated. It will take time to identify her at the best, and in the meantime, if a crime has been committed, the guilty person may escape. What I want now, right away, is action."

"Has nothing in her actions about the hotel offered any clue, no matter how slight?" asked Kennedy.

"Plenty of things," replied McBride quickly.

"For one thing, she didn't speak very much English and her maid seemed to do all the talking for her, even to ordering her meals, which were always served here. I did notice Madame a few times about the hotel, though she spent most of her time in her rooms. She was attractive as the deuce, and the men all looked at her whenever she stirred out. She never even noticed them. But she was evidently expecting some one, for her maid had left word at the desk that if a Mr. Gonzales called, she was at home; if any one else, she was out. For the first day or two she kept herself closely confined, except that at the end of the second day she took a short spin through the park in a taxicab—closed, even in this hot weather. Where she went I cannot say, but when they returned the maid seemed rather agitated. At least she was a few minutes later when she came all the way downstairs to telephone from a booth, instead of using the room telephone. At various times the maid was sent out to execute certain errands, but always returned promptly. Madame de Nevers was a genuine woman of mystery, but as long as she was a quiet mystery, I thought it no business of ours to pry into the affairs of Madame."

"Did she have any visitors? Did this Mr. Gonzales call?" asked Kennedy at length.

"She had one visitor, a woman who called and asked if a Madame de Nevers was stopping at the hotel," answered McBride. "That was what the clerk was telling me when I happened to catch sight of you. He says that, obedient to the orders from the maid, he told the visitor that Madame was not at home."

"Who was this visitor, do you suppose?" asked Craig. "Did she leave any card or message? Is there any clue to her?"

The detective looked at him earnestly for a time as if he hesitated to retail what might be merely pure gossip.

"The clerk does not know this absolutely, but from his acquaintance with society news and the illustrated papers he is sure that he recognised her. He says that he feels positive that it was Miss Catharine Lovelace."

"The Southern heiress," exclaimed Kennedy. "Why, the papers say that she is engaged——"

"Exactly," cut in McBride, "the heiress who is rumoured to be engaged to the Duc de Chateaurouge."

Kennedy and I exchanged glances. "Yes," I added, recollecting a remark I had heard a few days before from our society reporter on the *Star*, "I believe it has been said that Chateaurouge is in this country, incognito."

"A pretty slender thread on which to hang an identification," McBride hastened to remark. "Newspaper photographs are not the best means of recognising anybody. Whatever there may be in it, the fact remains that Madame de Nevers, supposing that to be her real name, has been dead for at least a day or two. The first thing to be determined is whether this is a death from natural causes, a suicide, or a murder. After we have determined that we shall be in a position to run down this Lovelace clue."

Kennedy said nothing and I could not gather whether he placed greater or less value on the suspicion of the hotel clerk. He had been making a casual examination of the body on the bed, and finding nothing he looked intently about the room as if seeking some evidence of how the crime had been committed.

To me the thing seemed incomprehensible, that without an outcry being overheard by any of the guests a murder could have been done in a crowded hotel in which the rooms on every side had been occupied and people had been passing through the halls at all hours. Had it indeed been a suicide, in spite of McBride's evident conviction to the contrary?

A low exclamation from Kennedy attracted our attention. Caught in the filmy lace folds of the woman's dress he had found a few small and thin pieces of glass. He was regarding them with an interest that was oblivious to everything else. As he turned them over and over and tried to fit them together they seemed to form at least a part of what had once been a hollow globe of very thin glass, perhaps a quarter of an inch or so in diameter.

"How was the body discovered?" asked Craig at length, looking up at McBride quickly.

"Day before yesterday Madame's maid went to the cashier," repeated the detective slowly as if rehearsing the case as much for his own information as ours, "and said that Madame had asked her to say to him that she was going away for a few days and that under no circumstances was her room to be disturbed in her absence. The maid was commissioned to pay the bill, not only for the time they had been here, but also for the remainder of the week, when Madame would most likely return, if not earlier. The bill was made out and paid.

"Since then only the chambermaid has entered this suite. The key to that closet over in the corner was gone, and it might have hidden its secret until the end of the week or perhaps a day or two longer, if the chambermaid hadn't been a bit curious. She hunted till she found another key that fitted, and opened the closet door, apparently to see what Madame had been so particular to lock up in her absence. There lay the body of Madame, fully dressed, wedged into the narrow space and huddled up in a corner. The chambermaid screamed and the secret was out."

"And Madame de Nevers's maid? What has become of her?" asked Kennedy eagerly.

"She has disappeared," replied McBride. "From the moment when the bill was paid no one about the hotel has seen her."

"But you have a pretty good description of her, one that you could send out in order to find her if necessary?"

"Yes, I think I could give a pretty good description."

Kennedy's eye encountered the curious gaze of McBride. "This may prove to be a most unusual case," he remarked in answer to the implied inquiry of the detective. "I suppose you have heard of the 'endormeurs' of Paris?"

McBride shook his head in the negative.

"It is a French word signifying a person who puts another to sleep, the sleep makers," explained Kennedy. "They are the latest scientific school of criminals who use the most potent, quickest-acting stupefying drugs. Some of their exploits surpass anything hitherto even imagined by the European police. The American police have been officially warned of the existence of the endormeurs and full descriptions of their methods and photographs of their paraphernalia have been sent over here.

"There is nothing in their repertoire so crude as chloral or knock-out drops. All the derivatives of opium such as morphine, codeine, heroine, dionine, narceine, and narcotine, to say nothing of bromure d'étyle, bromoform, nitrite d'amyle, and amyline are known to be utilised by the endormeurs to put their victims to sleep, and the skill which they have acquired in the use of these powerful drugs establishes them as one of the most dangerous groups of criminals in existence. The men are all of superior intelligence and daring; the chief requisite of the women is extreme beauty as well as unscrupulousness.

"They will take a little thin glass ball of one of these liquids, for instance, hold it in a pocket handkerchief, crush it, shove it under the nose of their victim, and—whiff!—the victim is unconscious. But ordinarily the endormeur does not kill. He is usually satisfied to stupefy, rob, and then leave his victim. There is something more to this case than a mere suicide or murder, McBride. Of course she may have committed suicide with the drugs of the endormeurs; then again she may merely have been rendered unconscious by those drugs and some other poison may have been administered. Depend on it, there is something more back of this affair than appears on the surface. Even as far as I have gone I do not hesitate to say that we have run across the work of one or perhaps a band of the most up-to-date and scientific criminals."

Kennedy had scarcely finished when McBride brought his right fist down with a resounding smack into the palm of his left hand.

"Say," he cried in great excitement, "here's another thing which may or may not have some connection with the case. The evening after Madame arrived, I happened to be walking through the café, where I saw a face that looked familiar to me. It was that of a dark-haired, olive-skinned man, a fascinating face, but a face to be afraid of. I remembered him, I thought, from my police experience, as a notorious crook who had not been seen in New York for years, a man who in the old days used to gamble with death in South American revolutions, a soldier of fortune.

"Well, I gave the waiter, Charley, the wink and he met me in the rear of the café, around a corner. You know we have a regular system in the hotel by which I can turn all the help into amateur sleuths. I told him to be very careful about the dark-faced man and the younger man who was with him, to be particular to wait on them well, and to pick up any scraps of conversation he could.

"Charley knows his business, and the barest perceptible sign from me makes him an obsequious waiter. Of course the dark man didn't notice it at the time, but if he had been more observant he would have seen that three times during his chat with his companion Charley had wiped off his table with lingering hand. Twice he had put fresh seltzer in his drink. Like a good waiter always working for a big tip he had hovered near, his face blank and his eyes unobservant. But that waiter was an important link in my chain of protection of the hotel against crooks. He was there to listen and to tip me off, which he did between orders.

"There wasn't much that he overheard, but what there was of it was so suspicious that I did not hesitate to conclude that the fellow was an undesirable guest. It was something about the Panama Canal, and a coaling station of a steamship and fruit concern on the shore of one of the Latin American countries. It was, he said, in reality to be the coaling station of a certain European power which he did not name but which the younger man seemed to understand. They talked of wharves and tracts of land, of sovereignty and blue prints, the Monroe Doctrine, value in case of war, and a lot of other things. Then they talked of money, and though Charley was most assiduous at the time all he overheard was something about 'ten thousand francs' and 'buying her off,' and finally a whispered confidence of which he caught the words, 'just a blind to get her over here, away from Paris.' Finally the dark man in an apparent burst of confidence said something about 'the other plans being the real thing after all,' and that the whole affair would bring him in fifty thousand francs, with which he could afford to be liberal. Charley could get no inkling about what that other thing was.

"But I felt sure that he had heard enough to warrant the belief that some kind of confidence game was being discussed. To tell the truth I didn't care much what it was, at the time. It might have been an attempt of the dark-visaged fellow to sell the Canal to a come-on. What I wanted was to have it known that the Vanderveer was not to be a resort of such gentry as this. But I'm afraid it was much more serious than I thought at the time.

"Well, the dark man finally excused himself and sauntered into the lobby and up to the desk, with me after him around the opposite way. He was looking over the day's arrivals on the register when I concluded that it was about time to do something. I was standing directly beside him lighting a cigar. I turned quickly on him and deliberately trod on the man's patent leather shoe. He faced me furiously at not getting any apology. 'Sacré,' he exclaimed, 'what the——' But before he could finish I moved still closer and pinched his elbow. A dull red glow of suppressed anger spread over his face, but he cut his words short. He knew and I knew he knew. That is the sign in the continental hotels when they find a crook and quietly ask him to move on. The man turned on his heel and stalked out of the hotel. By and by the young man in the café, considerably annoyed at the sudden inattention of the waiter who acted as if he wasn't satisfied with his tip, strolled through the lobby and not seeing his dark-skinned friend, also disappeared. I wish to heaven I had had them shadowed. The young fellow wasn't a come-on at all. There was something afoot between these two, mark my words."

"But why do you connect that incident with this case of Madame de Nevers?" asked Kennedy, a little puzzled.

"Because the next day, and the day that Madame's maid disappeared, I happened to see a man bidding good-bye to a woman at the rear carriage entrance of the hotel. The woman was Madame's maid and the man was the dark man who had been seated in the café."

"You said a moment ago that you had a good description of the maid or could write one. Do you think you could locate her?"

The hotel detective thought a minute or two. "If she has gone to any of the other hotels in this city, I could," he answered slowly. "You know we have recently formed a sort of clearing house, we hotel detectives, and we are working together now very well, though secretly. It is barely possible that she has gone to another hotel. The very brazenness of that would be its safeguard, she might think."

"Then I can leave that part of it to you, McBride?" asked Kennedy thoughtfully as if laying out a programme of action in his mind. "You will set the hotel detectives on the trail as well as the police of the city, and of other cities, will make the inquiries at the steamships and railroads, and all that sort of thing? Try to find some trace of the two men whom you saw in the café at the same time. But for the present I should say spare no effort to locate that girl."

"Trust it to me," agreed McBride confidently.

A heavy tap sounded at the door and McBride opened it. It was the coroner.

I shall not go into the lengthy investigation which the coroner conducted, questioning one servant and employee after another without eliciting any more real information than we had already obtained so concisely from the house man. The coroner was, of course, angry at the removal of the body from the closet to the bed because he wanted to view it in the position in which it had been found, but as that had been done by the servants before McBride could stop them, there was nothing to do about it but accept the facts.

"A very peculiar case," remarked the coroner at the conclusion of his examination, with the air of a man who could shed much light on it from his wide experience if he chose. "There is just one point that we shall have to clear up, however. What was the cause of the death of the deceased? There is no gas in the room. It couldn't have been illuminating gas, then. No, it must have been a poison of some kind. Then as to the motive," he added, trying to look confident but really shooting a tentative remark at Craig and the house detective, who said nothing. " It looks a good deal like that other suicide—at least a suicide which some one has endeavoured to conceal," he added, hastily recollecting the manner in which the body had been found and his criticisms of the removal from the closet.

" Didn't I tell you? " rejoined McBride dolefully after we had left the coroner downstairs a few minutes later. " I knew he would think the hotel was hiding something from him."

" We can't help what he thinks—yet," remarked Craig. " All we can do is to run down the clues which we have. I will leave the maid to be found by your organisation, McBride. Let me see, the theatres and roof gardens must be letting out by this time. I will see if I can get any information from Miss Lovelace. Find her address, Walter, and call a cab."

The Southern heiress, who had attracted more attention by her beauty than by her fortune which was only moderate as American fortunes go nowadays, lived in an apartment facing the park, with her mother, a woman whose social ambitions it was commonly known had no bounds and were often sadly imposed upon.

Fortunately we arrived at the apartment not very many minutes after the mother and daughter, and although it was late, Kennedy sent up his card with an urgent message to see them. They received us in a large drawing-room and were plainly annoyed by our visit, though that of course was susceptible of a natural interpretation.

" What is it that you wished to see me about? "

began Mrs. Lovelace in a tone which was intended to close the interview almost before it was begun.

Kennedy had not wished to see her about anything, but of course he did not even hint as much in his reply which was made to her but directed at Miss Lovelace.

"Could you tell me anything about a Madame de Nevers who was staying at the Vanderveer?" asked Craig, turning quickly to the daughter so as to catch the full effect of his question, and then waiting as if expecting the answer from her.

The young lady's face blanched slightly and she seemed to catch her breath for an instant, but she kept her composure admirably in spite of the evident shock of Craig's purposely abrupt question.

"I have heard of her," Miss Lovelace replied with forced calmness as he continued to look to her for an answer. "Why do you ask?"

"Because a woman who is supposed to be Madame de Nevers has committed suicide at the Vanderveer and it was thought that perhaps you could identify her."

By this time she had become perfect mistress of herself again, from which I argued that whatever knowledge she had of Madame was limited to the time before the tragedy.

"I, identify her? Why, I never saw her. I simply know that such a creature exists."

She said it defiantly and with an iciness which showed more plainly than in mere words that she scorned even an acquaintance with a demi-mondaine.

"Do you suppose the Duc de Chateaurouge would

be able to identify her?" asked Kennedy mercilessly. "One moment, please," he added, anticipating the blank look of amazement on her face. "I have reason to believe that the duke is in this country incognito—is he not?"

Instead of speaking she merely raised her shoulders a fraction of an inch.

"Either in New York or in Washington," pursued Kennedy.

"Why do you ask me?" she said at length. "Isn't it enough that some of the newspapers have said so? If you see it in the newspapers, it's so—perhaps—isn't it?"

We were getting nowhere in this interview, at least so I thought. Kennedy cut it short, especially as he noted the evident restlessness of Mrs. Lovelace. However, he had gained his point. Whether or not the duke was in New York or Washington or Spitzbergen, he now felt sure that Miss Lovelace knew of, and perhaps something about, Madame de Nevers. In some way the dead woman had communicated with her and Miss Lovelace had been the woman whom the hotel clerk had seen at the Vanderveer. We withdrew as gracefully as our awkward position permitted.

As there was nothing else to be done at that late hour, Craig decided to sleep soundly over the case, his infallible method of taking a fresh start after he had run up a cul-de-sac.

Imagine our surprise in the morning at being waited on by the coroner himself, who in a few words explained that he was far from satisfied with the progress his own office was making with the case.

"You understand," he concluded after a lengthy statement of confession and avoidance, "we have no very good laboratory facilities of our own to carry out the necessary chemical, pathological, and bacteriological investigations in cases of homicide and suicide. We are often forced to resort to private laboratories, as you know in the past when I have had to appeal to you. Now, Professor Kennedy, if we might turn over that research part of the case to you, sir, I will engage to see that a reasonable bill for your professional services goes through the office of my friend the city comptroller promptly."

Craig snapped at the opportunity, though he did not allow the coroner to gain that impression.

"Very well," agreed that official, "I shall see that all the necessary organs for a thorough test as to the cause of the death of this woman are sent up to the Chemistry Building right away."

The coroner was as good as his word, and we had scarcely breakfasted and arrived at Craig's scientific workshop before that official appeared, accompanied by a man who carried in uncanny jars the necessary materials for an investigation following an autopsy.

Kennedy was now in his element. The case had taken an unexpected turn which made him a leading factor in its solution. Whatever suspicions he may have entertained unofficially the night before he could now openly and quickly verify.

He took a little piece of lung tissue and with a sharp sterilised knife cut it up. Then he made it slightly alkaline with a little sodium carbonate, talking half to us and half to himself as he worked. The next step was to place the matter in a glass flask in a water bath where it was heated. From the flask a Bohemian glass tube led into a cool jar and on a part of the tube a flame was playing which heated it to redness for two or three inches.

Several minutes we waited in silence. Finally when the process had gone far enough, Kennedy took a piece of paper which had been treated with iodised starch, as he later explained. He plunged the paper into the cool jar. Slowly it turned a strong blue tint.

Craig said nothing, but it was evident that he was more than gratified by what had happened. He quickly reached for a bottle on the shelves before him, and I could see from the label on the brown glass that it was nitrate of silver. As he plunged a little in a test-tube into the jar a strong precipitate was gradually formed.

"It is the decided reaction for chloroform," he exclaimed simply in reply to our unspoken questions.

"Chloroform," repeated the coroner, rather doubtfully, and it was evident that he had expected a poison and had not anticipated any result whatever from an examination of the lungs instead of the stomach to which he had confined his own work so far. "Could chloroform be discovered in the lungs or viscera after so many days? There was one famous chloroform case for which a man is now serving a life term in Sing Sing which I have understood there was grave doubt in the minds of the experts. Mind, I am not trying to question the results of your work except as they might naturally be questioned in court. It seems to me that the volatility of chloroform might very possibly preclude its discovery after a short time. Then again, might not other substances be generated in a dead body which would give a reaction very much like chloroform? We must consider all these questions before we abandon the poison theory, sir. Remember, this is the summer time too, and chloroform would evaporate very much more rapidly now than in winter."

Kennedy smiled, but his confidence remained unshaken.

"I am in a position to meet all of your objections," he explained simply. "I think I could lay it down as a rule that by proper methods chloroform may be discovered in the viscera much longer after death than is commonly supposed—in summer from six days to three weeks, with a practical working range of say twelve days, while in winter it may be found even after several months—by the right method. Certainly this case comes within the average length of time. More than that, no substance is generated by the process of decomposition which will vitiate the test for chloroform which I have just made. Chloroform has an affinity for water and is also a preservative, and hence from all these facts I think it safe to conclude that sometimes traces of it may be found for two weeks after its administration, certainly for a few days."

"And Madame de Nevers?" queried the coroner, as if the turn of events was necessitating a complete reconstruction of his theory of the case.

"Was murdered," completed Kennedy in a tone that left nothing more to be said on the subject.

"But," persisted the coroner, "if she was murdered by the use of chloroform, how do you account for the fact that it was done without a struggle? There were no marks of violence and I, for one, do not believe that under ordinary circumstances any one will passively submit to such an administration without a hard fight."

From his pocket Kennedy drew a small pasteboard box filled with tiny globes, some bonbons and lozenges, a small hypodermic syringe, and a few cigars and cigarettes. He held it out in the palm of his hand so that we could see it.

"This," he remarked, "is the standard equipment of the endormeur. Whoever obtained admittance to Madame's rooms, either as a matter of course or secretly, must have engaged her in conversation, disarmed suspicion, and then suddenly she must have found a pocket handkerchief under her nose. The criminal crushed a globe of liquid in the handkerchief, the victim lost consciousness, the chloroform was administered without a struggle, all marks of identification were obliterated, the body was placed in the closet, and the maid—either as principal or accessory—took the most likely means of postponing discovery by paying the bill in advance at the office, and then disappeared."

Kennedy slipped the box back into his pocket. The coroner had, I think, been expecting Craig's verdict, although he was loath to abandon his own suicide theory and had held it to the last possible moment. At any rate, so far he had said little, apparently preferring to keep his own counsel as to his course of action and to set his own machinery in motion.

He drew a note from his pocket, however. "I suppose," he began tentatively, shaking the note as he glanced doubtfully from it to us, "that you have heard that among the callers on this unfortunate woman was a lady of high social position in this city?"

"I have heard a rumour to that effect," replied Kennedy as he busied himself cleaning up the apparatus he had just used. There was nothing in his manner even to hint at the fact that we had gone further and interviewed the young lady in question.

"Well," resumed the coroner, "in view of what you have just discovered I don't mind telling you that I believe it was more than a rumour. I have had a man watching the woman and this is a report I received just before I came up here."

We read the note which he now handed to us. It was just a hasty line: "Miss Lovelace left hurriedly for Washington this morning."

What was the meaning of it? Clearly, as we probed deeper into the case, its ramifications grew wider than anything we had yet expected. Why had

Miss Lovelace gone to Washington, of all places, at this torrid season of the year?

The coroner had scarcely left us, more mystified than ever, when a telephone message came from McBride saying that he had some important news for us if we would meet him at the St. Cenis Hotel within an hour. He would say nothing about it over the wire.

As Kennedy hung up the receiver he quietly took a pistol from a drawer of his desk, broke it quickly, and looked thoughtfully at the cartridges in the cylinder. Then he snapped it shut and stuck it into his pocket.

"There's no telling what we may run up against before we get back to the laboratory," he remarked and we rode down to meet McBride.

The description which the house man had sent out to the other hotel detectives the night before had already produced a result. Within the past two days a man answering the description of the younger man whom McBride had seen in the café and a woman who might very possibly have been Madame's maid had come to the St. Cenis as M. and Mme. Duval. Their baggage was light, but they had been at pains to impress upon the hotel that they were persons of some position and that it was going direct from the railroad to the steamer, after their tour of America. They had, as a matter of fact, done nothing to excite suspicion until the general request for information had been received.

The house man of the St. Cenis welcomed us cordially upon McBride's introduction and agreed to take us up to the rooms of the strange couple if they were not in. As it happened it was the lunch hour and they were not in the room. Still, Kennedy dared not be too particular in his search of their effects, for he did not wish to arouse suspicion upon their return, at least not yet.

"It seems to me, Craig," I suggested after we had nosed about for a few minutes, finding nothing, "that this is pre-eminently a case in which to use the dictograph as you did in that Black Hand case."

He shook his head doubtfully, although I could see that the idea appealed to him. "The dictograph has been getting too much publicity lately," he said. "I'm afraid they would discover it, that is, if they are at all the clever people I think them. Besides, I would have to send up to the laboratory to get one and by the time the messenger returned they might be back from lunch. No, we've got to do something else, and do it quickly."

He was looking about the room in an apparently aimless manner. On the side wall hung a cheap etching of a woodland scene. Kennedy seemed engrossed in it while the rest of us fidgeted at the delay.

"Can you get me a couple of old telephone instruments?" he asked at length, turning to us and addressing the St. Cenis detective.

The detective nodded and disappeared down the hall. A few minutes later he deposited the instruments on a table. Where he got them I do not know, but I suspect he simply lifted them from vacant rooms.

"Now some Number 30 copper wire and a couple of dry cells," ordered Kennedy, falling to work immediately on the telephones. The detective despatched a bellboy down to the basement to get the wire from the house electrician.

Kennedy removed the transmitters of the telephones, and taking the carbon capsules from them placed the capsules on the table carefully. Then he lifted down the etching from the wall and laid it flat on its face before us. Quickly he removed the back of the picture.

Pressing the transmitter fronts with the carbon capsules against the paper and the glass on the picture he mounted them so that the paper and glass acted as a large diaphragm to collect all the sounds in the room.

"The size of this glass diaphragm," he explained as we gathered around in intense interest at what he was doing, "will produce a strikingly sensitive microphone action and the merest whisper will be reproduced with startling distinctness."

The boy brought the wire up and also the news that the couple in whose room we were had very nearly finished luncheon and might be expected back in a few minutes.

Kennedy took the tiny wires, and after connecting them hung up the picture again and ran them up alongside the picture wires leading from the huge transmitter up to the picture moulding. Along the top of the moulding and out through the transom it was easy enough to run the wires and so down the hall to a vacant room, where Craig attached them quickly to one of the old telephone receivers.

Then we sat down in this room to await developments from our hastily improvised picture frame microphone detective.

At last we could hear the elevator door close on our floor. A moment later it was evident from the expression of Kennedy's face that some one had entered the room which we had just left. He had finished not a moment too soon.

"It's a good thing that I didn't wait to put a dictograph there," he remarked to us. "I thought I wasn't reckoning without reason. The couple, whoever they are, are talking in undertones and looking about the room to see if anything has been disturbed in their absence."

Kennedy alone, of course, could follow over his end of the telephone what they said. The rest of us could do nothing but wait, but from notes which Craig jotted down as he listened to the conversation I shall reproduce it as if we had all heard it. There were some anxious moments until at last they had satisfied themselves that no one was listening and that no dictograph or other mechanical eavesdropper, such as they had heard of, was concealed in the furniture or back of it.

"Why are you so particular, Henri?" a woman's voice was saying.

"Louise, I've been thinking for a long time that we are surrounded by spies in these hotels. You remember I told you what happened at the Vanderveer the night you and Madame arrived? I'm sure that waiter overheard what Gonzales and I were talking about."

"Well, we are safe now anyhow. What was it that you would not tell me just now at luncheon?" asked the woman, whom Kennedy recognised as Madame de Nevers's maid.

"I have a cipher from Washington. Wait until I translate it."

There was a pause. "What does it say?" asked the woman impatiently.

"It says," repeated the man slowly, "that Miss Lovelace has gone to Washington. She insists on knowing whether the death of Marie was a suicide or not. Worse than that the Secret Service must have wind of some part of our scheme, for they are acting suspiciously. I must go down there or the whole affair may be exposed and fall through. Things could hardly be worse, especially this sudden move on her part."

"Who was that detective who forced his way to see her the night they discovered Marie's body?" asked the woman. "I hope that that wasn't the Secret Service also. Do you think they could have suspected anything?"

"I hardly think so," the man replied. "Beyond the death of Madame they suspect nothing here in New York, I am convinced. You are sure that all her letters were secured, that all clues to connect her with the business in hand were destroyed, and particularly that the package she was to deliver is safe?"

"The package? You mean the plans for the

coaling station on the Pacific near the Canal? You see, Henri, I know."

"Ha, ha,—yes," replied the man. "Louise, shall I tell you a secret? Can you keep it?"

"You know I can, Henri."

"Well, Louise, the scheme is deeper than even you think. We are playing one country against another, America against—you know the government our friend Schmidt works for in Paris. Now, listen. Those plans of the coaling station are a fake—a fake. It is just a commercial venture. No nation would be foolish enough to attempt such a thing, yet. We know that they are a fake. But we are going to sell them through that friend of ours in the United States War Department. But that is only part of the coup, the part that will give us the money to turn the much larger coups we have in the future. You can understand why it has all to be done so secretly and how vexatious it is that as soon as one obstacle is overcome a dozen new ones appear. Louise, here is the big secret. By using those fake plans as a bait we are going to obtain something which when we all return to Paris we can convert into thousands of francs. There, I can say no more. But I have told you so much to impress upon you the extreme need of caution."

"And how much does Miss Lovelace know?"

"Very little—I hope. That is why I must go to Washington myself. She must know nothing of this coup nor of the real de Nevers, or the whole scheme may fall through. It would have fallen through before, Louise, if you had failed us and had let any of de Nevers's letters slip through to Miss Lovelace. She richly deserved her fate for that act of treachery. The affair would have been so simple, otherwise. Luck was with us until her insane jealousy led her to visit Miss Lovelace. It was fortunate the young lady was out when Madame called on her or all would have been lost. Ah, we owe you a great deal, Louise, and we shall not forget it, never. You will be very careful while I am gone?"

"Absolutely. When will you return to me, Henri?"

"To-morrow morning at the latest. This afternoon the false coaling station plans are to be turned over to our accomplice in the War Department and in exchange he is to give us something else—the secret of which I spoke. You see the trail leads up into high circles. It is very much more important than you suppose and discovery might lead to a dangerous international complication just now."

"Then you are to meet your friend in Washington to-night? When do you start, Henri? Don't let the time slip by. There must be no mistake this time as there was when we were working for Japan and almost had the blue prints of Corregidor at Manila only to lose them on the streets of Calcutta."

"Trust me. We are to meet about nine o'clock and therefore I leave on the limited at three-thirty, in about an hour. From the station I am going straight to the house on Z Street—let me see, the cipher says the number is 101—and ask for a man named Gonzales. I shall use the name Montez.

He is to appear, hand over the package—that thing I have told you about—then I am to return here by one of the midnight trains. At any cost we must allow nothing to happen which will reach the ears of Miss Lovelace. I'll see you early to-morrow morning, *ma chérie,* and remember, be ready, for the *Aquitania* sails at ten. The division of the money is to be made in Paris. Then we shall all go our separate ways."

Kennedy was telephoning frantically through the regular hotel service to find out how the trains ran for Washington. The only one that would get there before nine was the three-thirty; the next, leaving an hour later, did not arrive until nearly eleven. He had evidently had some idea of causing some delay that would result in our friend down the hall missing the limited, but abandoned it. Any such scheme would simply result in a message to the gang in Washington putting them on their guard and defeating his purpose.

"At all costs we must beat this fellow to it," exclaimed Craig, waiting to hear no more over his improvised dictograph. "Come, Walter, we must catch the limited for Washington immediately. McBride, I leave you and the regular house man to shadow this woman. Don't let her get out of your sight for a moment."

As we rode across the city to the new railroad terminus Craig hastily informed me of what he had overheard. We took up our post so that we could see the outgoing travellers, and a few minutes later Craig spotted our man from McBride's description, and succeeded in securing chairs in the same car in which he was to ride.

Taken altogether it was an uneventful journey. For five mortal hours we sat in the Pullman or toyed with food in the dining-car, never letting the man escape our sight, yet never letting him know that we were watching him. Nevertheless I could not help asking myself what good it did. Why did not Kennedy hire a special if the affair was so important as it appeared? How were we to get ahead of him in Washington better than in New York? I knew that some plan lurked behind the calm and inscrutable face of Kennedy as I tried to read and could not.

The train had come to a stop in the Union Station. Our man was walking rapidly up the platform in the direction of the cab stand. Suddenly Kennedy darted ahead and for a moment we were walking abreast of him.

"I beg your pardon," began Craig as we came to a turn in the shadow of the arc lights, "but have you a match?"

The man halted and fumbled for his match-box. Instantly Kennedy's pocket handkerchief was at his nose.

"Some of the medicine of your own gang of endormeurs," ground out Kennedy, crushing several of the little glass globes under his handkerchief to make doubly sure of their effect.

The man reeled and would have fallen if we had not caught him between us. Up the platform we led him in a daze.

"Here," shouted Craig to a cabman, "my friend is ill. Drive us around a bit. It will sober him up. Come on, Walter, jump in, the air will do us all good."

Those who were in Washington during that summer will remember the suppressed activity in the State, War, and Navy Departments on a certain very humid night. Nothing leaked out at the time as to the cause, but it was understood later that a crisis was narrowly averted at a very inopportune season, for the heads of the departments were all away, the President was at his summer home in the North, and even some of the under-secretaries were out of town. Hasty messages had been sizzling over the wires in cipher and code for hours.

I recall that as we rode a little out of our way past the Army Building, merely to see if there was any excitement, we found it a blaze of lights. Something was plainly afoot even at this usually dull period of the year. There was treachery of some kind and some trusted employee was involved, I felt instinctively. As for Craig he merely glanced at the insensible figure between us and remarked sententiously that to his knowledge there was only one nation that made a practice of carrying out its diplomatic and other coups in the hot weather, a remark which I understood to mean that our mission was more than commonly important.

The man had not recovered when we arrived within several blocks of our destination, nor did he show signs of recovery from his profound stupor. Kennedy stopped the cab in a side street, pressed a bill into the cabman's hand, and bade him wait until we returned.

We had turned the corner of Z Street and were approaching the house when a man walking in the opposite direction eyed us suspiciously, turned, and followed us a step or two.

"Kennedy!" he exclaimed.

If a fourteen-inch gun had exploded behind us I could not have been more startled. Here, in spite of all our haste and secrecy we were followed, watched, and beaten.

Craig wheeled about suddenly. Then he took the man by the arm. "Come," he said quickly, and we three dove into the shadow of an alley.

As we paused, Kennedy was the first to speak. "By Jove, Walter, it's Burke of the Secret Service," he exclaimed.

"Good," repeated the man with some satisfaction. "I see that you still have that memory for faces." He was evidently referring to our experiences together some months before with the portrait parlé and identification in the counterfeiting case which Craig cleared up for him.

For a moment or two Burke and Kennedy spoke in whispers. Under the dim light from the street I could see Kennedy's face intent and working with excitement.

"No wonder the War Department is a blaze of lights," he exclaimed as we moved out of the shadow again, leaving the Secret Service man. "Burke, I had no idea when I took up this case that I should be doing my country a service also. We must succeed at any hazard. The moment you hear a pistol shot, Burke, we shall need you. Force the door if it is not already open. You were right as to the street but not the number. It is that house over there. Come on, Walter."

We mounted the low steps of the house and a negress answered the bell. "Is Mr. Gonzales in?" asked Kennedy.

The hallway into which we were admitted was dark but it opened into a sitting-room, where a dim light was burning behind the thick portières. Without a word the negress ushered us into this room, which was otherwise empty.

"Tell him Mr. Montez is here," added Craig as we sat down.

The negress disappeared upstairs, and in a few minutes returned with the message that he would be down directly.

No sooner had the shuffle of her footsteps died away than Kennedy was on his feet, listening intently at the door. There was no sound. He took a chair and tiptoed out into the dark hall with it. Turning it upside down he placed it at the foot of the stairs with the four legs pointing obliquely up. Then he drew me into a corner with him.

How long we waited I cannot say. The next I knew was a muffled step on the landing above, then the tread on the stairs.

A crash and a deep volley of oaths in French followed as the man pitched headlong over the chair on the dark steps.

Kennedy whipped out his revolver and fired point-blank at the prostrate figure. I do not know what the ethics are of firing on a man when he is down, nor did I have time to stop to think.

Craig grasped my arm and pulled me toward the door. A sickening odour seemed to pervade the air. Upstairs there was shouting and banging of doors.

"Closer, Walter," he muttered, "closer to the door, and open it a little, or we shall both be suffocated. It was the Secret Service gun I shot off—the pistol that shoots stupefying gas from its vapour-filled cartridges and enables you to put a criminal out of commission without killing him. A pull of the trigger, the cap explodes, the gunpowder and the force of the explosion unite some capsicum and lycopodium, producing the blinding, suffocating vapour whose terrible effect you see. Here, you upstairs," he shouted, "advance an inch or so much as show your heads over the rail and I pump a shot at you, too. Walter, take the gun yourself. Fire at a move from them. I think the gases have cleared away enough now. I must get him before he recovers consciousness."

A tap at the door came, and without taking my eyes off the stairs I opened it. Burke slid in and gulped at the nauseous atmosphere.

"What's up?" he gasped. "I heard a shot. Where's Kennedy?"

I motioned in the darkness. Kennedy's electric bull's-eye flashed up at that instant and we saw him deftly slip a bright pair of manacles on the wrists of the man on the floor, who was breathing heavily, while blood flowed from a few slight cuts due to his fall.

Dexterously as a pickpocket Craig reached into the man's coat, pulled out a packet of papers, and gazed eagerly at one after another. From among them he unfolded one written in French to Madame Marie de Nevers some weeks before. I translate:

DEAR MARIE: Herr Schmidt informs me that his agent in the War Department at Washington, U. S. A., has secured some important information which will interest the Government for which Herr Schmidt is the agent—of course you know who that is.

It is necessary that you should carry the packet which will be handed to you (if you agree to my proposal) to New York by the steamer *Tripolitania.* Go to the Vandeveer Hotel and in a few days, as soon as a certain exchange can be made, either our friend in Washington or myself will call on you, using the name Gonzales. In return for the package which you carry he will hand you another. Lose no time in bringing the second package back to Paris.

I have arranged that you will receive ten thousand francs and your expenses for your services in this matter. Under no conditions betray your connection with Herr Schmidt. I was to have carried the packet to America myself and make the exchange but knowing your need of money I have secured the work for you. You had better take your maid, as it is much better to travel with distinction in this case. If, however, you accept this commission I shall consider you in honour bound to surrender your claim upon my name for which I agree to pay you fifty thousand francs upon my marriage with the American heiress of whom you know. Please let me know immediately through our mutual friend Henri Duval whether this proposal is satisfactory. Henri will tell you that fifty thousand is my ultimatum.

CHATEAUROUGE.

"Thc scoundrel," ground out Kennedy. "He lured his wife from Paris to New York, thinking the Paris police too acute for him, I suppose. Then by means of the treachery of the maid Louise and his friend Duval, a crook who would even descend to play the part of valet for him and fall in love with the maid, he has succeeded in removing the woman who stood between him and an American fortune."

"Marie," rambled Chateaurouge as he came blinking, sneezing, and choking out of his stupor, "Marie, you are clever, but not too clever for me. This blackmailing must stop. Miss Lovelace knows something, thanks to you, but she shall never know all—never—never. You—you—ugh!—Stop. Do you think you can hold me back now with those little white hands on my wrists? I wrench them loose—so—and—ugh!—What's this? Where am I?"

The man gazed dazedly at the manacles that held his wrists instead of the delicate hands he had been dreaming of as he lived over the terrible scene of his struggle with the woman who was his wife in the Vanderveer.

"Chateaurouge," almost hissed Kennedy in his righteous wrath, "fake nobleman, real swindler of five continents. Marie de Nevers alive stood in the way of your marriage to the heiress Miss Lovelace. Dead, she prevents it absolutely."

Craig continued to turn over the papers in his hand, as he spoke. At last he came to a smaller packet in oiled silk. As he broke the seal he glanced at it in surprise, then hurriedly exclaimed, "There, Burke. Take these to the War Department and tell them they can turn out their lights and stop their telegrams. This seems to be a copy of our government's plans for the fortification of the Panama Canal, heights of guns, location of searchlights, fire control stations, everything from painstaking search of official and confidential records. That is what this fellow obtained in exchange for his false blue prints of the supposed coaling station on the Pacific.

"I leave the Secret Service to find the leak in the War Department. What I am interested in is not the man who played spy for two nations and betrayed one of them. To me this adventurer who calls himself Chateaurouge is merely the murderer of Madame de Nevers."

X

THE SMUGGLER

It was a rather sultry afternoon in the late summer when people who had calculated by the calendar rather than by the weather were returning to the city from the seashore, the mountains, and abroad.

Except for the week-ends, Kennedy and I had been pretty busy, though on this particular day there was a lull in the succession of cases which had demanded our urgent attention during the summer.

We had met at the Public Library, where Craig was doing some special research at odd moments in criminology. Fifth Avenue was still half deserted, though the few pedestrians who had returned or remained in town like ourselves were, as usual, to be found mostly on the west side of the street. Nearly everybody, I have noticed, walks on the one side of Fifth Avenue, winter or summer.

As we stood on the corner waiting for the traffic man's whistle to halt the crush of automobiles, a man on the top of a 'bus waved to Kennedy.

I looked up and caught a glimpse of Jack Herndon, an old college mate, who had had some political aspirations and had recently been appointed to a position in the customs house of New York. Herndon, I may add, represented the younger and clean-cut generation which is entering official life with great advantage to both themselves and politics.

The 'bus pulled up to the curb, and Jack tore down the breakneck steps hurriedly.

"I was just thinking of you, Craig," he beamed as we all shook hands, "and wondering whether you and Walter were in town. I think I should have come up to see you to-night, anyhow."

"Why, what's the matter—more sugar frauds?" laughed Kennedy. "Or perhaps you have caught another art dealer red-handed?"

"No, not exactly," replied Herndon, growing graver for the moment. "We're having a big shake-up down at the office, none of your 'new broom' business, either. Real reform it is, this time."

"And you—are you going or coming?" inquired Craig with an interested twinkle.

"Coming, Craig, coming," answered Jack enthusiastically. "They've put me in charge of a sort of detective force as a special deputy surveyor to rout out some smuggling that we know is going on. If I make good it will go a long way for me—with all this talk of efficiency and economy down in Washington these days."

"What's on your mind now?" asked Kennedy observantly. "Can I help you in any way?"

Herndon had taken each of us by an arm and walked us over to a stone bench in the shade of the library building.

"You have read the accounts in the afternoon papers of the peculiar death of Mademoiselle Violette, the little French modiste, up here on Forty-sixth Street?" he inquired.

"Yes," answered Kennedy. "What has that to do with customs reform?"

"A good deal, I fear," Herndon continued. "It's part of a case that has been bothering us all summer. It's the first really big thing I've been up against and it's as ticklish a bit of business as even a veteran treasury agent could wish."

Herndon looked thoughtfully at the passing crowd on the other side of the balustrade and continued. "It started, like many of our cases, with the anonymous letter writer. Early in the summer the letters began to come in to the deputy surveyor's office, all unsigned, though quite evidently written in a woman's hand, disguised of course, and on rather dainty notepaper. They warned us of a big plot to smuggle gowns and jewellery from Paris. Smuggling jewellery is pretty common because jewels take up little space and are very valuable. Perhaps it doesn't sound to you like a big thing to smuggle dresses, but when you realise that one of those filmy lacy creations may often be worth several hundred, if not thousand, dollars, and that it needs only a few of them on each ship that comes in to run up into the thousands, perhaps hundreds of thousands in a season, you will see how essential it is to break up that sort of thing. We've been getting after the individual private smugglers pretty sharply this summer and we've had lots of criticism. If we could land a big fellow and make an object-lesson of the extent of the thing I believe it would leave our critics of the press without a leg to stand on.

"At least that was why I was interested in the letters. But it was not until a few days ago that we got a tip that gave us a real working clue, for the anonymous letters had been very vague as to names, dates, and places, though bold enough as to general charges, as if the writer were fearful of incriminating herself—or himself. Strange to say, this new clue came from the wife of one of the customs men. She happened to be in a Broadway manicure shop one day when she heard a woman talking with the manicurist about fall styles, and she was all attention when she heard the customer say, 'You remember Mademoiselle Violette's—that place that had the exquisite things straight from Paris, and so cheaply, too? Well, Violette says she'll have to raise her prices so that they will be nearly as high as the regular stores. She says the tariff has gone up, or something, but it hasn't, has it?'

"The manicurist laughed knowingly, and the next remark caught the woman's attention. 'No, indeed. But then, I guess she meant that she had to pay the duty now. You know they are getting much stricter. To tell the truth, I imagine most of Violette's goods were—well——'

"'Smuggled?' supplied the customer in an undertone.

"The manicurist gave a slight shrug of the shoulders and a bright little yes of a laugh.

"That was all. But it was enough. I set a

special customs officer to watch Mademoiselle, a clever fellow. He didn't have time to find out much, but on the other hand I am sure he didn't do anything to alarm Mademoiselle. That would have been a bad game. His case was progressing favourably and he had become acquainted with one of the girls who worked in the shop. We might have got some evidence, but suddenly this morning he walked up to my desk and handed me an early edition of an afternoon paper. Mademoiselle Violette had been discovered dead in her shop by the girls when they came to work this morning. Apparently she had been there all night, but the report was quite indefinite and I am on my way up there now to meet the coroner, who has agreed to wait for me."

"You think there is some connection between her death and the letters?" put in Craig.

"Of course I can't say, yet," answered Herndon dubiously. "The papers seem to think it was a suicide. But then why should she commit suicide? My man found out that among the girls it was common gossip that she was to marry Jean Pierre, the Fifth Avenue jeweller, of the firm of Lang & Pierre down on the next block. Pierre is due in New York on *La Montaigne* to-night or to-morrow morning.

"Why, if my suspicions are correct, it is this Pierre who is the brains of the whole affair. And here's another thing. You know we have a sort of secret service in Paris and other European cities which is constantly keeping an eye on purchases of goods by Americans abroad. Well, the chief of our men in Paris cables me that Pierre is known to have made extraordinarily heavy purchases of made-up jewellery this season. For one thing, we believe he has acquired from a syndicate a rather famous diamond necklace which it has taken years to assemble and match up, worth about three hundred thousand. You know the duty on made-up jewellery is sixty per cent., and even if he brought the stones in loose it would be ten per cent., which on a valuation of, say, two hundred thousand, means twenty thousand dollars duty alone. Then he has a splendid 'dog collar' of pearls, and, oh, a lot of other stuff. I know because we get our tips from all sorts of sources and they are usually pretty straight. Some come from dealers who are sore about not making sales themselves. So you see there is a good deal at stake in this case and it may be that in following it out we shall kill more than one bird. I wish you'd come along with me up to Mademoiselle Violette's and give me an opinion."

Craig had already risen from the bench and we were walking up the Avenue.

The establishment of Mademoiselle Violette consisted of a three-story and basement brownstone house in which the basement and first floor had been remodelled for business purposes. Mademoiselle's place, which was on the first floor, was announced to the world by a neat little oval gilt sign on the handrailing of the steps.

We ascended and rang the bell. As we waited I noticed that there were several other modistes on the same street, while almost directly across was a sign which proclaimed that on September 15 Mademoiselle Gabrielle would open with a high class exhibition of imported gowns from Paris.

We entered. The coroner and an undertaker were already there, and the former was expecting Herndon. Kennedy and I had already met him and he shook hands cordially.

Mademoiselle Violette, it seemed, had rented the entire house and then had sublet the basement to a milliner, using the first floor herself, the second as a workroom for the girls whom she employed, while she lived on the top floor, which had been fitted for light housekeeping with a kitchenette. It was in the back room of the shop itself on the first floor that her body had been discovered, lying on a davenport.

"The newspaper reports were very indefinite," began Herndon, endeavouring to take in the situation. "I suppose they told nearly all the story, but what caused her death? Have you found that out yet? Was it poison or violence?"

The coroner said nothing, but with a significant glance at Kennedy he drew a peculiar contrivance from his pocket. It had four round holes in it and through each hole he slipped a finger, then closed his hand, and exhibited his clenched fist. It looked as if he wore a series of four metal rings on his fingers.

"Brass knuckles?" suggested Herndon, looking hastily at the body, which showed not a sign of violence on the stony face.

The coroner shook his head knowingly. Suddenly he raised his fist. I saw him press hard with his thumb on the upper end of the metal contrivance. From the other end, just concealed under his little finger, there shot out as if released by a magic spring a thin keen little blade of the brightest and toughest steel. He was holding, instead of a meaningless contrivance of four rings, a most dangerous kind of stiletto or dagger upraised. He lifted his thumb and the blade sprang back into its sheath like an extinguished spark of light.

"An Apache dagger, such as is used in the underworld of Paris," broke out Kennedy, his eyes gleaming with interest.

The coroner nodded. "We found it," he said, "clasped loosely in her hand. But it is only by expert medical testimony that we can determine whether it was placed on her fingers before or after this happened. We have photographed it, and the prints are being developed."

He had now uncovered the slight figure of the little French modiste. On the dress, instead of the profuse flow of blood which we had expected to see, there was a single round spot. And in the white marble skin of her breast was a little, nearly microscopic puncture, directly over the heart.

"She must have died almost instantly," commented Kennedy, glancing from the Apache weapon to the dead woman and back again. "Internal hemorrhage. I suppose you have searched her effects. Have you found anything that gives a hint among them?"

"No," replied the coroner doubtfully, "I can't say we have—unless it is the bundle of letters from Pierre, the jeweller. They seem to have been engaged, and yet the letters stopped abruptly, and, well, from the tone of the last one from him I should say there was a quarrel brewing."

An exclamation from Herndon followed. "The same notepaper and the same handwriting as the anonymous letters," he cried.

But that was all. Go over the ground as Kennedy might he could find nothing further than the coroner and Herndon had already revealed.

"About these people, Lang & Pierre," asked Craig thoughtfully when we had left Mademoiselle's and were riding downtown to the customs house with Herndon. "What do you know about them? I presume that Lang is in America, if his partner is abroad."

"Yes, he is here in New York. I believe the firm has a rather unsavoury reputation; they have to be watched, I am told. Then, too, one or the other of the partners makes frequent trips abroad, mostly Pierre. Pierre, as you see, was very intimate with Mademoiselle, and the letters simply confirm what the girls told my detective. He was believed to be engaged to her and I see no reason now to doubt that. The fact is, Kennedy, it wouldn't surprise me in the least to learn that it was he who engineered the smuggling for her as well as himself."

"What about the partner? What rôle does he play in your suspicions?"

"That's another curious feature. Lang doesn't seem to bother much with the business. He is a sort of silent partner, although nominally the head of the firm. Still, they both seem always to be plentifully supplied with money and to have a good trade. Lang lives most of the time up on the west shore of the Hudson, and seems to be more interested in his position as commodore of the Riverledge Yacht Club than in his business down here. He is quite a sport, a great motor-boat enthusiast, and has lately taken to hydroplanes."

"I meant," repeated Kennedy, "what about Lang and Mademoiselle Violette. Were they—ah—friendly?"

"Oh," replied Herndon, seeming to catch the idea. "I see. Of course—Pierre abroad and Lang here. I see what you mean. Why, the girl told my man that Mademoiselle Violette used to go motor-boating with Lang, but only when her fiancé, Pierre, was along. No, I don't think she ever had anything to do with Lang, if that's what you are driving at. He may have paid attentions to her, but Pierre was her lover, and I haven't a doubt but that if Lang made any advances she repelled them. She seems to have thought everything of Pierre."

We had reached Herndon's office by this time. Leaving word with his stenographer to get the very latest reports from *La Montaigne,* he continued talking to us about his work.

"Dressmakers, milliners, and jewellers are our worst offenders now," he remarked as we stood gazing out of the window at the panorama of the bay off the sea-wall of the Battery. "Why, time and again we unearth what looks for all the world like a 'dressmakers' syndicate,' though this case is the first I've had that involved a death. Really, I've come to look on smuggling as one of the fine arts among crimes. Once the smuggler, like the pirate and the highwayman, was a sort of gentleman-rogue. But now it has become a very ladylike art. The extent of it is almost beyond belief, too. It begins with the steerage and runs right up to the absolute unblushing cynicism of the first cabin. I suppose you know that women, particularly a certain brand of society women, are the worst and most persistent offenders. Why, they even boast of it. Smuggling isn't merely popular—it's aristocratic. But we're going to take some of the flavour out of it before we finish."

He tore open a cable message which a boy had brought in. "Now, take this, for instance," he continued. "You remember the sign across the street from Mademoiselle Violette's, announcing that a Mademoiselle Gabrielle was going to open a salon or whatever they call it? Well, here's another cable from our Paris Secret Service with a belated tip. They tell us to look out for a Mademoiselle Gabrielle—on *La Montaigne,* too. That's another interesting thing. You know the various lines are all ranked, at least in our estimation, according to the likelihood of such offences being perpetrated by their passengers. We watch ships from London, Liverpool, and Paris most carefully. Scandinavian ships are the least likely to need watching. Well, Miss Roberts?"

"We have just had a wireless about *La Montaigne*," reported his stenographer, who had entered while he was speaking, "and she is three hundred miles east of Sandy Hook. She won't dock until to-morrow."

"Thank you. Well, fellows, it is getting late and that means nothing more doing to-night. Can you be here early in the morning? We'll go down the bay and 'bring in the ship,' as our men call it when the deputy surveyor and his acting deputies go down to meet it at Quarantine. I can't tell you how much I appreciate your kindness in helping me. If my men get anything connecting Lang with Mademoiselle Violette's case I'll let you know immediately."

It was a bright clear snappy morning, in contrast with the heat of the day before, when we boarded the revenue tug at the Barge Office. The waters of the harbour never looked more blue as they danced in the early sunlight, flecked here and there by a foaming whitecap as the conflicting tides eddied about. The shores of Staten Island were almost as green as in the spring, and even the haze over the Brooklyn factories had lifted. It looked almost like a stage scene, clear and sharp, new and brightly coloured.

Perhaps the least known and certainly one of the least recognised of the government services is that which includes the vigilant ships of the revenue service. It was not a revenue cutter, however, on which we were ploughing down the bay. The cutter lay, white and gleaming in the morning sun, at anchor off Stapleton, like a miniature warship, saluting as we passed. The revenue boats which steam down to Quarantine and make fast to the incoming ocean greyhounds are revenue tugs.

Down the bay we puffed and buffeted for about forty minutes before we arrived at the little speck of an island that is Quarantine. Long before we were there we sighted the great *La Montaigne* near the group of buildings on the island, where she had been waiting since early morning for the tide and the customs officials. The tug steamed alongside, and quickly up the high ladders swarmed the boarding officer and the deputy collectors. We followed Herndon straight to the main saloon, where the collectors began to receive the declarations which had been made out on blanks furnished to the passengers on the voyage over. They had had several days to write them out—the less excuse for omissions.

Glancing at each hastily the collector detached from it the slip with the number at the bottom and handed the number back, to be presented at the inspector's desk at the pier, where customs inspectors were assigned in turn.

"Number 140 is the one we want to watch," I heard Herndon whisper to Kennedy. "That tall dark fellow over there."

I followed his direction cautiously and saw a sparely built, striking looking man who had just filed his declaration and was chatting vivaciously with a lady who was just about to file hers. She was a clinging looking little thing with that sort of doll-like innocence that deceives nobody.

"No, you don't have to swear to it," he said. "You used to do that, but now you simply sign your name—and take a chance," he added, smiling and showing a row of perfect teeth.

"Number 156," Herndon noted as the collector detached the stub and handed it to her. "That was Mademoiselle Gabrielle."

The couple passed out to the deck, still chatting gaily.

"In the old days, before they got to be so beastly particular," I heard him say, "I always used to get the courtesy of the port, an official expedite. But that is over now."

The ship was now under way, her flags snapping in the brisk coolish breeze that told of approaching autumn. We had passed up the lower bay and the Narrows, and the passengers were crowded forward to catch the first glimpse of the skyscrapers of New York.

On up the bay we ploughed, throwing the spray proudly as we went. Herndon employed the time in keeping a sharp watch on the tall, thin man. Incidentally he sought out the wireless operator and from him learned that a code wireless message had been received for Pierre, apparently from his partner, Lang.

"There is no mention of anything dutiable in this declaration by 140 which corresponds with any of the goods mentioned in the first cable from Paris," a collector remarked unobtrusively to Herndon, "nor in 156 corresponding to the second cable."

"I didn't suppose there would be," was his laconic reply. "That's our job—to find the stuff."

At last *La Montaigne* was warped into the dock. The piles of first-class baggage on the ship were raucously deposited on the wharf and slowly the passengers filed down the plank to meet the line of white-capped uniformed inspectors and plain-clothes appraisers. The comedy and tragedy of the customs inspection had begun.

We were among the first to land. Herndon took up a position from which he could see without being seen. In the semi-light of the little windows in the enclosed sides of the pier, under the steel girders of the arched roof like a vast hall, there was a panorama of a huge mass of open luggage.

At last Number 140 came down, alone, to the roped-off dock. He walked nonchalantly over to the little deputy surveyor's desk, and an inspector was quickly assigned to him. It was all done neatly in the regular course of business apparently. He did not know that in the orderly rush the sharpest of Herndon's men had been picked out, much as a trick card player will force a card on his victim.

Already the customs inspection was well along. One inspector had been assigned to about each five passengers, and big piles of finery were being remorselessly tumbled out in shapeless heaps and exposed to the gaze of that part of the public which was not too much concerned over the same thing as to its own goods and chattels. Reticules and purses were being inspected. Every trunk was presumed to have a false bottom, and things wrapped up in paper were viewed suspiciously and unrolled. Clothes were being shaken and pawed. There did not seem to be much opportunity for concealment.

Herndon now had donned the regulation straw hat of the appraiser, and accompanied by us, posing as visitors, was sauntering about. At last we came within earshot of the spot where the inspector was going through the effects of 140.

Out of the corner of my eyes I could see that a dispute was in progress over some trifling matter. The man was cool and calm. "Call the appraiser," he said at last, with the air of a man standing on his rights. "I object to this frisking of passengers. Uncle Sam is little better than a pickpocket. Besides, I can't wait here all day. My partner is waiting for me uptown."

Herndon immediately took notice. But it was quite evidently, after all, only an altercation for the benefit of those who were watching. I am sure he knew he was being watched, but as the dispute proceeded he assumed the look of a man keenly amused. The matter, involving only a few dollars, was finally adjusted by his yielding gracefully and with an air of resignation. Still Herndon did not go and I am sure it annoyed him.

Suddenly he turned and faced Herndon. I could not help thinking, in spite of all that he must be so expert, that, if he really were a smuggler, he had all the poise and skill at evasion that would entitle him to be called a past master of the art.

"You see that woman over there?" he whispered. "She says she is just coming home after studying music in Paris."

We looked. It was the guileless ingénue, Mademoiselle Gabrielle.

"She has dutiable goods, all right. I saw her declaration. She is trying to bring in as personal effects of a foreign resident gowns which, I believe, she intends to wear on the stage. She's an actress."

There was nothing for Herndon to do but to act on the tip. The man had got rid of us temporarily, but we knew the inspector would be, if anything, more vigilant. I think he took even longer than usual.

Mademoiselle Gabrielle and her maid pouted and fussed over the renewed examination which Herndon ordered. According to the inspector everything was new and expensive; according to her, old, shabby, and cheap. She denied everything, raged and threatened. But when, instead of ordering the stamp "Passed" to be placed on her half dozen trunks and bags which contained in reality only a few dutiable articles, Herndon threatened to order them to the appraiser's stores and herself to go to the Law Division if she did not admit the points in dispute, there was a real scene.

"Generally, madame," he remonstrated, though I could see he was baffled at finding nothing of the goods he had really expected to find, "generally even for a first offence the goods are confiscated and the court or district attorney is content to let the person off with a fine. If this happens again we'll be more severe. So you had better pay the duty on these few little matters, without that."

If he had been expecting to "throw a scare" into her, it did not succeed. "Well, I suppose if I must, I must," she said, and the only result of the diversion was that she paid a few dollars more than had been expected and went off in a high state of mind.

Herndon had disappeared for a moment, after a whisper from Kennedy, to instruct two of his men to shadow Mademoiselle Gabrielle and, later, Pierre. He soon rejoined us and we casually returned to the vicinity of our tall friend, Number 140, for whom I felt even less respect than ever after his apparently ungallant action toward the lady he had been talking with. He seemed to notice my attitude and he remarked defensively for my benefit, "Only a patriotic act."

His inspector by this time had finished a most minute examination. There was nothing that could be discovered, not a false book with a secret spring that might disclose instead of reading matter a heap of almost priceless jewels, not a suspicious bulging of any garment or of the lining of a trunk or grip. Some of the goods might have been on his person, but not much, and certainly there was no excuse for ordering a personal examination, for he could not have hidden a tenth part of what we knew he had, even under the proverbial porous plaster. He was impeccable. Accordingly there was nothing for the inspector to do but to declare a polite armistice.

"So you didn't find 'Mona Lisa' in a false

bottom, and my trunks were not lined with smuggled cigars after all," he rasped savagely as the stamp "Passed" was at last affixed and he paid in cash at the little window with its sign, "Pay Duty Here: U. S. Custom House," some hundred dollars instead of the thousands Herndon had been hoping to collect, if not to seize.

All through the inspection, an extra close scrutiny had been kept on the other passengers as well, to prevent any of them from being in league with the smugglers, though there was no direct or indirect evidence to show that any of the others were.

We were about to leave the wharf, also, when Craig's attention was called to a stack of trunks still remaining.

"Whose are those?" he asked as he lifted one. It felt suspiciously light.

"Some of them belong to a Mr. Pierre and the rest to a Miss Gabrielle," answered an inspector. "Bonded for Troy and waiting to be transferred by the express company."

Here, perhaps, at last was an explanation, and Craig took advantage of it. Could it be that the real seat of trouble was not here but at some other place, that some exchange was to be made en route or perhaps an attempt at bribery?

Herndon, too, was willing to run a risk. He ordered the trunks opened immediately. But to our disappointment they were almost empty. There was scarcely a thing of value in them. Most of the contents consisted of clothes that had plainly been made in America and were being brought back here. It was another false scent. We had been played with and baffled at every turn. Perhaps this had been the method originally agreed on. At any rate it had been changed.

"Could they have left the goods in Paris, after all?" I queried.

"With the fall and winter trade just coming on?" Kennedy replied, with an air of finality that set at rest any doubts about his opinion on that score. "I thought perhaps we had a case of—what do you call it, Herndon, when they leave trunks that are to be secretly removed by dishonest expressmen from the wharf at night?"

"'Sleepers.' Oh, we've broken that up, too. No expressman would dare try it now. I must confess this thing is beyond me, Craig."

Kennedy made no answer. Evidently there was nothing to do but to await developments and see what Herndon's men reported. We had been beaten at every turn in the game. Herndon seemed to feel that there was a bitter sting in the defeat, particularly because the smuggler or smugglers had actually been in our grasp so long to do with as we pleased, and had so cleverly slipped out again, leaving us holding the bag.

Kennedy was especially thoughtful as he told over the facts of the case in his mind. "Of course," he remarked, "Mademoiselle Gabrielle wasn't an actress. But we can't deny that she had very little that would justify Herndon in holding her, unless he simply wants a newspaper row."

"But I thought Pierre was quite intimate with

her at first," I ventured. "That was a dirty trick of his."

Craig laughed. "You mean an old one. That was simply a blind, to divert attention from himself. I suspect they talked that over between themselves for days before."

It was plainly more perplexing than ever. What had happened? Had Pierre been a prestidigitator and had he merely said presto! when our backs were turned and whisked the goods invisibly into the country? I could find no explanation for the little drama on the pier. If Herndon's men had any genius in detecting smuggling, their professional opponent certainly had greater genius in perpetrating it.

We did not see Herndon again until after a hasty luncheon. He was in his office and inclined to take a pessimistic view of the whole affair. He brightened up when a telephone message came in from one of his shadows. The men trailing Pierre and Mademoiselle Gabrielle had crossed trails and run together at a little French restaurant on the lower West Side, where Pierre, Lang, and Mademoiselle Gabrielle had met and were dining in a most friendly spirit. Kennedy was right. She had been merely a cog in the machinery of the plot.

The man reported that even when a newsboy had been sent in by him with the afternoon papers displaying in big headlines the mystery of the death of Mademoiselle Violette, they had paid no attention. It seemed evident that whatever the fate of the little modiste, Mademoiselle Gabrielle had quite replaced her in the affections of Pierre. There was nothing for us to do but to separate and await developments.

It was late in the afternoon when Craig and I received a hurried message from Herndon. One of his men had just called him up over long distance from Riverledge. The party had left the restaurant hurriedly, and though they had taken the only taxicab in sight he had been able to follow them in time to find out that they were going up to Riverledge. They were now preparing to go out for a sail in one of Lang's motor-boats and he would be unable, of course, to follow them further.

For the remainder of the afternoon Kennedy remained pondering the case. At last an idea seemed to dawn on him. He found Herndon still at his office and made an appointment to meet on the waterfront near *La Montaigne's* pier, after dinner. The change in Kennedy's spirits was obvious, though it did not in the least enlighten my curiosity. Even after a dinner which was lengthened out considerably, I thought, I did not get appreciably nearer a solution, for we strolled over to the laboratory, where Craig loaded me down with a huge package which was wrapped up in heavy paper.

We arrived on the corner opposite the wharf just as it was growing dusk. The neighbourhood did not appeal to me at night, and even though there were two of us I was rather glad when we met Herndon, who was waiting in the shadow of a fruit stall.

But instead of proceeding across to the pier by

the side of which *La Montaigne* was moored, we cut across the wide street and turned down the next pier, where a couple of freighters were lying. The odour of salt water, sewage, rotting wood, and the night air was not inspiring. Nevertheless I was now carried away with the strangeness of our adventure.

Halfway down the pier Kennedy paused before one of the gangways that was shrouded in darkness. The door was opened and we followed gingerly across the dirty deck of the freight ship. Below we could hear the water lapping the piles of the pier. Across a dark abyss lay the grim monster *La Montaigne* with here and there a light gleaming on one of her decks. The sounds of the city seemed miles away.

"What a fine place for a murder," laughed Kennedy coolly. He was unwrapping the package which he had taken from me. It proved to be a huge reflector in front of which was placed a little arrangement which, under the light of a shaded lantern carried by Herndon, looked like a coil of wire of some kind.

To the back of the reflector Craig attached two other flexible wires which led to a couple of dry cells and a cylinder with a broadened end, made of vulcanised rubber. It might have been a telephone receiver, for all I could tell in the darkness.

While I was still speculating on the possible use of the enormous parabolic reflector, a slight commotion on the opposite side of the pier distracted my attention. A ship was coming in and was being carefully and quietly berthed alongside the other big iron freighter on that side. Herndon had left us.

"The *Mohican* is here," he remarked as he rejoined us. To my look of inquiry he added, "The revenue cutter."

Kennedy had now finished and had pointed the reflector full at *La Montaigne.* With a whispered hasty word of caution and advice to Herndon, he drew me along with him down the wharf again.

At the little door which was cut in the barrier guarding the shore end of *La Montaigne's* wharf Kennedy stopped. The customs service night watchman—there is always a watchman of some kind aboard every ship, passenger or freighter, all the time she is in port—seemed to understand, for he admitted us after a word with Kennedy.

Threading our way carefully among the boxes, and bales, and crates which were piled high, we proceeded down the wharf. Under the electric lights the longshoremen were working feverishly, for the unloading and loading of a giant trans-Atlantic vessel in the rush season is a long and tedious process at best, requiring night work and overtime, for every moment, like every cubic foot of space, counts.

Once within the door, however, no one paid much attention to us. They seemed to take it for granted that we had some right there. We boarded the ship by one of the many entrances and then proceeded down to a deck where apparently no one was working. It was more like a great house than a ship,

I felt, and I wondered whether Kennedy's search was not more of a hunt for a needle in a haystack than anything else. Yet he seemed to know what he was after.

We had descended to what I imagined must be the quarters of the steward. About us were many large cases and chests, stacked up and marked as belonging to the ship. Kennedy's attention was attracted to them immediately. All at once it flashed on me what his purpose was. In some of those cases were the smuggled goods!

Before I could say a word and before Kennedy had a chance even to try to verify his suspicions, a sudden approach of footsteps startled us. He drew me into a cabin or room full of shelves with ship's stores.

"Why didn't you bring Herndon over and break into the boxes, if you think the stuff is hidden in one of them?" I whispered.

"And let those higher up escape while their tools take all the blame?" he answered. "Sh-h."

The men who had come into the compartment looked about as if expecting to see some one.

"Two of them came down," a gruff voice said. "Where are they?"

From the noise I inferred that there must be four or five men, and from the ease with which they shifted the cases about some of them must have been pretty husky stevedores.

"I don't know," a more polished but unfamiliar voice answered.

The door to our hiding-place was opened roughly

and then banged shut before we realised it. With a taunting laugh, some one turned a key in the lock and before we could move a quick shift of packing cases against the door made escape impossible.

Here we were marooned, shanghaied, as it were, within sight if not call of Herndon and our friends. We had run up against professional smugglers, of whom I had vaguely read, disguised as stewards, deckhands, stokers, and other workers.

The only other opening to the cabin was a sort of porthole, more for ventilation than anything else. Kennedy stuck his head through it, but it was impossible for a man to squeeze out. There was one of the lower decks directly before us while a bright arc light gleamed tantalisingly over it, throwing a round circle of light into our prison. I reflected bitterly on our shipwreck within sight of port.

Kennedy remained silent, and I did not know what was working in his mind. Together we made out the outline of the freighter at the next wharf and speculated as to the location where we had left Herndon with the huge reflector. There was no moon and it was as black as ink in that direction, but if we could have got out I would have trusted to luck to reach it by swimming.

Below us, from the restless water lapping on the sides of the hulk of *La Montaigne,* we could now hear muffled sounds. It was a motor-boat which had come crawling up the river front, with lights extinguished, and had pushed a cautious nose into the slip where our ship lay at the quay. None of your romantic low-lying, rakish craft of the old smuggling yarns was this, ready for deeds of desperation in the dark hours of midnight. It was just a modern little motor-boat, up-to-date, and swift.

"Perhaps we'll get out of this finally," I grumbled as I understood now what was afoot, "but not in time to be of any use."

A smothered sound as of something going over the vessel's side followed. It was one of the boxes which we had seen outside in the storeroom. Another followed, and a third and a fourth.

Then came a subdued parley. "We have two customs detectives locked in a cabin here. We can't stay now. You'll have to take us and our things off, too."

"Can't do it," called up another muffled voice. "Make your things into a little bundle. We'll take that, but you'll have to get past the night-watchman yourselves and meet us at Riverledge."

A moment later something else went over the side, and from the sound we could infer that the engine of the motor-boat was being started.

A voice sounded mockingly outside our door. "Bon soir, you fellows in there. We're going up the dock. Sorry to leave you here till morning, but they'll let you out then. Au revoir."

Below I could hear just the faintest well-muffled chug-chug. Kennedy in the meantime had been coolly craning his neck out of our porthole under the rays of the arc light overhead. He was holding something in his hand. It seemed like a little silver-backed piece of thin glass with a flaring funnel-like thing back of it, which he held most particularly. Though he heard the parting taunt outside he paid no attention.

"You go to the deuce, whoever you are," I cried, beating on the door, to which only a coarse laugh echoed back down the passageway.

"Be quiet, Walter," ordered Kennedy. "We have located the smuggled goods in the storeroom of the steward, four wooden cases of them. I think the stuff must have been brought on the ship in the trunks and then transferred to the cases, perhaps after the code wireless message was received. But we have been overpowered and locked in a cabin with a port too small to crawl through. The cases have been lowered over the side of the ship to a motor-boat that was waiting below. The lights on the boat are out, but if you hurry you can get it. The accomplices who locked us in are going to disappear up the wharf. If you could only get the night watchman quickly enough you could catch them, too, before they reach the street."

I had turned, half expecting to see Kennedy talking to a ship's officer who might have chanced on the deck outside. There was no one. The only thing of life was the still sputtering arc light. Had the man gone crazy?

"What of it?" I growled. "Don't you suppose I know all that? What's the use of repeating it now? The thing to do is to get out of this hole. Come, help me at this door. Maybe we can batter it down."

Kennedy paid no attention to me, however, but

kept his eyes glued on the Cimmerian blackness outside the porthole.

He had done nothing apparently, yet a long finger of light seemed to shoot out into the sky from the pier across from us and begin waving back and forth as it was lowered to the dark waters of the river. It was a searchlight. At once I thought of the huge reflector which I had seen set up. But that had been on our side of the next pier and this light came from the far side where the *Mohican* lay.

"What is it?" I asked eagerly. "What has happened?"

It was as if a prayer had been answered from our dungeon on *La Montaigne*.

"I knew we should need some means to communicate with Herndon," he explained simply, "and the wireless telephone wasn't practicable. So I have used Dr. Alexander Graham Bell's photophone. Any of the lights on this side of *La Montaigne*, I knew, would serve. What I did, Walter, was merely to talk into the mouthpiece back of this little silvered mirror which reflects light. The vibrations of the voice caused a diaphragm in it to vibrate and thus the beam of reflected light was made to pulsate. In other words, this little thing is just a simple apparatus to transform the air vibrations of the voice into light vibrations.

"The parabolic reflector over there catches these light vibrations and focuses them on the cell of selenium which you perhaps noticed in the centre of the reflector. You remember doubtless that the element selenium varies its electrical resistance under light? Thus there are reproduced similar variations in the cell to those vibrations here in this transmitter. The cell is connected with a telephone receiver and batteries over there—and there you are. It is very simple. In the ordinary carbon telephone transmitter a variable electrical resistance is produced by pressure, since carbon is not so good a conductor under pressure. Then these variations are transmitted along two wires. This photophone is wireless. Selenium even emits notes under a vibratory beam of light, the pitch depending on the frequency. Changes in the intensity of the light focused by the reflector on the cell alter its electrical resistance and vary the current from the dry batteries. Hence the telephone receiver over there is affected. Bell used the photophone or radiophone over several hundred feet, Ruhmer over several miles. When you thought I was talking to myself I was really telling Herndon what had happened and what to do—talking to him literally over a beam of light."

I could scarcely believe it, but an exclamation from Kennedy as he drew his head in quickly recalled my attention. "Look out on the river, Walter," he cried. "The *Mohican* has her searchlight sweeping up and down. What do you see?"

The long finger of light had now come to rest. In its pathway I saw a lightless motor-boat bobbing up and down, crowding on all speed, yet followed relentlessly by the accusing finger. The river front was now alive with shouting.

Suddenly the *Mohican* shot out from behind the

pier where she had been hidden. In spite of Lang's expertness it was an unequal race. Nor would it have made much difference if it had been otherwise, for a shot rang out from the *Mohican* which commanded instant respect. The powerful revenue cutter rapidly overhauled the little craft.

A hurried tread down the passageway followed. Cases were being shoved aside and a key in the door of our compartment turned quickly. I waited with clenched fists, prepared for an attack.

"You're all right?" Herndon's voice inquired anxiously. "We've got that steward and the other fellows all right."

"Yes, come on," shouted Craig. "The cutter has made a capture."

We had reached the stern of the ship, and far out in the river the *Mohican* was now headed toward us. She came alongside, and Herndon quickly seized a rope, fastened it to the rail, and let himself down to the deck of the cutter. Kennedy and I followed.

"This is a high-handed proceeding," I heard a voice that must have been Lang's protesting. "By what right do you stop me? You shall suffer for this."

"The *Mohican*," broke in Herndon, "has the right to appear anywhere from Southshoal Lightship off Nantucket to the capes of the Delaware, demand an inspection of any vessel's manifest and papers, board anything from *La Montaigne* to your little motor-boat, inspect it, seize it, if necessary put a crew on it." He slapped the little cannon.

"That commands respect. Besides, you were violating the regulations—no lights."

On the deck of the cutter now lay four cases. A man broke one of them open, then another. Inside he disclosed thousands of dollars' worth of finery, while from a tray he drew several large chamois bags of glittering diamonds and pearls.

Pierre looked on, crushed, all his jauntiness gone.

"So," exclaimed Kennedy, facing him, "you have your jilted fiancée, Mademoiselle Violette, to thank for this—her letters and her suicide. It wasn't as easy as you thought to throw her over for a new soul mate, this Mademoiselle Gabrielle whom you were going to set up as a rival in business to Violette. Violette has her revenge for making a plaything of her heart, and if the dead can take any satisfaction she——"

With a quick movement Kennedy anticipated a motion of Pierre's. The ruined smuggler had contemplated either an attack on himself or his captor, but Craig had seized him by the wrist and ground his knuckles into the back of Pierre's clenched fist until he winced with pain. An Apache dagger similar to that which the little modiste had used to end her life tragedy clattered to the deck of the ship, a mute testimonial to the high class of society Pierre and his associates must have cultivated.

"None of that, Pierre," Craig muttered, releasing him. "You can't cheat the government out of its just dues even in the matter of punishment."

XI

THE INVISIBLE RAY

"I WON'T deny that I had some expectations from the old man myself."

Kennedy's client was speaking in a low, full-chested, vibrating voice, with some emotion, so low that I had entered the room without being aware that any one was there until it was too late to retreat.

"As his physician for over twelve years," the man pursued, "I certainly had been led to hope to be remembered in his will. But, Professor Kennedy, I can't put it too strongly when I say that there is no selfish motive in my coming to you about the case. There is something wrong—depend on that."

Craig had glanced up at me and, as I hesitated, I could see in an instant that the speaker was a practitioner of a type that is rapidly passing away, the old-fashioned family doctor.

"Dr. Burnham, I should like to have you know Mr. Jameson," introduced Craig. "You can talk as freely before him as you have to me alone. We always work together."

I shook hands with the visitor.

"The doctor has succeeded in interesting me greatly in a case which has some unique features," Kennedy explained. "It has to do with Stephen

Haswell, the eccentric old millionaire of Brooklyn. Have you ever heard of him?"

"Yes, indeed," I replied, recalling an occasional article which had appeared in the newspapers regarding a dusty and dirty old house in that part of the Heights in Brooklyn whence all that is fashionable had not yet taken flight, a house of mystery, yet not more mysterious than its owner in his secretive comings and goings in the affairs of men of a generation beyond his time. Further than the facts that he was reputed to be very wealthy and led, in the heart of a great city, what was as nearly like the life of a hermit as possible, I knew little or nothing. "What has he been doing now?" I asked.

"About a week ago," repeated the doctor, in answer to a nod of encouragement from Kennedy, "I was summoned in the middle of the night to attend Mr. Haswell, who, as I have been telling Professor Kennedy, had been a patient of mine for over twelve years. He had been suddenly stricken with total blindness. Since then he appears to be failing fast, that is, he appeared so the last time I saw him, a few days ago, after I had been superseded by a younger man. It is a curious case and I have thought about it a great deal. But I didn't like to speak to the authorities; there wasn't enough to warrant that, and I should have been laughed out of court for my pains. The more I have thought about it, however, the more I have felt it my duty to say something to somebody, and so, having heard of Professor Kennedy, I decided to consult him.

The fact of the matter is, I very much fear that there are circumstances which will bear sharp looking into, perhaps a scheme to get control of the old man's fortune."

The doctor paused, and Craig inclined his head, as much as to signify his appreciation of the delicate position in which Burnham stood in the case. Before the doctor could proceed further, Kennedy handed me a letter which had been lying before him on the table. It had evidently been torn into small pieces and then carefully pasted together.

The superscription gave a small town in Ohio and a date about a fortnight previous.

Dear Father [it read]: I hope you will pardon me for writing, but I cannot let the occasion of your seventy-fifth birthday pass without a word of affection and congratulation. I am alive and well—Time has dealt leniently with me in that respect, if not in money matters. I do not say this in the hope of reconciling you to me. I know that is impossible after all these cruel years. But I do wish that I could see you again. Remember, I am your only child and even if you still think I have been a foolish one, please let me come to see you once before it is too late. We are constantly travelling from place to place, but shall be here for a few days.

Your loving daughter,
GRACE HASWELL MARTIN.

" Some fourteen or fifteen years ago," explained the doctor as I looked up from reading the note, " Mr. Haswell's only daughter eloped with an artist named Martin. He had been engaged to paint a portrait of the late Mrs. Haswell from a photograph. It was the first time that Grace Haswell had ever been able to find expression for the artistic yearning which had always been repressed by the cold, practical sense of her father. She remembered her mother perfectly since the sad bereavement of her girlhood and naturally she watched and helped the artist eagerly. The result was a portrait which might well have been painted from the subject herself rather than from a cold photograph.

"Haswell saw the growing intimacy of his daughter and the artist. His bent of mind was solely toward money and material things, and he at once conceived a bitter and unreasoning hatred for Martin, who, he believed, had 'schemed' to capture his daughter and an easy living. Art was as foreign to his nature as possible. Nevertheless they went ahead and married, and, well, it resulted in the old man disinheriting the girl. The young couple disappeared bravely to make their way by their chosen profession and, as far as I know, have never been heard from since until now. Haswell made a new will and I have always understood that practically all of his fortune is to be devoted to founding the technology department in a projected university of Brooklyn."

"You have never seen this Mrs. Martin or her husband?" asked Kennedy.

"No, never. But in some way she must have learned that I had some influence with her father, for she wrote to me not long ago, enclosing a note for him and asking me to intercede for her. I did so. I took the letter to him as diplomatically as

I could. The old man flew into a towering rage, refused even to look at the letter, tore it up into bits, and ordered me never to mention the subject to him again. That is her note, which I saved. However, it is the sequel about which I wish your help."

The physician folded up the patched letter carefully before he continued. "Mr. Haswell, as you perhaps know, has for many years been a prominent figure in various curious speculations, or rather in loaning money to many curious speculators. It is not necessary to go into the different schemes which he has helped to finance. Even though most of them have been unknown to the public they have certainly given him such a reputation that he is much sought after by inventors.

"Not long ago Haswell became interested in the work of an obscure chemist over in Brooklyn, Morgan Prescott. Prescott claims, as I understand, to be able to transmute copper into gold. Whatever you think of it offhand, you should visit his laboratory yourselves, gentlemen. I am told it is wonderful, though I have never seen it and can't explain it. I have met Prescott several times while he was trying to persuade Mr. Haswell to back him in his scheme, but he was never disposed to talk to me, for I had no money to invest. So far as I know about it the thing sounds scientific and plausible enough. I leave you to judge of that. It is only an incident in my story and I will pass over it quickly. Prescott, then, believes that the elements are merely progressive variations of an original substance or base called 'protyle,' from which everything is derived. But this fellow Prescott goes much further than any of the former theorists. He does not stop with matter. He believes that he has the secret of life also, that he can make the transition from the inorganic to the organic, from inert matter to living protoplasm, and thence from living protoplasm to mind and what we call soul, whatever that may be."

"And here is where the weird and uncanny part of it comes in," commented Craig, turning from the doctor to me to call my attention particularly to what was about to follow.

"Having arrived at the point where he asserts that he can create and destroy matter, life, and mind," continued the doctor, as if himself fascinated by the idea, "Prescott very naturally does not have to go far before he also claims a control over telepathy and even a communication with the dead. He even calls the messages which he receives by a word which he has coined himself, 'telepagrams.' Thus he says he has unified the physical, the physiological, and the psychical—a system of absolute scientific monism."

The doctor paused again, then resumed. "One afternoon, about a week ago, apparently, as far as I am able to piece together the story, Prescott was demonstrating his marvellous discovery of the unity of nature. Suddenly he faced Mr. Haswell.

"'Shall I tell you a fact, sir, about yourself?' he asked quickly. 'The truth as I see it by means of my wonderful invention? If it is the truth, will you believe in me? Will you put money into my invention? Will you share in becoming fabulously rich?'

"Haswell made some noncommittal answer. But Prescott seemed to look into the machine through a very thick plate-glass window, with Haswell placed directly before it. He gave a cry. 'Mr. Haswell,' he exclaimed, 'I regret to tell you what I see. You have disinherited your daughter; she has passed out of your life and at the present moment you do not know where she is.'

"'That's true,' replied the old man bitterly, 'and more than that I don't care. Is that all you see? That's nothing new.'

"'No, unfortunately, that is not all I see. Can you bear something further? I think you ought to know it. I have here a most mysterious telepagram.'

"'Yes. What is it? Is she dead?'

"'No, it is not about her. It is about yourself. To-night at midnight or perhaps a little later,' repeated Prescott solemnly, 'you will lose your sight as a punishment for your action.'

"'Pouf!' exclaimed the old man in a dudgeon, 'if that is all your invention can tell me, good-bye. You told me you were able to make gold. Instead, you make foolish prophecies. I'll put no money into such tomfoolery. I'm a practical man,' and with that he stamped out of the laboratory.

"Well, that night, about one o'clock, in the silence of the lonely old house, the aged caretaker, Jane, whom he had hired after he banished his daughter from his life, heard a wild shout of 'Help! Help!' Haswell, alone in his room on the second floor, was groping about in the dark.

"'Jane,' he ordered, 'a light—a light.'

"'I have lighted the gas, Mr. Haswell,' she cried.

"A groan followed. He had himself found a match, had struck it, had even burnt his fingers with it, yet he saw nothing.

"The blow had fallen. At almost the very hour which Prescott, by means of his weird telepagram had predicted, old Haswell was stricken.

"'I'm blind,' he gasped. 'Send for Dr. Burnham.'

"I went to him immediately when the maid roused me, but there was nothing I could do except prescribe perfect rest for his eyes and keeping in a dark room in the hope that his sight might be restored as suddenly and miraculously as it had been taken away.

"The next morning, with his own hand, trembling and scrawling in his blindness, he wrote the following on a piece of paper:

"'MRS. GRACE MARTIN.—Information wanted about the present whereabouts of Mrs. Grace Martin, formerly Grace Haswell of Brooklyn.

STEPHEN HASWELL,
—— Pierrepont St., Brooklyn.

"This advertisement he caused to be placed in all the New York papers and to be wired to the leading Western papers. Haswell himself was a changed man after his experience. He spoke bitterly of Prescott, yet his attitude toward his daughter was completely reversed. Whether he admitted to himself a belief in the prediction of the inventor, I do not know. Certainly he scouted such an idea in telling me about it.

" A day or two after the advertisements appeared a telegram came to the old man from a little town in Indiana. It read simply: 'Dear Father: Am starting for Brooklyn to-day. Grace.'

" The upshot was that Grace Haswell, or rather Grace Martin, appeared the next day, forgave and was forgiven with much weeping, although the old man still refused resolutely to be reconciled with and receive her husband. Mrs. Martin started in to clean up the old house. A vacuum cleaner sucked a ton or two of dust from it. Everything was changed. Jane grumbled a great deal, but there was no doubt a great improvement. Meals were served regularly. The old man was taken care of as never before. Nothing was too good for him. Everywhere the touch of a woman was evident in the house. The change was complete. It even extended to me. Some friend had told her of an eye and ear specialist, a Dr. Scott, who was engaged. Since then, I understand, a new will has been made, much to the chagrin of the trustees of the projected school. Of course I am cut out of the new will, and that with the knowledge at least of the woman who once appealed to me, but it does not influence me in coming to you."

" But what has happened since to arouse suspicion?" asked Kennedy, watching the doctor furtively.

"Why, the fact is that, in spite of all this added care, the old man is failing more rapidly than ever. He never goes out except attended and not much even then. The other day I happened to meet Jane on the street. The faithful old soul poured forth a long story about his growing dependence on others and ended by mentioning a curious red discoloration that seems to have broken out over his face and hands. More from the way she said it than from what she said I gained the impression that something was going on which should be looked into."

"Then you perhaps think that Prescott and Mrs. Martin are in some way connected in this case?" I hazarded.

I had scarcely framed the question before he replied in an emphatic negative. "On the contrary, it seems to me that if they know each other at all it is with hostility. With the exception of the first stroke of blindness"—here he lowered his voice earnestly—"practically every misfortune that has overtaken Mr. Haswell has been since the advent of this new Dr. Scott. Mind, I do not wish even to breathe that Mrs. Martin has done anything except what a daughter should do. I think she has shown herself a model of forgiveness and devotion. Nevertheless the turn of events under the new treatment has been so strange that almost it makes one believe that there might be something occult about it—or wrong with the new doctor."

"Would it be possible, do you think, for us to see Mr. Haswell?" asked Kennedy, when Dr. Burnham had come to a full stop after pouring forth his suspicions. "I should like to see this Dr. Scott. But first I should like to get into the old house without exciting hostility."

The doctor was thoughtful. "You'll have to arrange that yourself," he answered. "Can't you think up a scheme? For instance, go to him with a proposal like the old schemes he used to finance. He is very much interested in electrical inventions. He made his money by speculation in telegraphs and telephones in the early days when they were more or less dreams. I should think a wireless system of television might at least interest him and furnish an excuse for getting in, although I am told his daughter discourages all tangible investment in the schemes that used to interest his active mind."

"An excellent idea," exclaimed Kennedy. "It is worth trying anyway. It is still early. Suppose we ride over to Brooklyn with you. You can direct us to the house and we'll try to see him."

It was still light when we mounted the high steps of the house of mystery across the bridge. Mrs. Martin, who met us in the parlour, proved to be a stunning looking woman with brown hair and beautiful dark eyes. As far as we could see the old house plainly showed the change. The furniture and ornaments were of a period long past, but everything was scrupulously neat. Hanging over the old marble mantel was a painting which quite evidently was that of the long since deceased Mrs. Haswell, the mother of Grace. In spite of the hideous style of dress of the period after the war, she had evidently been a very beautiful woman with large masses of light chestnut hair and blue eyes which the painter had succeeded in catching with almost life-likeness for a portrait.

It took only a few minutes for Kennedy, in his most engaging and plausible manner, to state the hypothetical reason of our call. Though it was perfectly self-evident from the start that Mrs. Martin would throw cold water on anything requiring an outlay of money Craig accomplished his full purpose of securing an interview with Mr. Haswell. The invalid lay propped up in bed, and as we entered he heard us and turned his sightless eyes in our direction almost as if he saw.

Kennedy had hardly begun to repeat and elaborate the story which he had already told regarding his mythical friend who had at last a commercial wireless "televue," as he called it on the spur of the moment, when Jane, the aged caretaker, announced Dr. Scott. The new doctor was a youthfully dressed man, clean-shaven, but with an undefinable air of being much older than his smooth face led one to suppose. As he had a large practice, he said, he would beg our pardon for interrupting but would not take long.

It needed no great powers of observation to see that the old man placed great reliance on his new doctor and that the visit partook of a social as well as a professional nature. Although they talked low we could catch now and then a word or phrase.

Dr. Scott bent down and examined the eyes of his patient casually. It was difficult to believe that they saw nothing, so bright was the blue of the iris.

"Perfect rest for the present," the doctor directed, talking more to Mrs. Martin than to the old man. "Perfect rest, and then when his health is good, we shall see what can be done with that cataract."

He was about to leave, when the old man reached up and restrained him, taking hold of the doctor's wrist tightly, as if to pull him nearer in order to whisper to him without being overheard. Kennedy was sitting in a chair near the head of the bed, some feet away, as the doctor leaned down. Haswell, still holding his wrist, pulled him closer. I could not hear what was said, though somehow I had an impression that they were talking about Prescott, for it would not have been at all strange if the old man had been greatly impressed by the alchemist.

Kennedy, I noticed, had pulled an old envelope from his pocket and was apparently engaged in jotting down some notes, glancing now and then from his writing to the doctor and then to Mr. Haswell.

The doctor stood erect in a few moments and rubbed his wrist thoughtfully with the other hand, as if it hurt. At the same time he smiled on Mrs. Martin. "Your father has a good deal of strength yet, Mrs. Martin," he remarked. "He has a wonderful constitution. I feel sure that we can pull him out of this and that he has many, many years to live."

Mr. Haswell, who caught the words eagerly, brightened visibly, and the doctor passed out. Kennedy resumed his description of the supposed wireless picture apparatus which was to revolutionise the newspaper, the theatre, and daily life in general. The old man did not seem enthusiastic and turned to his daughter with some remark.

"Just at present," commented the daughter, with an air of finality, "the only thing my father is much interested in is a way in which to recover his sight without an operation. He has just had a rather unpleasant experience with one inventor. I think it will be some time before he cares to embark in any other such schemes."

Kennedy and I excused ourselves with appropriate remarks of disappointment. From his preoccupied manner it was impossible for me to guess whether Craig had accomplished his purpose or not.

"Let us drop in on Dr. Burnham since we are over here," he said when we had reached the street. "I have some questions to ask him."

The former physician of Mr. Haswell lived not very far from the house we had just left. He appeared a little surprised to see us so soon, but very interested in what had taken place.

"Who is this Dr. Scott?" asked Craig when we were seated in the comfortable leather chairs of the old-fashioned consulting-room.

"Really, I know no more about him than you do," replied Burnham. I thought I detected a little of professional jealousy in his tone, though he went on frankly enough, "I have made inquiries and I can find out nothing except that he is supposed to be a graduate of some Western medical school and came to this city only a short time ago. He has hired a small office in a new building devoted entirely to doctors and they tell me that he is an eye and ear specialist, though I cannot see that he has any practice. Beyond that I know nothing about him."

"Your friend Prescott interests me, too," remarked Kennedy, changing the subject quickly.

"Oh, he is no friend of mine," returned the doctor, fumbling in a drawer of his desk. "But I think I have one of his cards here which he gave me when we were introduced some time ago at Mr. Haswell's. I should think it would be worth while to see him. Although he has no use for me because I have neither money nor influence, still you might take this card. Tell him you are from the university, that I have interested you in him, that you know a trustee with money to invest—anything you like that is plausible. When are you going to see him?"

"The first thing in the morning," replied Kennedy. "After I have seen him I shall drop in for another chat with you. Will you be here?"

The doctor promised, and we took our departure.

Prescott's laboratory, which we found the next day from the address on the card, proved to be situated in one of the streets near the waterfront under the bridge approach, where the factories and warehouses clustered thickly. It was with a great deal of anticipation of seeing something happen that we threaded our way through the maze of streets with the cobweb structure of the bridge carrying its endless succession of cars arching high over our heads. We had nearly reached the place when Kennedy paused and pulled out two pairs of glasses, those huge round tortoiseshell affairs.

"You needn't mind these, Walter," he explained. "They are only plain glass, that is, not ground. You can see through them as well as through air. We must be careful not to excite suspicion. Perhaps a disguise might have been better, but I think this will do. There—they add at least a decade to your age. If you could see yourself you wouldn't speak to your reflection. You look as scholarly as a Chinese mandarin. Remember, let me do the talking and do just as I do."

We had now entered the shop, stumbled up the dark stairs, and presented Dr. Burnham's card with a word of explanation along the lines which he had suggested. Prescott, surrounded by his retorts, crucibles, burettes, and condensers, received us much more graciously than I had had any reason to anticipate. He was a man in the late forties, his face covered with a thick beard, and his eyes, which seemed a little weak, were helped out with glasses almost as scholarly as ours.

I could not help thinking that we three bespectacled figures lacked only the flowing robes to be taken for a group of mediæval alchemists set down a few centuries out of our time in the murky light of Prescott's sanctum. Yet, though he accepted us at our face value, and began to talk of his strange discoveries there was none of the old familiar prating about matrix and flux, elixir, magisterium, magnum opus, the mastery and the quintessence, those alternate names for the philosopher's stone which Paracelsus, Simon Forman, Jerome Cardan, and the other mediæval worthies indulged in. This experience at least was as up-to-date as the Curies, Becquerel, Ramsay, and the rest.

"Transmutation," remarked Prescott, "was, as you know, finally declared to be a scientific absurdity in the eighteenth century. But I may say that it is no longer so regarded. I do not ask you to believe anything until you have seen; all I ask is that you maintain the same open mind which the most progressive scientists of to-day exhibit in regard to the subject."

Kennedy had seated himself some distance from a curious piece or rather collection of apparatus over which Prescott was working. It consisted of numerous coils and tubes.

"It may seem strange to you, gentlemen," Prescott proceeded, "that a man who is able to produce gold from, say, copper should be seeking capital from other people. My best answer to that old objection is that I am not seeking capital, as such. The situation with me is simply this. Twice I have applied to the patent office for a patent on my invention. They not only refuse to grant it, but they refuse to consider the application or even to give me a chance to demonstrate my process to them.

On the other hand, suppose I try this thing secretly. How can I prevent any one from learning my trade secret, leaving me, and making gold on his own account? Men will desert as fast as I educate them. Think of the economic result of that; it would turn the world topsy-turvy. I am looking for some one who can be trusted to the last limit to join with me, furnish the influence and standing while I furnish the brains and the invention. Either we must get the government interested and sell the invention to it, or we must get government protection and special legislation. I am not seeking capital; I am seeking protection. First let me show you something."

He turned a switch, and a part of the collection of apparatus began to vibrate.

"You are undoubtedly acquainted with the modern theories of matter," he began, plunging into the explanation of his process. "Starting with the atom, we believe no longer that it is indivisible. Atoms are composed of thousands of ions, as they are called,—really little electric charges. Again, you know that we have found that all the elements fall into groups. Each group has certain related atomic weights and properties which can be and have been predicted in advance of the discovery of missing elements in the group. I started with the reasonable assumption that the atom of one element in a group could be modified so as to become the atom of another element in the group, that one group could perhaps be transformed into another, and so on, if only I knew the force that would change the number or modify the vibrations of these ions composing the various atoms.

"Now for years I have been seeking that force or combination of forces that would enable me to produce this change in the elements—raising or lowering them in the scale, so to speak. I have found it. I am not going to tell you or any other man whom you may interest the secret of how it is done until I find some one I can trust as I trust myself. But I am none the less willing that you should see the results. If they are not convincing, then nothing can be."

He appeared to be debating whether to explain further, and finally resumed: "Matter thus being in reality a manifestation of force or ether in motion, it is necessary to change and control that force and motion. This assemblage of machines here is for that purpose. Now a few words as to my theory."

He took a pencil and struck a sharp blow on the table. "There you have a single blow," he said, "just one isolated noise. Now if I strike this tuning fork you have a vibrating note. In other words, a succession of blows or wave vibrations of a certain kind affects the ear and we call it sound, just as a succession of other wave vibrations affects the retina and we have sight. If a moving picture moves slower than a certain number of pictures a minute you see the separate pictures; faster it is one moving picture.

"Now as we increase the rapidity of wave vibration and decrease the wave length we pass from sound waves to heat waves or what are known as the infra-red waves, those which lie below the red in the spectrum of light. Next we come to light, which is composed of the seven colours as you know from seeing them resolved in a prism. After that are what are known as the ultra-violet rays, which lie beyond the violet of white light. We also have electric waves, the waves of the alternating current, and shorter still we find the Hertzian waves, which are used in wireless. We have only begun to know of X-rays and the alpha, beta, and gamma rays from them, of radium, radioactivity, and finally of this new force which I have discovered and call 'protodyne,' the original force.

"In short, we find in the universe Matter, Force, and Ether. Matter is simply ether in motion, is composed of corpuscles, electrically charged ions, or electrons, moving units of negative electricity about one one-thousandth part of the hydrogen atom. Matter is made up of electricity and nothing but electricity. Let us see what that leads to. You are acquainted with Mendeléeff's periodic table?"

He drew forth a huge chart on which all the eighty or so elements were arranged in eight groups or octaves and twelve series. Selecting one, he placed his finger on the letters "Au," under which was written the number, 197.2. I wondered what the mystic letters and figures meant.

"That," he explained, "is the scientific name for the element gold and the figure is its atomic weight. You will see," he added, pointing down the second vertical column on the chart, "that gold belongs to the hydrogen group—hydrogen, lithium, sodium, potassium, copper, rubidium, silver, caesium, then two blank spaces for elements yet to be discovered to science, then gold, and finally another unknown element."

Running his finger along the eleventh, horizontal series, he continued: "The gold series—not the group—reads gold, mercury, thallium, lead, bismuth, and other elements known only to myself. For the known elements, however, these groups and series are now perfectly recognised by all scientists; they are determined by the fixed weight of the atom, and there is a close approximation to regularity.

"This twelfth series is interesting. So far only radium, thorium, and uranium are generally known. We know that the radioactive elements are constantly breaking down, and one often hears uranium, for instance, called the 'parent' of radium. Radium also gives off an emanation, and among its products is helium, quite another element. Thus the transmutation of matter is well known within certain bounds to all scientists to-day like yourself, Professor Kennedy. It has even been rumoured but never proved that copper has been transformed into lithium—both members of the hydrogen-gold group, you will observe. Copper to lithium is going backward, so to speak. It has remained for me to devise this protodyne apparatus by which I can reverse that process of decay and go forward in the table, so to put it—can change lithium into copper and copper into gold. I can create and destroy matter by protodyne."

He had been fingering a switch as he spoke. Now he turned it on triumphantly. A curious snapping and crackling noise followed, becoming more rapid, and as it mounted in intensity I could smell a pungent odour of ozone which told of an electric discharge. On went the machine until we could feel heat radiating from it. Then came a piercing burst of greenish-blue light from a long tube which looked like a curious mercury vapour lamp.

After a few minutes of this Prescott took a small crucible of black lead. "Now we are ready to try it," he cried in great excitement. "Here I have a crucible containing some copper. Any substance in the group would do, even hydrogen if there was any way I could handle the gas. I place it in the machine—so. Now if you could watch inside you would see it change; it is now rubidium, now silver, now caesium. Now it is a hitherto unknown element which I have named after myself, presium, now a second unknown element, cottium—ah!—there we have gold."

He drew forth the crucible, and there glowed in it a little bead or globule of molten gold.

"I could have taken lead or mercury and by varying the process done the same thing with the gold series as well as the gold group," he said, regarding the globule with obvious pride. "And I can put this gold back and bring it out copper or hydrogen, or better yet, can advance it instead of cause it to decay, and can get a radioactive element which I have named morganium—after my first name, Morgan Prescott. Morganium is a radioactive element next in the series to radium and much more active. Come closer and examine the gold."

Kennedy shook his head as if perfectly satisfied to accept the result. As for me I knew not what to think. It was all so plausible and there was the bead of gold, too, that I turned to Craig for enlightenment. Was he convinced? His face was inscrutable.

But as I looked I could see that Kennedy had been holding concealed in the palm of his hand a bit of what might be a mineral. From my position I could see the bit of mineral glowing, but Prescott could not.

"Might I ask," interrupted Kennedy, "what that curious greenish or bluish light from the tube is composed of?"

Prescott eyed him keenly for an instant through his thick glasses. Craig had shifted his gaze from the bit of mineral in his own hand, but was not looking at the light. He seemed to be indifferently contemplating Prescott's hand as it rested on the switch.

"That, sir," replied Prescott slowly, "is an emanation due to this new force, protodyne, which I use. It is a manifestation of energy, sir, that may run changes not only through the whole gamut of the elements, but is capable of transforming the ether itself into matter, matter into life, and life into mind. It is the outward sign of the unity of nature, the——"

"The means by which you secure the curious

telepagrams I have heard of?" inquired Kennedy eagerly.

Prescott looked at him sharply, and for a moment I thought his face seemed to change from a livid white to an apoplectic red, although it may have been only the play of the weird light. When he spoke it was with no show of even suppressed surprise.

"Yes," he answered calmly. "I see that you have heard something of them. I had a curious case a few days ago. I had hoped to interest a certain capitalist of high standing in this city. I had showed him just what I have showed you, and I think he was impressed by it. Then I thought to clinch the matter by a telepagram, but for some reason or other I failed to consult the forces I control as to the wisdom of doing so. Had I, I should have known better. But I went ahead in self-confidence and enthusiasm. I told him of a long banished daughter with whom, in his heart, he was really wishing to become reconciled but was too proud to say the word. He resented it. He started to stamp out of this room, but not before I had another telepagram which told of a misfortune that was soon to overtake the old man himself. If he had given me a chance I might have saved him, at least have flashed a telepagram to that daughter myself, but he gave me no chance. He was gone.

"I do not know precisely what happened after that, but in some way this man found his daughter, and to-day she is living with him. As for my hopes of getting assistance from him, I lost them from the moment when I made my initial mistake of telling him something distasteful. The daughter hates me and I hate her. I have learned that she never ceases advising the old man against all schemes for investment except those bearing moderate interest and readily realised on. Dr. Burnham—I see you know him—has been superseded by another doctor, I believe. Well, well, I am through with that incident. I must get assistance from other sources. The old man, I think, would have tricked me out of the fruits of my discovery anyhow. Perhaps I am fortunate. Who knows?"

A knock at the door cut him short. Prescott opened it, and a messenger boy stood there. "Is Professor Kennedy here?" he inquired.

Craig motioned to the boy, signed for the message, and tore it open. "It is from Dr. Burnham," he exclaimed, handing the message to me.

"Mr. Haswell is dead," I read. "Looks to me like asphyxiation by gas or some other poison. Come immediately to his house. Burnham."

"You will pardon me," broke in Craig to Prescott, who was regarding us without the slightest trace of emotion, "but Mr. Haswell, the old man to whom I know you referred, is dead, and Dr. Burnham wishes to see me immediately. It was only yesterday that I saw Mr. Haswell and he seemed in pretty good health and spirits. Prescott, though there was no love lost between you and the old man, I would esteem it a great favour if you would accompany me to the house. You need not take any responsibility unless you desire."

His words were courteous enough, but Craig spoke in a tone of quiet authority which Prescott found it impossible to deny. Kennedy had already started to telephone to his own laboratory, describing a certain suitcase to one of his students and giving his directions. It was only a moment later that we were panting up the sloping street that led from the river front. In the excitement I scarcely noticed where we were going until we hurried up the steps to the Haswell house.

The aged caretaker met us at the door. She was in tears. Upstairs in the front room where we had first met the old man we found Dr. Burnham working frantically over him. It took only a minute to learn what had happened. The faithful Jane had noticed an odour of gas in the hall, had traced it to Mr. Haswell's room, had found him unconscious, and instinctively, forgetting the new Dr. Scott, had rushed forth for Dr. Burnham. Near the bed stood Grace Martin, pale but anxiously watching the efforts of the doctor to resuscitate the blue-faced man who was stretched cold and motionless on the bed.

Dr. Burnham paused in his efforts as we entered. "He is dead, all right," he whispered, aside. "I have tried everything I know to bring him back, but he is beyond help."

There was still a sickening odour of illuminating gas in the room, although the windows were now all open.

Kennedy, with provoking calmness in the excitement, turned from and ignored Dr. Burnham.

"Have you summoned Dr. Scott?" he asked Mrs. Martin.

"No," she replied, surprised. "Should I have done so?"

"Yes. Send Jame immediately. Mr. Prescott, will you kindly be seated for a few moments."

Taking off his coat, Kennedy advanced to the bed where the emaciated figure lay, cold and motionless. Craig knelt down at Mr. Haswell's head and took the inert arms, raising them up until they were extended straight. Then he brought them down, folded upward at the elbow at the side. Again and again he tried this Sylvester method of inducing respiration, but with no more result than Dr. Burnham had secured. He turned the body over on its face and tried the new Schaefer method. There seemed to be not a spark of life left.

"Dr. Scott is out," reported the maid breathlessly, "but they are trying to locate him from his office, and if they do they will send him around immediately."

A ring at the doorbell caused us to think that he had been found, but it proved to be the student to whom Kennedy had telephoned at his own laboratory. He was carrying a heavy suitcase and a small tank.

Kennedy opened the suitcase hastily and disclosed a little motor, some long tubes of rubber fitting into a small rubber cap, forceps, and other paraphernalia. The student quickly attached one tube to the little tank, while Kennedy grasped the tongue of the dead man with the forceps, pulled it up off the soft palate, and fitted the rubber cap snugly over his mouth and nose.

"This is the Draeger pulmotor," he explained as he worked, "devised to resuscitate persons who have died of electric shock, but actually found to be of more value in cases of asphyxiation. Start the motor."

The pulmotor began to pump. One could see the dead man's chest rise as it was inflated with oxygen forced by the accordion bellows from the tank through one of the tubes into the lungs. Then it fell as the oxygen and the poisonous gas were slowly sucked out through the other tube. Again and again the process was repeated, about ten times a minute.

Dr. Burnham looked on in undisguised amazement. He had long since given up all hope. The man was dead, medically dead, as dead as ever was any gas victim at this stage on whom all the usual methods of resuscitation had been tried and had failed.

Still, minute after minute, Kennedy worked faithfully on, trying to discover some spark of life and to fan it into flame. At last, after what seemed to be a half-hour of unremitting effort, when the oxygen had long since been exhausted and only fresh air was being pumped into the lungs and out of them, there was a first faint glimmer of life in the heart and a touch of colour in the cheeks. Haswell was coming to. Another half-hour found him muttering and rambling weakly.

"The letter—the letter," he moaned, rolling his

glazed eyes about. "Where is the letter? Send for Grace."

The moan was so audible that it was startling. It was like a voice from the grave. What did it all mean? Mrs. Martin was at his side in a moment.

"Father, father,—here I am—Grace. What do you want?"

The old man moved restlessly, feverishly, and pressed his trembling hand to his forehead as if trying to collect his thoughts. He was weak, but it was evident that he had been saved.

The pulmotor had been stopped. Craig threw the cap to his student to be packed up, and as he did so he remarked quietly, "I could wish that Dr. Scott had been found. There are some matters here that might interest him."

He paused and looked slowly from the rescued man lying dazed on the bed toward Mrs. Martin. It was quite apparent even to me that she did not share the desire to see Dr. Scott, at least not just then. She was flushed and trembling with emotion. Crossing the room hurriedly she flung open the door into the hall.

"I am sure," she cried, controlling herself with difficulty and catching at a straw, as it were, "that you gentlemen, even if you have saved my father, are no friends of either his or mine. You have merely come here in response to Dr. Burnham, and he came because Jane lost her head in the excitement and forgot that Dr. Scott is now our physician."

"But Dr. Scott could not have been found in time, madame," interposed Dr. Burnham with evident triumph.

She ignored the remark and continued to hold the door open.

"Now leave us," she implored, "you, Dr. Burnham, you, Mr. Prescott, you, Professor Kennedy, and your friend Mr. Jameson, whoever you may be."

She was now cold and calm. In the bewildering change of events we had forgotten the wan figure on the bed still gasping for the breath of life. I could not help wondering at the woman's apparent lack of gratitude, and a thought flashed over my mind. Had the affair come to a contest between various parties fighting by fair means or foul for the old man's money—Scott and Mrs. Martin perhaps against Prescott and Dr. Burnham? No one moved. We seemed to be waiting on Kennedy. Prescott and Mrs. Martin were now glaring at each other implacably.

The old man moved restlessly on the bed, and over my shoulder I could hear him gasp faintly, "Where's Grace? Send for Grace."

Mrs. Martin paid no attention, seemed not to hear, but stood facing us imperiously as if waiting for us to obey her orders and leave the house. Burnham moved toward the door, but Prescott stood his ground with a peculiar air of defiance. Then he took my arm and started rather precipitately, I thought, to leave.

"Come, come," said somebody behind us, "enough of the dramatics."

It was Kennedy, who had been bending down, listening to the muttering of the old man.

"Look at those eyes of Mr. Haswell," he said. "What colour are they?"

We looked. They were blue.

"Down in the parlour," continued Kennedy leisurely, "you will find a portrait of the long deceased Mrs. Haswell. If you will examine that painting you will see that her eyes are also a peculiarly limpid blue. No couple with blue eyes ever had a black-eyed child. At least, if this is such a case, the Carnegie Institution investigators would be glad to hear of it, for it is contrary to all that they have discovered on the subject after years of study of eugenics. Dark-eyed couples may have light-eyed children, but the reverse, never. What do you say to that, madame?"

"You lie," screamed the woman, rushing frantically past us. "I *am* his daughter. No interlopers shall separate us. Father!"

The old man moved feebly away from her.

"Send for Dr. Scott again," she demanded. "See if he cannot be found. He must be found. You are all enemies, villains."

She addressed Kennedy, but included the whole room in her denunciation.

"Not all," broke in Kennedy remorselessly. "Yes, madame, send for Dr. Scott. Why is he not here?"

Prescott, with one hand on my arm and the other on Dr. Burnham's, was moving toward the door.

"One moment, Prescott," interrupted Kennedy,

detaining him with a look. " There was something I was about to say when Dr. Burnham's urgent message prevented it. I did not take the trouble even to find out how you obtained that little globule of molten gold from the crucible of alleged copper. There are so many tricks by which the gold could have been 'salted' and brought forth at the right moment that it was hardly worth while. Besides, I had satisfied myself that my first suspicions were correct. See that?"

He held out the little piece of mineral I had already seen in his hand in the alchemist's laboratory.

"That is a piece of willemite. It has the property of glowing or fluorescing under a certain kind of rays which are themselves invisible to the human eye. Prescott, your story of the transmutation of elements is very clever, but not more clever than your real story. Let us piece it together. I had already heard from Dr. Burnham how Mr. Haswell was induced by his desire for gain to visit you and how you had most mysteriously predicted his blindness. Now, there is no such thing as telepathy, at least in this case. How then was I to explain it? What could cause such a catastrophe naturally? Why, only those rays invisible to the human eye, but which make this piece of willemite glow—the ultra-violet rays."

Kennedy was speaking rapidly and was careful not to pause long enough to give Prescott an opportunity to interrupt him.

"These ultra-violet rays," he continued, "are

always present in an electric arc light though not to a great degree unless the carbons have metal cores. They extend for two octaves above the violet of the spectrum and are too short to affect the eye as light, although they affect photographic plates. They are the friend of man when he uses them in moderation as Finsen did in the famous blue light treatment. But they tolerate no familiarity. To let them—particularly the shorter of the rays—enter the eye is to invite trouble. There is no warning sense of discomfort, but from six to eighteen hours after exposure to them the victim experiences violent pains in the eyes and headache. Sight may be seriously impaired, and it may take years to recover. Often prolonged exposure results in blindness, though a moderate exposure acts like a tonic. The rays may be compared in this double effect to drugs, such as strychnine. Too much of them may be destructive even to life itself."

Prescott had now paused and was regarding Kennedy contemptuously. Kennedy paid no attention, but continued: "Perhaps these mysterious rays may shed some light on our minds, however. Now, for one thing, ultra-violet light passes readily through quartz, but is cut off by ordinary glass, especially if it is coated with chromium. Old Mr. Haswell did not wear glasses. Therefore he was subject to the rays—the more so as he is a blond, and I think it has been demonstrated by investigators that blonds are more affected by them than are brunettes.

"You have, as a part of your machine, a peculiarly shaped quartz mercury vapour lamp, and the mercury vapour lamp of a design such as that I saw has been invented for the especial purpose of producing ultra-violet rays in large quantity. There are also in your machine induction coils for the purpose of making an impressive noise, and a small electric furnace to heat the salted gold. I don't know what other ingenious fakes you have added. The visible bluish light from the tube is designed, I suppose, to hoodwink the credulous, but the dangerous thing about it is the invisible ray that accompanies that light. Mr. Haswell sat under those invisible rays, Prescott, never knowing how deadly they might be to him, an old man.

"You knew that they would not take effect for hours, and hence you ventured the prediction that he would be stricken at about midnight. Even if it was partial or temporary, still you would be safe in your prophecy. You succeeded better than you hoped in that part of your scheme. You had already prepared the way by means of a letter sent to Mr. Haswell through Dr. Burnham. But Mr. Haswell's credulity and fear worked the wrong way. Instead of appealing to you he hated you. In his predicament he thought only of his banished daughter and turned instinctively to her for help. That made necessary a quick change of plans."

Prescott, far from losing his nerve, turned on us bitterly. "I knew you two were spies the moment I saw you," he shouted. "It seemed as if in some way I knew you for what you were, as if I knew you had seen Mr. Haswell before you came to me. You, too, would have robbed an inventor as I am sure he would. But have a care, both of you. You may be punished also by blindness for your duplicity. Who knows?"

A shudder passed over me at the horrible thought contained in his mocking laugh. Were we doomed to blindness, too? I looked at the sightless man on the bed in alarm.

"I knew that you would know us," retorted Kennedy calmly. "Therefore we came provided with spectacles of Euphos glass, precisely like those you wear. No, Prescott, we are safe, though perhaps we may have some burns like those red blotches on Mr. Haswell, light burns."

Prescott had fallen back a step and Mrs. Martin was making an effort to appear stately and end the interview.

"No," continued Craig, suddenly wheeling, and startling us by the abruptness of his next exposure, "it is you and your wife here—Mrs. Prescott, not Mrs. Martin—who must have a care. Stop glaring at each other. It is no use playing at enemies longer and trying to get rid of us. You overdo it. The game is up."

Prescott made a rush at Kennedy, who seized him by the wrist and held him tightly in a grasp of steel that caused the veins on the back of his hands to stand out like whipcords.

"This is a deep-laid plot," he went on calmly, still holding Prescott, while I backed up against the door and cut off his wife; "but it is not so difficult to see it after all. Your part was to destroy the eyesight of the old man, to make it necessary for him to call on his daughter. Your wife's part was to play the role of Mrs. Martin, whom he had not seen for years and could not see now. She was to persuade him, with her filial affection, to make her the beneficiary of his will, to see that his money was kept readily convertible into cash.

"Then, when the old man was at last out of the way, you two could decamp with what you could realise before the real daughter, cut off somewhere across the continent, could hear of the death of her father. It was an excellent scheme. But Haswell's plain, material newspaper advertisement was not so effective for your purposes, Prescott, as the more artistic 'telepagram,' as you call it. Although you two got in first in answering the advertisement, it finally reached the right person after all. You didn't get away quickly enough.

"You were not expecting that the real daughter would see it and turn up so soon. But she has. She lives in California. Mr. Haswell in his delirium has just told of receiving a telegram which I suppose you, Mrs. Prescott, read, destroyed, and acted upon. It hurried your plans, but you were equal to the emergency. Besides, possession is nine points in the law. You tried the gas, making it look like a suicide. Jane, in her excitement, spoiled that, and Dr. Burnham, knowing where I was, as it happened, was able to summon me immediately. Circumstances have been against you from the first, Prescott."

Craig was slowly twisting up the hand of the

inventor, which he still held. With his other hand he pulled a paper from his pocket. It was the old envelope on which he had written upon the occasion of our first visit to Mr. Haswell when we had been so unceremoniously interrupted by the visit of Dr. Scott.

"I sat here yesterday by this bed," continued Craig, motioning toward the chair he had occupied, as I remembered. "Mr. Haswell was telling Dr. Scott something in an undertone. I could not hear it. But the old man grasped the doctor by the wrist to pull him closer to whisper to him. The doctor's hand was toward me and I noticed the peculiar markings of the veins.

"You perhaps are not acquainted with the fact, but the markings of the veins in the back of the hand are peculiar to each individual—as infallible, indestructible, and ineffaceable as finger prints or the shape of the ear. It is a system invented and developed by Professor Tamassia of the University of Padua, Italy. A superficial observer would say that all vein patterns were essentially similar, and many have said so, but Tamassia has found each to be characteristic and all subject to almost incredible diversities. There are six general classes—in this case before us, two large veins crossed by a few secondary veins forming a V with its base near the wrist.

"Already my suspicions had been aroused. I sketched the arrangement of the veins standing out on that hand. I noted the same thing just now on the hand that manipulated the fake apparatus in the laboratory. Despite the difference in make-up Scott and Prescott are the same.

"The invisible rays of the ultra-violet light may have blinded Mr. Haswell, even to the recognition of his own daughter, but you can rest assured, Prescott, that the very cleverness of your scheme will penetrate the eyes of the blindfolded goddess of justice. Burnham, if you will have the kindness to summon the police, I will take all the responsibility for the arrest of these people."

XII

THE CAMPAIGN GRAFTER

"WHAT a relief it will be when this election is over and the newspapers print news again," I growled as I turned the first page of the *Star* with a mere glance at the headlines.

"Yes," observed Kennedy, who was puzzling over a note which he had received in the morning mail. "This is the bitterest campaign in years. Now, do you suppose that they are after me in a professional way or are they trying to round me up as an independent voter?"

The letter which had called forth this remark was headed, "The Travis Campaign Committee of the Reform League," and, as Kennedy evidently intended me to pass an opinion on it, I picked it up. It was only a few lines, requesting him to call during the morning, if convenient, on Wesley Travis, the candidate for governor and the treasurer of his campaign committee, Dean Bennett. It had evidently been written in great haste in longhand the night before.

"Professional," I hazarded. "There must be some scandal in the campaign for which they require your services."

"I suppose so," agreed Craig. "Well, if it is business instead of politics it has at least this merit—it is current business. I suppose you have no objection to going with me?"

Thus it came about that not very much later in the morning we found ourselves at the campaign headquarters, in the presence of two nervous and high-keyed gentlemen in frock coats and silk hats. It would have taken no great astuteness, even without seeing the surroundings, to deduce instantly that they were engaged in the annual struggle of seeking the votes of their fellow-citizens for something or other, and were nearly worn out by the arduous nature of that process.

Their headquarters were in a tower of a skyscraper, whence poured forth a torrent of appeal to the moral sense of the electorate, both in printed and oral form. Yet there was a different tone to the place from that which I had ordinarily associated with political headquarters in previous campaigns. There was an absence of the old-fashioned politicians and of the air of intrigue laden with tobacco. Rather, there was an air of earnestness and efficiency which was decidedly prepossessing. Maps of the state were hanging on the walls, some stuck full of various coloured pins denoting the condition of the canvass. A map of the city in colours, divided into all sorts of districts, told how fared the battle in the stronghold of the boss, Billy McLoughlin. Huge systems of card indexes, loose leaf devices, labour-saving appliances for getting out a vast mass of campaign "literature" in a hurry, in short a perfect system, such as a great, well-managed business might have been proud of, were in evidence everywhere.

Wesley Travis was a comparatively young man,

a lawyer who had early made a mark in politics and had been astute enough to shake off the thraldom of the bosses before the popular uprising against them. Now he was the candidate of the Reform League for governor and a good stiff campaign he was putting up.

His campaign manager, Dean Bennett, was a business man whose financial interests were opposed to those usually understood to be behind Billy McLoughlin, of the regular party to which both Travis and Bennett might naturally have been supposed to belong in the old days. Indeed the Reform League owed its existence to a fortunate conjunction of both moral and economic conditions demanding progress.

"Things have been going our way up to the present," began Travis confidentially, when we were seated democratically with our campaign cigars lighted. "Of course we haven't such a big 'barrel' as our opponents, for we are not frying the fat out of the corporations. But the people have supported us nobly, and I think the opposition of the vested interests has been a great help. We seem to be winning, and I say 'seem' only because one can never be certain how anything is going in this political game nowadays.

"You recall, Mr. Kennedy, reading in the papers that my country house out on Long Island was robbed the other day? Some of the reporters made much of it. To tell the truth, I think they had become so satiated with sensations that they were sure that the thing was put up by some muckrakers and that there would be an exposé of some kind. For the thief, whoever he was, seems to have taken nothing from my library but a sort of scrap-book or album of photographs. It was a peculiar robbery, but as I had nothing to conceal it didn't worry me. Well, I had all but forgotten it when a fellow came into Bennett's office here yesterday and demanded—tell us what it was, Bennett. You saw him."

Bennett cleared his throat. "You see, it was this way. He gave his name as Harris Hanford and described himself as a photographer. I think he has done work for Billy McLoughlin. At any rate, his offer was to sell us several photographs, and his story about them was very circumstantial. He hinted that they had been evidently among those stolen from Mr. Travis and that in a roundabout way they had come into the possession of a friend of his without his knowing who the thief was. He said that he had not made the photographs himself, but had an idea by whom they were made, that the original plates had been destroyed, but that the person who made them was ready to swear that the pictures were taken after the nominating convention this fall which had named Travis. At any rate the photographs were out and the price for them was $25,000."

"What are they that he should set such a price on them?" asked Kennedy, keenly looking from Bennett quickly to Travis.

Travis met his look without flinching. "They are supposed to be photographs of myself," he replied slowly. "One purports to represent me in a group on McLoughlin's porch at his farm on the south shore of the island, about twenty miles from my place. As Hanford described it, I am standing between McLoughlin and J. Cadwalader Brown, the trust promoter who is backing McLoughlin to save his investments. Brown's hand is on my shoulder and we are talking familiarly. Another is a picture of Brown, McLoughlin, and myself riding in Brown's car, and in it Brown and I are evidently on the best of terms. Oh, there are several of them, all in the same vein. Now," he added, and his voice rose with emotion as if he were addressing a cart-tail meeting which must be convinced that there was nothing criminal in riding in a motor-car, "I don't hesitate to admit that a year or so ago I was not on terms of intimacy with these men, but at least acquainted with them. At various times, even as late as last spring, I was present at conferences over the presidential outlook in this state, and once I think I did ride back to the city with them. But I know that there were no pictures taken, and even if there had been I would not care if they told the truth about them. I have frankly admitted in my speeches that I knew these men, that my knowledge of them and breaking from them is my chief qualification for waging an effective war on them if I am elected. They hate me cordially. You know that. What I do care about is the sworn allegation that now accompanies these—these fakes. They were not, could not have been taken after the independent convention that nominated me. If the photographs were true I would be a fine traitor. But I haven't even seen McLoughlin or Brown since last spring. The whole thing is a——"

"Lie from start to finish," put in Bennett emphatically. "Yes, Travis, we all know that. I'd quit right now if I didn't believe in you. But let us face the facts. Here is this story, sworn to as Hanford says and apparently acquiesced in by Billy McLoughlin and Cad. Brown. What do they care anyhow as long as it is against you? And there, too, are the pictures themselves—at least they will be in print or suppressed, according as we act. Now, you know that nothing could hurt the reform ticket worse than to have an issue like this raised at this time. We were supposed at least to be on the level, with nothing to explain away. There may be just enough people to believe that there is some basis for this suspicion to turn the tide against us. If it were earlier in the campaign I'd say accept the issue, fight it out to a finish, and in the turn of events we should really have the best campaign material. But it is too late now to expose such a knavish trick of theirs on the Friday before election. Frankly, I believe discretion is the better part of valour in this case and without abating a jot of my faith in you, Travis, well, I'd pay first and expose the fraud afterward, after the election, at leisure."

"No, I won't," persisted Travis, shutting his square jaw doggedly. "I won't be held up."

The door had opened and a young lady in a very stunning street dress, with a huge hat and a tantalising veil, stood in it for a moment, hesitated, and then was about to shut it with an apology for intruding on a conference.

"I'll fight it if it takes my last dollar," declared Travis, "but I won't be blackmailed out of a cent. Good-morning, Miss Ashton. I'll be free in a moment. I'll see you in your office directly."

The girl, with a portfolio of papers in her hand, smiled, and Travis quickly crossed the room and held the door deferentially open as he whispered a word or two. When she had disappeared he returned and remarked, "I suppose you have heard of Miss Margaret Ashton, the suffragette leader, Mr. Kennedy? She is the head of our press bureau." Then a heightened look of determination set his fine face in hard lines, and he brought his fist down on the desk. "No, not a cent," he thundered.

Bennett shrugged his shoulders hopelessly and looked at Kennedy in mock resignation as if to say, "What can you do with such a fellow?" Travis was excitedly pacing the floor and waving his arms as if he were addressing a meeting in the enemy's country. "Hanford comes at us in this way," he continued, growing more excited as he paced up and down. "He says plainly that the pictures will of course be accepted as among those stolen from me, and in that, I suppose, he is right. The public will swallow it. When Bennett told him I would prosecute he laughed and said, 'Go ahead. I didn't steal the pictures. That would be a great joke for Travis to seek redress from the courts he is criticising. I guess he'd want to recall the decision if it went against him—hey?' Hanford says that a hundred copies have been made of each of the photographs and that this person, whom we do not know, has them ready to drop into the mail to the one hundred leading papers of the state in time for them to appear in the Monday editions just before Election Day. He says no amount of denying on our part can destroy the effect—or at least he went further and said 'shake their validity.'

"But I repeat. They are false. For all I know, it is a plot of McLoughlin's, the last fight of a boss for his life, driven into a corner. And it is meaner than if he had attempted to forge a letter. Pictures appeal to the eye and mind much more than letters. That's what makes the thing so dangerous. Billy McLoughlin knows how to make the best use of such a roorback on the eve of an election, and even if I not only deny but prove that they are a fake, I'm afraid the harm will be done. I can't reach all the voters in time. Ten see such a charge to one who sees the denial."

"Just so," persisted Bennett coolly. "You admit that we are practically helpless. That's what I have been saying all along. Get control of the prints first, Travis, for God's sake. Then raise any kind of a howl you want—before election or after. As I say, if we had a week or two it might be all right to fight. But we can make no move without making fools of ourselves until they are published Monday as the last big thing of the campaign. The rest of Monday and the Tuesday morning papers do *not* give us time to reply. Even if they were published to-day we should hardly have time to expose the plot, hammer it in, and make the issue an asset instead of a liability. No, you must admit it yourself. There isn't time. We must carry out the work we have so carefully planned to cap the campaign, and if we are diverted by this it means a let-up in our final efforts, and that is as good as McLoughlin wants anyhow. Now, Kennedy, don't you agree with me? Squelch the pictures now at any cost, then follow the thing up and, if we can, prosecute after election?"

Kennedy and I, who had been so far little more than interested spectators, had not presumed to interrupt. Finally Craig asked, "You have copies of the pictures?"

"No," replied Bennett. "This Hanford is a brazen fellow, but he was too astute to leave them. I saw them for an instant. They look bad. And the affidavits with them look worse."

"H'm," considered Kennedy, turning the crisis over in his mind. "We've had alleged stolen and forged letters before, but alleged stolen and forged photographs are new. I'm not surprised that you are alarmed, Bennett,—nor that you want to fight, Travis."

"Then you will take up the case?" urged the latter eagerly, forgetting both his campaign manager and his campaign manners, and leaning forward almost like a prisoner in the dock to catch the words of the foreman of the jury. "You will trace down the forger of those pictures before it is too late?"

" I haven't said I'll do that—yet," answered Craig measuredly. " I haven't even said I'd take up the case. Politics is a new game to me, Mr. Travis. If I go into this thing I want to go into it and stay in it—well, you know how you lawyers put it, with clean hands. On one condition I'll take the matter up, and on only one."

" Name it," cried Travis anxiously.

" Of course, having been retained by you," continued Craig with provoking slowness, " it is not reasonable to suppose that if I find—how shall I put it—bluntly, yes?—if I find that the story of Hanford has some—er—foundation, it is not reasonable to suppose that I should desert you and go over to the other side. Neither is it to be supposed that I will continue and carry such a thing through for you regardless of truth. What I ask is to have a free hand, to be able to drop the case the moment I cannot proceed further in justice to myself, drop it, and keep my mouth shut. You understand? These are my conditions and no less."

" And you think you can make good? " questioned Bennett rather sceptically. " You are willing to risk it? You don't think it would be better to wait until after the election is won? "

" You have heard my conditions," reiterated Craig.

" Done," broke in Travis. " I'm going to fight it out, Bennett. If we get in wrong by dickering with them at the start it may be worse for us in the end. Paying amounts to confession."

Bennett shook his head dubiously. " I'm afraid

this will suit McLoughlin's purpose just as well. Photographs are like statistics. They don't lie unless the people who make them do. But it's hard to tell what a liar can accomplish with either in an election."

"Say, Dean, you're not going to desert me?" reproached Travis. "You're not offended at my kicking over the traces, are you?"

Bennett rose, placed a hand on Travis's shoulder, and grasped his other. "Wesley," he said earnestly, "I wouldn't desert you even if the pictures were true."

"I knew it," responded Travis heartily. "Then let Mr. Kennedy have one day to see what he can do. Then if we make no progress we'll take your advice, Dean. We'll pay, I suppose, and ask Mr. Kennedy to continue the case after next Tuesday."

"With the proviso," put in Craig.

"With the proviso, Kennedy," repeated Travis. "Your hand on that. Say, I think I've shaken hands with half the male population of this state since I was nominated, but this means more to me than any of them. Call on us, either Bennett or myself, the moment you need aid. Spare no reasonable expense, and—and get the goods, no matter whom it hits higher up, even if it is Cadwalader Brown himself. Good-bye and a thousand thanks —oh, by the way, wait. Let me take you around and introduce you to Miss Ashton. She may be able to help you."

The office of Bennett and Travis was in the centre of the suite. On one side were the cashier and clerical force as well as the speakers' bureau, where spellbinders of all degrees were getting instruction, tours were being laid out, and reports received from meetings already held.

On the other side was the press bureau with a large and active force in charge of Miss Ashton, who was supporting Travis because he had most emphatically declared for "Votes for Women" and had insisted that his party put this plank in its platform. Miss Ashton was a clever girl, a graduate of a famous woman's college, and had had several years of newspaper experience before she became a leader in the suffrage cause. I recalled having read and heard a great deal about her, though I had never met her. The Ashtons were well known in New York society, and it was a sore trial to some of her conservative friends that she should reject what they considered the proper "sphere" for women. Among those friends, I understood, was Cadwalader Brown himself.

Travis had scarcely more than introduced us, yet already I scented a romance behind the ordinarily prosaic conduct of a campaign press bureau. It is far from my intention to minimise the work or the ability of the head of the press bureau, but it struck me, both then and later, that the candidate had an extraordinary interest in the newspaper campaign, much more than in the speakers' bureau, and I am sure that it was not solely accounted for by the fact that publicity is playing a more and more important part in political campaigning.

Nevertheless such innovations as her card index

system by election districts all over the state, showing the attitude of the various newspaper editors, of local political leaders, and changes of sentiment, were very full and valuable. Kennedy, who had a regular pigeon-hole mind for facts, was visibly impressed by this huge mechanical memory built up by Miss Ashton. Though he said nothing to me I knew he had also observed the state of affairs between the reform candidate and the suffrage leader.

It was at a moment when Travis had been called back to his office that Kennedy, who had been eyeing Miss Ashton with marked approval, leaned over and said in a low voice, "Miss Ashton, I think I can trust you. Do you want to do a great favour for Mr. Travis?"

She did not betray even by a fleeting look on her face what the true state of her feelings was, although I fancied that the readiness of her assent had perhaps more meaning than she would have placed in a simple "Yes" otherwise.

"I suppose you know that an attempt is being made to blackmail Mr. Travis?" added Kennedy quickly.

"I know something about it," she replied in a tone which left it for granted that Travis had told her before even we were called in. I felt that not unlikely Travis's set determination to fight might be traceable to her advice or at least to her opinion of him.

"I suppose in a large force like this it is not impossible that your political enemies may have a spy or two," observed Kennedy, glancing about at the score or more clerks busily engaged in getting out " literature."

" I have sometimes thought that myself," she agreed. " But of course I don't know. Still, I have to be pretty careful. Some one is always over here by my desk or looking over here. There isn't much secrecy in a big room like this. I never leave important stuff lying about where any of them could see it."

" Yes," mused Kennedy. " What time does the office close? "

" We shall finish to-night about nine, I think. To-morrow it may be later."

" Well, then, if I should call here to-night at, say, half-past nine, could you be here? I need hardly say that your doing so may be of inestimable value to—to the campaign."

" I shall be here," she promised, giving her hand with a peculiar straight arm shake and looking him frankly in the face with those eyes which even the old guard in the legislature admitted were vote-winners.

Kennedy was not quite ready to leave yet, but sought out Travis and obtained permission to glance over the financial end of the campaign. There were few large contributors to Travis's fund, but a host of small sums ranging from ten and twenty-five dollars down to dimes and nickels. Truly it showed the depth of the popular uprising. Kennedy also glanced hastily over the items of expense—rent, salaries, stenographer and office force, advertising, printing and stationery, postage, telephone, telegraph, automobile and travelling expenses, and miscellaneous matters.

As Kennedy expressed it afterwards, as against the small driblets of money coming in, large sums were going out for expenses in lumps. Campaigning in these days costs money even when done honestly. The miscellaneous account showed some large indefinite items, and after a hasty calculation Kennedy made out that if all the obligations had to be met immediately the committee would be in the hole for several thousand dollars.

"In short," I argued as we were leaving, "this will either break Travis privately or put his fund in hopeless shape. Or does it mean that he foresees defeat and is taking this way to recoup himself under cover of being held up?"

Kennedy said nothing in response to my suspicions, though I could see that in his mind he was leaving no possible clue unnoted.

It was only a few blocks to the studio of Harris Hanford, whom Kennedy was now bent on seeing. We found him in an old building on one of the side streets in the thirties which business had captured. His was a little place on the top floor, up three flights of stairs, and I noticed as we climbed up that the room next to his was vacant.

Our interview with Hanford was short and unsatisfactory. He either was or at least posed as representing a third party in the affair, and absolutely refused to permit us to have even a glance at the photographs.

"My dealings," he asserted airily, "must all be

with Mr. Bennett, or with Mr. Travis, direct, not with emissaries. I don't make any secret about it. The prints are not here. They are safe and ready to be produced at the right time, either to be handed over for the money or to be published in the newspapers. We have found out all about them; we are satisfied, although the negatives have been destroyed. As for their having been stolen from Travis, you can put two and two together. They are out and copies have been made of them, good copies. If Mr. Travis wishes to repudiate them, let him start proceedings. I told Bennett all about that. To-morrow is the last day, and I must have Bennett's answer then, without any interlopers coming into it. If it is yes, well and good; if not, then they know what to expect. Good-bye."

It was still early in the forenoon, and Kennedy's next move was to go out on Long Island to examine the library at Travis's from which the pictures were said to have been stolen. At the laboratory Kennedy and I loaded ourselves with a large oblong black case containing a camera and a tripod.

His examination of the looted library was minute, taking in the window through which the thief had apparently entered, the cabinet he had forced, and the situation in general. Finally Craig set up his camera with most particular care and took several photographs of the window, the cabinet, the doors, including the room from every angle. Outside he snapped the two sides of the corner of the house in which the library was situated. Partly by trolley and partly by carriage we crossed the island to the south shore, and finally found McLoughlin's farm, where we had no trouble in getting half a dozen photographs of the porch and house. Altogether the proceedings seemed tame to me, yet I knew from previous experience that Kennedy had a deep laid purpose.

We parted in the city, to meet just before it was time to visit Miss Ashton. Kennedy had evidently employed the interval in developing his plates, for he now had ten or a dozen prints, all of exactly the same size, mounted on stiff cardboard in a space with scales and figures on all four sides. He saw me puzzling over them.

"Those are metric photographs such as Bertillon of Paris takes," he explained. "By means of the scales and tables and other methods that have been worked out we can determine from those pictures distances and many other things almost as well as if we were on the spot itself. Bertillon has cleared up many crimes with this help, such as the mystery of the shooting in the Hotel Quai d'Orsay and other cases. The metric photograph, I believe, will in time rank with the portrait parlé, finger prints, and the rest.

"For instance, in order to solve the riddle of a crime the detective's first task is to study the scene topographically. Plans and elevations of a room or house are made. The position of each object is painstakingly noted. In addition, the all-seeing eye of the camera is called into requisition. The plundered room is photographed, as in this case. I might have done it by placing a foot rule on a table and taking that in the picture, but a more scientific and accurate method has been devised by Bertillon. His camera lens is always used at a fixed height from the ground and forms its image on the plate at an exact focus. The print made from the negative is mounted on a card in a space of definite size, along the edges of which a metric scale is printed. In the way he has worked it out the distance between any two points in the picture can be determined. With a topographical plan and a metric photograph one can study a crime as a general studies the map of a strange country. There were several peculiar things that I observed to-day, and I have here an indelible record of the scene of the crime. Preserved in this way it cannot be questioned.

"Now the photographs were in this cabinet. There are other cabinets, but none of them has been disturbed. Therefore the thief must have known just what he was after. The marks made in breaking the lock were not those of a jimmy but of a screwdriver. No amazing command of the resources of science is needed so far. All that is necessary is a little scientific common sense, Walter.

"Now, how did the robber get in? All the windows and doors were supposedly locked. It is alleged that a pane was cut from this window at the side. It was, and the pieces were there to show it. But take a glance at this outside photograph. To reach that window even a tall man must have stood on a ladder or something. There are no marks of a ladder or of any person in the soft soil under the window. What is more, that window was cut from the inside. The marks of the diamond which cut it plainly show that. Scientific common sense again."

"Then it must have been some one in the house or at least some one familiar with it?" I exclaimed.

Kennedy nodded. "One thing we have which the police greatly neglect," he pursued, "a record. We have made some progress in reconstructing the crime, as Bertillon calls it. If we only had those Hanford pictures we should be all right."

We were now on our way to see Miss Ashton at headquarters, and as we rode downtown I tried to reason out the case. Had it really been a put-up job? Was Travis himself faking, and was the robbery a "plant" by which he might forestall exposure of what had become public property in the hands of another, no longer disposed to conceal it? Or was it after all the last desperate blow of the Boss?

The whole thing began to assume a suspicious look in my mind. Although Kennedy seemed to have made little real progress, I felt that, far from aiding Travis, it made things darker. There was nothing but his unsupported word that he had not visited the Boss subsequent to the nominating convention. He admitted having done so before the Reform League came into existence. Besides it seemed tacitly understood that both the Boss and Cadwalader Brown acquiesced in the sworn statement of the man who said he had made the pictures. Added to that the mere existence of the actual pictures themselves was a graphic clincher to the story. Personally, if I had been in Kennedy's place I think I should have taken advantage of the proviso in the compact with Travis to back out gracefully. Kennedy, however, now started on the case, hung to it tenaciously.

Miss Ashton was waiting for us at the press bureau. Her desk was at the middle of one end of the room in which, if she could keep an eye on her office force, the office force also could keep an eye on her.

Kennedy had apparently taken in the arrangement during our morning visit, for he set to work immediately. The side of the room toward the office of Travis and Bennett presented an expanse of blank wall. With a mallet he quickly knocked a hole in the rough plaster, just above the baseboard about the room. The hole did not penetrate quite through to the other side. In it he placed a round disc of vulcanised rubber, with insulated wires leading down back of the baseboard, then out underneath it, and under the carpet. Some plaster quickly closed up the cavity in the wall, and he left it to dry.

Next he led the wires under the carpet to Miss Ashton's desk. There they ended, under the carpet and a rug, eighteen or twenty huge coils several feet in diameter disposed in such a way as to attract no attention by a curious foot on the carpet which covered them.

"That is all, Miss Ashton," he said as we watched for his next move. "I shall want to see you early to-morrow, and,—might I ask you to be sure to wear that hat which you have on?"

It was a very becoming hat, but Kennedy's tone clearly indicated that it was not his taste in inverted basket millinery that prompted the request. She promised, smiling, for even a suffragette may like pretty hats.

Craig had still to see Travis and report on his work. The candidate was waiting anxiously at his hotel after a big political mass meeting on the East Side, at which capitalism and the bosses had been hissed to the echo, if that is possible.

"What success?" inquired Travis eagerly.

"I'm afraid," replied Kennedy, and the candidate's face fell at the tone, "I'm afraid you will have to meet them, for the present. The time limit will expire to-morrow, and I understand Hanford is coming up for a final answer. We must have copies of those photographs, even if we have to pay for them. There seems to be no other way."

Travis sank back in his chair and regarded Kennedy hopelessly. He was actually pale. "You—you don't mean to say that there is no other way, that I'll have to admit even before Bennett—and others that I'm in bad?"

"I wouldn't put it that way," said Kennedy mercilessly, I thought.

"It is that way," Travis asserted almost fiercely. "Why, we could have done that anyhow. No, no,—I don't mean that. Pardon me. I'm upset by this. Go ahead," he sighed.

"You will direct Bennett to make the best terms

he can with Hanford when he comes up to-morrow. Have him arrange the details of payment and then rush the best copies of the photographs to me."

Travis seemed crushed.

We met Miss Ashton the following morning entering her office. Kennedy handed her a package, and in a few words, which I did not hear, explained what he wanted, promising to call again later.

When we called, the girls and other clerks had arrived, and the office was a hive of industry in the rush of winding up the campaign. Typewriters were clicking, clippings were being snipped out of a huge stack of newspapers and pasted into large scrap-books, circulars were being folded and made ready to mail for the final appeal. The room was indeed crowded, and I felt that there was no doubt, as Kennedy had said, that nothing much could go on there unobserved by any one to whose interest it was to see it.

Miss Ashton was sitting at her desk with her hat on directing the work. "It works," she remarked enigmatically to Kennedy.

"Good," he replied. "I merely dropped in to be sure. Now if anything of interest happens, Miss Ashton, I wish you would let me know immediately. I must not be seen up here, but I shall be waiting downstairs in the corridor of the building. My next move depends entirely on what you have to report."

Downstairs Craig waited with growing impatience. We stood in an angle in which we could see without being readily seen, and our impatience was not diminished by seeing Hanford enter the elevator.

I think that Miss Ashton would have made an excellent woman detective, that is, on a case in which her personal feelings were not involved as they were here. She was pale and agitated as she appeared in the corridor, and Kennedy hurried toward her.

"I can't believe it. I won't believe it," she managed to say.

"Tell me, what happened?" urged Kennedy soothingly.

"Oh, Mr. Kennedy, why did you ask me to do this?" she reproached. "I would almost rather not have known it at all."

"Believe me, Miss Ashton," said Kennedy, "you ought to know. It is on you that I depend most. We saw Hanford go up. What occurred?"

She was still pale, and replied nervously, "Mr. Bennett came in about quarter to ten. He stopped to talk to me and looked about the room curiously. Do you know, I felt very uncomfortable for a time. Then he locked the door leading from the press bureau to his office, and left word that he was not to be disturbed. A few minutes later a man called."

"Yes, yes," prompted Kennedy. "Hanford, no doubt."

She was racing on breathlessly, scarcely giving one a chance to inquire how she had learned so much.

"Why," she cried with a sort of defiant ring in her tone, "Mr. Travis is going to buy those pictures after all. And the worst of it is that I met him in the hall coming in as I was coming down here, and he tried to act toward me in the same old way—and that after all I know now about him. They have fixed it all up, Mr. Bennett acting for Mr. Travis, and this Mr. Hanford. They are even going to ask me to carry the money in a sealed envelope to the studio of this fellow Hanford, to be given to a third person who will be there at two o'clock this afternoon."

"You, Miss Ashton?" inquired Kennedy, a light breaking on his face as if at last he saw something.

"Yes, I," she repeated. "Hanford insisted that it was part of the compact. They—they haven't asked me openly yet to be the means of carrying out their dirty deals, but when they do, I—I won't——"

"Miss Ashton," remonstrated Kennedy, "I beg you to be calm. I had no idea you would take it like this, no idea. Please, please. Walter, you will excuse us if we take a turn down the corridor and out in the air. This is most extraordinary."

For five or ten minutes Kennedy and Miss Ashton appeared to be discussing the new turn of events earnestly, while I waited impatiently. As they approached again she seemed calmer, but I heard her say, "I hope you're right. I'm all broken up by it. I'm ready to resign. My faith in human nature is shaken. No, I won't expose Wesley Travis for his sake. It cuts me to have to admit it, but Cadwalader used always to say that every man has his price. I am afraid this will do great harm to the cause of reform and through it to the woman suffrage cause which cast its lot with this party. I—I can hardly believe——"

Kennedy was still looking earnestly at her. "Miss Ashton," he implored, "believe nothing. Remember one of the first rules of politics is loyalty. Wait until——"

"Wait?" she echoed. "How can I? I hate Wesley Travis for giving in—more than I hate Cadwalader Brown for his cynical disregard of honesty in others."

She bit her lip at thus betraying her feelings, but what she had heard had evidently affected her deeply. It was as though the feet of her idol had turned to clay. Nevertheless it was evident that she was coming to look on it more as she would if she were an outsider.

"Just think it over," urged Kennedy. "They won't ask you right away. Don't do anything rash. Suspend judgment. You won't regret it."

Craig's next problem seemed to be to transfer the scene of his operations to Hanford's studio. He was apparently doing some rapid thinking as we walked uptown after leaving Miss Ashton, and I did not venture to question him on what had occurred when it was so evident that everything depended on being prepared for what was still to occur.

Hanford was out. That seemed to please Kennedy, for with a brightening face, which told more surely than words that he saw his way more and more clearly, he asked me to visit the agent and hire the vacant office next to the studio while he went uptown to complete his arrangements for the final step.

I had completed my part and was waiting in the empty room when he returned. He lost no time in getting to work, and it seemed to me as I watched him curiously in silence that he was repeating what he had already done at the Travis headquarters. He was boring into the wall, only this time he did it much more carefully, and it was evident that if he intended putting anything into this cavity it must be pretty large. The hole was square, and as I bent over I could see that he had cut through the plaster and laths all the way to the wallpaper on the other side, though he was careful to leave that intact. Then he set up a square black box in the cavity, carefully poising it and making measurements that told of the exact location of its centre with reference to the partitions and walls.

A skeleton key took us into Hanford's well-lighted but now empty studio. For Miss Ashton's sake I wished that the photographs had been there. I am sure Kennedy would have found slight compunction in a larceny of them, if they had been. It was something entirely different that he had in mind now, however, and he was working quickly for fear of discovery. By his measurements I guessed that he was calculating as nearly as possible the centre of the box which he had placed in the hole in the wall on the other side of the dark wallpaper. When he had quite satisfied himself he took a fine pencil from his pocket and made a light cross on the paper to indicate it. The dot fell to the left of a large calendar hanging on the wall.

Kennedy's appeal to Margaret Ashton had evidently had its effect, for when we saw her a few moments after these mysterious preparations she had overcome her emotion.

"They have asked me to carry a note to Mr. Hanford's studio," she said quietly, "and without letting them know that I know anything about it I have agreed to do so."

"Miss Ashton," said Kennedy, greatly relieved, "you're a trump."

"No," she replied, smiling faintly, "I'm just feminine enough to be curious."

Craig shook his head, but did not dispute the point. "After you have handed the envelope to the person, whoever it may be, in Hanford's studio, wait until he does something—er,—suspicious. Meanwhile look at the wall on the side toward the next vacant office. To the left of the big calendar you will see a light pencil mark, a cross. Somehow you must contrive to get near it, but don't stand in front of it. Then if anything happens stick this little number 10 needle in the wall right at the intersection of the cross. Withdraw it quickly, count fifteen, then put this little sticker over the cross, and get out as best you can, though we shan't be far away if you should need us. That's all."

We did not accompany her to the studio for fear of being observed, but waited impatiently in the next office. We could hear nothing of what was said, but when a door shut and it was evident that she had gone, Kennedy quickly removed something from the box in the wall covered with a black cloth.

As soon as it was safe Kennedy had sent me posting after her to secure copies of the incriminating photographs which were to be carried by her from the studio, while he remained to see who came out. I thought a change had come over her as she handed me the package with the request that I carry it to Mr. Bennett and get them from him.

The first inkling I had that Kennedy had at last been able to trace back something in the mysterious doings of the past two days came the following evening, when Craig remarked casually that he would like to have me call on Billy McLoughlin if I had no engagement. I replied that I had none—and managed to squirm out of the one I really had.

The Boss's office was full of politicians, for it was the eve of "dough day," when the purse strings were loosed and a flood of potent argument poured forth to turn the tide of election. Hanford was there with the other ward heelers.

"Mr. McLoughlin," began Kennedy quietly, when we were seated alone with Hanford in the little sanctum of the Boss, "you will pardon me if I seem a little slow in coming to the business that has brought me here to-night. First of all, I may say, and you, Hanford, being a photographer will appreciate it, that ever since the days of Daguerre photography has been regarded as the one infallible means of portraying faithfully any object, scene, or action. Indeed a photograph is admitted in court as irrefutable evidence. For when everything else fails, a picture made through the photographic lens almost invariably turns the tide. However, such a picture upon which the fate of an important case may rest should be subjected to critical examination for it is an established fact that a photograph may be made as untruthful as it may be reliable. Combination photographs change entirely the character of the initial negative and have been made for the past fifty years. The earliest, simplest, and most harmless photographic deception is the printing of clouds into a bare sky. But the retoucher with his pencil and etching tool to-day is very skilful. A workman of ordinary skill can introduce a person taken in a studio into an open-air scene well blended and in complete harmony without a visible trace of falsity.

"I need say nothing of how one head can be put on another body in a picture, nor need I say what a double exposure will do. There is almost no limit to the changes that may be wrought in form and feature. It is possible to represent a person crossing Broadway or walking on Riverside Drive, places he may never have visited. Thus a person charged with an offence may be able to prove an alibi by the aid of a skilfully prepared combination photograph.

"Where, then, can photography be considered as irrefutable evidence? The realism may convince all, will convince all, except the expert and the initiated after careful study. A shrewd judge will insist that in every case the negative be submitted and examined for possible alterations by a clever manipulator."

Kennedy bent his gaze on McLoughlin. "Now, I do not accuse you, sir, of anything. But a photograph has come into the possession of Mr. Travis in which he is represented as standing on the steps of your house with yourself and Mr. Cadwalader Brown. He and Mr. Brown are in poses that show the utmost friendliness. I do not hesitate to say that that was originally a photograph of yourself, Mr. Brown, and your own candidate. It is a pretty raw deal, a fake in which Travis has been substituted by very excellent photographic forgery."

McLoughlin motioned to Hanford to reply. "A fake?" repeated the latter contemptuously. "How about the affidavits? There's no negative. You've got to prove that the original print stolen from Travis, we'll say, is a fake. You can't do it."

"September 19th was the date alleged, I believe?" asked Kennedy quietly, laying down the bundle of metric photographs and the alleged photographs of Travis. He was pointing to a shadow of a gable on the house as it showed in the metric photographs and the others.

"You see that shadow of the gable? Perhaps you never heard of it, Hanford, but it is possible to tell the exact time at which a photograph was taken from a study of the shadows. It is possible in principle and practice and can be trusted. Almost any scientist may be called on to bear testimony in court nowadays, but you would say the astronomer is one of the least likely. Well, the shadow in this picture will prove an alibi for some one.

"Notice. It is seen very prominently to the right, and its exact location on the house is an easy matter. You could almost use the metric photograph for that. The identification of the gable casting the shadow is easy. To be exact it is 19.62 feet high. The shadow is 14.23 feet down, 13.10 feet east, and 3.43 feet north. You see I am exact. I have to be. In one minute it moved 0.080 feet upward, 0.053 feet to the right, and 0.096 feet in its apparent path. It passes the width of a weatherboard, 0.37 foot, in four minutes and thirty-seven seconds."

Kennedy was talking rapidly of data which he had derived from his metric photograph, from plumb line, level, compass, and tape, astronomical triangle, vertices, zenith, pole and sun, declination, azimuth, solar time, parallactic angles, refraction, and a dozen bewildering terms.

"In spherical trigonometry," he concluded, "to solve the problem three elements must be known. I knew four. Therefore I could take each of the known, treat it as unknown, and have four ways to check my result. I find that the time might have been either three o'clock, twenty-one minutes and twelve seconds, in the afternoon, or 3:21:31, or 3:21:29, or 3:21:33. The average is 3:21:26, and there can therefore be no appreciable error except for a few seconds. For that date must have been one of two days, either May 22 or July 22. Between these two dates we must decide on evidence other than the shadow. It must have been in May, as the immature condition of the foliage shows. But even if it had been in July, that is far from being September. The matter of the year I have also settled. Weather conditions, I find, were favourable on all these dates except that in September. I can really answer, with an assurance and accuracy superior to that of the photographer himself—even if he were honest—as to the real date. The real picture, aside from being doctored, was actually taken last May. Science is not fallible, but exact in this matter."

Kennedy had scored a palpable hit. McLoughlin and Hanford were speechless. Still Craig hurried on.

"But, you may ask, how about the automobile picture? That also is an unblushing fake. Of course I must prove that. In the first place, you know that the general public has come to recognise the distortion of a photograph as denoting speed. A picture of a car in a race that doesn't lean is rejected—people demand to see speed, speed, more speed even in pictures. Distortion does indeed show speed, but that, too, can be faked.

"Hanford knows that the image is projected upside down by the lens on the plate, and that the bottom of the picture is taken before the top. The camera mechanism admits light, which makes the picture, in the manner of a roller blind curtain. The slit travels from the top to the bottom and the image on the plate being projected upside down, the bottom of the object appears on the top of the plate. For instance, the wheels are taken before the head of the driver. If the car is moving quickly the image moves on the plate and each successive part is taken a little in advance of the last. The whole leans forward. By widening the slit and slowing the speed of the shutter, there is more distortion.

"Now, this is what happened. A picture was taken of Cadwalader Brown's automobile, probably at rest, with Brown in it. The matter of faking Travis or any one else by his side is simple. If with an enlarging lantern the image of this faked picture is thrown on the paper like a lantern slide, and if the right hand side is a little further away than the left, the top further away than the bottom, you can print a fraudulent high speed ahead picture. True, everything else in the picture, even if motionless, is distorted, and the difference between this faking and the distortion of the shutter can be seen by an expert. But it will pass. In this case, however, the faker was so sure of that that he was careless. Instead of getting the plate further from the paper on the right he did so on the left. It was further away on the bottom than on the top. He got distortion all right, enough still to satisfy the uninitiated. But it was distortion in the wrong way! The top of the wheel, which goes fastest and ought to be most indistinct, is, in the fake, as sharp as any other part. It is a small mistake, but fatal. That picture is really at high speed—backwards! It is too raw, too raw."

"You don't think people are going to swallow all that stuff, do you?" asked Hanford coolly, in spite of the exposures.

Kennedy paid no attention. He was looking at McLoughlin. The Boss was regarding him surlily. "Well," he said at length, "what of all this? I had nothing to do with it. Why do you come to me? Take it to the proper parties."

"Shall I?" asked Kennedy quietly.

He had uncovered another picture carefully. We could not see it, but as he looked at it McLoughlin fairly staggered.

"Wh—where did you get that?" he gasped.

"I got it where I got it, and it is no fake," replied Kennedy enigmatically. Then he appeared to think better of it. "This," he explained, "is what is known as a pinhole photograph. Three hundred years ago della Porta knew the camera obscura, and but for the lack of a sensitive plate would have made photographs. A box, thoroughly light-tight, slotted inside to receive plates, covered with black, and glued tight, a needle hole made by a number 10 needle in a thin sheet of paper—and you have the apparatus for lensless photography. It has a correctness such as no image-forming means by lenses can have. It is literally rectigraphic, rectilinear, it needs no focussing, and it takes a wide angle with equal effect. Even pinhole snapshots are possible where the light is abundant, with a ten to fifteen second exposure.

"That picture, McLoughlin, was taken yesterday at Hanford's. After Miss Ashton left I saw who came out, but this picture shows what happened before. At a critical moment Miss Ashton stuck a needle in the wall of the studio, counted fifteen, closed the needle-hole, and there is the record. Walter, Hanford,—leave us alone an instant."

When Kennedy passed out of the Boss's office

there was a look of quiet satisfaction on his face which I could not fathom. Not a word could I extract from him either that night or on the following day, which was the last before the election.

I must say that I was keenly disappointed by the lack of developments, however. The whole thing seemed to me to be a mess. Everybody was involved. What had Miss Ashton overheard and what had Kennedy said to McLoughlin? Above all, what was his game? Was he playing to spare the girl's feelings by allowing the election to go on without a scandal for Travis?

At last election night arrived. We were all at the Travis headquarters, Kennedy, Travis, Bennett, and myself. Miss Ashton was not present, but the first returns had scarcely begun to trickle in when Craig whispered to me to go out and find her, either at her home or club. I found her at home. She had apparently lost interest in the election, and it was with difficulty that I persuaded her to accompany me.

The excitement of any other night in the year paled to insignificance before this. Distracted crowds everywhere were cheering and blowing horns. Now a series of wild shouts broke forth from the dense mass of people before a newspaper bulletin board. Now came sullen groans, hisses, and catcalls, or all together with cheers as the returns swung in another direction. Not even baseball could call out such a crowd as this. Lights blazed everywhere. Automobiles honked and ground their gears. The lobster palaces were thronged. Police were everywhere. People with horns and bells and all manner of noise-making devices pushed up one side of the thoroughfares and down the other. Hungrily, ravenously they were feeding on the meagre bulletins of news.

Yet back of all the noise and human energy I could only think of the silent, systematic gathering and editing of the news. High up in the League headquarters, when we returned, a corps of clerks was tabulating returns, comparing official and semi-official reports. As first the state swung one way, then another, our hopes rose and fell. Miss Ashton seemed cold and ill at ease, while Travis looked more worried and paid less attention to the returns than would have seemed natural. She avoided him and he seemed to hesitate to seek her out.

Would the up-state returns, I had wondered at first, be large enough to overcome the hostile city vote? I was amazed now to see how strongly the city was turning to Travis.

"McLoughlin has kept his word," ejaculated Kennedy as district after district showed that the Boss's pluralities were being seriously cut into.

"His word? What do you mean?" we asked almost together.

"I mean that he has kept his word given to me at a conference which Mr. Jameson saw but did not hear. I told him I would publish the whole thing, not caring whom or where or when it hit if he did not let up on Travis. I advised him to read his Revised Statutes again about money in elections, and I ended up with the threat, 'There will be no dough day, McLoughlin, or this will be prosecuted to the limit.' There was no dough day. You see the effect in the returns."

"But how did you do it?" I asked, not comprehending. "The faked photographs did not move him, that I could see."

The words, "faked photographs," caused Miss Ashton to glance up quickly. I saw that Kennedy had not told her or any one yet, until the Boss had made good. He had simply arranged one of his little dramas.

"Shall I tell, Miss Ashton?" he asked, adding, "Before I complete my part of the compact and blot out the whole affair?"

"I have no right to say no," she answered tremulously, but with a look of happiness that I had not seen since our first introduction.

Kennedy laid down a print on a table. It was the pinhole photograph, a little blurry, but quite convincing. On a desk in the picture was a pile of bills. McLoughlin was shoving them away from him toward Bennett. A man who was facing forward in the picture was talking earnestly to some one who did not appear. I felt intuitively, even before Kennedy said so, that the person was Miss Ashton herself as she stuck the needle into the wall. The man was Cadwalader Brown.

"Travis," demanded Kennedy, "bring the account books of your campaign. I want the miscellaneous account particularly."

The books were brought, and he continued, turning the leaves, "It seemed to me to show a shortage of nearly twenty thousand dollars the other day. Why, it has been made up. How was that, Bennett?"

Bennett was speechless. "I will tell you," Craig proceeded inexorably. "Bennett, you embezzled that money for your business. Rather than be found out, you went to Billy McLoughlin and offered to sell out the Reform campaign for money to replace it. With the aid of the crook, Hanford, McLoughlin's tool, you worked out the scheme to extort money from Travis by forged photographs. You knew enough about Travis's house and library to frame up a robbery one night when you were staying there with him. It was inside work, I found, at a glance. Travis, I am sorry to have to tell you that your confidence was misplaced. It was Bennett who robbed you—and worse.

"But Cadwalader Brown, always close to his creature, Billy McLoughlin, heard of it. To him it presented another idea. To him it offered a chance to overthrow a political enemy and a hated rival for Miss Ashton's hand. Perhaps into the bargain it would disgust her with politics, disillusion her, and shake her faith in what he believed to be some of her 'radical' notions. All could be gained at one blow. They say that a check-book knows no politics, but Bennett has learned some, I venture to say, and to save his reputation he will pay back what he has tried to graft."

Travis could scarcely believe it yet. "How did you get your first hint?" he gasped.

Kennedy was digging into the wall with a bill

file at the place where he had buried the little vulcanised disc. I had already guessed that it was a dictograph, though I could not tell how it was used or who used it. There it was, set squarely in the plaster. There also were the wires running under the carpet. As he lifted the rug under Miss Ashton's desk there also lay the huge circles of wire. That was all.

At this moment Miss Ashton stepped forward. "Last Friday," she said in a low tone, "I wore a belt which concealed a coil of wire about my waist. From it a wire ran under my coat, connecting with a small dry battery in a pocket. Over my head I had an arrangement such as the telephone girls wear with a receiver at one ear connected with the battery. No one saw it, for I wore a large hat which completely hid it. If any one had known, and there were plenty of eyes watching, the whole thing would have fallen through. I could walk around; no one could suspect anything; but when I stood or sat at my desk I could hear everything that was said in Mr. Bennett's office."

"By induction," explained Kennedy. "The impulses set up in the concealed dictograph set up currents in these coils of wire concealed under the carpet. They were wirelessly duplicated by induction in the coil about Miss Ashton's waist and so affected the receiver under her very becoming hat. Tell the rest, Miss Ashton."

"I heard the deal arranged with this Hanford," she added, almost as if she were confessing something, "but not understanding it as Mr. Kennedy did, I very hastily condemned Mr. Travis. I heard talk of putting back twenty thousand into the campaign accounts, of five thousand given to Hanford for his photographic work, and of the way Mr. Travis was to be defeated whether he paid or not. I heard them say that one condition was that I should carry the purchase money. I heard much that must have confirmed Mr. Kennedy's suspicion in one way, and my own in an opposite way, which I know now was wrong. And then Cadwalader Brown in the studio taunted me cynically and—and it cut me, for he seemed right. I hope that Mr. Travis will forgive me for thinking that Mr. Bennett's treachery was his——"

A terrific cheer broke out among the clerks in the outer office. A boy rushed in with a still unblotted report. Kennedy seized it and read: "McLoughlin concedes the city by a small majority to Travis, fifteen election districts estimated. This clinches the Reform League victory in the state."

I turned to Travis. He was paying no attention except to the pretty apology of Margaret Ashton.

Kennedy drew me to the door. "We might as well concede Miss Ashton to Travis," he said, adding gaily, "by induction of an arm about the waist. Let's go out and watch the crowd."

CPSIA information can be obtained
at www.ICGtesting.com
Printed in the USA
LVHW012001070119
603018LV00011B/272/P

APR 29 2019